His Good Opinion

Nancy Kelley

Smokey Rose Press

Dedicated to my parents, Mark and Jan Kelley.
Thank you for always believing in me.

Chapter One

"**I WILL NEVER** understand, Darcy, why you insist on going out in Society, only to be displeased with everyone you meet."

Fitzwilliam Darcy poured two glasses of brandy and handed one to his friend before he took the chair opposite him. "I go out because it is expected of me, Bingley. You know that."

Charles Bingley pointed at him. "Ah, but that does not answer the question, does it?"

Darcy conceded the point with the barest shrug of his shoulders. Here, in the comfort of his own study, there was no need to pretend. "I admit that I find little in Society of which to approve."

"Only because you are determined to disapprove," Bingley protested. "What of the young lady you sat out with tonight? Let me hear your opinion of her."

Darcy ran his fingers down the side of his glass. "Her aunt approached me and said her niece had sprained her ankle, and would I be willing to keep her company. Good manners forbade I refuse, though you know how little I enjoy making conversation with someone I am not intimately acquainted with. I have not your ease of speaking on subjects in which I have little or no interest." His lips curled in disdain, and he took a sip of brandy to wash the sour taste from his mouth.

"That is a commentary on your own character, not the lady's."

Darcy ignored the familiar needling. "After two minutes of idle chatter, I inquired after her injury."

Satisfaction gleamed in Bingley's eyes. "Ah, you are capable of courtesy after all."

Darcy leaned forward, his forehead creased in a frown. "Perhaps you will not be so victorious, Bingley, when you hear the rest of the story. She did not understand what I spoke of. When she returned to her aunt shortly thereafter, she did not have a limp. The entire incident was manufactured so she could gain my attention. No doubt they have heard that I do not dance often —"

"Or ever."

The leather chair creaked in protest when Darcy stood. He took Bingley's glass and strode to the table, glad to have something to do, even if it was only refilling their drinks. This topic never failed to rile him, but he found a measure of calm in pouring the liquor into their glasses.

"They sought a way to gain time with me, and they found it. You wish to know why I so seldom give my good opinion to those I meet; it is this dishonesty, this deception of which I cannot approve. I cannot—I will not—marry a woman I do not trust."

Bingley took his refilled glass, and Darcy noted his frown with some vexation. "You are being a bit presumptuous, Darcy. How can you be so certain she wished to marry you? It was simply a dance."

Darcy set the decanter down on the tray with a hard clang. "Surely even you will acknowledge that a single woman in possession of no brothers must be in want of a husband."

Bingley shook his head and laughed. "You can hardly claim that to be a universal truth."

Darcy ran his hands through his close-cropped dark curls. *Has it truly escaped his notice that he too has received such attentions?* Though it was this very ability to see nothing but the good in people that recommended Bingley to him, at times his amiable nature bordered on naiveté.

"Perhaps not universal, but a truth nonetheless." He paced the confines of the study. The paneled walls, usually calming, pressed in on him tonight. London always wore on his nerves, but this Season had been worse than most. "I need to leave town, Bingley."

Bingley eyed Darcy over the edge of his glass. "You sound as if you have a plan in mind."

Darcy stood in front of the empty fireplace and tapped his fingers on the mantle. "I believe it is time I visited Georgiana in Ramsgate."

"Is that what has made you so tense of late? I know you take great care of her."

Bingley's insight startled Darcy. "Yes, I imagine so. I trust Mrs. Younge, of course, or I would not have consented to the plan. Still, I will feel better once I see for myself how she is getting on." He turned back to his friend, at ease for the first time in weeks.

"When will you leave?"

"Tomorrow morning."

Bingley raised his eyebrows. "That is rather spontaneous, Darcy—indeed, it is the kind of precipitous decision you often tease me for."

Darcy tossed back the rest of his brandy before he answered. "In truth, I have been thinking about it some weeks," he replied. "I just did not realize it until tonight."

"Well, if you are decided, then I wish you safe travels."

Bingley rose and shook his hand in farewell, and Darcy retired for the night soon after. He slept well, content with the knowledge he would soon be free of the artifice of town.

Chapter Two

DARCY DID NOT go to Ramsgate the following morning. News of a farm accident arrived from Pemberley, and he returned home to tend to the matter. Two of his best tenants had nearly been crippled. Neither family could afford to lose the profit they would gain on the year's harvest, so Darcy forgave their rent until they healed.

This was all done easily enough, but as often happened, his presence at home brought other concerns to light. Darcy's dual roles of Master of Pemberley and guardian to his sister had always complemented each other. Now it seemed that to do his duty by one he must neglect the other. Each night he went to bed determined to leave for Ramsgate the next day. Each morning, his steward arrived in his study with some new issue that needed his attention.

At last, however, he was able to leave. As Darcy approached the shore, the salt air eased the remaining vestiges of tension from his shoulders. He had not seen Georgiana since her companion, Mrs. Younge, had convinced both him and his cousin Richard that spending the summer in the resort town would be the best way to gently ease her into Society, and he missed her.

However, when the townhouse door opened, what he witnessed was far from the calm oasis of gentility he expected. Two maids scurried across the foyer in a flurry of activity, their arms laden with packages. They chattered unceasingly, though Darcy was unable to make out any of the words.

The normally indomitable butler looked harried, but he drew himself up to his full height when he saw his employer standing on the doorstep. "Mr. Darcy. The ladies are in the morning room, sir. Shall I announce you?"

"No, thank you. Allow me to surprise my sister." Through the open door of the drawing room, Darcy spied the same two maids frantically cleaning. *What is going on?*

He shook his head and pushed open the door to the morning room. Both ladies turned toward the door with looks of expectation when he walked in; Georgiana's expression quickly shifted to surprise and then pleasure when she realized it was he. "Fitzwilliam! I did not know you were coming."

"But surely you are expecting someone," he said. An inscrutable expression fell over Mrs. Younge's features and roused Darcy's curiosity. "I vow I have never seen anyone watch a door open with such interest before."

His sister blushed, and he felt the first stirrings of alarm. "I confess, I did think you were someone else."

Darcy glanced at Mrs. Younge, then back at his sister. He began to suspect there was news to be imparted which he would not want to learn in the presence of a woman who, for all her credentials, was still but a servant. "Mrs. Younge, will you leave us please? I believe I can act as a perfectly proper chaperone to Miss Darcy and her visitor when he arrives—it is a gentleman, is it not, Georgiana?" he queried gently. She bit her lip and nodded slightly.

Mrs. Younge rose from her position on the far settee and slowly crossed the room. At the door, she turned and shared a long, speaking gaze with Georgiana. Darcy could not interpret it, but his sister flushed and smiled. "Very well, sir," the companion said. "I shall inform the cook that we have an extra person for dinner this evening."

Darcy schooled his features into an impassive expression before he turned back to Georgiana. It would not do to let her see the depth of his concern. Neither he nor Richard had been informed of her attachment to a young man. *That is definitely the kind of information a companion is expected to pass on to her charge's guardians.* "So, Georgiana, is there anything you would like to tell me?"

Georgiana twisted her handkerchief into tight knots. Her hesitation told him more than that he wanted to know about the strength of her attachment, but it did not tell the most important piece of information. "Perhaps you should start from the beginning." He took her hands and led her to the light blue brocade settee. "For instance, who is this young man you were so looking forward to seeing when I walked in?"

She graced him with a radiant smile. "You will be so surprised when I tell you his name. Indeed, I was surprised myself when he found us on one of our beach walks and remembered me from childhood. He says that even then..."

A dark suspicion formed in the back of Darcy's mind. "His name, Georgiana."

Her gaze fell back to her lap. "George Wickham."

Had Georgiana been looking at him, she could not have missed the pale anger that suffused over her brother's face at the name. He had not seen George Wickham in some time, and their last encounter had not improved his opinion of him. Wickham was a spendthrift and a profligate—not the kind of man he wanted his sister to associate with. "George Wickham?" he said. Georgiana started at the rough harshness in his voice, and he took a deep breath before he continued. "What exactly is your relationship with him?"

What little smile remained on her face wilted. "He has asked me to marry him," she whispered.

Darcy could not answer immediately; so many arguments rose to his tongue that he did not know which to speak first. Even if the character of the gentleman had not been so questionable, there was still the matter of his birth. It would be insupportable to see his sister joined with a man who was the son of their father's former steward.

However, before he could express that opinion, he remembered the joy in her earlier smile. *He has convinced her to care for him. How can I make her see what he truly is—a rogue, using her in the basest of manners?*

After a moment of silence, Georgiana continued. "We were to elope, but now I know that would not do. I would not want to do something that would bring you shame or disappoint you in any way."

"Was the elopement his idea or yours?" Darcy asked, though he already knew the answer.

Georgiana gnawed on her lower lip. "He suggested it. A trip to Scotland seemed so exciting, and then we could visit you in London and he could introduce me to you as his wife."

Even through her uncertainty, he could still detect a hint of schoolgirl hopes in her voice, and he somehow managed to keep his voice calm at such a repellent thought. "Does it still sound exciting?"

She shook her head, her blue eyes filled with tears. "No. I have disappointed you, have I not, Fitzwilliam?"

Darcy knelt in front of his sister and took her hands in his. "No, dearest. He has. No gentleman of quality would suggest an elopement to a young lady, not when there are family members who might be worried about her. Wickham knew I would not accept his suit if he asked in the customary manner."

Georgiana tilted her head, a quizzical frown wrinkling her brow. "Why not? I thought you were friends."

Darcy rose and turned toward the window, his hands clasped behind his back. "I have not spoken to Wickham in almost two years, and we did not part on good terms. He had come to ask for money, and I refused his request."

It did not take Georgiana long to put the pieces together.

"Then you believe he is only after my fortune."

The pain in her voice brought him back to her side. Loathe as he was to injure her tender heart, he would not lie to her. Her fortune of thirty thousand pounds was undoubtedly Wickham's chief motive in wooing her. "I am afraid so." A single tear rolled down her cheek. Others soon followed, and Darcy held her close while she cried.

"No harm was done," he reassured her, his voice soft and soothing. "I will write Wickham and inform him your engagement is over, and that will be the end of it." Inwardly, he seethed with rage. *The blackguard! How I wish I could introduce him to the business end of my blade.*

Georgiana soon pulled back and wiped her tears, though she could not mend the damage done to her coiffure. "I am sorry, Fitzwilliam. When Mrs. Younge introduced him as a gentleman —"

"Mrs. Younge introduced him?" Darcy interrupted. "You said earlier that you met him on the beach."

She swallowed and nodded her head. "And we did, but he was known to Mrs. Younge before that. She told me I could not attract a more worthy gentleman; that, combined with my knowledge of your relationship, was enough to recommend him to me."

Darcy pressed his lips into a thin line. He had wondered how his sister's chaperone could have allowed such a relationship to progress without notifying himself or Richard. *She was part of the plot from the beginning.* "Georgiana, I believe I need to speak with Mrs. Younge. Could you send her to me please?"

"Yes, of course." She left the room, and a minute later Mrs. Younge appeared, her hands twisting nervously in her apron.

"You asked for me, sir?"

"Mrs. Younge. Please have a seat." He waited until she had done so before speaking again. "Allow me to be frank. I am most displeased that you chose to keep Miss Darcy's attachment from her guardians."

Mrs. Younge returned Darcy's gaze without flinching. "What do you mean, sir?"

Darcy narrowed his eyes. "Do not be coy with me, madam, I have little patience for it. My sister tells me you introduced her to George Wickham and encouraged his calls. Surely her cousin and I should have been consulted in the matter."

She glared at him over crossed arms. "Aye, and what would you have done if you'd known? Ye would have turned him down flat, and him as nice a young man as ever lived. Oh, to be sure he's had his share of hard times, and who's to blame for that? You and your stingy ways." She smirked at Darcy's involuntary start. "Oh yes, he told me all about his previous dealings with you, how ye wouldn't give him the living what was promised to him and turned him out cold after he'd been such a favorite of your father. What kind of gentleman would do such a thing, I ask?"

"The same kind who will turn you off without a reference." Darcy pointed at the door, his hand shaking slightly. "You will leave here at once, madam. Do not bother to pack your things; they will be forwarded to you."

Mrs. Younge rose from her seat, her nose stuck high in the air. "As if I would want to work for the likes of you." She stalked from the room in a manner reminiscent of his aunt, Lady Catherine de Bourgh, a comparison which would have amused him if his temper were not so high.

Darcy was tempted, now that he was alone, to give way to the violence of his feelings. However, there was still business to be done and he pulled paper, pen, and ink from the writing desk.

His letter to George Wickham was brief; all that was needed to end the match was his disapproval, and both men knew that. It crossed Darcy's mind briefly that Wickham might make Georgiana's folly known, but it would do him no good to be known as a debaucher of innocents. He sealed the letter and pressed his signet ring into the hot wax, a grim smile on his face when he pictured Wickham's reaction to that familiar impression.

He rang the bell and a footman soon appeared. "See to it this is delivered to George Wickham. I am afraid I do not know his direction; perhaps—"

"I know where he lives, sir."

"Do you indeed? Very well then, take it to him at once."

That unpleasant business resolved, Darcy went upstairs and knocked on Georgiana's door. "Are you ready to go down, Georgiana?"

She was dressed for dinner, and though he detected a hint of sadness in her eyes, her maid at least had tamed her blonde curls and pulled them back into a bun. "Yes, Fitzwilliam." Georgiana took his arm and they went down the stairs together.

The table was simply laid, as was their custom when they ate alone. Brother and sister took their seats, and Darcy nodded to the footmen to begin serving the first course. "Are we not going to wait for Mrs. Younge, Brother?" Georgiana asked.

Darcy did not answer until the servant had left the room. "Mrs. Younge is no longer your companion, Georgiana. You do understand why, do you not?"

Georgiana looked down at her plate. "Yes," she replied. "I am sorry, Fitzwilliam; I did not know what he was."

The guilt he heard took Darcy by surprise. "I have no doubt you were deceived most grievously, Georgiana."

She looked up and offered him a tremulous smile. "Will I be coming back to London with you?"

"I think that is the best thing to do. Richard and I can begin looking for another companion for you once we arrive."

"I would rather go home," she said, her voice wistful.

"Georgiana, there is no one at home to keep you company, and I do want you to be accustomed to Society before your debut. I am sorry; perhaps we can return to Pemberley for an extended visit before the Season starts."

Georgiana pushed the food around her plate with a fork, though none of it made it into her mouth. "Of course, I know it is not possible now," she said finally. "I simply dread the questions people will ask when they find out."

"No one will find out," he bit out. She flinched, and he softened his voice. "Besides you and me, no one knows of this but Mrs. Younge and Wickham himself. They could not expose you without likewise exposing themselves."

She nodded slowly. "I do wish there was a way to keep Cousin Richard from knowing, but I suppose that cannot be avoided."

How deeply has Wickham wounded her? Darcy wished once more for his sword, but he reined in his anger. "Georgiana, why does that bother you? Richard will see the situation as I do—that Wickham is a rake of the worst kind who attempted to take advantage of a young girl's affectionate heart."

"I do not wish him to think me naïve!" she burst out suddenly. "I do not wish..." She took a deep breath and focused her eyes on her plate. "I find I am not hungry after all. May I be excused, please?"

The request bemused Darcy, but he would not refuse her. "Yes, of course. Get some rest; we will be leaving for London on the morrow."

Chapter Three

DARCY SENT HIS cousin a message by express before he and Georgiana left Ramsgate the next morning, and Colonel Fitzwilliam arrived in London the following Monday. Darcy had ordered Remington, his butler, to show his cousin into the study without delay. Relief caught him by surprise when Richard appeared in the doorway, and he realized again how right his father had been to split the charge of his daughter between the cousins.

Though the military man appeared relaxed, his uniform gave him an air of command. "I came as soon as I received your letter, Darcy. What was urgent enough to require my immediate presence in town? I can only assume it has something to do with Georgie, since the last I knew, she was in Ramsgate with Mrs. Younge."

"Sit down, Richard."

"This begins to sound serious, Darcy," he teased. Darcy did not laugh, and Richard sat in a leather chair in front of the fireplace. "How serious is it?"

Darcy looked him straight in the eye. "It is very nearly as serious as it can be. Do you remember George Wickham?"

"I do. He was a great friend of your father's, was he not? Perhaps not the most decorous of gentlemen once he got to school, but then so many find that the freedom of being away from home loosens their morals." Richard sat up ramrod straight and said, "Good God! You do not mean to tell me…"

"I am afraid so."

"Where is she? Is she hurt? What did he do to her?"

Familiar with his cousin's rapid-fire method of questioning, Darcy did not blink. "She is in her bedchamber putting away her belongings. She is not hurt—at least not physically. He coerced her into an elopement, but I arrived just in time to spoil his well-laid plans. Naturally, I sent a letter to the reprobate expressing my disapproval of the match and immediately removed Georgiana from Ramsgate."

Richard jumped from his seat with an oath. "The cur! How dare he play with her feelings. I do wish I had been the one that found them—I would dearly love to have run him through."

Darcy watched him pace in front of the fireplace with some amazement. Of all the cousins, Richard had the calmest temperament. His cool head was the reason he had risen so quickly in the officers' ranks. Darcy had never seen him so riled.

"I admit the thought did cross my mind," Darcy said after a minute. "I cannot guarantee my restraint will hold if I ever meet with him again."

Richard pivoted back toward Darcy, anger drawn across his face in stark lines and fire in his dark eyes. "Where was Mrs. Younge in all of this?"

Darcy's lips tightened. "She was complicit in the scheme. He joined them in Ramsgate at her invitation, and it was by her design that they conveniently met during one of their walks."

Richard clenched his hand into a fist. "I take it she is no longer in our employ."

"No, so we will need to once again find a suitable companion for her. I confess I do not relish the chore."

A stifled cry alerted them to Georgiana's presence. The men turned to see her standing by the door, her hand over her mouth and tears in her eyes. "I am sorry," she cried. "I did not mean to be such a bother. He said he loved me, that he wished to marry me."

Before either gentleman could say a word, she fled down the long corridor. After her swishing skirts disappeared from view, Richard looked at Darcy in amazement. "What exactly was that about?"

Darcy shoved his hand through his hair. This was the area where he most desired his cousin's help. "I am afraid this has left Georgiana rather blue-deviled. She seems to believe the whole affair—" Richard winced, and Darcy shrugged apologetically—"this whole… business is her fault."

Richard sighed. "I will speak to her. I know you have told her she is not to blame, but perhaps she needs to hear the truth from someone else." He smiled wryly at Darcy. "Besides, words have never been your strength, cousin."

Darcy breathed a sigh of relief. *Perhaps she will believe the truth more from Richard.* "Thank you. I have tried, but…"

"Then it is up to me. You may begin writing the notice for the papers." Richard placed a supportive hand on Darcy's shoulder, and the cousins shared a quick smile before he left the room.

Despite his confident words, when Richard returned downstairs, he was alone. "She will not leave her room. I have asked a tray to be sent to her—let us leave her alone for the evening, William."

But it was not just for an evening. Over the next few days, Georgiana withdrew until she scarcely resembled the laughing child Darcy remembered. He turned all his attention to finding a companion for her, in hope a female influence would help matters.

Their notice attracted many applicants, but after their previous experience, he and Richard exercised even greater caution. One by one they eliminated candidates, until Darcy feared no one would meet their standards.

He pinched the bridge of his nose; there was no time for such doubts now. "Who is next, Richard?"

His cousin checked the list. "A widow named Mrs. Annesley."

"Her recommendations?"

"Several, including Mrs. Upton-Sinclair and Lady Stanton."

Darcy straightened up in his chair. "Lady Stanton is quite the stickler. She would not recommend anyone who did not meet the most rigorous of requirements."

"My thoughts exactly."

"Very well then, call her in."

Richard left the room and returned a moment later, accompanied by a woman. Her apparent youth startled Darcy—she did not look much older than he was. However, her upright bearing and sensible blue walking dress (coupled with the recommendations she possessed) convinced him to listen with an open mind.

He rose from his chair and bowed slightly when she entered the room. "Good day, Mrs. Annesley. I am Mr. Darcy and this is my cousin, Colonel Fitzwilliam."

She smiled and took her seat. "Good afternoon, gentlemen."

"May we offer you some refreshment before we begin? A cup of tea perhaps?"

"Thank you; that is not necessary."

As per their arrangement, Darcy observed while Richard asked the questions. "Your references are glowing, madam. May I ask how you came to be in need of a new position?"

"My previous charge is to marry Lord Rathbourne next month."

Darcy raised his eyebrows a little. Rathbourne's engagement had been the talk of the Season. Mrs. Annesley clearly felt at home in the highest circles; that was good. As the granddaughter of an earl, Georgiana could marry very well.

"Your position with Miss Darcy might be slightly different from what you are accustomed. Mr. Darcy and I are often away from town on business. During those times, we would depend on you to provide any guidance she might need. If that makes you at all uneasy, we need not go any further." Once again, Darcy was grateful for Richard's military precision; his words cut straight to the heart of the matter.

"Not at all," she said, and her calm, unaffected manner struck Darcy favorably. He could not imagine this genteel woman yelling at him as Mrs. Younge had.

Her next words cemented his high opinion of her. "In fact, my very first position was quite similar to what you just described. Estate duties kept the father often from London. With regular correspondence, I informed him of anything that required his attention, and he in turn trusted me implicitly."

Darcy shared a look with his cousin. She had just answered their most important question without prompting. Richard nodded almost imperceptibly, and Darcy turned back to Mrs. Annesley. "Thank you very much for your time," he told her. "By your answers, I believe you would be a good fit for the post. We will, of course, need to check into your references, but I do not imagine there will be any problem there. Expect to hear from us in the next few days to finalize the matter."

She stood and both gentleman followed suit. "Thank you, Colonel Fitzwilliam and Mr. Darcy. I look forward to hearing from you."

"Colonel Fitzwilliam will see you to the door."

It was a simple matter to check the references, and within a week Mrs. Annesley was installed at their townhouse in Grosvenor Square. Her presence forced Georgiana to be social, but Darcy noticed a hesitancy in her manner that told him all was still not well. He would not leave her yet so vulnerable, but he did not relish the thought of summer in the city. As little as he enjoyed London during the Season, the capital was even more unpleasant in the sultry heat. The stench alone was almost unbearable.

The one consolation Darcy had was that with the Ton largely absent, there were very few social obligations. There were no parties or soirees, no simpering misses to be avoided. In truth, it was almost too solitary for Darcy, and he was glad when Bingley paid a visit about a week after Mrs. Annesley's arrival.

"I did not think to find you in town, Darcy. I was most pleasantly surprised to see your card when I returned."

"The sea air did not agree with Georgiana, so I found it necessary to reestablish her here in London." Darcy hated the lie more with every repetition, but he would not expose his sister to gossip.

"Ah, that is too bad." Bingley rocked back on his heels, his eyes crinkled in a broad smile. "Oh, but this is a wonderful coincidence. I can issue my invitation in person."

Darcy tilted his head. "Invitation?"

"Yes. I just signed the lease on a lovely estate in Hertfordshire, and I would be honored if you would stay with me for a time this autumn."

Darcy hid a smile. Bingley frequently stated his desire to purchase an estate of his own, but Darcy privately wondered if his friend's easy personality gave him the drive for such an undertaking. If there was an estate to be let, it was doubtful he would ever feel it necessary. "What is the estate called?"

"Netherfield Park. It is but half a day's ride from London. Will you join me, Darcy?"

Darcy's smile slipped. In his amusement, he had forgotten Bingley's question. "I am afraid I have business that keeps me here for the present, Bingley."

He knew his friend too well to think this would dissuade him, and he was not disappointed. Bingley laughed and said, "You must rest sometime, Darcy. I leave for Netherfield on Sunday next, but I shall return the week following and will persuade you to join me."

"You have my permission to try, but I do not promise that you will succeed."

"That is as much as I can hope for today. I have business of my own to attend to, so I bid you farewell. I shall see you again Monday fortnight."

Darcy breathed a sigh when Bingley was gone. Though he hated lying to his friend, Georgiana's reputation demanded it. He had a notion that Bingley would make a fine husband for her, but even a man of his easy humor might be swayed by an aborted elopement.

As to leaving London to rusticate in Hertfordshire, that was utterly out of the question. Georgiana had not regained enough confidence for him to leave her alone. His heart ached when he saw her shy timidity, so different from the warm, happy child she had been not too long ago.

Richard, however, took a different view on the matter and let Darcy know his feelings over port two days later. "You cannot stay always in town, William. You know you will go mad in a matter of weeks if you do not return to the country."

Darcy tugged on his ear. His impatience with town life was indeed growing, but he would not relinquish his responsibilities. "If I remove Georgiana to Pemberley so soon, she will never be at ease in Society. She will see my actions as proof I do not trust her."

Richard snorted. "She already believes that."

Darcy looked up, startled. "She thinks what?"

"Watch her when we rejoin the ladies. She shies away from your gaze, thinking you only watch her because you doubt her judgment. Can you not see she is afraid of disappointing you again? That fear only increases the longer you stay, watching her like a mother hen."

Darcy did not want to believe it, but when they entered the drawing room, he saw immediately what Richard meant. Georgiana glanced away from Mrs. Annesley to him, met his gaze, and then looked away. Her speech faltered for a moment, and he suddenly felt like an imbecile.

He turned to Richard and said in a low voice, "What shall

I do?"

"Do not go to Pemberley if you feel that it is too far, but do leave London. I will keep watch over Georgie so long as I am not needed elsewhere; you know she looks on me differently than she does you. You are the brother who is nearly a father to her. I am merely the beloved cousin."

Darcy contemplated for moment. "Bingley did ask if I cared to winter with him in Hertfordshire."

Richard shook his head and slapped Darcy on the shoulder. "Go! For God's sake man, go."

Darcy nodded decisively. "I will."

He told Georgiana the next morning, and she took the announcement with quiet resignation. "How long will you remain with Mr. Bingley and his sisters?"

"Of that I am not certain. Bingley, I know, plans to remain all through the winter, but I would like to be back in town for Christmas." Darcy and his father had always striven to make Christmas special for Georgiana, and in recent years it had become one of the few times of the year brother and sister were together.

"Very well, I will see you in December. Do greet them for me."

Georgiana's dispassionate response to his departure assured Darcy he did the right thing. If she could regard his absence with such calm, then his presence in London was not needed.

A short trip back to Pemberley was necessary, and he arrived back in London just in time to join Bingley's party as they journeyed to Hertfordshire. The carriage being full of Bingley's two sisters and the husband of one, he and Bingley opted to ride alongside. The open air suited his temperament better than being trapped inside a carriage for hours on end with Bingley's sisters, and he was glad of Bingley's company. His friend's gift for turning idle chatter into meaningful conversation kept him from worrying about Georgiana the whole ride to Hertfordshire, and for that at least he was grateful.

Chapter Four

DARCY HAD BEEN in Hertfordshire less than a day when he first wondered if he had made the right choice in accepting his friend's invitation. "I have promised our presence at the local assembly," Bingley announced at breakfast the morning after they arrived.

"A country ball?" Every inch of Miss Bingley's refined appearance, from her perfectly coiffed chestnut hair to the fine lace ruffle on her gown, proclaimed her disapprobation with such a scheme. "Really, Charles, you might have consulted us first."

Though Darcy did not speak, he was in private agreement. Public balls were an unpleasantness he avoided at all costs—the people were just as supercilious as the members of the Ton, but without enough manners and good breeding to make the engagement even tolerable.

When they entered the uncomfortably cramped assembly hall that evening, his worst prejudices were confirmed. Even in the low light provided by too few candles, he could discern the country styles and high spirits he disdained.

Though the dancing did not stop when they walked in, the room otherwise became noticeably quieter as people observed their arrival, and then steadily louder as they began to talk and speculate amongst themselves. Clearly, Bingley's arrival had been long anticipated, and with the flock of young ladies of marriageable age, Darcy did not wonder why.

Bingley led the way to the front of the room where a cheerful gentleman with a florid nose presided over the assembly. "Mr. Bingley, it is a pleasure to see you again."

"I am pleased to be here, Sir William. May I introduce my party? My sister and her husband, Mr. and Mrs. Hurst, and my younger sister, Miss Bingley. The gentleman is our friend, Mr. Darcy. "

Sir William's low bow gave Darcy an excellent view of his balding head. "Ah, splendid! Mr. Darcy, I am pleased to make your acquaintance. Where are you from, sir?"

"From Derbyshire, sir." Darcy made no mention of his estate. It was bad enough to have town mamas crying after him; it would be unbearable in the midst of such low company.

Despite his efforts, whispers soon reached his ears:

"Fitzwilliam Darcy…"

"Ten thousand a year…"

"A large estate in Derbyshire."

He glanced at the door, but he knew very well there was no escape. The sensation of being trapped unawares added heat to his glower, and his curt refusals soon put off even the most stalwart parents. No, he did not wish to be introduced to the local daughters—no matter how pretty or amiable they may be.

His mouth turned down in disapproval as two young ladies danced by him, heedless of the spectacle they created. *No indeed, I do not wish to meet any of the young ladies.*

Duty required him to dance once with each of Bingley's sisters. Caroline Bingley tried to tease him into leading her out a second time, but he bowed and moved to the edge of the room. Laughter caught his attention, and the same two girls skipped across the room in a most unladylike fashion.

"Mama! Mama!" they called out in unison, and Darcy sneered when he recognized the lady they addressed. *Now I understand the lack of parental control.* Mrs. Bennet had been absolutely brazen in her attempt to attach Bingley to one of her five daughters. She had even tried to approach him, but he had moved away before she could reach his side. To think he would be willing to join himself to such a family insulted everything he believed in.

Much to his displeasure, his peace was soon interrupted yet again by a lady he did not recognize. "May I sit by you, Mr. Darcy?" the matron said on her approach. He nodded coolly, and she sat. "Thank you, sir. I am Mrs. Long."

The impudence of her manner disgusted him, and he turned slightly away. That, however, did not deter her. "My, this room is not quite large enough for the number of couples, is it?" She opened her fan to cool herself. "How unfortunate that there are so few gentlemen present. I see several young ladies sitting out the dance."

Darcy pressed his lips into a thin line. He knew from her tone that one of these young ladies was a relation to her. Courtesy dictated he should offer to lead said young lady out, but he stubbornly refused to be so blatantly manipulated.

The silence stretched on, and eventually she changed the subject to one he could not avoid answering. "I do hope you find Netherfield Park to your liking. Your friend will, I believe, be staying in Hertfordshire for a while?"

"I find nothing lacking in my accommodation. As to

Mr. Bingley's plans, you will have to inquire of him." The terseness of Darcy's reply at last quieted the babbling woman. She remained by his side for a few more minutes, before making up the excuse that a friend beckoned her from across the room.

Soon after, Bingley joined him in between the dances of a set. "Come, Darcy, I must have you dance. I hate to see you standing about by yourself in this stupid manner. You had much better dance."

Darcy crossed his arms. He should have known Bingley would not let him sit quietly. "I certainly shall not. You know how I detest it, unless I am particularly acquainted with my partner. At such an assembly as this it would be insupportable." He frowned. "Your sisters are engaged, and there is not another woman in the room whom it would not be a punishment to me to stand up with."

Bingley's jaw dropped for an instant before he snapped it shut. "I would not be so fastidious as you are for a kingdom! Upon my honor, I never met with so many pleasant girls in my life as I have this evening; and there are several of them you see uncommonly pretty."

Darcy gave a cursory glance around him and found nothing to contradict his own opinion. He nodded at the eldest Bennet girl, a graceful, fair-haired maiden. "*You* are dancing with the only handsome girl in the room."

"Oh! She is the most beautiful creature I ever beheld!" The beatific smile on his friend's face was a familiar one—Bingley was in the habit of believing himself in love with every pretty woman. "But there is one of her sisters sitting down just behind you who is very pretty, and I dare say very agreeable. Do let me ask my partner to introduce you."

"Which do you mean?" Darcy turned around and

leveled a disinterested gaze at the young lady seated behind him. Where her sister was fair, she was dark— plain brown hair, brown eyes, and skin he could tell received too much sun. Her features altogether lacked symmetry, but above all, it was her eyes that bothered him. They caught his gaze, and something in her expression discomfited him. He turned back to Bingley and said, "She is tolerable, but not handsome enough to tempt *me;* I am in no humor at present to give consequence to young ladies who are slighted by other men."

Even as Darcy said the words, he knew they were ungenerous. There were far more ladies present than gentlemen, and every young lady had taken her turn without a partner. Eager to end the conversation, he said, "You had better return to your partner and enjoy her smiles, for you are wasting your time with me."

Bingley laughed and returned to Miss Bennet, and Darcy finally gained the peace he desired. With the exception of a few remarks from Miss Bingley, no one spoke to him. The evening drew to a close a short while later, to Darcy's relief and Bingley's dismay. The carriage ride back to Netherfield was short, and soon they were comfortably ensconced in the drawing room.

"Was that not a most delightful evening, Darcy?" Bingley said. "I never expected to find such pleasant people in the country. It was so nice to be in company lacking all the stiffness one so often finds in town."

"And equally lacking in manners and taste," Darcy countered.

"Indeed, Charles, Mr. Darcy is correct." Miss Bingley's derisive tone was equally ill mannered.

Bingley was momentarily taken aback by this evaluation, but he quickly shrugged it off. "Darcy, I do not understand why you sat by yourself all evening. You say you will not dance with ladies not of your acquaintance, but everyone was so personable, I soon felt that I had known them for quite some time."

Darcy knew his friend well enough to know that he could state his own mind without fear of giving insult. The ability to be honest was one of the things he valued most about Bingley's friendship. "I am afraid I saw none of that. There was little in their manner to be admired, and nothing in their fashion. It was entirely as I imagined a small country assembly to be."

Bingley pursued the conversation with dogged interest. "And the young ladies were quite pretty. Miss Bennet especially, of course."

"She is pretty," Darcy conceded, "though she smiles too much."

"Smiles too much! My word, Darcy, is there nothing or no one you do not find fault with? Next you will be complaining because her eyes opened too widely, or she blinked too often."

"Do not be ridiculous, Bingley. I merely pointed out the complacency of her temper makes it difficult to tell what she is really feeling. She seems a pleasant enough young lady, however, not as insipid or silly as her two younger sisters."

"Yes, indeed," Mrs. Hurst agreed. "Caroline and I talked with her for a time, and we can say that Jane Bennet is a sweet girl."

"Indeed. I should not mind getting to know her better," Miss Bingley chimed in.

Whatever reply the gentlemen might have given was cut off by a loud snore from Mr. Hurst, and the evening was at a close.

Chapter Five

AS A VISITOR in Bingley's home, Darcy did not feel obligated to take part in the round of social calls, which must needs follow their arrival in the neighborhood. With concern for Georgiana heavy on his mind, he took advantage of his freedom and avoided everyone but Bingley for the next few days.

Regrettably, there were some modes of polite society he could not avoid. Dinner invitations followed the social calls, and Bingley announced on their fourth morning at Netherfield that they would dine with the Bennet family that evening. If Darcy had a remote hope of the Bennets' behavior being more modulated at home, they were put to rest the moment the Netherfield party arrived at Longbourn.

The modest, two-story home spoke of good sense and taste that were entirely lacking in most members of the family. The lady of the house fluttered around them, her effusions almost too much to bear. "Mr. Bingley, it is so good to see you! You are most welcome, sir, along with your fine sisters."

She then half turned and looked at Darcy over the tip of her well-shaped nose. "And good evening to you as well, sir."

In the blink of an eye, she focused attention back on Bingley. Darcy was not sure how he should take being so summarily dismissed. *Does her disapprobation bother you?* he chided himself. *You have at last achieved your goal.* With five daughters, Mrs. Bennet was exactly the kind of woman Darcy sought to avoid.

Bingley, he observed, was not lucky enough to escape Mrs. Bennet's attentions; when they moved into the dining room, she seated him on her right and monopolized his attention. "It was so good of you to accept our dinner invitation, sir, and with such short notice. I did wonder if we should wait a few days, but my Jane would not hear of it. 'We do not want Mr. Bingley to think we do not understand the courtesies of Society,' she said. But then, Jane has ever been my sweet, wise girl."

Darcy set his lips in a firm line. *Does she mean to imply her daughter actively seeks gentleman callers?*

He could not tell if the sudden pink tint in Jane Bennet's face was simply a reflection of the candlelight, or if her mother's comment embarrassed her. However, when he heard her sister's quick indrawn breath, he guessed it to be the latter.

"Mama, that was not at all what Jane meant." Miss Elizabeth smiled at Mr. Bingley. "My mother was fretting over the courses, and Jane simply said that she could not imagine you would mind mutton."

The grace with which Miss Elizabeth jumped to her sister's defense unfortunately proved to be the only pleasant moment of the evening. Once the courses were laid on the table, the two youngest girls joined in the conversation. "Mama, do you know what we learned from our Aunt Philips today?"

"Tell me, Lydia, my love."

Miss Lydia's light brown curls shook as she trembled with unrestrained excitement. "The Militia are coming to Meryton!"

Darcy's eyes widened when Mrs. Bennet clapped

her hands like a giddy schoolgirl. "The militia!"

"Yes." Miss Catherine placed her elbows on the table and leaned into her cupped hands. "They are to remain here for the whole winter."

Sighs of delight followed this intelligence. "Oh my dears, what an exciting thing for you. Officers in Meryton!"

Darcy glanced down at Mr. Bennet. *Why does he not step in to check this idle prattle?* That gentleman watched the proceedings with an amused smile. He seemed to positively delight in the ridiculous behavior of his wife and daughters, and Darcy's disapproval of the family was firmly set.

The evening left Darcy in a foul frame of mind, and it did not end when they left Longbourn. Even in the comfort of the Netherfield drawing room, he could not escape mention of the Bennet family. Miss Bingley dismissed her brother-in-law's suggestion of cards —"For we have far too much to talk of to pay attention to what we are playing," she explained.

Unperturbed, Mr. Hurst sat in the far corner of the room, and Mr. Darcy took the seat nearest him, not even minding the draught he felt when he sat down. *The less I hear of the Bennets, the better.*

Alas, the room was not large enough for him to miss the conversation between his companions. "The more I meet with Jane Bennet, the more I take a liking to her," Miss Bingley said, a self-satisfied smile on her face.

"Indeed, she is a very sweet creature." Mrs. Hurst wrinkled her nose. "But her family."

"Oh yes, the mother and those two younger sisters; so unrefined! Miss Mary Bennet was described to me as accomplished, so imagine my surprise to discover she can neither draw nor paint. Her one skill seems to be playing the pianoforte."

"Do not forget quoting from Fordyce's sermons."

Their merry laughter grated on Darcy's nerves.

Bingley frowned at them both. "You do not give enough credit to the Bennet sisters, I think. They have not had all the advantages of town and education that you have, and yet they are all pleasant, genteel girls."

All of them pleasant, Bingley? Darcy shook his head, and from Miss Bingley's smirk and barely muffled giggle, he knew he was not the only one who doubted this statement.

The room was quiet for a moment, and Darcy thought perhaps they had left the subject of the Longbourn family behind them. Then Miss Bingley spoke again. "I have heard Elizabeth Bennet referred to as one of the great beauties of the county."

"Elizabeth Bennet?" Darcy at last lost all patience with the conversation. "I should as soon call her mother a wit."

Both sisters tittered at this pronouncement, but Bingley was not amused. "Darcy, you are too harsh. Perhaps Miss Elizabeth is not quite the standard beauty you see in town, but I vow, there is something about her which draws the eye."

"Oh no, not quite the standard beauty at all," Miss Bingley said snidely. Her brother turned to glare at her, and she quickly modulated her answer. "However, Miss Eliza too is a pleasant, well-bred girl. I would not mind getting to know her better."

"Nor I," agreed Mrs. Hurst.

To the dismay of everyone but Bingley, becoming better acquainted with the elder Bennet girls came at the cost of time spent with the entire clan. Over the following weeks, they dined with the Longbourn family three times. By the end of the fortnight, Darcy was quite out of patience with the entire family, with the singular exception of Miss Elizabeth Bennet.

His good opinion of her took him quite by surprise.

At the second dinner between the two families, he noticed a blush of mortification creep across her face after one of her mother's more brazen attempts to attach Bingley to her older sister. Darcy found himself in sympathy with the lady, who obviously did not approve of scheming for a husband.

The third time the two parties met, he paid more attention to Miss Elizabeth and noticed the many glances she exchanged with her father. While Darcy still believed the gentleman should stir himself to control his family, he found himself on this occasion more struck by how uncommonly intelligent Miss Elizabeth's eyes were. When lit with laughter as they so often were, they were quite fine indeed.

Fine? Was it not just last week that you expressed yourself unmoved by her supposed beauty, Darcy? That thought followed him throughout the next week, until they once again dined at Longbourn. He watched Elizabeth for some minutes, trying to see the flaws in her appearance which he had so recently disapproved of, but he could not. When the Bennets joined them at Netherfield a few evenings later, he admired the easy, graceful way she carried herself and realized he could deny his attraction to Miss Elizabeth Bennet no longer.

Mortifying though such an attraction was, it did make future social obligations less odious. They were promised to a party at Lucas Lodge, an engagement Darcy had not looked on with much pleasure; however, as he scanned the room when he arrived, his gaze soon lit on the lady in question and he found it difficult to look elsewhere.

This will not do, Darcy. Despite the stern reminder to himself, he found his way near her. She was in conversation with Colonel Forster of the local militia, and though Darcy wished to join in, he knew not what to say. He had never been very good at speaking with those he did not know; he faltered and stumbled as he attempted to find a subject that would please them both. In truth, he had never been bothered enough to learn, but for the first time, he wished he possessed greater skill in conversing with young ladies.

Elizabeth smiled up at the Colonel, and her charm dazzled both men. "Colonel Forster," said she, "I believe it quite shameful that you have not entertained yourself."

The military man returned her smile. "Do you, Miss Eliza?"

"Indeed, sir. For as the commander of the militia, you are, of course, one of the leading personages in the area, and you must take the position Society has seen fit to bestow upon you."

"And what kind of entertainment would you have me offer? A card party?"

She shook her head, revealing for a moment the graceful curve of her neck. "Oh no, sir, for anyone can give a card party. No, from one of your standing nothing less than a ball would suffice."

"A ball!" Colonel Forster offered her his arm and they walked out of Darcy's earshot.

The impropriety of his own behavior in eavesdropping struck Darcy then, and he stayed where he was, at least for a time. He never let Miss Elizabeth out of his sight, however, and he was pleased when, some minutes later, she came back his direction in the company of Charlotte Lucas.

The soft cadence of Miss Elizabeth's voice drew Darcy closer. He thought he heard a hint of amusement, and he looked over at her to find those intelligent eyes fixed on him. "Did not you think, Mr. Darcy, that I expressed myself uncommonly well just now, when I was teasing Colonel Forster to give us a ball at Meryton?"

Darcy was dismayed to realize she had discerned his eavesdropping, but once discovered he could not pretend he had been doing otherwise. "With great energy," he agreed, "but it is a subject which always makes a lady energetic."

Her eyes laughed at him, and he hoped he was forgiven. "You are severe on us."

"It will be her turn soon to be teased," said Miss Lucas. "I am going to open the instrument, Eliza, and you know what follows."

Miss Elizabeth turned back to her friend, and if a frown could be merry, that was the expression she wore when she addressed Miss Lucas. "You are a very strange creature by way of a friend, always wanting me to play and sing before anybody and everybody! If my vanity had taken a musical turn, you would have been invaluable, but as it is, I would really rather not sit down before those who must be in the habit of hearing the very best performers."

Never before had Darcy seen a young lady turn down an opportunity to display her talents. Miss Elizabeth had yet again captured his attention, and he very much desired to hear her play. *Surely she possesses more skill than she is willing to acknowledge.*

He watched with some interest as Miss Lucas cajoled and eventually prevailed upon her friend. "Very well; if it must be so, it must," Miss Elizabeth said finally. She gave Darcy a sly glance and said, "There is a fine old saying, which everybody here is of course familiar with—'keep your breath to cool your porridge,'—and I shall keep mine to swell my song."

Despite Elizabeth's protestations, Darcy found nothing lacking in her performance—in fact, quite the opposite. *Her voice is clear and pleasant to listen to, and her playing light and unaffected.*

The same could not easily be said of Miss Mary

Bennet, who succeeded her at the pianoforte. If Miss Elizabeth's playing reflected her easy manners, then Miss Mary's was as pedantic as she, and about as pleasant to listen to as the sermons she favored. At the inducement of her two younger sisters, Miss Mary soon switched from sonatas to light airs, good for dancing. Darcy watched with a sense of mild astonishment as the two young girls danced about the room, their open smiles inviting the officers to join them—an invitation the men did not quickly turn down.

Gay laughter broke into his thoughts, and Miss Lydia sailed past him in the arms of an officer. From the grin on the young man's face, it was clear whatever comment he had just offered had not been entirely appropriate. *Why does her father not take control of her? If Georgiana ever behaved so...*

His ruminations were interrupted by their host, and Darcy braced himself for a supercilious display. He had discovered quite early in their stay in Hertfordshire that Sir William Lucas felt the distinction of his presentation at court a bit too strongly.

The gentleman did not disappoint. "What a charming amusement for young people this is, Mr. Darcy! There is nothing like dancing after all. I consider it as one of the first refinements of polished societies."

Darcy did not turn from the frolicking couples. "Certainly, sir; and it has the advantage also of being in vogue amongst the less polished societies in the world. Every savage can dance."

This subtle setdown would have told an astute man to leave the subject alone, but intelligence was not one of Sir William's fine qualities. The man smiled and said, "Your friend performs delightfully," as they both watched Bingley take the eldest Miss Bennet to the floor, "and I doubt not that you are an adept in the science yourself, Mr. Darcy."

Years of experience told Darcy where this was going. Sir William Lucas had two daughters of marriageable age, the eldest nearly twenty-seven, which would be considered firmly on the shelf in London society. If he admitted he could dance, he would soon be coerced into dancing with one of the Miss Lucases, but Darcy would not lie. "You saw me dance at Meryton, I believe, sir."

The jovial man rocked back on his heels. "Yes, indeed, and received no inconsiderable pleasure from the sight. Do you often dance at St. James's?"

Darcy's brows snapped together. *Of all the insinuating...* "Never, sir."

But Sir William would not be dissuaded. "Do you not think it would be a proper compliment to the place?"

"It is a compliment which I never pay to any place if I can avoid it," Darcy replied, his words both honest and brusque.

Sir William continued to speak, but Darcy knew not what the subject was. Something far more interesting than the gentleman's courteous comments caught his attention—Miss Elizabeth was walking back toward them, this time alone. *If I could but ask her to dance...*

Darcy took half a step toward her as she drew near, but Sir William, ever attentive, beat him to it. "My dear Miss Eliza, why are you not dancing? Mr. Darcy, you must allow me to present this young lady to you as a very desirable partner. You cannot refuse to dance, I am sure, when so much beauty is before you."

Darcy would have been glad to oblige Sir William, but Elizabeth withdrew her hand before he could take it. "Indeed, sir," she said to Sir William, a pretty smile on her face, "I have not the least intention of dancing. I entreat you not to suppose that I moved this way in order to beg for a partner."

Unbeknownst to Elizabeth, her words drew Darcy's admiration more than anything else could have. How many London ladies had not done exactly that? "It would be a great honor if you would dance with me, Miss Elizabeth," he told her, speaking the words in earnest for the first time in his life.

Miss Elizabeth smiled and shook her head, and the stab of disappointment surprised him. Sir William seemed to feel it too, for he launched into an embarrassing speech. "You excel so much in the dance, Miss Eliza, that it is cruel to deny me the happiness of seeing you; and though this gentleman dislikes the amusement in general, he can have no objection, I am sure, to oblige us for one half hour."

"Mr. Darcy is all politeness," Elizabeth answered with another smile.

"He is indeed—but considering the inducement, my dear Miss Eliza, we cannot wonder at his complaisance; for who would object to such a partner?"

In answer to Sir William's obsequiousness, Miss Elizabeth merely raised an eyebrow and turned away. In so doing, she may not have given Sir William what he desired, but she had wholly impressed Darcy. She was utterly unlike any female he had ever met.

He pictured again the laughing intelligence in her eyes. *Perhaps it is her eyes which render the rest of her face so attractive,* he mused. *They are so alive with emotion, so full of wit and good humor; one cannot help but be caught by them.*

So absorbed was he in his own thoughts that he did not notice Miss Bingley approach from the side. "I can guess the subject of your reverie," she said in a low tone.

He looked at her and then back across the room to

where Miss Elizabeth once again spoke with Miss Lucas. "I should imagine not."

Miss Bingley gazed out at the room, disdain evident on her features. "You are considering how insupportable it would be to pass many evenings in this manner—in such society; and indeed I am quite of your opinion. I was never more annoyed! The insipidity and yet the noise; the nothingness and yet the self-importance of all these people! What would I give to hear your strictures on them!"

She only echoed Darcy's earlier thoughts, but after his conversation with Miss Elizabeth, he could not agree with her. "Your conjecture is totally wrong, I assure you. My mind was more agreeably engaged. I have been meditating on the very great pleasure which a pair of fine eyes in the face of a pretty woman can bestow."

Miss Bingley raised her fan in a coy gesture. "Pray, tell me which of the young ladies has inspired such reflections?"

She now stood between Darcy and Elizabeth, so it was possible for him to look at her while she spoke and still observe Miss Elizabeth. His attention thus divided, it did not occur to him to dissemble. "Miss Elizabeth Bennet."

Surprise flashed through Miss Bingley's eyes, and Darcy realized too late the trap he had set for himself. "Miss Elizabeth Bennet! I am all astonishment." She flipped her fan open with a snap. "How long has she been such a favorite—and pray, when am I to wish you joy?"

The trap tightened, and Darcy winced. "That is exactly the question which I expected you to ask. A lady's imagination is very rapid; it jumps from admiration to love, from love to matrimony in a moment. I knew you would be wishing me joy."

He hoped to put her off by pointing out the ridiculous nature of her charge, but Miss Bingley showed her teeth in a feline smile. "Nay, if you are serious about it, I shall consider the matter as absolutely settled. You will have a charming mother-in-law, indeed, and of course she will be always at Pemberley with you."

This was too absurd to deserve an answer, and Darcy allowed her to continue to tease him on his future felicity. As long as she was thus employed, he remained at his leisure to watch Miss Elizabeth.

Chapter Six

"DARCY, YOU ARE wearing a path in what used to be a very fine rug."

Darcy continued pacing between the two leather chairs, heedless of Bingley's mild chastisement. "Why has she not written?" His fingers tapped a nervous rhythm against his leg as he considered all the dire occurrences which could have kept Georgiana from sending a letter.

"What has you so on edge?"

Darcy glanced back at Bingley. "I have yet to hear from Georgiana."

Bingley leaned back into his chair and assessed his friend. "I begin to think there is more to her removal from Ramsgate than you originally told me. Did something happen there?"

The lie sprung to his lips, but Darcy would not give it in the face of such a direct question. *Still, I cannot tell him the whole truth...* Bingley raised his cigar to his lips while he waited for an answer, and Darcy finally said, "I fear Georgiana received attentions from an unworthy suitor."

Bingley let out his breath on a long hiss. "That certainly explains your reluctance to leave London."

"Precisely. However, Richard is with her and he assured me... I just do not understand—"

"Why there has been no letter," Bingley finished.

Darcy did not have time to respond before a footman entered the room with a letter on a tray. "For you, Mr. Darcy."

Darcy snatched it up and gave a sigh of relief when he recognized Georgiana's elegant hand and his cousin's seal. He sat down in a chair by the window and began to read:

My dear brother,

I hope this letter finds you well and enjoying your stay with Mr. Bingley and his sisters. Please pass my regards on to them all.

I believe I am finally settling into life in town. Cousin Richard has been ever so kind since you left. He has even taken me to the Museum. I am sure I am a great trial, but he never complains.

Tell me a little of Hertfordshire, Fitzwilliam. Is the countryside as beautiful as Derbyshire? I confess; I cannot believe anyplace could compare, but then I am biased.

I will be glad to return home to Pemberley. I cannot believe eight months have passed since I left. Oh Brother— how I long to see the sunrise over the Derwent again. Fitzwilliam, do let us be home this spring in time to see the crocuses bloom. As fond as I have become of London, I do not think anything in the world as lovely as those sweet blossoms peeking above the frosty ground in February.

I hope you are enjoying yourself as much in Hertfordshire as I am in London. Keep yourself well, and write to me when you can.

Your devoted sister,
Georgiana

Darcy reached the end of the letter and returned to the first page immediately. A second reading revealed no hidden sorrow, none of the reserve which had characterized the last few weeks he had spent with his sister. He breathed a sigh of relief and relaxed against the back of the chair.

Bingley, who had remained silent while Darcy read, finally said, "By the smile on your face, I trust the letter contains good news."

Darcy folded the paper and placed it in his breast pocket. "Indeed, Bingley."

"Perhaps I may impose on your good mood then. Colonel Forster has invited us to dine with the officers tonight. Of course I will go, but I would be glad of your company."

Normally Darcy would refuse such an invitation. He had nothing against the Colonel, but some of his officers had proven less genteel. Today, however, his mood was complacent. "I believe I will join you, Bingley."

"Join Charles where Mr. Darcy?" said Miss Bingley, who entered the room just in time to hear that last pronouncement. "Surely not at Colonel Forster's, for I know how little you care for such coarse manners."

"Nevertheless, I do mean to dine there tonight."

Her attempt at a pout looked more like a grimace. "But what of Louisa and me? We will be left quite alone if all the gentlemen are gone, for Mr. Hurst intends to go as well."

"Invite Miss Bennet to share the evening meal with you," Bingley suggested. "I am sure she would be willing, and you have said you enjoy her company."

Irritation flashed quickly across his sister's face, but she had no choice but to agree. A servant was dispatched with a letter for Miss Bennet shortly before the gentlemen left.

The evening passed much as Darcy had expected, coarse company with worse manners, but the food was surprisingly good. Colonel Forster reminded him a great deal of Richard, and between him and the two gentlemen there soon subsisted an easy camaraderie which made Darcy willing to overlook the roughness of the general party.

"Well, Darcy?" Bingley inquired when they were on their way back to Netherfield. "Was the evening as objectionable as you anticipated?"

"I admit, Bingley, it was not."

"Indeed not," Mr. Hurst interjected, with far more energy than he usually displayed. "I have not seen a better level of card play since entering the neighborhood."

Darcy leaned back against the carriage seat. "That is hardly surprising, sir. From what my cousin has told me, militiamen often have little to do in the way of regular duties. With so much time on their hands, of course they develop an aptitude for cards."

Mr. Hurst snorted. "Aptitude! Devilish skill is more like it. Bingley, if we ever have the opportunity to invite them to Netherfield, I should like a chance to play again with Mr. Denny in particular."

"I am sure Caroline would be delighted to host a true party," Bingley said. "I will ask her about it tonight."

However, they found Miss Bennet still at Netherfield when they arrived, and her presence drove all else from Bingley's mind. She smiled at them in apology when they entered the house. "I am so sorry to impose, but I wonder if I might borrow your carriage, Mr. Bingley. I am afraid I did not anticipate the rain, and rode over on horseback."

Her dismay caught even Darcy's sympathy, and Bingley tripped over his words when he invited her to stay the night instead. "Then when morning comes, we will send you on home."

When morning came, however, it was clear to

everyone that Miss Bennet would not be going anywhere. The dampness in which she had been forced to remain for the whole of the previous afternoon had settled in her bones, leaving her with a chill and a nasty cough. Bingley insisted on calling for Mr. Jones, the local apothecary, and Miss Bennet was equally insistent that she must send a letter to her family, letting them know what had become of her.

After those messages were sent, the party sat down to breakfast, sans Miss Bennet, who had been made comfortable in her room. They were just finishing their coffee when a footman entered and cleared his throat. "Miss Elizabeth Bennet is here, sir," he told Bingley.

"Well, show her in."

The gentlemen rose when Miss Elizabeth entered, dressed in a gown whose soiled hem told plainly that the road was still wet. Then she brushed a wayward strand of hair from her face, and Darcy saw her eyes, bright with exercise, and her loveliness banished all other thoughts from Darcy's mind.

His sudden awareness of her caught him off guard, and he moved to the side of the room, where he could observe her freely. Her windblown hair clung to her cheeks in a most beguiling fashion, and he realized with a start that she was one of the handsomest women of his acquaintance.

"I am sorry to trouble you so early," Miss Elizabeth said, and Darcy's attention was drawn to her lips. "I received a note from Jane. Please, is she very ill?"

Concern added a note of sweetness to her voice, and the disdain Darcy heard in Miss Bingley's reply set his teeth on edge. "Do not trouble yourself with the time, Miss Eliza. It is quite natural you should come to see your sister."

"Jane is not well at all," Mrs. Hurst provided. "She slept ill, and as you can see, she was not well enough to leave her room."

Worry darkened Miss Elizabeth's eyes. "Is she feverish?"

Miss Bingley nodded. "I am afraid so."

Bingley walked toward Miss Elizabeth and took her hands in his. "We have called for Mr. Jones," he said comfortingly. "I have hopes he will tell us our concerns are exaggerated and that Miss Bennet will be returned to health in a few days' time."

Elizabeth managed a weak smile. "Thank you. May I see her?"

Miss Bingley rose from her seat. "Of course, Miss Eliza. I will take you to her room."

The ladies moved toward the stairs, and as Miss Elizabeth left the room, it was evident that the back of her petticoat was coated in mud. The thought of a lady walking such rough roads alone bordered on indelicate. *Was it quite necessary for her to expose herself to the elements, just to visit her sister?*

"I believe we must find some way of amusing ourselves today, gentlemen." Bingley's voice cut into Darcy's thoughts. "If we remain indoors, we will only get in the way."

Darcy was very willing to absent himself from the house and the disconcerting effect of Miss Elizabeth's presence. "Hertfordshire offers excellent hunting."

"A capital suggestion, Darcy. Mr. Hurst, will you join us?"

The lazy gentleman grunted his assent. His wife said, "Caroline and I will, of course, spend most of our day with the Bennet sisters."

"I trust you to treat them both with every politeness," Bingley said. The plans for the day were shared with Miss Bingley when she returned, and then the gentlemen departed to change.

They gathered in the entryway fifteen minutes later,

dressed in warm hunting clothes. A footman held the rifles and a bag to carry any birds they might hit. Bingley opened the door, and the early November sunshine seeped into the house. "Are we ready, gentlemen?"

Darcy and Hurst nodded, and they set out for the wooded area which surrounded Netherfield on three sides. From their rides across the property, Darcy and Bingley knew of a small pond where they might conceivably find fowl.

Their destination was approximately thirty minutes away on foot, over some rather steep hills. For Darcy and Bingley it was but an easy walk, but Hurst was puffing when they reached the water's edge. "Is this it?" he said, disappointment clear in his voice.

"It is." Bingley gestured for the footman to hand out rifles, but though Darcy readily accepted one, Hurst held up his hands in refusal.

"I think not. I have no intention of standing here in the shade on a cool November afternoon, with nothing to do but wait for a bird to appear." He surveyed the area and then pointed to a large tree on the bank. "There is a spot of sunshine; I am going to sit down for a rest. That walk left me entirely fatigued." He was asleep within moments, and Darcy and Bingley shared a look of amusement.

However, it did not take Darcy long to realize Bingley did not have much more interest in the hunting than did his brother-in-law. Birds came and went without Bingley's notice, and of the ones he shot at, he missed more than he hit. After his fifth missed shot, Darcy said, "Where are your thoughts, Bingley? For it is clear they are not here."

His friend smiled sheepishly. "You have caught me, I am afraid. I am worried about Miss Bennet. Do you think Mr. Jones has been to visit her yet?"

Darcy raised an eyebrow. Though it was plain to everyone in the neighborhood that Bingley preferred Miss Bennet, this was a new level of solicitude. He glanced at the sun and judged it to be mid-afternoon. "We should return to the house to change for dinner. Perhaps you will be able to inquire after her."

Bingley brightened. "Yes, let us. Hurst, are you ready?" They roused the gentleman and the whole party returned to the house, where Bingley immediately set out to find someone who could tell him the state of Miss Bennet's health.

That evening as he dressed for dinner, Darcy considered once again the Bennet ladies. He had escaped to the privacy of his own rooms when they returned to the house, and he had not heard anything about the apothecary's visit. He eyed his valet in the mirror and finally said, "Vincent, how does Miss Bennet fare?"

Vincent took a step back. "I beg your pardon, Mr. Darcy?"

Darcy flushed lightly. He was well aware his question was outside his normal behavior. He did not encourage gossip among his servants, and he never participated in it. *But I need to know if she...* "Come, man. I know you are aware of what goes on in this house. How ill is Miss Bennet?"

Vincent narrowed his eyes, and Darcy forced himself not to squirm under his servant's examination. "She has caught a violent cold, as was to be expected," he said finally. "Miss Elizabeth would go home, but Miss Bennet was so concerned when she announced her departure that Miss Bingley invited her to stay." Vincent snorted. "I do not imagine she enjoyed that."

Darcy's brow wrinkled in a frown. "Why would Miss Elizabeth not wish to stay, if her sister is truly ill?"

Vincent raised an eyebrow, and Darcy realized he

had referred to Miss Bingley. He nodded to show he understood, though this was every bit as confusing as what he had first believed. *Why would Miss Bingley begrudge giving every consideration to her sick guest?*

Vincent said no more, and Darcy respected his circumspection, though he felt he had missed something. A few minutes more, and he was ready to go down for dinner.

When Darcy exited his room, he heard the quiet snick of a door closing on the adjacent corridor, where he knew Miss Bennet's room was. Unwilling to encounter Miss Elizabeth on the stairs, he waited a moment to allow her to reach the dining room before he did.

In fact, Darcy was the last to arrive. Upon his entry Bingley gestured for the footmen to bring in the first course. "And how is Jane doing?" Miss Bingley asked, and Darcy gathered she was continuing a conversation with Miss Elizabeth that his arrival had interrupted.

"She feels quite ill, I am afraid. She wished me to send her apologies for keeping to her room."

"Well, of course we could not expect her to join us," Mrs. Hurst exclaimed. "The poor dear, to have a cold. It is quite a miserable experience."

"Oh yes," Miss Bingley chimed in. "I declare there is nothing so wretched as lying ill in bed. And to be in a strange house as well! When I am sick, I wish for nothing more than the comforts of home."

Miss Bingley did not wait for a reply from Elizabeth, but turned to Darcy instead. "Mr. Darcy, I hear you received a letter from your sister yesterday. Tell me, how does she fare in London?"

The rapid change of topic caught Darcy off guard, but he answered her question tolerably well. Unfortunately, his answer led to another question, and he quickly found himself locked in conversation with the two people in the room he least wished to converse with—Miss Bingley and Mrs. Hurst.

Elizabeth's light laugh caught his attention, and he looked over at her. She and Bingley spoke with some animation, he supposed about something for the elder Miss Bennet's comfort. He had been glad when he sat down to be on the opposite side of the table from her, but now he wished he could be closer.

At last, the footmen collected the dishes from the final course of the evening. Miss Elizabeth rose to her feet when they exited the room and said, "I believe it is time I returned to Jane. She was asleep when I left, but I am sure she is awake now and wanting my company."

"We must make every effort to give her some home comforts," Bingley said. "Miss Elizabeth, is there anything in particular, anything your mother would do for your sister that we can offer?"

Miss Elizabeth smiled. "I fear my mother is not the most tender of nursemaids. Jane is so very agreeable; I cannot think of anything we might lack."

"If anything comes to mind, please just let the servants know."

"Pray come down to join us if she sleeps again," Miss Bingley added, and Miss Elizabeth nodded her thanks before she left the room.

Darcy caught the half-smile on Miss Elizabeth's face and wondered at it. A minute later, her reason became clear. No sooner had she gone than Miss Bingley began to abuse her.

"I declare, I have never been so surprised by the manners of the lady as I have been by Miss Eliza Bennet," Miss Bingley remarked. "They are very bad indeed, a mixture of pride and impertinence that is utterly without fashion. And did she really just leave us to tend to her sick sister? She truly has no conversation. I pity Jane her company. Of course, her style is lacking, but no one expects that in the country —even from one reputed as a great beauty."

The sisters shared a laugh, and then Mrs. Hurst offered her observations. "She has nothing, in short, to recommend her, but being an excellent walker. I shall never forget her appearance this morning. She really looked almost wild."

Wild is not the word I would use. Darcy shifted uncomfortably at the memory of Miss Elizabeth's appearance that morning.

"She did indeed, Louisa! I could hardly keep my countenance. Very nonsensical to come at all!" Miss Bingley *tsked* softly. "Why must *she* be scampering about the country, because her sister had a cold? Her hair so untidy, so blowsy!"

The ladies laughed again, and then Mrs. Hurst continued. "Yes, and her petticoat; I hope you saw her petticoat, six inches deep in mud, I am absolutely certain; and the gown which had been let down to hide it, not doing its office."

"Your picture may be very exact, Louisa," Bingley countered, "but this was all lost upon me. I thought Miss Elizabeth Bennet looked remarkably well when she came into the room this morning. Her dirty petticoat quite escaped my notice."

Miss Bingley turned to Darcy, and her arch smile seemed very smug when compared with Miss Elizabeth's genuine expressions. "You observed it, Mr. Darcy, I am sure, and I am inclined to think that you would not wish to see *your sister* make such an exhibition."

"Certainly not." There was no way to deny it, but he kept any hint of censure from his voice when he agreed. *After all, the difference in age and station of life quite excuses Miss Elizabeth from any wrongdoing in this case.*

He had thought this would end the conversation, but Miss Bingley took his comment as license to continue. "To walk three miles, or four miles, or five miles, or whatever it is, above her ankles in dirt, and alone, quite alone! What could she mean by it? It seems to me to show an abominable sort of conceited independence, a most country town indifference to decorum."

Darcy pressed his lips together to hold in a stinging retort, but Bingley was not as restrained. "It shows an affection for her sister that is very pleasing."

She ignored her brother and turned instead to Darcy. "I am afraid, Mr. Darcy, that this adventure has rather affected your admiration of her fine eyes."

He now regretted that wayward comment, for honesty compelled him to say, "Not at all, they were brightened by the exercise."

Miss Bingley stared at him, her lips compressed in a thin line. *What did I say?* He went over his words again, and realized with some chagrin how they might be taken. *And yet I said nothing but the truth. If she chooses to believe I am smitten by Miss Elizabeth, that is her own problem.*

After a minute, Mrs. Hurst picked the conversation up at its original topic. "I have an excessive regard for Jane Bennet, she is really a very sweet girl, and I wish with all my heart she were well settled. But with such a father and mother, and such low connections, I am afraid there is no chance of it."

Miss Bingley's energy revived at this. "I think I have heard you say that their uncle is an attorney in Meryton."

"Yes, and they have another, who lives somewhere near Cheapside."

"That is capital!"

Bingley frowned. "If they had uncles enough to fill all Cheapside," said he, "it would not make them one jot less agreeable."

For the first time, Darcy felt uneasy about Bingley's affection for Miss Bennet. He had not before considered her as a true rival with Georgiana for Bingley's affections. "But it must very materially lessen their chance of marrying men of any consideration in the world," he explained.

Bingley gave no sign of hearing him, but from his sisters, however, Darcy's remark received ready agreement. "Exactly so, Mr. Darcy," Mrs. Hurst said.

"You do have such a way stating things," said Miss Bingley.

Something in the compliment struck Darcy as odd. He remembered Vincent's words, and for the first time it occurred to him that Miss Bingley might believe she stood a chance at gaining his favor. *And yet, if that is the case, what can I do? Bingley is my friend and I am a guest in his home.*

Darcy still did not know the answer when Miss Bingley stood a moment later and glanced at the clock. "Louisa and I will leave you gentlemen to your cigars while we visit Jane. We will join you in the drawing room in approximately half an hour. Perhaps we might play cards this evening."

To Darcy's relief, conversation over port was minimal. Bingley appeared deep in thought, and Hurst settled himself into a chair by the fire for a brief nap. It was not difficult to wake him at the appointed time, however, for the promise of cards provided ample inducement.

They played loo, the stakes growing higher with each hand. After four rounds Miss Elizabeth appeared at the door. "Would you care to join us at cards, Miss Eliza?" Miss Bingley asked.

Elizabeth glanced at the table and shook her head. "Thank you but no. I will not stay below long enough to play. I shall amuse myself with a book before I need to return to my sister."

Mr. Hurst leaned forward, his mouth agape. "Do you prefer reading to cards? That is rather singular."

Darcy privately agreed, but not in the sense Hurst meant. It was his opinion that ladies in general were too much in need of outside stimulus, rather than being able to amuse themselves. Miss Elizabeth's enjoyment of a good book was singular indeed.

Miss Bingley smirked. "Miss Eliza Bennet despises cards. She is a great reader, and has no pleasure in anything else."

The insult was clear. Darcy was almost tempted to speak out in Miss Elizabeth's defense, but she raised one eyebrow and he knew she could handle herself. "I deserve neither such praise nor such censure. I am *not* a great reader, and I have pleasure in many things."

Well answered, Darcy thought. *How I would love to see you go against Lady Catherine.*

"In nursing your sister I am sure you have pleasure, and I hope it will soon be increased by seeing her quite well," Bingley said, using his role as host to steer the conversation in a more genial manner. Elizabeth smiled and thanked him, and then picked Fanny Burney's *Cecilia* up from a nearby table. "Is there something here to your taste? If not, I can easily go to the library and bring you something else. And I wish my collection were larger for your benefit and my own credit; but I am an idle fellow, and though I have not many, I have more than I ever look into."

"No, thank you. These here will be just fine."

Miss Bingley laid her next card on the table. "I am astonished that my father should have left so small a collection of books. What a delightful library you have at Pemberley, Mr. Darcy!"

"It ought to be good. It has been the work of many generations." There was something about Miss Bingley that always brought out Darcy's public manners—that is, his practiced air of boredom and disinterest. No matter what she said, he could not bring himself to have a real conversation with her.

"And then you have added so much to it yourself; you are always buying books."

He shrugged off her simpering compliment and played a card. "I cannot comprehend the neglect of a family library in such days as these."

"Neglect! I am sure you neglect nothing that can add to the beauties of that noble place. Charles, when you build your house, I wish it may be half as delightful as Pemberley."

The friends exchanged an amused look. "I wish it may," Bingley said.

Miss Bingley would not give up. "But I would really advise you to make your purchase in that neighborhood, and take Pemberley for a kind of model. There is not a finer county in England than Derbyshire."

Bingley grinned at Darcy and voiced the thought the two gentlemen shared. "With all my heart; I will buy Pemberley itself if Darcy will sell it."

Miss Bingley pursed her lips. "I am talking of possibilities, Charles."

"Upon my word, Caroline, I should think it more possible to get Pemberley by purchase than by imitation."

Darcy had noticed several minutes ago that their conversation had caught Miss Elizabeth's attention. Now she set her book down and took a seat at the table between Bingley and Mrs. Hurst. Her nearness distracted Darcy from play for a brief moment, but the ever-vigilant Miss Bingley soon called him back to himself. "Is Miss Darcy much grown since the spring? Will she be as tall as I am?"

Darcy tilted his head back and considered. "I think she will. She is now about Miss Elizabeth Bennet's height, or rather taller," he said, eyeing the lady in question.

Miss Bingley sighed, and Darcy wondered what she would say now. "How I long to see her again! I never met with anybody who delighted me so much. Such a countenance, such manners, and so extremely accomplished for her age! Her performance on the pianoforte is exquisite."

Bingley spoke before Darcy had fully processed this long recitation of his sister's charms. "It is amazing to me," he said, "how young ladies can have patience to be so very accomplished, as they all are."

Miss Bingley placed her hand on her chest. "All young ladies accomplished! My dear Charles, what do you mean?"

"Yes, all of them, I think. They all paint tables, cover screens, and net purses. I scarcely know anyone who cannot do all this, and I am sure I have never heard a young lady spoken of for the first time, without being informed that she was very accomplished."

Though Darcy had little liking for the conversation, Bingley's naïveté forced him to break in. "Your list of the common extent of accomplishments has too much truth," he agreed. "The word is applied to many a woman who deserves it no otherwise than by netting a purse or covering a screen. But I am very far from agreeing with you in your estimation of ladies in general. I cannot boast of knowing more than half a dozen, in the whole range of my acquaintance, that are really accomplished."

Miss Bingley's agreement was instantaneous. "Nor I,

I am sure."

Miss Elizabeth did not attempt to hide the incredulity spreading across her face. "Then you must comprehend a great deal in your idea of an accomplished woman."

Her honest question interested him far more than Caroline Bingley's instant agreement, and he warmed to the conversation. "Yes. I do comprehend a great deal in it."

"Oh, certainly!" cried Miss Bingley, before he could finish his thought, or allow Miss Elizabeth to question him further. "No one can really be esteemed accomplished who does not greatly surpass what is usually met with. A woman must have a thorough knowledge of music, singing, drawing, dancing, and the modern languages, to deserve the word; and besides all this, she must possess a certain something in her air and manner of walking, the tone of her voice, her address and expressions, or the word will be but half-deserved."

Darcy eyed Miss Elizabeth, whose smile had widened with each quality listed. He glanced down at the book she still held in her lap, and a sudden desire to tease her with a compliment seized him. "All this she must possess, and to all this she must yet add something more substantial, in the improvement of her mind by extensive reading."

Miss Elizabeth's fine eyes danced with amusement. "I am no longer surprised at your knowing *only* six accomplished women. I rather wonder now at your knowing *any*."

He set his cards down on the table and turned fully toward her. "Are you so severe on your own sex, as to doubt the possibility of all this?" It was an honest question; most ladies he knew—nay, most people—would take this opportunity for self-gratulation, claiming all these qualities for themselves.

She shook her head. "I never saw such a woman. I never saw such capacity, and taste, and application, and elegance, as you describe, united."

Instantly, Miss Bingley and Mrs. Hurst launched into the tirade he would have expected before, listing off all the women they knew who fit this mold. In doing so, they not only belied their earlier statement that only a few women deserved to be known as accomplished, Darcy believed they also put themselves in very poor contrast to Miss Bennet. Her decorous humility was even more attractive in comparison to their vain cries of outrage.

Mr. Hurst soon called them back to the card table, and Darcy was not sorry to see the conversation end. *Miss Elizabeth has an astonishing ability to discompose me.*

He was grateful when, a few minutes later, that lady rose from her own seat and walked toward the door. "Oh, Miss Eliza, you are not leaving so soon," Miss Bingley exclaimed, but this time, Darcy could hear the note of falseness in her voice.

"I am afraid I must," Miss Elizabeth said. "You understand, my first concern is Jane."

"Of course it is," Bingley said. "We could credit you with nothing less. Pray tell me if there is anything that can be done for her."

Miss Elizabeth smiled in receipt of this request and curtsied prettily. On the whole, there was nothing in her manner of which Darcy could disapprove, and if he could but master his own attraction to her, he would be very glad of her company.

Darcy's approbation of the lady was not shared by all in the room. Miss Bingley tossed a card down on the table and then rested her chin on her hand as she surveyed her companions. "Eliza Bennet is one of those young ladies who seek to recommend themselves to the other sex by undervaluing their own, and with many men, I daresay, it succeeds. But in my opinion, it is a paltry device, a very mean art."

She looked directly at Darcy when she leveled this accusation, no doubt hoping for some reaction from him. But Darcy refused to be baited. Tonight had shown him a smallness of character about her which he had not previously known. "Undoubtedly there is meanness in *all* the arts which ladies sometimes condescend to employ for captivation. Whatever bears an affinity with cunning is despicable."

Miss Bingley's gaze dropped to the table, and Darcy had all the satisfaction of knowing that he was understood. *And let us see if that does not put an end to her sniping,* he thought.

Miss Elizabeth returned before Miss Bingley could find her tongue. Her hands were clenched tightly in front of her, and she worried her lower lip between her teeth. "I am afraid Jane is feeling worse, rather than better as I had hoped," she said, her face drawn with tension.

Bingley rose to his feet with alacrity. "Let us call for Mr. Jones immediately," he suggested.

"No, this is not something a simple country doctor can advise on," Miss Bingley protested.

Mrs. Hurst chimed in quickly. "Clearly we must send to town for a physician."

"I am sure that will not be necessary," Miss Elizabeth said, "but if she does not feel better in the morning, I will gladly accept your offer to send for Mr. Jones."

Bingley frowned and cajoled, but the lady would not be moved. She soon left the room to go back to her sister. Bingley was quite out of sorts for the rest of the evening, while his sisters, after dramatic declarations of their misery, somehow managed to assuage their

own feelings by singing duets until the evening drew
to a close.

Chapter Seven

THE LADIES HAD already retreated to Miss Bennet's room when Darcy came in for breakfast the next morning, and by the time he realized Miss Elizabeth had sent for not only Mr. Jones but her mother, it was too late for escape.

Muffled giggles caught his attention before the door of the breakfast room opened to admit Caroline Bingley, Mrs. Bennet, and her daughters. Darcy frowned at the younger girls, who sidled off to a corner to whisper to one another. *If they are to be out in public, they should be taught to behave with propriety.*

Ever polite, Bingley joined them in conversation. "I hope you have not found Miss Bennet worse than you expected," he said, addressing Mrs. Bennet, who stood in the middle of the room with only Miss Elizabeth beside her.

The woman smiled and simpered at Bingley like a young lady at her first ball. "Indeed I have, sir. She is a great deal too ill to be moved. Mr. Jones said we must not think of moving her. We must trespass a little longer on your kindness."

Darcy raised his eyebrows—as far as he knew, no one had suggested Miss Bennet be moved. The possibility that the mother had actually engineered her daughter's stay at Netherfield occurred to him. *Is she truly that desperate to gain Bingley as her son-in-law?* he wondered with dawning horror.

Bingley, however, was far too kind to suspect such a thing. "Removed!" he cried. "It must not be thought of. My sister, I am sure, will not hear of her removal."

Darcy's sympathies were with Miss Bingley, who had no choice but to answer as her brother had dictated. "You may depend upon it, madam, that Miss Bennet shall receive every possible attention while she remains with us."

"You are too good to us, and especially to my Jane," Mrs. Bennet said. "I am sure if it was not for such good friends I do not know what would become of her, for she is very ill indeed, and suffers a vast deal, though with the greatest patience in the world—which is always the way with her, for she has, without exception, the sweetest temper I ever met with. I often tell my other girls they are nothing to *her*."

Every word from the woman's mouth sunk Darcy's opinion of her lower still. Degrading younger daughters in favor of the eldest was a trick he had seen many times, and one he despised.

Mrs. Bennet continued, oblivious to his thoughts. "You have a sweet room here, Mr. Bingley, and a charming prospect over the gravel walk. I do not know a place in the country that is equal to Netherfield Park. You will not think of quitting it in a hurry, I hope, though you have but a short lease."

Here at least Bingley disappointed her. "Whatever I do is done in a hurry, and therefore if I should resolve to quit Netherfield Park, I should probably be off in five minutes. At present, however, I consider myself as quite fixed here," he said in the off-handed manner Darcy knew so well.

Elizabeth joined in the conversation. "That is exactly what I should have supposed of you."

Bingley smiled at her. "You begin to comprehend me, do you?"

"Oh, yes! I understand you perfectly." Her lovely eyes sparkled at Bingley, and Darcy pursed his lips. That Miss Elizabeth should comprehend any man so well did not sit well with him, and that the man was Bingley somehow made it worse.

"I wish I might take this for a compliment; but to be so easily seen through I am afraid is pitiful," Bingley said.

Darcy crossed his arms. The easy familiarity in Bingley's tone rankled him, and for the first time, he was not inclined to disagree with his friend's ready self-deprecation. *Indeed, you are quite pitiful,* he agreed silently.

"That is as it happens," Miss Elizabeth said, and Darcy was gratified she did not immediately offer the commendation Bingley asked for. "It does not necessarily follow that a deep, intricate character is more or less estimable than such a one as yours."

Mrs. Bennet's shrill voice startled Darcy. "Lizzy, remember where you are, and do not run on in the wild manner that you are suffered to do at home."

Bingley continued on as if Mrs. Bennet had not spoken. "I did not know before that you were a studier of character. It must be an amusing study."

"Yes, but intricate characters are the *most* amusing. They have at least that advantage."

Finally Darcy felt it necessary to break into their private conversation, though he could not say why. "The country can in general supply but few subjects for such a study. In a country neighborhood you move in a very confined and unvarying society."

At last, she turned those laughing brown eyes on him, and Darcy suddenly did not mind the topic of conversation in the slightest. "But people themselves alter so much, there is something new to be observed in them forever," she countered.

Her face was serious, but for a smile that played with the ends of her mouth. Darcy was so caught by the dimples that seemed to appear and disappear at will that he missed his opportunity to refute her latest assertion.

Instead, it was Mrs. Bennet who next added her voice to the conversation. "Yes, indeed! I assure you there is quite as much of *that* going on in the country as in town."

Her vitriol took the whole room by surprise, Darcy in particular. He stared at her for a moment, and then, not trusting himself to say anything pleasant to her, he turned away. Not even the surprisingly intriguing conversation with Miss Elizabeth was worth tangling with her mother.

Mrs. Bennet, however, was incapable of perceiving the snub. Instead, she took his lack of response as a victory and continued on the same line of thought. "I cannot see that London has any great advantage over the country for my part, except the shops and public places. The country is a vast deal pleasanter, is not it, Mr. Bingley?"

Darcy barely restrained a snort. Her motives were patently obvious; she sought to turn her perceived victory over him into a promise from Bingley that he would remain in Hertfordshire indefinitely. *I shall have to prise him from here—this is no company for a lady like Georgiana.*

He was not unaware that he made assumptions on his friend's intentions, but the match between Bingley and Georgiana was so equal on both sides, that Darcy had come to regard it as something of a settled thing. Now that relationship offered yet another benefit, as Bingley's courtship of Georgiana would necessarily pull him away from Hertfordshire.

As always, Bingley managed to be polite without lying—diplomatic, Darcy supposed. "When I am in the country I never wish to leave it; and when I am in town it is pretty much the same. They each have their advantages, and I can be equally happy in either."

"Aye—that is because you have the right disposition. But that gentleman —" from the corner of his eye, Darcy saw her direct a glare at him—"seemed to think the country was nothing at all."

That was not at all what he had said, but he cared too little for Mrs. Bennet's opinion to explain himself. *Let her misunderstand my every word, if it keeps her from directing her superciliousness at me.*

"Indeed, Mama, you are mistaken," said Elizabeth. "You quite mistook Mr. Darcy. He only meant that there were not such a variety of people to be met with in the country as in town, which you must acknowledge to be true."

Her quick defense and understanding of him gratified Darcy. He caught a glimpse of her reflection in the window, and her reddened cheeks drew his sympathy. *You are a charming young lady, Miss Elizabeth, but I fear few men will wish to attach themselves to your family.*

As if to prove his point, her mother continued without heeding her much wiser daughter. "Certainly, my dear, nobody said there were; but as to not meeting with many people in this neighborhood, I believe there are few neighborhoods larger. I know we dine with four and twenty families."

From where he stood, Darcy could easily hear the sudden coughs and whispers between Bingley's sisters, and he shook his head. Ridiculous as the statement was, one did not mock a guest to her face.

"Has Charlotte Lucas called at Longbourn since I

left, Mama?" Miss Elizabeth asked, in an obvious attempt to turn her attention to another topic.

It almost worked. "Yes, she called yesterday with her father. What an agreeable man Sir William is, Mr. Bingley—is not he? So much the man of fashion, so genteel and so easy! He always has something to say to everybody. *That* is my idea of good breeding; and those persons who fancy themselves very important, and never open their mouths, quite mistake the matter."

Better to keep one's mouth shut and appear ill-bred than to open it and remove all doubt, Darcy thought, with some indignation. Really! That he should be compared to Sir William and found lacking.

"Did Charlotte dine with you?"

Miss Elizabeth seemed determined to turn the focus of the conversation away from Darcy, and he admired her efforts. He knew he did not bear up well under public scrutiny, though in this case he cared little enough for the result.

"No, she would go home. I fancy she was wanted about the mince pies. For my part, Mr. Bingley, *I* always keep servants that can do their own work; *my* daughters are brought up differently. But everybody is to judge for themselves, and the Lucases are a very good sort of girls, I assure you. It is a pity they are not handsome! Not that *I* think Charlotte so *very* plain— but then she is our particular friend."

Darcy was not sure which was worse: the invectives on his own character, or this fawning after Bingley and his good opinion. The woman seemed unable to hold any other thoughts in her head, and she would bounce back and forth between the two subjects and nothing else.

"She seems a very pleasant young woman," Bingley said generously of Charlotte Lucas, naturally oblivious to the undercurrents in the conversation.

Darcy sometimes wished Bingley would be more aware of the machinations of scheming mamas—*But if he were,* he thought, *he would not be Bingley.* It was plain to him what such a commendation of another young lady would lead to, and his assumption was correct.

"Oh dear, yes! But you must own she is very plain. Lady Lucas herself has often said so, and envied me Jane's beauty. I do not like to boast of my own child —" here Darcy could not help but snort quietly, for it seemed that was all Mrs. Bennet did like to do—"but to be sure, Jane—one does not often see anybody better looking. It is what everybody says. I do not trust my own partiality. When she was only fifteen, there was a gentleman at my brother Gardiner's in town so much in love with her that my sister-in- law was sure he would make her an offer before we came away. But, however, he did not. Perhaps he thought her too young. However, he wrote some verses on her, and very pretty they were."

"And so ended his affection," Elizabeth interrupted, and Darcy marveled at the way she controlled her mother. "There has been many a one, I fancy, overcome in the same way. I wonder who first discovered the efficacy of poetry in driving away love!"

Such a contrary way of thinking compelled Darcy to turn around, and he rejoined the conversation, almost against his will. "I have been used to consider poetry as the *food* of love."

Elizabeth smiled at him, and Darcy's heart stopped, stuttered, and then raced. "Of a fine, stout, healthy love it may. Everything nourishes what is strong already. But if it be only a slight, thin sort of inclination, I am convinced that one good sonnet will drive it entirely away."

That she could express such a ridiculous belief caught his attention; that she could make it sound reasonable made him smile. *Here is a young lady I would gladly meet in conversation, were it not for the presence of her mother.*

A moment later, Mrs. Bennet spoke again, and Darcy cringed for an instant before realizing that she merely thanked Bingley, however obsequiously, for keeping Jane at Netherfield Park during her illness. "I do apologize that you must have Lizzy too, but they are so close, you know; when she heard Jane was ill there was nothing for it—she must walk to Netherfield Park that very hour."

Darcy glanced over at Elizabeth, who blushed warmly under her mother's criticism. Little did either woman know that it was this considerate nature of Elizabeth's that had first recommended her to Darcy. The friendship he had witnessed between the sisters that first evening at Longbourn had called to mind his relationship with his own sister, and he knew that were he in Elizabeth's position and Georgiana was ill, he would do whatever lay in his power to ease her discomfort.

Bingley obviously agreed. "Of course she must," he said warmly. "I assure you, Mrs. Bennet, neither of your daughters are a burden on my household. We are glad to have them here until such time as Miss Bennet is fit to travel home."

"Yes, indeed, Mrs. Bennet. Jane and Eliza are very welcome here," Miss Bingley said, though Darcy could easily hear the lie in her words.

"Well, I cannot thank you enough for such hospitality. I suppose, though, we must be getting back to our own home. Would you be so good as to have your servant call the carriage?"

The two younger Bennet sisters had, until this time, been talking between themselves off to the side of the room. Apparently, their mother's words were a signal for the youngest to step forward and speak in a manner entirely too bold. "Mr. Bingley, when are you to give a ball here at Netherfield Park?" She gazed up at him through flirtatiously lowered lashes. "For you promised you would, sir—indeed, you did—and it would be quite shameful if you did not keep your word."

Bingley was far more cordial in the face of such impropriety than Darcy would have been. "I am perfectly ready, I assure you, to keep my engagement, and when your sister is recovered, you shall if you please, name the very day of the ball. But you would not wish to be dancing while she is ill."

"Oh! Yes—it would be much better to wait until Jane was well, and by that time most likely Captain Carter would be at Meryton again," Miss Lydia replied, her broad, jovial tone indicating her complaisance with the suggestion. Darcy thought he could see a hint of excitement brewing in the mother's eyes, which he found even more distasteful, but Miss Lydia was not done speaking. "And when you have given your ball, I shall insist on their giving one also. I shall tell Colonel Forster that it will be quite a shame if he does not."

Before anyone could answer that, a servant appeared to announce the Bennets' carriage was ready. Darcy rejoiced to see them leave; he did not think he had ever been forced to suffer through a more inane conversation in his life.

Miss Elizabeth followed her family to the door and then went upstairs to sit with Jane, so the breakfast room was free of Bennets for a time. Miss Bingley and Mrs. Hurst took advantage of this and began discussing with great animation the vagaries of their visitors.

Even Bingley, mild-mannered though he was, could not argue with many of the statements his sisters made. The family had shown themselves to be entirely unrefined, and Darcy was glad to see his friend's usual good humor was dampened by their visit. *Perhaps this has shown him the lack of wisdom in pursuing a relationship with Miss Bennet.*

He was surprised, however, when Miss Bingley addressed the conversation toward him. "Did you notice how you were shunned by Mrs. Bennet, Mr. Darcy? I am sure it pains you deeply that you have not met with her exacting standards."

"The only thing that woman is qualified to have exacting standards on is ridiculousness and impropriety," he said, letting his disdain show clearly.

Bingley at last was driven to respond. "Darcy, that is ungenerous. She is not perhaps as discerning in tastes as a lady in town would be, but she does care for her children."

"Charles, if she truly cared for her children she would teach them some discretion." Miss Bingley rolled her eyes.

"Miss Elizabeth was perfectly refined," Bingley said, refusing to grant the point.

"Yes, of course she was," Mrs. Hurst agreed. "Poor Miss Eliza, having such a family as that."

"Oh yes, indeed, Louisa. She is not perhaps the prettiest of ladies—though her eyes might be called fine—" this, with a sly glance up at Darcy—"but she is a very nice young lady. It is too bad that her family situation makes her so undesirable to any one of consequence."

Miss Bingley looked to him for a reply, but he was not sure if she wished him to agree or disagree. He refused to answer in any way, either by words or expression. Commenting on Miss Elizabeth Bennet was not a task he felt up to at the moment, no matter what she might say about that lady's *fine eyes*.

Chapter Eight

WHEN THE GENTLEMEN rejoined the ladies in the drawing room after dinner that evening, Darcy sat down with pen and paper to reply to Georgiana's letter. It should have been a solitary activity, but to his consternation, Miss Bingley would not leave him in peace.

"How delighted Miss Darcy will be to receive such a letter." When he did not reply, she said, "You write uncommonly fast."

That was so patently untrue, he could not remain silent. "You are mistaken. I write rather slowly."

He knew too much of Caroline Bingley to suppose this rebuff would dissuade her. "How many letters you must have occasion to write in the course of the year! Letters of business too! How odious I should think them!"

Having spoken once, it seemed he could not ignore her again. "It is fortunate, then, that they fall to my lot instead of to yours."

"Pray tell your sister that I long to see her."

"I have already done so once, by your desire."

The hairs on the back of his neck pricked with awareness; he glanced up from his letter just long enough to ascertain that Miss Bennet, apparently engrossed in her needlework, barely managed to hide a smile. *Unless her stitchery is unusually amusing, she must be attending to Miss Bingley's incessant chatter. Let us see if I am correct.*

He waited eagerly for Miss Bingley's next remark; it was not long in coming. "I am afraid you do not like your pen. Let me mend it for you. I mend pens remarkably well."

"Thank you—but I always mend my own."

There—though her eyes were still fastened on the cloth she held, she smiled yet again. Miss Bingley's commentary, previously annoying to Darcy, now offered a chance to admire Miss Bennet's quick wit.

"How can you contrive to write so even?"

Miss Bennet pursed her lips in an effort to hold in her laughter, and her dimple ruined Darcy's concentration once more. Thankfully, Miss Bingley did not seem to need a response. "Tell your sister I am delighted to hear of her improvement on the harp, and pray let her know that I am quite in raptures with her beautiful little design for a table, and I think it infinitely superior to Miss Grantley's."

With utter solemnity, he said, "Will you give me leave to defer your raptures till I write again? At present I have not the room to do them justice."

"Oh! It is of no consequence. I shall see her in January. But do you always write such charming long letters to her, Mr. Darcy?"

From the corner of his eye, Darcy saw Elizabeth bow her head low over her needlework to hide her amusement. This dance of interacting with her without actually speaking directly to her stimulated Darcy more than he had imagined conversation with a lady ever could.

By chance, Miss Bennet's eyes met his for a bare instant before dropping back to her lap. The sparkle there stole his breath, and he paused to catch it before he could answer Miss Bingley's question. "They are generally long; but whether always charming, it is not for me to determine."

Miss Bingley smiled coyly. "It is a rule with me, that a person who can write a long letter, with ease, cannot write ill."

Bingley, lounging in a chair by the fire, took this opportunity to join the conversation. "That will not do for compliment to Darcy, Caroline, because he does *not* write with ease. He studies too much for words of four syllables—do you not, Darcy?"

Darcy realized with a start he had almost forgotten anyone else was in the room, so intent was he on his game with Elizabeth. His discomfort acute, he said, "My style of writing is very different from yours."

Eager that she should not be forgotten, Miss Bingley interjected. "Oh! Charles writes in the most careless way imaginable. He leaves out half his words, and blots the rest."

Bingley shrugged; clearly the epithet against him did not bother him. "My ideas flow so rapidly that I have not time to express them—by which means my letters sometimes convey no ideas at all to my correspondents."

Miss Bennet joined the conversation then but Mr. Darcy had little liking for the subject. "Your humility, Mr. Bingley, must disarm reproof."

Her continued praise of Bingley throughout the day provoked Darcy in a way little else could, and for once, he spoke without thinking. "Nothing is more deceitful than the appearance of humility. It is often only carelessness of opinion, and sometimes an indirect boast."

Bingley raised an eyebrow. "And which of the two do you call *my* little recent piece of modesty?"

Darcy put his pen down and leaned back in his

chair. "The indirect boast—for you are really proud of your defects in writing, because you consider them as proceeding from a rapidity of thought and carelessness of execution, which, if not estimable, you think at least highly interesting."

The idea that Elizabeth might find Bingley fascinating added a bite to his tone. "The power of doing anything with quickness is always much prized by the possessor, and often without any attention to the imperfection of the performance. When you told Mrs. Bennet this morning that if you ever resolved on quitting Netherfield Park you should be gone in five minutes, you meant it to be a sort of panegyric, a compliment to yourself—and yet what is there so very laudable in a precipitance which must leave very necessary business undone, and can be of no real advantage to yourself or anyone else?"

Bingley blinked, but quickly rallied to defend himself. "Nay, this is too much, to remember at night all the foolish things that were said in the morning. And yet, upon my honor, I believed what I said of myself to be true, and I believe it at this moment. At least, therefore, I did not assume the character of needless precipitance merely to show off before the ladies."

For some unfathomable reason, this upset Darcy even more. "I dare say you believed it; but I am by no means convinced that you would be gone with such celerity. Your conduct would be quite as dependent on chance as that of any man I know; and if, as you were mounting your horse, a friend were to say, 'Bingley, you had better stay till next week,' you would probably do it, you would probably not go—and, at another word, you might stay a month."

"You have only proved by this that Mr. Bingley did not do justice to his own disposition." Miss Bennet set her needlework down in her basket and leaned forward. "You have shown him off now much more than he did himself."

Bingley answered her, but he did not turn from Darcy. "I am exceedingly gratified by your converting what my friend says into a compliment on the sweetness of my temper. But I am afraid you are giving it a turn which that gentleman did by no means intend; for he would certainly think the better of me, if under such a circumstance I were to give a flat denial, and ride off as fast as I could."

Miss Bennet shook her head slightly, and Darcy felt the full weight of her disapproval before she spoke a word. "Would Mr. Darcy then consider the rashness of your original intention as atoned for by your obstinacy in adhering to it?"

"Upon my word I cannot exactly explain the matter; Darcy must speak for himself."

Though Bingley's depiction of his character stung, Darcy readily took the opportunity to break into his discussion with Miss Bennet. "You expect me to account for opinions which you choose to call mine, but which I have never acknowledged."

He paused, wanting that point to stand alone for a moment. Only when his audience nodded slightly did he reply to Bingley's commentary. "Allowing the case, however, to stand according to your representation, you must remember, Miss Bennet, that the friend who is supposed to desire his return to the house, and the delay of his plan, has merely desired it, asked it without offering one argument in favor of its propriety."

She rested her chin in one hand, her gaze fixed on Darcy. "To yield readily—easily—to the *persuasion* of a friend is no merit with you."

"To yield without conviction is no compliment to the

understanding of either."

"You appear to me, Mr. Darcy, to allow nothing for the influence of friendship and affection. A regard for the requester would often make one readily yield to a request without waiting for arguments to reason one into it."

Darcy opened his mouth to protest this point, but she raised a hand to forestall his words. "I am not particularly speaking of such a case as you have supposed about Mr. Bingley. We may as well wait, perhaps, till the circumstance occurs before we discuss the discretion of his behavior thereupon."

He smiled at her wisdom and her clever words, but before he could reply, she continued. "But in general and ordinary cases between friend and friend, where one of them is desired by the other to change a resolution of no very great moment, should you think ill of that person for complying with the desire, without waiting to be argued into it?"

Once again, the lady's intellect caught his attention. *How far can we take this discussion?* "Would it not be advisable, before we proceed on this subject, to arrange with rather more precision the degree of importance which is to appertain to the request, as well as the degree of intimacy subsisting between the parties?"

By the spark in Miss Bennet's eyes, he knew she was willing to carry the debate farther, but before she could, Bingley cut in. "By all means! Let us hear all the particulars, not forgetting their comparative height and size; for that will have more weight in the argument, Miss Bennet, than you may be aware of. I assure you that if Darcy were not such a great tall fellow, in comparison with myself, I should not pay him half so much deference. I declare I do not know a more awful object than Darcy, on particular occasions, and in particular places, at his own house especially, and of a

Sunday evening when he has nothing to do."

Bingley had managed to turn the joke on him, and social convention demanded that he smile. Inwardly, however, he felt hurt that his friend thought so little of him that he could make him such an object of ridicule in front of their guest. *Did you not do the same to him?* his conscience asked, but the reminder did little to sooth his pride.

"Charles!" Miss Bingley reprimanded her brother. "You should not speak so of Mr. Darcy. You know he is everything that is good and kind to us, the very best of friends."

Darcy ignored her defense. "I see your design, Bingley. You dislike an argument and want to silence this."

Bingley shrugged, apology in his eyes. "Perhaps I do. Arguments are too much like disputes. If you and Miss Bennet will defer yours until I am out of the room, I shall be very thankful; and then you may say whatever you like of me."

"What you ask is no sacrifice on my side," Miss Bennet said, "and Mr. Darcy had much better finish his letter."

Elizabeth's apparent lack of interest in their conversation was more of a letdown than Darcy wished to acknowledge. However, after her statement the best he could do was return to the long forgotten letter to Georgiana. He glanced up at Miss Bennet, who had turned her attention back to her book.

He tapped his pen against the paper a few times before he dipped it back in the ink and continued:

We have met a few young ladies I think you would enjoy socializing with, however: a pair of sisters by the last name of Bennet. Miss Elizabeth in particular possesses a wit and vivacity I think you would find refreshing, especially after

*the stilted conversations and manners of town ladies. Since
you are not likely to meet either of them, you shall have to
know them through me.*

He continued for a few minutes, telling Georgiana
of the people in Hertfordshire and sharing some of the
more humorous incidents he had witnessed, though he
was careful not to mention any names. When the page
was full, he signed the letter and carefully removed
any excess ink with a sheet of blotting paper.

The letter then tucked away in his pocket, he sought
another means of entertainment. He glanced around
the room and spotted Hurst asleep beside the fire.
Preferably one that does not employ the card table.

His eyes lit on the pianoforte, and he remembered
how well he had enjoyed listening to Elizabeth play at
Lucas Lodge. "Miss Bingley, Miss Bennet, perhaps you
would be good enough to grace us with your musical
talents."

His brow tightened in a frown when Miss Bingley
moved toward the instrument with unladylike haste.
She recalled her manners just in time and turned to her
guest with false politeness. "I would be delighted if
you would entertain us first, Miss Bennet," she said, the
lie patently obvious by the look on her face.

Miss Bennet's half-smile seemed to say that she felt
the insult just as keenly as Darcy did, but she would
not acknowledge it. "No, indeed, Miss Bingley, I am
quite satisfied to be the listener this evening. Please,
you go ahead."

So she truly does not care to perform. Darcy had
wondered if the attitude she showed at the Lucas party
was typical for her. His admiration of her rose; Miss
Bingley had bordered on bad manners in first her
eagerness to perform and then the obvious
afterthought with which she offered the instrument to

her guest, but Miss Bennet was gracious enough to ignore both slights.

He listened to Miss Bingley and Mrs. Hurst play and sing with half an ear, but his attention was focused on Miss Bennet as she strolled the room, eventually walking up to the pianoforte and perusing the music lying on top of it. She swayed slightly to the song, and he was struck by the impulse to dance with her.

He approached her and said, "Do not you feel a great inclination, Miss Bennet, to seize such an opportunity of dancing a reel?" He waited a minute for her answer, sure of what it would be. Though she smiled, she remained silent. Finally, he repeated his request, unable to keep the surprise out of his voice. *I had thought all young ladies ready to dance when asked.*

Elizabeth set her music down and looked at him, her eyes lit with mischief. "Oh! I heard you before; but I cannot immediately determine what to say in reply. You wanted me, I know, to say 'Yes,' that you might have the pleasure of despising my taste; but I always delight in overthrowing those kinds of schemes, and cheating a person of their premeditated contempt. I have, therefore, made up my mind to tell you that I do not want to dance a reel at all—and now despise me if you dare."

Her words elicited a smile from him. "Indeed, I do not dare," he promised her, taking pleasure in the bemusement he saw in her own eyes. Miss Elizabeth Bennet evidently took great pleasure in a sort of verbal sparring and had expected him to offer a parry in answer to her riposte. However, there was something about her manner that drew him in, rather than upsetting or unsettling him. *Were it not for the inferiority of her connections, I would be in some danger of falling in love,* he realized with surprise.

The next afternoon, Darcy tried to take a solitary

walk. He was not used to being so constantly in the company of others, and he greatly desired time to himself. Though the Netherfield library might be lacking, its gardens certainly were not. Here, among the twisting paths and walkways, Darcy was able to lose himself for a time. Surrounded by peace and quiet, he took a few deep breaths and finally began to relax.

However, just as he started to contemplate his rather unexpected response to Miss Elizabeth Bennet, his privacy was most unwelcomingly interrupted when Miss Bingley joined him from one of the side garden paths.

"Mr. Darcy! Why, I never expected to see you out walking on such a day as this."

Her lips curled into a coy smile, and Darcy knew she lied. The only thing which could persuade Miss Bingley to leave the comfort of her private sitting room was the company of a gentleman, and he realized with a start that her attentions to him were becoming quite marked.

"Miss Bingley," he said with the utmost civility, "I must tell you, you have not found me at the best of moments. I have several things on my mind and will not be a very good companion."

She took his arm and he went cold at her touch. "I can only imagine what things must be occupying your thoughts at present, Mr. Darcy. Why, your impending marriage into the Bennet family is of great interest even to myself, and I am not a concerned party." Miss Bingley walked farther down the path, and as she had possession of his arm, Darcy had no choice but to join her.

"I am afraid I do not follow."

"Oh, I do not mean that I am not interested in your future happiness!" cried she. "On the contrary, it is a subject which I have given much thought, and I have a few suggestions if I may."

There did not seem to be a polite way to avoid further conversation, so he bowed his head in acquiescence.

Miss Bingley's face took on the expression of a governess scolding a naughty child. It was completely out of place with her flirtatious tone of voice, and Darcy nearly laughed at the odd pairing. "I hope you will give your mother-in-law a few hints, when this desirable event takes place, as to the advantage of her holding her tongue; and if you can compass it, do cure the younger girls of running after the officers. And, if I may mention so delicate a subject, endeavor to check that little something bordering on conceit and impertinence, which your lady possesses."

Perhaps if Miss Bingley had not added this last about Elizabeth, her words would have landed on fertile ground. Instead, Darcy experienced a mad desire to discount everything she had said and do the opposite of what she wished. "Have you anything else to propose for my domestic felicity?" he asked, keeping his tone disinterested.

She tilted her head in consideration, a gesture he knew was designed to draw his gaze to the graceful curve of her neck. "Oh yes!" She squeezed his arm and Darcy fought the urge to shake her off. "Do let the portraits of your Uncle and Aunt Phillips be placed in the gallery at Pemberley. Put them next to your great uncle, the judge. They are in the same profession, you know, only in different lines. As for your Elizabeth's picture, you must not attempt to have it taken, for what painter could do justice to those beautiful eyes?"

His own indignation finally rose to the surface, and he expressed it in a manner he knew would most upset his partner. "It would not be easy, indeed, to catch their expression." He had not intended to say anything else, but once he began, he found he could not stop. "But their color and shape, and the eyelashes, so remarkably fine, might be copied." Miss Bingley blushed in vexation and her step faltered, and he took great pleasure in knowing that his words had upset her.

It was perhaps to his advantage that they were at that moment joined by the young lady in question, who was walking with Mrs. Hurst. There was much Darcy could have said in general approbation of Miss Elizabeth that he might have regretted sharing with anyone, especially Miss Bingley.

"I did not know that you intended to walk," Miss Bingley said, and Darcy noted in her tone a general unease that Miss Elizabeth might have perceived some of their conversation. He had the benefit of being able to read Elizabeth's expression well enough to know that she had not, so he was comfortable in the knowledge that she had not heard his praise of her, nor Miss Bingley's censure of her family.

Mrs. Hurst pouted. "You used us abominably ill," she answered her sister, "in running off without telling us that you were coming out."

Then, before Darcy could object, Mrs. Hurst took the arm that Miss Bingley was not holding, leaving them to walk three abreast on the path, with no room for Miss Elizabeth to join them. He instantly saw the insult of their behavior and was ashamed of them, on Bingley's behalf. "This walk is not wide enough for our party," said he. "We had better go into the avenue."

But it seemed Miss Elizabeth was unable to be offended. Instead of encouraging such an action, she laughed and said, "No, no; stay where you are. You are charmingly grouped, and appear to uncommon advantage. The picturesque would be spoilt by admitting a fourth. Goodbye."

Darcy's gaze followed her down the path until she

was out of sight, and when his companions again began their idle chatter, he wished mightily that he had been able to join her instead.

Chapter Nine

DARCY WAS STILL thinking of Elizabeth's calm, easy manner a few hours later when the dinner hour was announced. When he entered the dining room, he was surprised to find the eldest Miss Bennet had joined them. At the general exclamations of the party, she smiled and said that she felt much better.

Darcy noticed with some displeasure that Bingley could not keep his eyes off Jane Bennet, and later when the ladies had withdrawn and the gentlemen were enjoying their port, Bingley continually glanced at the clock. After the tenth time, his face broke into a broad smile, and he said, "Ah, I believe it is time we rejoin the ladies, gentlemen!"

Bingley led the way to the drawing room, and Darcy frowned at his back. *His attentions are becoming quite decided.*

However, Darcy could not keep his friend away from Miss Bennet, because Miss Bingley sidled up to him as soon as they entered the drawing room. *Her manners are nearly as bold as those of the younger Bennet sisters.*

"Mr. Darcy," he forced himself not to physically recoil from the purr in her voice, "it seems we will soon have Netherfield to ourselves once more."

He ignored her insinuations and presented himself

to Miss Bennet. "Miss Bennet, it is good to see you are well enough to be about."

She smiled graciously. "Thank you, Mr. Darcy. I confess I had rather wearied of the four walls of my room."

Beside Darcy, Mr. Hurst sketched a respectable bow. "Yes indeed, Miss Bennet, we are very glad to see you in company once more." Hurst hovered near his sister-in-law, and Darcy knew he would soon ask for the card table.

Darcy looked around the room for Bingley and found him stoking the fire. Amusement warred with concern when he saw his friend pull a comfortable armchair closer to the hearth and then approach the lady.

"Miss Bennet! I am so relieved to see you are on the mend. I declare I was quite miserable at the thought of your discomfort."

Jane Bennet lowered her eyes demurely. "You are too kind, Mr. Bingley."

Darcy tapped his fingers against his leg. *Is this to be her only response to all of Bingley's efforts on her behalf?*

"Please, will you not move farther away from the door? We would not want you to take a chill from the draught and fall ill again. See, I have positioned a chair for you by the fire."

"Yes, I believe the warmth would feel nice." Her smile was sweet, but to Darcy, it did not appear to hold any affection she had not shown either Hurst or himself.

Darcy took the seat Miss Bennet had just abandoned. Its proximity to the door did not bother him in the slightest, and it had something more to recommend it: as Miss Elizabeth occupied the only other chair near it, Miss Bingley could not easily disturb him.

When the tea things were removed, Mr. Hurst made his request. "How shall we spend our time this evening?" Miss Bingley ignored him, and he asked once more. "Miss Bingley, might we play cards this evening?"

"Oh no, Mr. Hurst. I am afraid no one intends to play," Miss Bingley quickly assured him before she turned back to the rest of the party.

Darcy knew she had asked Bingley if he wished for cards. Her attentions grated on him far more than her brother's toward Miss Bennet, and he felt rather like a fox among the hounds.

Desiring to ignore the company for a time, Darcy selected a book from the table. Even that attempt was thwarted, however, for Miss Bingley, too, stood and chose a book. Darcy bit back a smile when he saw she had the companion to his book. *Volume two of Don Quixote will do you little good without having read the first.*

His amusement soon turned to irritation for every minute she was interrupting him with a question or remark, often calling from across the room to ask for explanation of a passage. Miss Bingley's disruptions were of double annoyance, as they kept him from the true purpose of reading, which was to distract himself from the presence of Miss Elizabeth. Each time she asked a question or sighed over Cervantes' language, his gaze unerringly fell on that lady.

Her loveliness tonight surpassed what he had seen in the previous days, and after some surreptitious glances, he realized the worry lines on her forehead had eased. She smiled over at her sister, and he could well understand how concern for a loved one might mar her own enjoyment of simple entertainments.

Miss Bingley, meanwhile, did not appreciate being ignored. Each comment was a little louder, each sigh more pronounced. Still he did not reply. It did not surprise Darcy, therefore, when some fifteen minutes later, she held her volume up and said, with a practiced yawn, "How pleasant it is to spend an evening in this way! I declare after all there is no enjoyment like reading! How much sooner one tires of anything than of a book! When I have a house of my own, I shall be miserable if I have not an excellent library."

She glanced at Darcy with a sly smile. The words, "Like yours at Pemberley" hung in the air so loudly that he thought for moment she had actually spoken them. *Impertinent!* Darcy fixed his eyes on his book.

After a few minutes of silence, Miss Bingley threw aside the book—that which she would never tire of—and sought something else to hold her attention. Darcy did not hold out much hope that she would not return to bother him more later, but for now at least she was easily drawn into the conversation between her brother and Miss Elizabeth regarding the promised ball.

"By the bye, Charles, are you really serious in meditating a dance at Netherfield Park? I would advise you, before you determine on it, to consult the wishes of the present party; I am very much mistaken if there are not some among us to whom a ball would be rather a punishment than a pleasure."

She tilted her head in Darcy's direction, and he cringed at the obvious reference to himself. He would have responded had Bingley not beat him to it. "If you mean Darcy, he may go to bed, if he chooses, before it begins—but as for the ball, it is quite a settled thing; and as soon as Nicholls has made white soup enough I shall send round my cards."

Miss Bingley persisted, undaunted. "I should like balls infinitely better if they were carried on in a different manner; but there is something insufferably tedious in the usual process of such a meeting. It would surely be much more rational if conversation instead of dancing made the order of the day."

It is only with the greatest of restraint that Darcy could keep his amusement from showing. Never before had the lady shown any dislike of balls; in fact, her enthusiasm for them was well known among their circle of friends. *As for conversation, it seems the only time she enjoys that is when she can gain something by it.*

As her brother, Bingley was not so constrained by the rules of propriety. "Much more rational, my dear Caroline, I daresay, but it would not be near so much like a ball." It was the perfect answer, and Darcy mentally took his hat off to him.

A moment later, tired of pursuing a conversation which was not gaining her the end she sought, Miss Bingley rose from her seat and started walking around the room. It was easy for him to ascertain her intent in doing so; she had a pleasant figure and was hoping to draw attention to that fact. Darcy took advantage of her momentary silence to attend to his book.

"Miss Eliza Bennet, let me persuade you to follow my example, and take a turn about the room. I assure you it is very refreshing after sitting so long in one attitude." Here at last Miss Bingley succeeded in gaining his attention. When Miss Elizabeth stood, Darcy's eyes followed her, and when Miss Bingley took her arm and they began to parade around the room together, he set down his book and leaned forward slightly.

Miss Bingley could not have known how she would show in comparison to Miss Elizabeth, or she would not have invited the lady to join her. Though Miss Bingley's figure looked quite fine while walking, there was again something about Miss Elizabeth Bennet that he could not take his eyes from. Her form was nothing out of the common way, but the ease and confidence with which she carried herself was extraordinary.

When engaged in conversation, she tilted her head toward her partner, her whole being focused on that invidual. *Why does she not turn that expression toward me?*

The desire surprised and discomfited him, and for once he was glad when Miss Bingley spoke. "Would you care to join us, Mr. Darcy? I believe there is room for three to walk together here."

The reference to their walk the previous day and the rudeness which had concluded it chilled his feelings toward her even further, and he declined. "I am afraid you must excuse me—you could have only two motives for walking about the room, and I would interfere with either."

Miss Bingley turned to her companion and said, with all sense of confidence, "What could he mean? I am dying to know what could be his meaning. Miss Eliza, can you at all understand him?"

Miss Elizabeth tilted her head toward him and said with laughing eyes, "Not at all, but depend upon it, he means to be severe on us, and our surest way of disappointing him will be to ask nothing about it."

There was a certain wisdom in her words that made Darcy smile. She began to understand him, a thought which pleased him more than he cared to admit. Miss Bingley, however, was not content to leave it thus and turned to him. "Mr. Darcy, you have utterly confused us both by your odd words. Pray, sir, what are the two motives you speak of?"

Darcy leaned back in his seat and, keeping his attention focused on Miss Elizabeth, answered easily. "I have not the smallest objection to explaining them. You either choose this method of passing the evening because you are in each other's confidence and have secret affairs to discuss —" he greatly enjoyed the flash of annoyance in Miss Bingley's eyes when he suggested it—"or because you are conscious that your figures appear to the greatest advantage in walking; if the first, I should be completely in your way; and if the second, I can admire you much better as I sit by the fire."

The amusement in Miss Elizabeth's eyes made it difficult for him to keep a straight face. He had quickly determined that she was one who enjoyed espousing opinions she did not hold, simply to see the reaction she got from others. As such, he had suspected she would see through his words and enjoy sharing the joke.

Miss Bingley, however, understood only what was actually said, not the meaning behind the words. "Oh, shocking! I have never heard anything so abominable. How shall we punish him for such a speech?"

If Darcy thought he had actually offended his friend's sister, he would have been mortified, but he knew Miss Bingley well enough to know that her intent in walking had, in fact, been to draw his eyes to her figure, and she would be satisfied knowing that she had succeeded. Instead, he waited eagerly for Miss Elizabeth's response.

She turned back toward Miss Bingley, and Darcy felt the strangest pique toward that lady—why should Elizabeth continually be giving her the favor of her countenance, and not him? "Nothing so easy, if you have but inclination. We can all plague and punish one another. Tease him—laugh at him. Intimate as you are, you must know how it is to be done."

Torn between disgust at the thought of intimacy with Miss Bingley and discomfort at the notion of being teased, Darcy waited to hear what the lady in question had to say. "But upon my honor, I do *not*. I do assure you that my intimacy has not yet taught me *that*." He cringed of implication that their intimacy would increase, but she was not yet finished. "Tease calmness of temper and presence of mind! No, no—I feel he may defy us there. And as to laughter, we will not expose ourselves, if you please, by attempting to laugh without a subject. Mr. Darcy may hug himself."

Darcy allowed Miss Bingley's simpering praise to roll off his back. He was more interested what Miss Elizabeth would say to such a statement; certainly she would not follow her companion's example.

She did not disappoint. Her words gave voice to the laughter he could see in her lovely eyes. "Mr. Darcy is not to be laughed at! That is an uncommon advantage, and uncommon I hope it will continue, for it would be a great loss to *me* to have many such acquaintances. I dearly love a laugh."

Darcy reveled in the novelty of a shared joke. "Miss Bingley has given me credit for more than can be. The wisest and the best of men, nay, the wisest and best of their actions, may be rendered ridiculous by a person whose first object in life is a joke." He knew this was not what she had meant, but there was something about Miss Elizabeth Bennet that enticed him into a duel of words, and he could not resist baiting her, just to see her intelligence rise to the occasion.

"Certainly, there are such people, but I hope I am not one of *them*. I hope I never ridicule what is wise or good. Follies and nonsense, whims and inconsistencies, *do* divert me, I own, and I laugh at them whenever I can." She cocked her head slightly and said, with just the right sardonic lilt, "But these, I suppose, are precisely what you are without."

He slipped into the role of her devil's advocate as if he had been doing it all his life. "Perhaps that is not possible for anyone. But it has been the study of my life to avoid those weaknesses which often expose a strong understanding to ridicule."

"Such as vanity and pride."

Darcy had the vague sense that he was being led somewhere, that she wished him to say something specific, but he did not yet know what it was. "Yes, vanity is a weakness indeed. But pride—where there is a real superiority of mind, pride will always be under good regulation."

He chose his words carefully, revealing nothing in order to force her to give away what she wanted him to say. But it was Miss Bingley, not Miss Elizabeth, who replied. "Your examination of Mr. Darcy is over, I presume, and pray, what is the result?"

Miss Elizabeth shrugged in answer to Miss Bingley's question, and Darcy knew he would not learn what had been on her mind. "I am perfectly convinced by it that Mr. Darcy has no defect. He owns it himself without disguise."

Something in her tone compelled him to shed his usual rectitude. Under normal circumstances, he would not reveal himself in public, but for some reason, Darcy needed her to know that he did not consider himself so far above the world as that.

"No, I made no such pretension," he protested. "I have faults enough, but they are not, I hope, of understanding. My temper I dare not vouch for—it is, I believe, too little yielding—certainly too little for the convenience of the world. I cannot forget the follies and vices of others so soon as I ought, nor their offenses against myself. My feelings are not puffed about with every attempt to move them. My temper would perhaps be called resentful. My good opinion, once lost, is lost forever."

Elizabeth shook her head, and Darcy was sorry to see some of the teasing light leave her eyes. "*That* is a failing indeed! Implacable resentment *is* a shade in a character. But you have chosen your fault well—I really cannot *laugh* at it. You are safe from me."

Though it was true that resentment is not be laughed at, he wondered if there was some other reason she could not. *Does she, perhaps, share the same failing? Against whom might she be holding a grudge?* A moment later, he discounted the notion; he could not believe it of her. Her every word, every gesture, indicated her to be kind and generous. However...

"There is, I believe, in every disposition a tendency to some particular evil—a natural defect, which not even the best education can overcome." Perhaps she would share her own as he had shared his.

Elizabeth raised an eyebrow in challenge. "And *your* defect is a propensity to hate everybody."

He almost laughed at the easy way she caught him out. "And yours is willfully to misunderstand them."

They might have continued on in such a manner until supper, had not Miss Bingley interrupted them once more. "Do let us have a little music. Louisa, you will not mind my waking Mr. Hurst."

"I have no objection whatsoever." Darcy and Bingley shared a look of amusement; they had often commented in private that Mrs. Hurst did not possess much in the way of wifely cares for her husband.

Miss Bingley and Mrs. Hurst once again opened the pianoforte and began to sing, and though Darcy at first resented their interruption, a moment's contemplation showed him the wisdom in it. *Miss Bingley seeks to gain my attention, because I have been giving it exclusively to Miss Elizabeth. It is a dangerous thing, Darcy, for a gentleman to single out a lady he does not intend to marry.*

With that fact in mind, he resolved to ignore Miss Elizabeth for the rest of her stay at Netherfield. When he learned the next morning at breakfast of the Bennet sisters' wish to leave as soon as possible, he breathed a sigh of relief. *Surely I can avoid her for one day. Perhaps I will simply closet myself in the library with a book.*

He had forgotten that one thing Miss Elizabeth shared with him was a love of good literature. He had scarcely been in the room for ten minutes when the door opened and she walked in.

So firm was his resolve to be neutral that he did not even feel a quiver of dismay at her arrival. He merely nodded his head to her and then returned his attention to his book while she selected one of her own.

He braced himself for the continual chatter of Miss Bingley, but instead, she sat down in a chair by the window and read quietly. He watched in some fascination when, a few minutes later, she absently curled her feet under her legs and rested her head against the seat back so she could read more comfortably.

Pay attention to your book, Darcy—not to Elizabeth Bennet. The thought that he might raise hopes he could not fulfill drove his gaze back to the page, and after a few minutes he was sufficiently engrossed in the story to almost forget she sat not twenty feet away.

About a half hour later, she rose from her seat and replaced her book on its shelf before leaving the room. After she had gone, he found he had lost all enjoyment in his book. He set it down on the side table where he might find it again later and left the room as well. A quick glance around told him Miss Bingley was nowhere to be found, and he went directly out of doors.

Today, he was afforded the solitude he had wished for earlier in the week, and by the time he reentered the house a few hours later, his mind was once again in order. At the dinner table that night, he spoke more to Miss Bingley than to anyone else, though he said little at all. The eldest Miss Bennet took up Bingley's attention, and Darcy rejoiced in the thought that the sisters would soon be gone from Netherfield.

Chapter Ten

DARCY AVOIDED THE leave-taking the next morning. It was not merely Miss Elizabeth he did not wish to see; Miss Bingley's advances had severely tried his patience.

However, after the Bennet sisters were gone, Miss Bingley found him sitting with her brother in his study. Her presence forced him to set down a letter he had received from his steward at Pemberley, and he frowned in vexation.

If she noticed the forbidding look on his face, she did not heed it. "It is so nice to have one's house to oneself again, do you not think, Mr. Darcy?"

"I confess I am never happier than when I am with family at Pemberley." Satisfaction lit her face. *Does she believe I include her in a family party? I have had quite enough of her presumption.* "There is a peace about the place when none but Georgiana and I are there that I cherish."

Heat flushed Miss Bingley's cheeks, and she changed course. "I am sorry Charles allowed himself to be goaded into hosting a ball."

Bingley set his newspaper down and glared at his sister. "I say, Caroline, you need not talk about me as if I were not here."

Darcy looked over at his friend. "Netherfield is

Bingley's home, and he may do as he pleases. I am surprised you are so unenthusiastic, Miss Bingley—I had thought all ladies longed to give a ball of their own."

The words had their desired effect. Miss Bingley left them alone and immediately set about making preparations for a ball at Netherfield. Were it not for the disquieting notion that she was attempting to show him her skills as a hostess, Darcy would have been most satisfied with himself.

It had been Darcy's belief that once the Bennet sisters were removed from Netherfield, he would be able to put Elizabeth Bennet out of his mind. To his surprise and dismay, he found this was not the case. In her short stay, she had stamped her presence on the place, and there were very few rooms in the house that did not hold some memory of her. The uneasy sense that she had gained more than his good opinion grew in his mind.

Thus, when Bingley announced at luncheon two days later that he intended to ride to Longbourn that afternoon, Darcy's instinctive reaction was retreat. Miss Bingley, however, spoke before he could. "Oh, I am sure Mr. Darcy has had quite his fill of the Bennet family, have you not, sir?"

Darcy pursed his lips in a frown, and then turned to Bingley. "I would be glad to join you at Longbourn this afternoon."

It was only later, as they approached Meryton, that he regretted the moment of pique which had driven him to accept the invitation. Bingley had been praising the elder Miss Bennet's beauty and charm since they had left Netherfield, and in the quiet of his own mind, Darcy had likewise reflected on Miss Elizabeth. *I must overcome this,* he told himself and yanked so hard on the reins that his horse grunted and tossed his head.

"Look, Darcy!" exclaimed Bingley as they rode sedately down High Street. "Perhaps we need not ride to Longbourn after all." Darcy looked where his friend indicated and saw four of the Bennet sisters standing off to the side of the street with a group of officers in the regimental. He and Bingley dismounted and led their horses to where the little party stood.

Bingley spoke first. "Miss Bennet," he said with a bow, "how fortunate this is. We are just on our way to Longbourn for the very purpose of seeing you and inquiring after your health, and here we find you in Meryton. You must be better then?"

Miss Elizabeth stood to the right of her elder sister, and Darcy carefully avoided looking at her. Miss Bennet smiled at Bingley's speech and said, "Mr. Bingley, Mr. Darcy, how good it is to see you, and how very kind you are to still be concerned for me."

Darcy missed Bingley's reply entirely, for one of the gentlemen turned toward them and recognition struck him forcibly. *George Wickham!* Suddenly, Elizabeth was the last person on his mind. Anger heated his face and his hand involuntarily clenched. *What I would give to hit him, just once.*

Wickham knew him well enough to perceive his thoughts, and it gave Darcy some satisfaction to see the pale ghost of fear cast a shadow over his countenance. Even that pleasure was short-lived, however, for it told him Wickham knew very well he deserved to be on the receiving end of whatever Darcy dealt him, and he remembered how upset Georgiana had been to discover how he had used her.

Wickham raised his hands to his hat in a polite salute, and after a moment, Darcy returned the gesture. He knew Miss Lydia rattled on about something, but he could not hear her over the blood rushing in his head. *George Wickham here in Hertfordshire! Will I never be quit of the man?*

He caught a movement out of the corner of his eye and realized that Bingley had gotten back up on his horse. He remounted as well, but stayed silent when Bingley said their goodbyes to the ladies. He did not trust himself to speak with Wickham around.

Darcy stayed quiet the whole ride back to Netherfield Park. When they returned, he allowed the stable hand to take his horse for him, but when Bingley gestured back to the house, he declined. "No, Bingley, I need some time alone to think. You go on, I will be in before dark."

He took to the garden paths. More troubled him than simply the meeting with Wickham, though several moments passed before he allowed himself to admit it. Wickham's behavior toward Georgiana was enough to make Darcy hate the sight of him, but equally distressing was the fact that he had been in company with the Bennet sisters—particularly with Elizabeth—his Elizabeth!

His possessiveness surprised him, and it was with some effort that he turned his mind back to Wickham. *Can I stay in this country while he is here?* There was always the possibility that he would not be staying long in the area. There certainly were not any wealthy young ladies to tempt him in Meryton, so perhaps he was only visiting a friend and would soon be gone. "Bingley may know—he certainly attended to the conversation more closely than I did."

When the ladies withdrew after dinner, Darcy took his chance to speak with Bingley. "Bingley, I feel as if I owe you an apology for my behavior this afternoon." He cleared his throat. "I was rather shocked to see someone I have the misfortune of knowing—George Wickham, the son of my father's late steward."

Bingley furrowed his brow. "I heard the name, but I

confess I did not make the connection. Is that not the young man who abused your generosity most grievously?"

Darcy took in a deep breath—Bingley did not know the extent to which Wickham had trespassed upon him. "Indeed. There is more, but I cannot share the whole, for it is a rather delicate nature and involves another's reputation. Suffice to say, I cannot stand to be in his presence."

Bingley looked down at his glass and swirled the port around before taking a sip. "Darcy, he has joined the –shire militia regiment. The younger Bennet sisters announced his intentions to us this afternoon."

This was unwelcome news indeed, but Darcy did not see how it should affect him overmuch. "This is unfortunate, but I believe I shall find a way to avoid the militia."

Bingley pinched the bridge of his nose. "Darcy, you know I am sending the militia an invitation to the ball. I cannot single him out; everyone would wonder why. Can you be in the same house with him?"

Darcy started to say no, that he would bow out of the ball if Wickham was to be there. Then he had a sudden vision of Wickham being able to monopolize Elizabeth's time. He would fill her dance card, sit at supper with her, and woo her with his smooth words.

"Yes, I will be there," he heard himself say.

Darcy second-guessed that decision every day for the next week, and were it not for the arrival of a second letter from Georgiana, he likely would have changed his mind. To even breathe the same air as Wickham was an injury to his sense of justice, to the duty he owed his sister. Could he be present in a room with Wickham? Her letter assured him he could.

Dearest Fitzwilliam,

Your letter arrived today, and I am much intrigued by what you say of Hertfordshire. It sounds quite different from the country around home. I do wish I could meet the people you have met there, especially the Bennets. There are not enough ladies my age in London at this time, and it would be nice to have someone to talk to.

Fitzwilliam, I must talk on a subject which may give pain to us both. You were right to bring me back to London after... after Wickham. I could not let him control my life. I see that now. There is so much in the world that is good; one man should not taint it all. Thank you, brother, for your wisdom.

I do not say that I am completely over the hurt he dealt me, for that would not be honest. However, I am coming to understand that perhaps... perhaps there was nothing I could do differently. I do believe he used me most grievously, and I do not truly understand why any man would do that. However, if it was not me... then perhaps it was him?

Oh, Brother, I do not wish to speak of him any longer! He has dominated our lives for far too long. Let us discuss other things.

When do you return to town? I miss you dearly, and look forward to the holiday season with great anticipation.

Your loving sister,
Georgiana

It was clear Georgiana still felt the wound from Wickham's blow, but it was equally obvious she was determined to move on with her life as best she could. If she could look on Wickham with such equanimity, then so could Darcy.

Caroline Bingley had apparently taken Darcy's earlier words regarding the ball to heart. Not an evening passed without some discussion of the preparations she'd made. On the day in question, even

Mr. Hurst escaped into the fields to hunt and get away from her shrill voice piercing the air as she yelled at some hapless servant.

Alas, the good weather did not last, and the clouds opened up shortly after noon. Darcy, Bingley, and Hurst tromped across the fields back to the house, where they were greeted by the shrieks of the lady demanding they walk through the servants' entry so as not to soil her freshly cleaned carpets. "And do not think of coming downstairs until you are clean!" she ordered.

After Darcy had dressed, he found himself still with time on his hands before the ball began. His fingers tapped the side of his leg for a minute, and then he left his room for the sanctuary of the library.

This proved to be an ill thought-out decision. This room, like so many others, held memories of Miss Elizabeth Bennet, and Darcy only made it through a few pages of his book before he snapped it shut in frustration. "This will not do!" He paced the length of the room, his scowl deepening with each pass. "I cannot continue to think of Miss Elizabeth; I will put her from my mind henceforth."

Chapter Eleven

DARCY GLANCED AT his watch one last time. Guests had begun arriving over half an hour ago, and he had purposely delayed his own entrance in order to avoid the Bennet family. *For Mrs. Bennet surely saw to it they were among the first to arrive.*

He walked through the open doors, and all his good intentions were lost. Elizabeth Bennet stood not ten feet away. Her back was to him, and though Darcy told himself to turn away, to pretend he had not seen her, he could not.

She took his breath away. The delicate fabric of her ball gown revealed more of the lithe lines of her figure than he had previously seen, and the candlelight caught and reflected off the jewels in her hair.

Darcy approached her slowly, gauging his own reaction. Only when he was certain he could maintain his usual reserve did he speak. "Miss Elizabeth?"

She turned, and he wondered if perhaps he had overestimated his own control. Up close, he could see the smooth texture of her creamy skin, and he clenched a fist to keep himself from taking her hand to see if it felt as satiny as it looked.

"Yes, Mr. Darcy?"

He flushed at the question in her voice; how long had he stood without saying a word? "I trust the weather has not dampened your spirits this evening?"

He thought her smile was a little forced, but as he himself struggled to find enjoyment in balls, he did not wonder at it. "You will find, sir, that I rarely allow anything to interfere with my enjoyment."

He bowed and walked away to hide the emotions those words stirred in him. "You will find..." *Could this be a hint that she would welcome further attentions from me?* Darcy had thought himself immune to her charms, inured against them by the knowledge of her family connections. However, the idea that she would encourage his suit enthralled him.

His mood was made still better when Bingley told him in low tones that Wickham had opted not to attend the ball. *An evening spent in the company of Miss Elizabeth, without the aggravation brought by George Wickham. Excellent.*

Duty kept Miss Bingley at the door during the first dance, greeting the late arrivals, and her absence allowed Darcy to wander the floor, mulling over the possibilities. There was nothing he could do... she was not... and her family. Just as he made the decision, he looked up and saw her lovely face, smiling at her partner with a certain amount of forbearance—and forbearance was required, for the stout gentleman made a horrible muddle of the dance.

Still, some strange beast rose up in his chest when he saw that smile directed at another man. *She should be smiling at me!*

He took half a step toward them, but his sense of decorum held him in place. *What would you do, wrest Elizabeth from his arms?* He was surprised by the satisfaction that thought gave, and decided it might be best if he quit the ballroom for the card table.

However, he could not attend to his play, and rather than annoy his fellows and lose more money, he returned to the ballroom after only a few hands. He found Elizabeth easily, on the far side of the room with Charlotte Lucas, and he approached them, pulled to her side by his own desires.

He did not know what he planned to say to her, but after he had bowed to them, the words came to his lips naturally. "Miss Elizabeth, I pray you will grant me the pleasure of a dance. Are you available for the two next?"

She blinked, and her surprise gratified him. At least he had kept his weakness for her a secret from others, if not from himself.

"I am, sir," she answered finally.

"Then will you allow me to claim you for the set?"

"I will. Thank you, Mr. Darcy."

"No, Miss Elizabeth, thank you." He bowed again and retreated before he could say anything that would give away the depth of his attraction to her.

Regrettably, he paid no attention to where he walked, and he wandered across the path of Caroline Bingley. "And how are you enjoying the ball, Mr. Darcy?"

"Quite well, Miss Bingley. You have done an excellent job."

She preened, and Darcy could not help but think that in comparison to Elizabeth's refreshing simplicity, Miss Bingley's ensemble was fussy and overdone. "Thank you, sir. I confess I was not sure I could manage in the wilds of Hertfordshire. I imagined many a disaster in the last weeks."

"It is strange the fancies our minds can take if we do not regulate our thoughts with common sense."

She placed a hand on her chest and simpered up at him. "Oh sir, I fear you will find that my fancies are quite wild tonight. Why, I thought I saw you talking with Miss Eliza just now, but surely that cannot be."

He regarded Miss Bingley coolly, wondering how much he ought to tell her. "In fact, you did see me talking to Miss Elizabeth," he said at last. "She has done me the honor of agreeing to stand up with me for the two next."

Her lips pressed into a thin smile. "Ah, of course. Her fine eyes have drawn you in, I see."

"Miss Bingley, I would be glad to discuss this at another time, but I believe the dance is about to begin. If you will excuse me, I must collect my partner." Darcy left without waiting for a response, a rudeness he knew he would pay for later.

"Miss Elizabeth, I believe this is our dance. May I?" She took his outstretched hand without hesitation, and he led her onto the dance floor.

As he did so, he heard the whispers around them. *Let them wonder that I should choose to dance,* he thought, for once giving no care to the thoughts or attentions of others. *They will see a very well contented man.*

Their position in the dance allowed them some time before the pattern reached them, and Darcy took advantage of those still moments to quietly admire his partner. She looked up the dance to where her sister danced with Bingley, a smile on her face. After some minutes, however, she turned to him.

"This dance is one of my favorites; I am afraid, though, that I do not often get the chance to dance it."

"I am glad you can do so now," he said, and then, not knowing what else to say, he was quiet once more.

Miss Elizabeth watched him for a few moments, a gleam in her intelligent eyes. *What is she thinking?* he wondered. *I do not know if I can manage our verbal parry and thrust in the middle of a dance floor.*

Their turn in the dance came, and for a minute the steps kept them occupied. But if he thought the action would protect him from her satirical eye, he was mistaken. "It is *your* turn to say something now, Mr. Darcy. *I* talked about the dance, and *you* ought to make some sort of remark on the size of the room, or the number of couples."

He recognized the common forms of conversation on the dance floor, but he also heard the challenge in her voice. *She does not think I can move past those. I shall prove to her I am more than her match.*

He smiled blandly and said, "I am glad to oblige you. Which of those subjects would please you more?"

She did not hide her amusement so well; her eyes sparkled with ready wit. "Very well. That reply will do for the present. Perhaps by and by I may observe that private balls are much pleasanter than public ones. But now we may be silent."

Darcy pressed his advantage. "Do you talk by rule then, while you are dancing?" he asked.

She tilted her head and pretended to consider. "Sometimes. One must speak a little, you know. It would look odd to be entirely silent for half an hour together, and yet for the advantage of *some*, conversation ought to be so arranged as that they may have the trouble of saying as little as possible."

Against his will, his lips quirked up and he had to swallow a laugh. *What a delight she is!* "Are you consulting your own feelings in the present case, or do you imagine you are gratifying mine?"

"Both, for I have always seen a great similarity in the turn of our minds. We are each of an unsocial, taciturn disposition, unwilling to speak, unless we expect to say something that will amaze the whole room, and be handed down to posterity with all the éclat of a proverb."

His lips quirked up briefly in a smile. *That last sounds more like Caroline Bingley than either Elizabeth or myself.* "This is no very striking resemblance of your own character, I am sure. How near it may be to *mine*, I cannot pretend to say. *You* think it a faithful portrait undoubtedly."

She shook her head slightly, and he watched, mesmerized, as loose curls danced about her face. In that moment, Darcy would have accepted any judgment of his character or person from Elizabeth, no matter how harsh or ridiculous. He was so taken by her appearance that he entirely missed her answer and had nothing to say in response.

Darcy's earlier words to Sir William had been honest. He had never seen the great appeal of dancing —until now. To be so close to Elizabeth, every moment taking her hand or feeling her pass behind him, was an almost unbearable pleasure.

At this moment, Elizabeth was perfection. Her every movement was gracefulness itself, her every smile pleasing to his eye. Her warmth invited camaraderie with the other couples on the floor and she charmed them all with her laugh, but none so much as him.

When they had gone back up the dance, Darcy realized with a start that he had been silent for several minutes. He pursed his lips slightly as he sought a topic of conversation that would be appropriate to the dance floor. "Do you and your sisters often walk to Meryton?" he finally asked, remembering the last time he had seen her.

"We do," she replied. "Our aunt enjoys our company, and as you can imagine, there is nothing in our small village to amuse my younger sisters." A curious light entered her eyes, and he realized what she was going to say a moment too late. "When you met us there the other day, we had just been forming a new acquaintance."

All of Darcy's happy thoughts of the evening vanished. He barely called back the violent accusations that sprung to his lips, and he compressed his mouth into a thin line. The effort of holding his tongue made him red in the face, but he would not expose his sister's folly, no matter how much he trusted Elizabeth Bennet.

Finally, he deemed himself master enough of his emotions to speak. "Mr. Wickham is blessed with such happy manners as may ensure his *making* friends," he said, a tinge of bitterness coloring his voice. "Whether he may be equally capable of *retaining* them is less certain." The reminder that Georgiana had dropped Wickham's acquaintance once she knew his character brought back a hint of warmth to his heart, which Elizabeth's next words dispersed entirely.

"He has been so unlucky as to lose *your* friendship, and in a manner which he is likely to suffer from all his life."

It did not take much thought to work out her meaning. Wickham had been spreading his old lies regarding the living. *But surely the truth will come out at some point,* he consoled himself. *Elizabeth will learn in the future that I am not so mean as to withhold help from a friend of my father's, even one as undeserving as Wickham.*

Still, he resented the man for intruding into his time with Elizabeth, even in his absence. Sir William appeared at his side before either of them spoke again, and for the first time since he had met the gentleman, Darcy was grateful for his presence and volubility, for it gave him an excuse to remain quiet while he gathered the rest of his composure.

Sir William bowed low to Darcy and said, "I have been most highly gratified indeed, my dear sir. Such very superior dancing is not often seen. It is evident that you belong to the first circles. Allow me to say, however, that your fair partner does not disgrace you, and that I must hope to have this pleasure often repeated, especially when a certain desirable event, my dear Miss Eliza, shall take place."

He glanced down the dance at Miss Bennet and Bingley when saying the last, and Darcy realized with a start that Bingley's attentions to Miss Bennet had been so marked as to give rise to general expectations in the neighborhood. *How could I have been so lax in my friendship to him?* he berated himself. *Was I so entranced by Miss Elizabeth that I could not keep Bingley from involving himself too deeply with her sister?*

Sir William did not notice the sudden hauteur on Darcy's face and continued blithely along. "What congratulations will then flow in! I appeal to Mr. Darcy —but let me not interrupt you, sir. You will not thank me for detaining you from the bewitching converse of that young lady, whose bright eyes are also upbraiding me."

Darcy, however, did not turn back to the gentleman but continued to watch Miss Bennet and Bingley. *How could I not have noticed that his affections were truly engaged? Have I become so used to him merely being attracted to various young ladies that I simply did not think it possible? Or...* He glanced at his own partner ... *did I not wish to acknowledge that the Bennet sisters could exert such a pull against a gentleman's better judgment?*

He recognized the truth in this last thought, and it took him some minutes after Sir William's departure to gain command of himself again. "Sir William's interruption has made me forget what we were talking of," he said by way of excusing his silence.

"I do not think we were speaking at all," Elizabeth said airily. "Sir William could not have interrupted any two people in the room who had less to say for themselves. We have tried two or three subjects already without success, and what we are to talk of next I cannot imagine."

Anxious to give his mind somewhere to turn, Darcy

considered all the times they had shared together, and quickly found a subject he thought they could discuss in some depth. "What think you of books?"

He was startled when she said, "Books? Oh no! I am sure we never read the same, or not with the same feelings."

"I am sorry you think so," he said, though he privately believed her to be much mistaken; "but if that be the case, there can at least be no want of subject. We may compare our different opinions."

"No. I cannot talk of books in a ballroom; my head is always full of something else."

For the first time since he had made her acquaintance, Darcy did not believe Miss Elizabeth was being wholly honest with him. "The *present* always occupies you in such scenes—does it?" He could not keep a hint of skepticism from his voice. *What is she thinking?*

"Yes, always."

The steps of the dance took her from him at that moment, and Darcy stared at her doubtfully. *Is that all she has to say? Perhaps when she turns back, she might admit she is simply speaking out of nerves.* He would admire her the more for it, given his own state of mind. There was something agitated about her manner, and though he could not pinpoint the cause, he knew she was not quite herself.

That cause soon was made clear. "I remember hearing you once say, Mr. Darcy," said she, "that you hardly ever forgave; that your resentment once created was unappeasable. You are very cautious, I suppose, as to its *being created.*"

Elizabeth had hit on the greatest weakness of his temperament, and though he could wish for a kinder turn of conversation, he could not disagree. "I am."

This answer was not enough for her. She waited

until the dance brought them face-to-face and then asked, "And you never allow yourself to be blinded by prejudice?"

He remembered then what she had said about pride on that day, and he wondered if that was her concern. "I hope not."

"It is particularly incumbent on those who never change their opinion," she said as she passed behind him, "to be secure of judging properly at first."

Darcy took her hand and led her up the dance. "May I ask to what these questions tend?" he inquired, with more of a clip in his voice than he usually used when addressing her.

"Merely to the illustration of *your* character. I am trying to make it out." She smiled, but he was not fooled. Something bothered her.

"And what is your success?"

She shook her head, and though the gesture was playful, there was an edge to her voice. "I do not get on at all. I hear such different accounts of you as to puzzle me exceedingly."

Darcy's quick mind easily pieced the conversation together. *Wickham! Why is it that he always manages to appear the injured party in our disputes, and what devilry is it that would lead him to entice the very young lady I…*

Darcy could not finish the sentence, even in his mind. There was a longing deep in his breast that he could not understand, one that wished her to know and believe only the best of him. "I can readily believe that report may vary greatly with respect to me; and I could wish, Miss Bennet, that you were not to sketch my character at the present moment, as there is reason to fear that the performance would reflect no credit on either."

He had a vague thought as he spoke the words that he might find a way to meet her privately on the following morning and explain the truth of the matter, and her next words displeased him exceedingly. "But if I do not take your likeness now, I may never have another opportunity."

In all their short acquaintance, Darcy had never known her to be so disobliging. However, he would not beg. "I would by no means suspend any pleasure of yours."

An uneasy silence hung between them for the rest of the dance. For his part, Darcy was equally dissatisfied with the distance between them as he was with the subject of George Wickham, and on that count he quickly absolved her.

He felt how unequal he was to further conversation, and after he returned his partner to her friends, he withdrew from the ballroom to Bingley's study. His friend kept a particularly fine brandy there, and Darcy poured himself a measure. The cool glass in his hand calmed his thoughts. "Once again Wickham has insinuated himself with a young lady I value. Am I never to be free of his presence?"

He took a sip of brandy and paced the semi-dark room. "But Elizabeth is wise and insightful. She will see Wickham's true nature before long."

Hearing the words did more to ease his mind than anything else, and he knew he should return to the ball. He did not much relish the thought, but his sense of duty was too strong to allow him to remain hidden away for the rest of the evening. He looked regretfully about the quiet room, finished his brandy, and stepped back into the hallway.

His thoughts took a decidedly more cheerful turn on the way back, for the faint strains of music called to mind his dance with Elizabeth. His heart raced when he thought of her loveliness, so near and so vibrant, and his steps quickened to carry him back to her.

Unfortunately, instead of finding Elizabeth, he was approached by the same awkward young man he had seen dancing with her earlier. The gentleman had won no warm feelings from him at that time, and he did not improve upon acquaintance. Without even the courtesy of an introduction, he walked right up to him and bowed, as if they were equals. "I must beg your apology," he said, his tone most solemn, "for the duty I have neglected. I am Mr. Collins, the rector at Hunsford parish, near Rosings Park. Your noble aunt, Lady Catherine de Bourgh, is my patroness."

The connection explained much about the air of servility that surrounded the man. His aunt surrounded herself with people who bowed and scraped with an obsequiousness that Darcy found disgusting. "I am sure my aunt could not have the discernment to bestow that favor without merit, sir," he said, hoping his cold tone would discourage further familiarity.

But Mr. Collins bowed again, lower this time if it were possible. "It is with great pleasure that I can tell you Lady Catherine and her daughter were doing quite well on the Sunday sennight past. Indeed, I had the honor of filling out a table for quadrille just that previous Saturday, and found her ladyship to be in fine health and spirits both."

Darcy eyed the man with a barely hidden repugnance when he finished speaking. This time, he gave the briefest of bows and then turned away. Thankfully, Mr. Collins did not follow.

Shortly after this unwelcome intrusion, the guests were called to sit down to dinner. Darcy gladly took a seat that was directly across the table from Elizabeth, unaware that her mother sat beside her. That woman started talking when the first course was brought out and she continued until the meal ended, the feather on her head bobbing in time to the movements of her mouth.

"Oh! My dear Lady Lucas, do you not think Jane looks very well tonight? There is a certain glow about her this evening, would you not agree?" Lady Lucas barely had time to voice her assent before Mrs. Bennet continued. "I am glad, for perhaps seeing her at her finest will spur Mr. Bingley on. I do expect some kind of arrangement to be made very soon, and would it not be lovely if he were to use the opportunity of a ball—such a romantic occasion—to ask for her hand?"

Lady Lucas's smile was as strained as Darcy's was. To hear Bingley's name bantered around in this manner insulted his friend and disturbed Darcy. *Thankfully, Bingley's sisters are not in earshot,* he thought. Caroline sat at the far end of the table in the hostess's seat, and he shuddered to think how she would react to such presumption.

Darcy, however, could not avoid Mrs. Bennet's pronouncements. "Mr. Bingley is such a charming man, I am sure Mr. Bennet will agree that we could not get a finer son-in-law—nor a richer one, to be sure."

The impropriety of this comment nearly shocked Darcy into speech. His gut clenched; his own experience with a fortune hunter was still fresh enough to make him deeply feel Bingley's peril.

Only the sight of Elizabeth's mortification induced him to hold his tongue. *I must not lay the sins of the parent entirely on the feet of her children,* he reminded himself. *Just because Mrs. Bennet is mercenary does not mean her daughter does not have a strong affection for Bingley.*

Mrs. Bennet now prattled on about the solicitude Miss Bennet received from Bingley's sisters, and Darcy looked down the table to where they all sat. Miss Bingley was talking to her, to be sure, but he could tell her smile was artificial from twenty feet away. There was no questioning what the woman thought about having such a country nobody for a sister-in-law. She may like Jane Bennet very well as a friend, but as a member of the family was a different question altogether.

Mrs. Bennet's shrill voice drew his attention away from her daughter. "Oh! And how nice it will be for my other girls, if Jane marries Mr. Bingley!"

"Whatever do you mean, Mrs. Bennet?" Lady Lucas inquired, echoing Darcy's own question.

"Why my dear Lady Lucas, I mean, of course, that this must throw them in the path of other rich men! Just think what fine gentleman Kitty and Lydia might meet, if they spend time with Jane and Mr. Bingley."

Darcy almost choked on his wine. Thinking of those two girls being thrown into London society was not to be borne. They were the silliest pieces of farididdle he had ever had the misfortune to come across, and though any man who married them would richly deserve what he got, Darcy would not wish either of them on his worst enemy.

Mrs. Bennet placed a hand on her friend's arm and leaned in slightly. The gesture of secrecy was meaningless, for her voice still carried across the room. "Of course, it will be nice for Mr. Bennet and myself as well. We are getting far too old to go out in the evenings, and if Jane married, she could chaperone the rest of the girls at the parties. I do wish you might have a daughter settled half so well."

Elizabeth whispered something in Mrs. Bennet's ear, and Darcy guessed she urged her mother to lower her own voice. Mrs. Bennet, however, said, in her same voluble tone, "What is Mr. Darcy to me, pray, that I should be afraid of him? I am sure we owe him no such particular civility as to be obliged to say nothing *he* may not like to hear."

Darcy pulled back in surprise when he heard his own name, and from the look on her face, he knew Miss Elizabeth had not mentioned it. Her teeth clenched, she spoke again. "For heaven's sake, madam, speak lower—what advantage can it be to you to offend Mr. Darcy? You will never recommend yourself to his friend by so doing."

That Elizabeth shared her mother's hopes for Bingley and Miss Bennet was clear, and it was the only thing that might have convinced Darcy to give his approval of the match. Of all the Bennets, her opinion and judgment alone did he value.

Her endorsement of the match also led to a new consideration. *Is it possible Miss Bennet truly cares for Bingley?* This thought gave Darcy an occupation for his mind; rather than listening to Mrs. Bennet, he focused his attention on Bingley and Miss Bennet, trying to ascertain any symptoms of affection on the side of the latter.

When the meal ended, the entertainment began. Miss Bingley had scarcely said, "I wonder if any of the young ladies would like to entertain us with a song?" when Miss Mary Bennet rose from her seat at the table and approached the pianoforte with a haste that showed an indecorous eagerness. Darcy watched her prepare her music with little expectation of pleasure. He well remembered the last time he had heard the young lady play, and he did not imagine her style had much improved since that time.

Indeed, it had not. When it began, her playing was as forced and stilted as it had been some weeks earlier. He saw on the faces of his companions the same discomfort, and they all wished the song to end.

But when her song ended, some of the audience took the polite applause to the next level. "How delightful, Miss Mary. Perhaps you might be able to play for us again."

Darcy had only known the young lady for a few short months, but that was enough time for him to know what she would do with such encouragement. Rather than get up and let another young lady have a turn, she smiled primly and turned the pages of her music to another song. Across the table, Elizabeth blushed, and he could only guess at her mortification. She glanced down the table, and when he followed her gaze, he saw Jane Bennet calmly speaking with Bingley.

That sight convinced him of one thing: It would not be easy to move Jane Bennet to heights of emotion. If she could not feel even a little self-conscious at the spectacle her sisters were making of themselves—for the two younger sisters pointed at Miss Mary and openly laughed at her—then how was anyone to know if she had fallen in love? He watched her closely for some time and saw that although she smiled freely at Bingley, there did not seem to be any additional warmth or spark in her expression that would lead one to believe she felt anything deeper than admiration.

Miss Mary abused the pianoforte for another minute, and Elizabeth caught her father's eye and indicated he should for once take control of his family. Though Darcy agreed that Mr. Bennet should not allow his middle daughter to bring any more of Society's disdain on his family, he doubted the gentleman's ability to subtly handle the situation.

All of Darcy's prejudices against Mr. Bennet were confirmed a moment later. When Miss Mary's second song ended, he rose from his seat and said, "That will do extremely well, child. You have delighted us long enough. Let the other young ladies have time to exhibit."

Though he cared little for the young lady in question, Darcy felt the full weight of her humiliation, as he was sure Elizabeth did. Miss Mary flushed a little and fumbled with her music when she stood. Minutes before Darcy had scorned her; now she had his sympathy. Mr. Bennet, however... *He allows his family to make an exhibition of themselves for his own amusement.*

Mr. Collins, whose relationship with the Bennet family Darcy had still not managed to figure out, spoke now. "If I were so fortunate as to be able to sing, I should have great pleasure, I am sure, in obliging the company with an air; for I consider music as a very innocent diversion, and perfectly compatible with the profession of a clergyman."

This bit of exposition was odd enough, but the man did not stop there. He clasped his hands behind his back and paced a little alongside the tables. He expounded at length on the duties of a clergyman, from the writing of sermons to the collection of tithes, and when that was finished, he turned toward Darcy.

"And I do not think it of light importance that he should have attentive and conciliatory manners towards everybody, especially towards those to whom he owes his preferment. I cannot acquit him of that duty; nor could I think well of the man who should omit an occasion of testifying his respect towards anybody connected with the family."

Darcy watched in abject horror as the absurd man bowed to him before seating himself again. Mr. Collins had impressed Darcy earlier as one who dearly loved the sound of his own voice. His speech was filled with panegyrics, and though he had constantly spoken of those better than him, it was clear he believed himself to be quite good enough for the current society, and better than most.

Darcy could not avoid hearing Mrs. Bennet whisper,

"I do think Mr. Collins is a remarkably clever, good kind of young man, do you not, Lady Lucas?" Her companion did not offer a reply, none clearly being needed, and the obvious answer not being what she would expect to hear.

At long last, the ball came to a close. The evening had brought Darcy nothing but greater pain, and he greatly desired its end. He had watched for another forty-five minutes as Bingley made evident the depths of his affection for Miss Bennet, and Mr. Collins showed himself to be even more ridiculous than he had thought possible.

The latter brought him no pleasure, for he made a fool of himself at the expense of his cousin Elizabeth, whose side he barely left for the whole of the rest of the evening. Darcy did not enjoy watching the two of them together, regardless of how little the lady clearly appreciated his company.

A sudden thought occurred to Darcy as he observed them. *By all ordinary standards, Mr. Collins would be viewed as a good match for Elizabeth.* His chest tightened and he had to step out of the ballroom to take a quick breath of fresh air. *What can it matter to me who she marries? Have I not already decided...*

Darcy leaned against the wall in the darkened corridor. He *had* already made his decision. He had no business questioning Elizabeth's choice of partner in her future life.

Still, the possibility that she might marry such an unworthy man ruined the last bit of enjoyment he might have found in the ball, and when the evening finally came to a close, he rejoiced.

When at last the guests began to leave, Darcy thought he would have his peace in short order. He had not reckoned with Mrs. Bennet. By some trick, she managed to have their party be the last to leave, and even then to extend their visit by the period of another fifteen minutes. Darcy did not know how she had contrived to have their carriage take so long in coming, but he did not doubt it was her handiwork.

Earlier in the evening, Darcy would have been embarrassed by the behavior of Bingley's two sisters. They yawned prodigiously, and every sentence they spoke was an issuance of exhaustion and of how glad they would be to get to sleep after such an evening. He knew their behavior was excessively rude, but he could not bring himself to disagree with them. Mrs. Bennet had taxed him to the extreme; he could not even be prevailed upon to intercede for the sake of Elizabeth, who did not deserve such treatment.

Finally, they were gone. The Netherfield Park party watched them drive away and then closed the doors. "I believe I must be to bed," Bingley announced. "It has been a long day—though you would have been good to not mention it in front of our guests, Caroline—and I have an early morning and a ride to London in front of me. Good night Caroline, Louisa, Darcy."

Darcy sketched his own bow to the ladies. "I am afraid I too must retire. Good night, Miss Bingley, Mrs. Hurst. Thank you for hosting a delightful evening."

"I do believe it might have been more delightful if there had been fewer Bennets present," Miss Bingley muttered as they climbed the stairs.

Chapter Twelve

EVERY TIME DARCY closed his eyes, some member of the Bennet family invaded his thoughts. Mrs. Bennet's presumptuous chatter, the improprieties of the three younger daughters, and Mr. Bennet's amused indolence—they all played across his mind in vivid detail. *Is this what my friend is to marry into?*

He finally drifted off near dawn, but his dreams were no less troubling. Bingley, dressed in his finest morning coat, stood in front of the Longbourn church. Darcy stood by his side. The door opened, and all but the eldest of the Miss Bennets trailed up the aisle, Elizabeth last of all. She held Darcy's gaze for half a second, and the question he saw there smote him.

The organ struck a chord, and another figure appeared at the back of the church. Jane Bennet, radiant in bridal white, held her father's arm. Darcy watched her proceed down the aisle, a protest building in his throat. *"No! This cannot be,"* he longed to declare, but loyalty to his friend held his tongue. He could not, in front of all these people... *Why did I not speak before?*

Darcy woke with a start. The first fingers of weak sunlight lightened the room through the curtains, and he swung his legs out of bed. The cold stones under his feet sped him through his morning routine, and he was dressed in under ten minutes.

He walked quietly down the stairs, not wanting to wake any of the family. However, Bingley himself met him at the door. "Darcy! You are up early, even for you."

Darcy could not look at his friend without seeing him as he had appeared in his dream. He shook his head to clear the image of Bingley dressed for his wedding and said, "I am afraid I could not sleep. Are you leaving for London?"

Bingley nodded. "I wish to complete my business as quickly as possible, so I might return. There are some matters here which I cannot pursue until my affairs in London are tidied up a bit."

His meaning could not be clearer. Bingley intended to see a solicitor regarding marriage settlements while he was in town. Darcy bit back all his arguments against the match and instead said, "Then I hope we shall see you sooner, rather than later."

Bingley clapped him on the shoulder and laughed. "I believe you will. Now, I take it by your attire that you plan to ride. Walk with me to the stable."

Darcy hesitated for a bare instant before he shook his head. "You will excuse me, Bingley. I have something on my mind and I need time alone to think. I will let you continue on to London. We shall see you within a week."

"Or less," Bingley corrected with a grin.

"Or less." The two men exited the house, and Darcy turned toward the woods. Though the sky was cloudless, the blustery November wind stole all the warmth from the sun's rays. Darcy shivered and pulled his coat closer, but he did not give up his notion of taking a walk.

His dream still troubled him. The question in Miss Elizabeth's eyes had taunted him since he woke up —"When will you declare yourself?"

Darcy did not like to admit fault on his own part, even to himself, but his attentions toward the lady had been too marked to avoid notice. *Were it not for her family, I would gladly marry Elizabeth. But I will not expose the Darcy name to such low connections and gross improprieties.*

"And what of Bingley?" Darcy asked, voicing his frustration to the rocks and trees. "Am I to allow him to stay in Hertfordshire and marry Miss Bennet?" A glimpse of the dream wedding flashed through his mind, when he stood up beside Bingley and Elizabeth beside her sister. An ache built in his chest at the thought of standing across from her in the church, wanting to take her hand but unable to do so.

Elizabeth's laughing eyes brought to mind Jane Bennet's easy, complacent manner, and he frowned at the contrast. "Is Bingley then to be forced into a marriage of unequal affection?" The previous night had convinced him Miss Bennet's regard for Bingley did not extend to romantic attachment. "It would wound a sensitive man like Bingley to discover his wife did not care for him."

His stomach growled before he could find an answer. He realized with some surprise that the sun had risen to almost midday while he walked, and he turned back toward the house. Darcy found the Bingley sisters seated in the breakfast room. "I hope you did not wait for me," he said, noting they had only begun to eat.

"Oh no, Mr. Darcy," Mrs. Hurst assured him. "I am afraid dear Caroline and I did not rise at our usual time this morning after all the excitement of the ball last night."

Darcy poured his coffee in silence. The ball was the last subject Darcy wished to discuss. *Perhaps I might take a tray to my room,* he considered.

Behind him, Miss Bingley spoke. "I did not like what I saw last night, Louisa."

Or perhaps they might help me convince Bingley to leave Hertfordshire. Darcy took a seat across from them at the table.

"Nor I, Sister—nor I." Mrs. Hurst shook her head.

"Charles was far too free with his attentions to Miss Bennet. I do dote on her, but I do not wish to have her for a sister. Imagine having Mrs. Bennet at our brother's wedding!"

Darcy grimaced. Mrs. Bennet would not confine her interference in the family to just the wedding. If Bingley married Miss Bennet and they resided at Netherfield, they would never be free of her company.

Louisa Hurst shuddered delicately and spread more jam on her bread before answering. "But what can we do? He is of age, and there is no one in the family who could possible forbid him to marry her."

Miss Bingley sighed. "True, and even if they were to try, you know Charles would simply argue they do not know Jane—that if they were to meet her, they would understand her sweet temper and know why he must marry her."

The sisters were silent for a minute, and then Mrs. Hurst spoke again. "If only there was someone... someone who could persuade him of the folly of the match."

"Yes, but who would he listen to? No, Louisa. I am afraid we must resign ourselves to Mrs. Phillips as an aunt."

Darcy finished his coffee and rose from his seat. "I hope you will excuse me, ladies, I have some things I need to attend to this morning." He bowed and left the room without another word.

He knew very well what Bingley's sisters desired, and though it fell in line nicely with his own plans, he did not like the way they had attempted to manipulate him. *I will get Bingley out of this, but let them first wonder for a while. It would do them some good.*

He called Vincent as soon as he arrived in his room. "Yes, Mr. Darcy?" the valet asked.

"Vincent, we return to London on the morrow. See to it that my things are packed."

"Yes, Mr. Darcy."

Out of a desire to teach the sisters a lesson, Darcy purposely avoided them both until dinner. As a result, Miss Bingley fairly pounced on him when he entered the dining room that night. "Mr. Darcy, I must ask: what do you think of my brother's affection for Miss Bennet?"

Darcy took his seat before answering. "I do not like it," he said, and both sisters let out a breath. "However, as Bingley is an adult, I am not sure we can keep him from acting as he sees fit."

Mrs. Hurst drooped slightly in her seat, but Miss Bingley straightened and leveled a steady gaze at him. "Mr. Darcy, I am sure of my brother's faith in your opinion. Were you to tell him you did not believe Miss Bennet to be a worthy match for him, I do not doubt he would see reason."

Darcy thought for a moment of how he would respond, were someone to confront him with the utter lack of sense in his attachment to Miss Elizabeth Bennet, and his own confidence was shaken. *Are we right to separate them?*

"Of course," Miss Bingley added, sharing a long look with her sister, "if we were persuaded she truly cared for Charles we might feel differently. But is it not clear that the dear girl is being imposed on by her mother to make an advantageous connection?"

"Perhaps a more subtle play is required," Darcy suggested, his momentary hesitation forgotten. "Why do we not simply return to London ourselves, rather than remaining here to argue with him on his return?"

Miss Bingley smiled up at him. "You are far too kind, Mr. Darcy, and far too good a friend to our brother."

"What do you mean, Miss Bingley?"

Her smile widened and her eyes narrowed to cat-like slits. "Why, I do not believe many men would give up the attentions of their lady in order to help a friend."

Darcy stiffened. "I am sure I do not take your meaning."

Miss Bingley ignored the warning in his voice. "Oh, that is right—Miss Bennet is no longer *your* lady, is she? You passed that pleasure on to her cousin. My, but Mr. Collins was attentive to her last night! I half expected him to propose in the middle of the ballroom."

Darcy pressed his lips into a thin line. "I beg you ladies will excuse me; I must see to the details of our departure." Their mouths were agape, and it was no wonder. They had barely finished the first course of the meal. However, Darcy had little appetite remaining, and no desire to remain in the company of the ladies.

In the relative privacy of the hallway, Darcy loosened the knot of his cravat. It was one thing to accept Elizabeth would not be his wife, but quite another to realize she might marry someone else—and that odious Mr. Collins, Lady Catherine's parson! Was Elizabeth to be brought so low?

A second thought followed quickly, more unpleasant than the last. Were she to marry Mr. Collins, Darcy would see her every year on his annual visits to Rosings. "Would to God we had never come here," he muttered and took the stairs two at a time.

The troublesome thought still occupied his mind the

next day as they returned to London, and his quiet brooding did not go unnoticed by Miss Bingley. "Mr. Darcy, you have hardly spoken a word to us since dinner yesterday evening! I declare, Louisa and I did not know what to think when you quit the room so suddenly."

"I explained the necessity of my actions at the time; if we wished to depart this morning, there were things that needed to be done. I believe we can all agree that time is of the essence in this particular case."

The sisters looked at each other. "Yes, of course," Mrs. Hurst agreed. "We did wonder, Mr. Darcy—that is, Caroline believes—"

Miss Bingley sighed and tossed her head. "What my sister is trying to say, Mr. Darcy, is that we have decided it would be best if I were the one to speak to Charles."

Darcy frowned. "I understood my presence was necessary to convince him."

"Oh, and it is," she assured him with a pretty smile. "Your presence will only add weight to my words. However, this will mean more to him coming from a beloved sister, one who will be materially damaged by a reckless marriage on his part."

There was a certain amount of truth to that statement, so Darcy nodded his head in acquiescence. They had not been in London for an hour when he learned to regret his uncharacteristic complaisance.

"But Charles, surely you understand..."

Darcy winced; the whine in Miss Bingley's voice hurt his ears as much as Bingley's far more strident tones.

"I do not, Caroline, and I grow weary of this conversation!"

Darcy saw the mulish light in his friend's eye and knew it was time to step in, before the sisters completely ruined their chances of prising Bingley from Hertfordshire and Miss Bennet. "Miss Bingley, Mrs. Hurst, might I have a word with your brother in private?"

Miss Bingley flushed almost imperceptibly, but she did not argue. After the two sisters had left, Darcy turned to the sidebar and poured two glasses of the scotch whiskey Bingley kept there. He handed one to his friend, an apologetic smile on his face. "I am afraid your sister has very decided notions about things, Bingley."

Bingley shook his head. "You need not apologize to me for my own sister, Darcy." He tossed back the drink and poured another. "I should apologize to you for exposing you to her vulgar obsession with money and connections."

He sat down heavily in a chair by the fire, and Darcy regarded him carefully. *How shall I proceed?* At last he said, "I am sure she only thinks of your happiness."

Bingley sighed. "If I could believe that, I might consider her words. However…"

His dark frown told Darcy their plan was in danger of collapsing around him. "Can you not see how her warnings proceed from affection?" Darcy said, determined that he should not fail. He leaned forward in his chair, an earnest expression on his face. "An unequal marriage lends itself toward great unhappiness."

Bingley rubbed at the crease in his forehead. "I fail to see how marriage to Jane Bennet would be unequal."

Darcy took a breath; he stood on shaky ground. "Forgive my impertinence, Bingley, but have you forgotten your family was recently in trade?" His friend recoiled, so he hastened to add, "I assure you, that does not signify with most of our set. However, that is in part because your father married a gentleman's daughter."

"Jane is —"

Darcy held up his hand. "Yes, but what was her mother? What of *her* father, *her* sister and brother?" Bingley looked away and Darcy pressed his advantage. "Your wife will have a great hand in shaping the future of your family, for good or for evil. Could you be happy if your marriage made your sister's social position precarious? Do you not wish for a good match for her?"

Bingley laughed. "Caroline will make her own match, with little help or hindrance from me." He looked over at Darcy. "I must warn you, Darcy, I suspect she has her mind set on marrying you."

"You need not tell *me* that," Darcy said. He took the seat across from Bingley. If his pleas were to work, he must appear the concerned friend, rather than one who dictated his own wishes and expected others to follow. "But you know I wish for marriage with true affection, such as my parents shared."

Bingley smiled. "And that is why I will marry Jane."

Darcy tapped the side of his glass and then looked up at Bingley. "You love her, of that I am certain. But what of her feelings for you? Has she told you she loves you?"

Bingley flushed and looked down at his half-full glass. "Of course not. Jane—Miss Bennet—is a lady, and ladies do not…"

"I am sure she is everything that is proper," Darcy reassured him. "However, you have told her of your regard, have you not?"

"I have told her I admire her greatly."

"And she did not then answer in a way to give you no doubt of her feelings?"

Bingley crossed his arms in defiance and nearly

spilled whiskey on himself in the process. "To what do these questions attend, Darcy?"

Darcy thought he saw a hint of uncertainty in Bingley's eyes, and he pressed his advantage. "I observed Miss Bennet the other night, and though she received your attentions with perfect serenity, I could discern no particular regard on her part."

Bingley paled, and Darcy felt a moment of pity for his friend. "You do not believe she cares for me—at all?"

Darcy hesitated, honesty warring with a desire to keep Bingley from Hertfordshire. "That she esteems you is evident," he finally said. "However, she is universally pleased by all she meets, and I am convinced it would be difficult to recognize symptoms of peculiar regard in her."

"I see." Bingley walked to the window and stared into the night.

Darcy looked at his friend's back for a moment and said, "You see why you should remain in town..."

"You may settle your concerns on that account," Bingley said, his voice tired. "I find I have suddenly lost all desire to return to Hertfordshire."

"It is for the best, Bingley," Darcy said.

"It will be difficult to convince me of that. Now, if you will excuse me, Darcy, I am rather weary."

Darcy blinked. Bingley had never dismissed him before. *Though perhaps under the circumstances it is understandable.* "Very well. Good night, Bingley."

Chapter Thirteen

DARCY HOUSE WAS too well run for the unexpected arrival of the master to throw the household into an uproar. "Welcome home, Mr. Darcy," the butler said placidly when Darcy entered the house that evening, long after the supper hour had passed.

"Thank you, Remington. I trust all is well?"

"Of course, sir."

A familiar figure strode around the corner as a footman took Darcy's cloak. "Well hello, William," Richard said. He looked Darcy up and down. "Have you been traveling all day? Come, join me for a brandy."

Darcy followed him down the hallway to his own library. He watched with amusement as Richard poured two drinks and then sat down, his legs stretched out in front of them. "I must say, Cousin, you certainly seem to be treating my home as your own."

"And I must say, Cousin," Richard shot back, "that your manner of arriving late in the evening and unannounced is far more like my style than your own. What brings you from Hertfordshire in such a rush?"

Darcy sipped his brandy and considered his answer. It was not his place to tell anyone of Bingley's most recent *affaire de coeur*, so he finally settled for a half-truth. "The country was just as tedious as I expected.

When Bingley returned to town, I seized the opportunity to follow."

Richard rolled his eyes. "You are always so determined not to give your good opinion, it is a wonder anyone or anything meets with your approval."

The jest was a familiar one between the cousins, but tonight Darcy did not laugh. The words too closely mirrored those of another—"your good opinion, once lost, is lost forever." Elizabeth's face flashed before him, and he took another long drink of the brandy to hide his jumbled emotions.

Richard leaned forward. "It is good that you have come, though," he said. "I received word this evening that my presence is required in France for a short time."

Darcy had long ago learned not to question Richard's frequent trips across the Channel. Though his cousin was an army officer, he strongly suspected his primary role in the military was of a more clandestine nature. "When do you leave?"

Richard swirled the brandy around in his glass and did not look at Darcy when he answered. "My ship leaves Portsmouth on Monday. I had a letter ready to send you by express in the morning."

Darcy set his glass down and steepled his hands in front of him. *This is even shorter notice than usual.* "I am glad I have returned, though Georgie will be sad to see you go. Have you any idea how long you will be gone?"

Richard shrugged. "I cannot say for sure, but I believe I will be home in time to join you at Rosings in the spring."

"I should certainly hope so. Our aunt would never forgive you otherwise."

Richard's shoulders relaxed, and Darcy knew he had said the right thing. "I do not believe that for a second. As long as you are present, she does not care who else is there."

Darcy ran his hand through his hair. "Please let us speak of something more pleasant."

Richard glanced at the clock. "Actually, I believe it is time we turned in for the night. I will see you in the morning for breakfast."

"Good night, Richard."

When Darcy woke the next morning, he felt more like himself than he had in over a month. Georgiana's delight in seeing him only added to his pleasure in being home. "Fitzwilliam! We did not expect you home so soon."

He poured himself a cup of coffee and sat down opposite her and Richard. "Bingley returned to town himself, and without a host, I had no reason to stay in Hertfordshire."

"Mr. Bingley has returned? But I thought he planned to live in Hertfordshire."

She takes an eager interest in his affairs; that is good. She will easily form an attachment to Bingley. "I believe his plans were never fully settled. He would still like to purchase his own estate, if you recall."

Her frown cleared. "Of course. Oh, it is so good to have you home. I have missed you."

Darcy smiled. "And I have missed you, Georgie. Tell me, how did you pass the long lonely days awaiting my return?" He was delighted when she wrinkled her nose at his joke—the Georgiana of two months ago would not have done so.

"You know very well that Mrs. Annesley requested I return to my studies. Unless Cousin Richard stole me away to the museum or for a walk in the park, I have done little but read and sew and play."

"And what was the last book you read?" he asked.

"*Cecilia.*"

"Indeed?" For a moment, Darcy was back in the library at Netherfield, watching Elizabeth read the same book. "By Mrs. Burney?"

She nodded. "Have you read it, Brother?"

"No, another young lady I know read it recently."

Richard raised an eyebrow and Darcy shook his head slightly. He did not wish to discuss Elizabeth with his family. *Indeed, there is nothing to share.*

"I believe you had more enjoyment in London than I had in Hertfordshire, my dear," he said before Richard could open his mouth. "Now, tell me—would you mind very much if we invited Mr. Bingley and his sisters to dine with us tonight?"

Georgiana turned to Richard. "Would you mind a few additional guests, Cousin?"

Richard put his fork down and cleared his throat. "Actually, Georgie, I received orders to return to France on Monday. I must excuse myself from dinner tonight so I can prepare to leave."

Georgiana bit her lip and concern filled her blue eyes. "Will you be in any danger, Richard?"

Darcy and Richard shared a glance across the table, and then Richard placed his hand over hers and squeezed lightly. "I will be as safe as I can, sweet Cuz. After all, I would not want to leave you with only your brother as a guardian. You might end up as dour and disapproving as he is."

Darcy frowned. "Richard —" Laughter cut him off, and when he realized he had proven his cousin's point, he joined in.

Richard left a moment later, and Darcy raised his original question again. "Shall we have the Bingleys over for dinner?"

Georgiana lifted one shoulder in a gesture of listless acquiescence. "If you wish."

He heard worry under her disinterest and knew

concern for Richard would dampen her already quiet spirits. *She will do Bingley no good in this frame of mind.* "Perhaps we should have a family dinner instead. I have not heard all you did while I was away."

"Perhaps... perhaps we might invite them over after Richard leaves?" Her eyes darted to the door and back to Darcy. "When does he leave?"

"He needs to be in Portsmouth Sunday evening. Shall I see if the Bingleys and Hursts can pull us out of our doldrums that evening?"

Her cheeks had lost all their color, but she nodded. "Yes, that would be quite good."

Darcy visited Bingley that afternoon, and the butler showed him directly to the library, where his friend sat with a glass of claret. "Good afternoon, Bingley. I trust you are doing well?"

Bingley's smile lacked its usual cheer. "Of course. It is always good to be back in London after being away."

Darcy shook his head, a slight smile on his face. Despite Bingley's evidently low spirits, he could tell his friend truly meant that. *He had been telling Mrs. Bennet the truth then, when he said he could be just as happy in the country as in the city. I envy his easy temper at times.*

"Yes, it is," Darcy agreed. "I am anxious to return to Pemberley, but business dictates we remain in town. As we are all to be in London some time, Georgiana and I hoped you and your family might join us for dinner this coming Sunday."

Bingley considered. "I believe we could join you then," he said. "I know of no other engagements."

"Excellent. Georgiana will be pleased—Richard leaves London that day, and I am afraid the thought has left her a little melancholy." Darcy set his glass down and shook Bingley's hand in farewell.

The carriage ride home was just long enough for Darcy to tamp down any niggling concerns regarding Bingley's state of mind. *Of course he is unhappy,* he told himself. *What man would not be, when faced with the true nature of a woman's affections?*

When he arrived at home, he found Georgiana in the sitting room, in a dreadfully dull state. She pretended to do needlework, but even he could see she had done nothing on it since he had left. Her attempt to hide her distress disturbed Darcy. *Does she fear my disapproval when left without Richard's calming influence?*

Darcy knew he could not mimic Richard's easy manner with Georgiana, but he had thought previously that she understood the affection behind his occasional dictates. However, she clearly felt she must hide her upset from him, and he immediately sought a way to put her mind at ease. His gaze traveled the room and settled on the sunshine streaming in through the front windows. "Georgiana, would you care for a walk in the park? It is quite lovely outside today. We should take advantage of the sun, for I am sure the rain will come soon."

Georgiana set her stitching down and looked out the window. "Yes, of course," she said.

Darcy hid a sigh; he had hoped for a smile, but it seemed he must satisfy himself with quiet agreement instead. "Come, change into a walking dress and I will order the coach."

Hyde Park was quite busy for a November afternoon—clearly they were not the only ones enjoying the fine weather. Georgiana took the arm he offered, and they walked in silence for a while.

He glanced sideways at his sister and realized with a start that with her height and in her new green wool coat, she looked quite grown-up. He shook his head quickly, but the picture did not change.

"How do you like London?" Darcy asked finally.

For several minutes, the only indication she had heard was a slight tightening of her grip on his arm. He glanced sideways and could see by the tilt of her head that she was considering what to say. "I wish I knew some young ladies here," she said finally. "I am sure Cousin Richard grew weary of my company, and I confess it would have been nice to have female companionship."

He frowned and turned slightly toward her. "Does Mrs. Annesley not satisfy you?"

"Oh yes!" she said in a rush. "But it is not the same as another young lady, close to my own age..."

Georgiana bit her lip and looked away, and Darcy covered her hand with his. "Next year, you will be in London during the Season and you will make some friends. And then the year after that will be your own debut —" he halted when she flushed scarlet. "Georgie, you knew that would come, did you not?"

Her step faltered, and Darcy drew up beside her. Her head was bowed, and he had to bend down to hear her whisper. "I was not sure, after..."

Her low voice wrenched his heart. "Ah, dearest, must I remind you? That was not your fault, and you are wiser for it." He glanced around the people milling about them. "Now, speaking of wise, we should not discuss this in such a public place."

He placed his hand under her chin. "Come, Georgie, let us enjoy the sunshine while it lasts."

Her smile was weak but genuine. They walked for a while in silence before she returned to her earlier topic. "You believe there will be young ladies my own age in town next spring, Fitzwilliam?"

"I am sure of it," he said. "Ladies just as yourself, not quite out formally, but old enough to be in town with their families. Perhaps we might find a way to introduce you to some of them."

Darcy voice trailed off on the last word. A couple had joined the path from a different direction, and the silhouette of the lady was hauntingly familiar. He took a step toward her, and then she turned and his shoulders drooped. *Of course it was not Elizabeth; she is at home in Hertfordshire, not here in Hyde Park. What a fool you are, Darcy.*

"Fitzwilliam?"

He turned to Georgiana, who eyed him with curiosity, and he flushed when he realized how foolish he must look, staring after an unknown lady. "I believe it is time we turned back, Georgiana."

She accepted this without argument. The entire walk back to the carriage, Darcy relived that moment when he thought he had seen Elizabeth Bennet standing before him once more, and he finally understood Bingley's inability to let go of Jane Bennet. *What is the hold these sisters possess, that they can so ensnare a man?*

The rain returned the next day, and Darcy spent the afternoon in his library. When he had been in Hertfordshire, he had remembered London to be filled with entertainment. However, on a cold winter day, there was very little difference between the country and the city. Only the promise of company on the morrow relieved the monotony of town.

The library was not far from the music room, and when Georgiana's music master arrived, he opened the door so he could listen without embarrassing her. They did vocal exercises first, and then she sang a sweet country song of love and friendship.

"Where have I heard this recently?" It was not until she reached the chorus that he knew—Elizabeth had sung the song at the Lucas's party.

He reached out to slam the door shut, but realized just in time that the sound would give away his eavesdropping. He dropped instead into a chair, his book lying on the floor, utterly forgotten.

Georgiana continued to sing, but it was another's voice Darcy heard. He buried his face in his hands, but he could not erase the image of Elizabeth Bennet from his mind's eye.

Chapter Fourteen

DARCY AND GEORGIANA barely exerted themselves for the whole of December. The first evening with Bingley and his sisters was enough to show Darcy that she was not ready to be courted, or even to have the suggestion made to her. She nearly jumped out of her skin when Bingley approached her, and she remained on edge for the whole of the meal. Unwilling to see her suffer, he cut the evening short as early as he could.

Between Georgiana and the sisters, however, there grew a certain degree of familiarity, and he hoped they would pull her into their family circle. He knew they shared his wish—Miss Bingley no doubt hoped one marriage between their families would lead to another.

Therefore, he was not surprised to find the ladies with Georgiana in the blue salon one afternoon in early January. "Mr. Darcy, you must join us," Caroline Bingley called out.

He stepped into the salon. "Ladies," he said with a bow. "How may I be of service?"

Miss Bingley leaned forward, and she sat so close that Georgiana was forced to shift slightly away from her. "Oh, it is nothing so serious, I assure you. I have just received a letter from Longbourn with news that will interest you."

She pulled the letter from her reticule and handed it

to Darcy, who took it with a degree of unwillingness. *Please, let it not be an announcement of Elizabeth's engagement,* he prayed.

It was not. He read Jane Bennet's letter with growing consternation—"I am happy to say I shall arrive in town on January tenth..."

Miss Bingley, who had watched his face avidly as he read the letter, said, "How shall I reply?"

He handed the letter back and deliberated for a moment. If the ladies called on Miss Bennet in Gracechurch Street, it would be difficult to keep word of her presence in town from Bingley.

"Do not," he said finally, and she nodded her agreement. "Now, if you will excuse me..." Darcy bowed and left the room.

He returned to his library and paced the floor in front of the fireplace. Not for the first time, he cursed the very existence of the Bennet family. All his plans— for Bingley, for Georgiana, even for himself—had been going along quite well until the ill-advised sojourn to Hertfordshire. Now Bingley fancied himself in love with a lady wholly unsuitable, and he...

He flung himself into a chair. "I will overcome this... this weakness for Elizabeth Bennet!" he muttered. "I will not be so caught up by a woman I cannot have, that the mere thought of her sends my pulse racing."

Darcy rose abruptly and walked back down the hallway to the salon. The few minutes gave him time to compose himself, and he satisfied himself that none could detect his earlier torment when he asked, "Mrs. Hurst, is your brother at home today?"

"He is, sir."

"I believe I will ask him to ride with me tomorrow."

As winter slowly passed, Darcy kept Bingley too occupied to discover Jane Bennet was in town. Every afternoon they rode, or Bingley joined Darcy at his club for an early dinner and conversation after.

Darcy's reason was simple: though he had convinced Bingley once that Miss Bennet did not share his affection, he did not trust his friend not to fall in love with her a second time if he were to see her again. *And this time, my efforts at separating them might not be so successful,* he mused. As much as he hated to admit to such weakness in himself, he knew instinctively that his own defenses would crumble were he to meet Elizabeth again.

One evening in early February, Georgiana broached the subject of a visit to Pemberley. "For you never answered my earlier petition," she added.

It took him a moment to realize she referred to the letter she had sent him while he was at Netherfield. He recalled her desire to spend the spring at Pemberley, and he sighed. "I did not, did I?"

Georgiana turned slightly away, one hand playing with the folds of her gown. "You need not say anything else, Brother," she said. "I can hear in your voice that we are not to return to Pemberley before the Season begins."

Darcy took her hand in his, and she looked up at him. "I am sorry, Georgiana, but I cannot leave London right now. I am needed here on a matter of some delicacy."

Her ears reddened. "It is not... You have not seen..."

"No, it is nothing whatsoever to do with Wickham," he assured her, and her color receded. "In truth, my dear, a friend of mine is considering a bad decision, and I fear that if I leave, he will allow his emotions to sway him from a rational course of action."

"Then of course you must stay, if Mr. Bingley needs you," she said immediately. When he raised an eyebrow, she said, "Do you think I have not noticed you spend all your time with them? You are a good friend, Fitzwilliam."

Georgiana tapped her chin thoughtfully. "If I am not to go to Pemberley, I might bring Pemberley to London."

"How do you mean?"

"Mrs. Annesley and my painting master would like me to begin a landscape. I believe I will paint Pemberley in the spring, surrounded by green and flowers."

Darcy smiled at her. "I look forward to seeing it completed." He grimaced. "I cannot blame you for wishing to return home, but I quite envy you London. In six weeks, I shall have to make my annual trip to Rosings Park."

Georgiana wrinkled her nose. "I am glad I need not join you. Our aunt makes me quite nervous. I am always afraid she will find fault with something I do."

"Lady Catherine has decided opinions on everything," Darcy pointed out, "but you need not fear her rebuke."

Georgiana played with a fork for moment. "Are you going to m...marry Anne?"

The question was so unexpected, Darcy nearly choked. "I beg your pardon?" he said once he cleared his airway.

Georgiana returned his gaze. "I do not think you would at all suit, Brother." This time, she did not stammer. "Anne is not strong enough to care for the tenants or walk the estate with you. I do not think her little phaeton and ponies could quite make the full circle of the park."

She blushed a little under Darcy's disbelief. "I do not mean to speak ill of our cousin," she said hurriedly. "Indeed, I quite like Anne... At least I think I do. I am not sure I really know her."

"I am not sure Anne knows herself, Georgiana,"

Darcy said quietly. "You must understand, though we only see Lady Catherine once or twice a year, poor Anne has lived with her all her life."

Georgiana paled. "Oh, to always be told who you are to like, what you are to think. I do feel sorry for her."

"As do I. And to answer your most impertinent question, no, I do not plan to marry Anne. I have many reasons, but your point is a valid one. She could not manage the walk..."

Darcy's voice trailed off, his mind on another young lady who loved to walk, who would rather cross three miles of fields on foot than ride on horseback. He glanced at Georgiana, but she had turned back to her food, believing the conversation to be over. *Ah Elizabeth, what must I do to forget you?*

Chapter Fifteen

As FEBRUARY ENDED, Darcy was glad for Georgiana's painting on two counts: first, it brought a little light and sunshine into the dreary London winter, and second, it distracted them both from Richard's continued absence. That Richard had hesitated when Darcy asked when he might return did not make him feel any better.

When a knock on his study door disturbed him late one evening, he knew without being told who it was. "Come in, Richard," he called out and rose to pour some brandy. "You know," he said, his back to the door, "this manner of returning late and unannounced..."

The words died in his throat when he turned and caught sight of his cousin leaning heavily on the doorframe, his arm up in a sling. "Good God! What happened? Never mind," he said hastily when Richard opened his mouth. "Just sit down before you fall over."

Richard limped over to a chair and sank into it gratefully. "I believe I will take that brandy, William—thank you." He took a sip and released a sigh of satisfaction. "Excellent, as always. I hope you do not mind if I stay here for a while. I stopped by my rooms first, but they were cold and lonely." He did not explain why he avoided the Fitzwilliam townhouse—both men knew he could not show up there looking so haggard, not without enduring a long line of questions from the Earl and Countess.

"Of course not. You will want to clean up as much as possible before breakfast, however. I believe your current state would concern Georgiana a great deal."

"I should be able to dispense with the sling come morning. It was really only necessary to keep my arm from being jolted during travel. That injury at least is nearly healed."

"What exactly are your injuries? Were you shot?"

"Shot *at*," Richard corrected, "which scared my horse. Losing my seat was somewhat ignoble, but it likely saved my life, as the next shot might not have missed. However, I landed awkwardly—you can imagine—and injured my leg."

"And your arm?"

Richard's face darkened. "A knife."

Darcy's fingers tightened on the arm of his chair. "There were two attempts made on your life?" He knew Richard's occupation was dangerous, but he had never expected this.

"Yes, and it was the second which decided my superiors on returning me to England. An agent of the Crown whose identity has been discovered is of no use."

"Understandable. Well, I will have Johnston bring you hot water for a bath."

Richard stood gingerly. "Actually, I already requested one. It should be ready now. Good night, William—I might not make breakfast tomorrow."

In fact, it was nearly teatime before he showed his face. Darcy and Georgiana were in the salon when he appeared. "Richard!" She half rose, a ready smile on her face. However, a look from Mrs. Annesley settled her back in her seat. "I am glad to see you, Cousin. It has been far too long."

Richard glanced between Darcy and the companion. "Oh no, this will never do," he said in mock dismay. "I am gone for four months, and the only greeting I receive is one of a decorous young lady? Was I not missed, sweet Georgie, not even a little?"

"Wretch!" she said on a laugh. "You know you were missed very much. Does the Army not allow you to write, Colonel?" she asked pertly.

Richard hesitated, and Darcy wondered how he would answer the question. It was not certain to Darcy if he could not write because of the sensitivity of his work, or if he had in fact written and those letters had been intercepted.

The pause had just become noticeable when Richard smiled. "I did not stay in any one place long enough to write, nor could I receive any letters. If I had, I am sure I would have known how much taller you have become."

Georgiana straightened in her chair and smiled at him. "I am now nearly as tall as Miss Bingley."

"Yes, I can see that."

Richard settled into a chair, and Darcy indicated that Georgiana should order tea. When she had done so, he turned to Richard. "Will you be ready to leave for Kent in a week?"

Georgiana pouted. "Are you to leave so soon?"

"I fear we must. Imagine Lady Catherine's displeasure were she to learn you kept us from her side." Georgiana sighed and Richard patted her hand. "Fret not, sweet Cuz, we shall return as soon as we can."

"I am glad you took my advice and left London for a while—though it will be some time before she is back to her old self, Georgiana is much better than she was before. I imagine some of that is just the passage of time, of course."

Darcy looked across the carriage at his cousin. Though Richard claimed his arm no longer bothered him, he kept his leg stretched out in front of him. "You were right, as you usually are. My presence kept her from regaining her self-confidence." He shook his head. "I do wish she would laugh again. I miss her laughter."

"She will, Darcy. Just trust her, and yourself."

Darcy tapped his fingers against his leg. He had not told Richard about seeing Wickham in Hertfordshire, but if they did not change the subject, he would not be able to avoid it. "Yes, well, it seems I am destined to save all those I care about from imprudent matches of late."

"Really? I could use a good tale. Come, tell me what you have been doing while I was away."

Darcy shifted in his seat. He had said those words more to himself than to Richard. Mention of Bingley and Miss Bennet would take the conversation far closer to Elizabeth than he wished. Still, this was the most animated he had seen Richard since his return from France.

"I do not know that there is a great deal to tell," he said with a shrug. "A friend of mine came quite close to offering for a young lady this winter, but I was able to persuade him to do otherwise."

Richard raised one dark eyebrow. "I value your opinion, William, but when I choose my bride, I would appreciate it if you did not interfere."

Darcy snorted. "When you choose your bride, she will be worthy of the name. I know you, Richard. You are not a romantic. You are far too practical."

Richard laughed. "True—that is one thing the Army has given me, at least. So tell me, what was lacking in this young lady? Fortune?"

"Yes, though that was not my primary concern. My friend has more than enough to provide for a wife and children. Her family, however…" Darcy shuddered.

"Was she not a gentleman's daughter?"

Darcy flinched at the echo of Bingley's own words. "She was, but her family connections would do nothing for his standing in Society."

Richard carefully stretched his leg out in front of him. "William, you know that not everyone is looking for the same high connections you are."

"Yes, but I imagine most men would like to see a semblance of propriety in their family," he countered.

"Was the lady herself lacking?"

Darcy pursed his lips. "No, most of the objections were against her family. I cannot tell you the vulgar displays I was forced to witness. Why, I believe her mother already had the wedding planned."

Richard grinned, and Darcy was relieved to see his cousin's playful spirit returning. "By that count, you must despise most of the women in town. They have all had you married to their daughters for years."

Darcy laughed and shook his head. "It will take more than the will of the matchmaking mama to convince me to marry."

"True, or you would be wed to our cousin by now. Tell me, how long will you let her continue to believe you will marry her?"

"I beg your pardon," Darcy said stiffly. "I have never misled Anne."

"Oh no, not Anne—I am sure she is very aware you do not intend to marry her. But what of our aunt?"

Darcy raked his hand through his hair. "That is not a

conversation I relish. I prefer to postpone it until I can present my engagement as a *fait accompli*."

"So much for the vaunted Darcy integrity!"

"As a military man, you will, I am sure, be familiar with the phrase, 'Discretion is the better part of valor.'"

Their laughter softened the jolts as the carriage passed over ruts left by spring rains, and the hours of their journey passed swiftly by. All too soon, they reached the palings of Rosings Park, and Richard put a hand on Darcy's shoulder. "Are you ready to see your future bride?" he jested.

"Alas, I fear she will not have me," he joked in return.

They rounded a bend and Hunsford rectory came into view. A figure of a man was visible standing outside along the road, and Darcy stiffened with a sudden certainty that he knew who it was. Sure enough, Mr. Collins sketched one of his odd little bows as they passed. Darcy nodded in reply, and Richard looked at him curiously.

"Do you know him, William?"

"He is Mr. Collins, our aunt's new parson. He introduced himself to me in Hertfordshire."

Richard's eyes widened. "He introduced himself to you?"

"He did."

"I see. And how did you meet him in Hertfordshire, if he is the rector of Hunsford?"

Darcy ran his hand over the soft satin lining of the carriage. The conversation veered dangerously close to the Bennets, and for a moment he thought he could change the subject. A glance at Richard revealed an intent expression, and he shrugged. "He visited family in the neighborhood."

"How lucky for him to meet a family member of his patroness."

"I believe that is precisely what he thought." Darcy groaned and rested his head against the side of the carriage. "You cannot comprehend how ridiculous a man he is, you truly cannot. I would be glad to avoid his presence for the whole of our visit."

They arrived at Rosings before Richard could reply. The butler's familiar face greeted them at the door. "Mr. Darcy, Colonel Fitzwilliam, her ladyship has asked you to join her for tea in the small salon."

"Of course, Brewster. Thank you."

The butler bowed, and the gentleman walked down a short hallway and into the room indicated. "Darcy, Fitzwilliam. Come here at once! What has detained you —we expected you half an hour ago, did we not, Anne?"

Darcy bowed over his aunt's outstretched hand and kissed it. "We were not detained, Aunt. We had fine weather the entire way from London. However, I do wish you had let us clean up before we greeted you; I am sure our journey did not leave us fresh."

She waved her hand at him. "Anne would not hear of any delay in seeing you after so long. She has missed you both excessively, have you not, Anne?"

Darcy turned to his cousin, whose faint blush strongly reminded him of someone, though he could not quite figure out whom. "And how have you been, Cousin?" he asked felicitously.

Anne raised her hands to her neck, where they fluttered uselessly for a minute before they dropped back to her lap. "I have been well enough, William," she replied, her voice so soft he had to strain to hear it.

"Winter is the greatest discomfort to Anne, Darcy," Lady Catherine said, as if the Lord had created the season to vex her child, "but she bears up admirably."

"The cold does seem to settle in my bones," the young lady admitted.

"Then it is good we had a mild winter this year," Darcy observed. He took a seat next to Richard, who, except for that first greeting, had been completely ignored until this point. "Indeed, we were saying on the journey here that we have never known an earlier spring."

"Ah, but you do not recall spring four years ago then," Lady Catherine said. "Why, I had roses blooming in April that year."

Her soliloquy on spring lasted some minutes, and Darcy paid only the barest amount of attention. Anne caught his eye and shrugged apologetically; he smiled in return. He felt nothing but pity for his cousin, trapped by a mother who could only embarrass her.

He sat upright. *That is who she reminded me of—Jane Bennet, when her mother was so obviously attempting to snare Bingley.*

The conversation took a turn then that drew his attention. "Though, the Bishops are in town for the Season, which leaves us with paltry company. Of course, there is the rector Mr. Collins and his wife..."

"Mr. Collins is married?" Darcy broke in. *Surely not Elizabeth...*

"Of course. I advised him to take a wife, and he saw the wisdom in my suggestion. He went to Hertfordshire last fall for the express purpose."

"I had the pleasure of meeting Mr. Collins when I visited my friend Mr. Bingley in that neighborhood, but I had not heard of his marriage. Pray, tell me which of the local ladies became his wife?"

"Mrs. Collins was Miss Charlotte Lucas before her marriage," Lady Catherine answered, and Darcy fought to remain upright against the onslaught of relief. "Did you meet with her there?"

"Only in passing. I believe her to be a very practical sort of lady." *Except in her choice of spouse.*

Richard stood abruptly and bowed. "Thank you for your forbearance, Aunt, but I believe Darcy and I have tarried long enough. If we do not retire to our rooms now, we will not have time to change for dinner."

She looked down her nose at the elder of her nephews. "Very well, Fitzwilliam," she conceded. "But you will remember we dine early —"

"So as not to tax Anne," he finished smoothly and bowed over his cousin's hand. "We shall see you in a few hours, I hope?"

The tired lines on her forehead eased and she graced him with a small but genuine smile. "Of course, Richard. We will see you at dinner."

After the gentlemen left the salon, Richard turned to Darcy. "I have a question for you, William, if you have a minute."

"Of course. Shall we go to the study?" The study at Rosings Park was largely unused, there being no male in residence. Even Lady Catherine would not interrupt them there. "What did you wish to ask?" Darcy said once the door was shut.

Richard leaned against the wall, his arms folded in front of him. "You showed an unusual interest in Mrs. Collins. Is there anything regarding your stay in Hertfordshire you wish to tell me?"

Darcy's pulse sped up, but he remained outwardly calm. "What do you mean?"

"You did not form an attachment to Miss Lucas yourself, did you?"

Darcy laughed—Richard was so close and yet so wildly off target. "Not at all, I assure you. If we have the opportunity to meet Mrs. Collins, you will see she is as far from my ideal wife as you could imagine. I was merely curious," he repeated.

Richard put his hand on the door and looked Darcy over. Apparently he was satisfied Darcy told the truth, for he smiled and said, "Very well then. I shall leave you to dress for dinner."

Darcy grinned. "Yes, thank you for getting us away from Aunt Catherine."

Richard shook his head. "Do not thank me yet. I have not the patience to be ignored on this trip, and I am likely to make you uncomfortable." Before Darcy could ask what he meant, the door swung shut in his face.

Chapter Sixteen

RICHARD'S MEANING BECAME abundantly clear at breakfast the next morning.

Aware of their aunt's habit of lying in bed with her chocolate until late morning, the two cousins always made sure to rise with the dawn. Those morning hours were often their only moments of peace and quiet.

On this morning, however, Brewster interrupted their solitude with an announcement. "Mr. Collins is here to see you, Mr. Darcy."

Before Darcy could order him sent away, Richard said, "Show him in, Brewster." The butler bowed and retreated, and Richard looked over at Darcy. "I did tell you I would likely make you uncomfortable, did I not?"

"You did," Darcy acknowledged, "but in this particular instance I believe you will come to regret your penchant for teasing me."

"Oh? What do you mean?"

Darcy gestured to the door, which opened to admit Mr. Collins. "Mr. Darcy!" He bowed to the appropriate level for a duke, and the cousins exchanged amused glances over his back. "I am glad to see you in good health, sir. How good it is of you to give attendance to your noble aunt. I have often told her ladyship that if a member of the court were to come to Kent, it would be to pay honor to her, rather than the other way around."

"Quite so, sir," Darcy said, enjoying the look on Richard's face. "I understand you have lately married. Allow me to wish you happy."

The parson's face suffused with pride. "Oh, my dear Charlotte could not make me otherwise! She is the wisest and most amiable of females—excepting her ladyship, of course."

"Of course," Richard agreed gravely, and Darcy was confident only those who knew him would see this slight twitch of a smile. "Tell me, sir, what business took you to Hertfordshire? You were quite lucky to find such a paragon in a distant county."

Mr. Collins bowed again of this observation. "You are entirely correct, Colonel Fitzwilliam. It was Providence which led me there—well, Providence and the small matter of an estate I shall one day inherit. Imagine my surprise when I visited my cousins and found in that neighborhood the one lady destined to make my life complete!"

Unwilling to hear more of the Bennets, Darcy opened his mouth to redirect conversation. However, before he could, Mr. Collins continued. "In fact, one of my fair cousins stays with us now, along with my sister Maria. Do you remember my cousin Elizabeth, Mr. Darcy?"

"Yes —" he cleared his throat—"yes, of course. Miss Elizabeth is at Hunsford?"

"Indeed she is. She is quite the intimate friend of my dear Charlotte, if you will recall, and nothing less than a wedding visit could persuade her of her friend's happiness."

Darcy heard the petulant undertone and knew immediately that either Elizabeth had spoken against their engagement, or she herself had refused to marry Collins. The latter thought cheered him greatly, and without thought for the implications he said, "I wonder, sir, if we might accompany you back to the rectory. It has been some months since I visited with my acquaintances from Hertfordshire."

Mr. Collins positively beamed with delight. "Oh yes! That would be very good of you. Of course, it is nothing less than I would expect from someone associated with the noble house of de Bourgh."

Nothing but the thought of seeing Elizabeth that afternoon could have prevented Darcy from commenting that the house of de Bourgh benefited more from the connection with the Darcys and Fitzwilliams than the other way around. However, he nodded slightly, and all three gentlemen left the breakfast room together.

Darcy allowed Mr. Collins to lead them to his home, though it took all his self-control not to speed past him to the Parsonage where Elizabeth waited. *Elizabeth!* He thought of her rich dark eyes and his heart raced. *My Elizabeth, how I have missed you.*

The sardonic edge in Richard's voice pulled him from his thoughts. "You must forgive my cousin, Mr. Collins. He has such long legs that he nearly always outstrips whoever walks with him. Why, I sometimes find myself running just to keep up."

Darcy looked behind him and realized he had indeed passed them both. "I do apologize, Mr. Collins," he said, his ears warm. "Colonel Fitzwilliam is correct —I forget at times that I walk faster than most men."

Mr. Collins caught up and smiled. "I assure you, I was not in the least bit offended," he said. "We are almost to the rectory; allow me to go in and inform the ladies of the honor of your visit."

Darcy and Richard let the man precede them into the house, and then Richard turned toward Darcy. "You have a great deal of explaining to do when we return to

Rosings, Cousin," he said, and the promise of such teasing was almost enough to send Darcy back down the road without seeing Elizabeth. But Mr. Collins returned with his wife and Elizabeth, and Darcy's chance for escape ended.

Darcy clenched his hands into fists and released them, hoping to stop the shaking. "Mrs. Collins, Miss Elizabeth, I am pleased to see you both. I had not thought to have the pleasure of seeing you again after I left Hertfordshire last winter."

He was vaguely aware of Mrs. Collins accepting his greeting and returning it, but the whole of his vision had narrowed to Elizabeth. *Did her mouth always curve in such a deliciously appealing smile?*

Elizabeth curtsied, but said not a word. Darcy thought he saw a hint of discomfort in her manner, and his heart soared. He was overcome by the moment, and the thought that Elizabeth was also thrilled to see him.

Richard bowed low to the ladies. "Mrs. Collins, a pleasure to meet you, ma'am. And Miss Bennet, how delightful to meet you. Darcy has told me much about Hertfordshire, but he did not tell me that the prettiest women in the kingdom hid there."

Elizabeth smiled at him, and jealousy glued Darcy's tongue to the roof of his mouth. *I do not mind much his ability to make Georgiana and Anne smile, but this is too much.*

He sought for a topic of conversation he knew would interest her, but before he could find something to say, Richard spoke again. "I spent many winters in Hertfordshire, encamped in various villages. I remember the countryside as being truly lovely."

"Why thank you, Colonel Fitzwilliam," Miss Elizabeth said. "I am sure I do not know a prettier part of England, though I admit I am biased."

Richard smiled. "We are all inclined to believe our

home to be the prettiest, loveliest place in the world, do you not agree, Darcy?"

At a complete loss, Darcy merely nodded while frantically searching for something to say to join in the conversation. "This house is very nice, Mrs. Collins," he finally managed. "I caught sight of a garden out back as well, I believe."

"The garden is Mr. Collins's domain, but I will take your compliment on the house, Mr. Darcy. Thank you."

He nodded again and then fell silent.

After some minutes, he realized one thing he could say to Elizabeth that would not arouse the suspicion of anyone. "How is your family? Are they all in health?"

She nodded and then said, "My eldest sister has been in town these three months. Have you never happened to see her there?"

The innocent question blindsided Darcy, and for an instant he knew not how to respond. "No, I am afraid I have not had the pleasure," he said, a split second later.

It was the truth, yet when she accepted it without question he felt all the guilt of his deception. Indeed, he was almost glad when Richard rose a moment later and said, "I fear we have intruded too long, and our aunt will be wondering where we have gone. Good day to you all; it was a pleasure to make your acquaintance, and I trust we will see you often while we are in Kent." Mr. Collins accepted this courtesy with his usual odd mix of self-absorption and obsequious thanks and led them to the door.

Once they were on the road and well out of earshot of the house, Darcy braced himself for his cousin's teasing. He knew his behavior had been unusual enough to draw Richard's attention—*Did I not say just yesterday that I hoped to avoid Mr. Collins? Then this morning I practically ran in my eagerness to reach his house.*

But Richard was silent. Darcy glanced over at him

and saw the crease in his brow, which indicated he was deep in thought. "What could you have found in the Parsonage to put that frown on your face, Cousin?"

"Did Mr. Collins say he is to inherit Mr. Bennet's estate?"

Darcy thought it an odd question, but he answered anyway. "He did."

Richard nodded. "Then Miss Bennet has no brothers?"

"No, only four sisters, one elder and three younger."

"I see."

They walked farther in silence, but when they reached the gate to Rosings Park, Darcy could stand the suspense no longer. "I am curious, Richard; to what exactly do these questions tend?"

"Miss Elizabeth is a lovely, amiable young lady," Richard said, and Darcy nodded noncommittally. "Is all her father's estate entailed away?"

"Yes, I believe so," he answered.

"Hmmm…" Richard said, and Darcy fought the urge to grab him and demand to know what he was thinking.

"It is a shame, then." Richard said finally.

"Excuse me?"

"She is a fine young lady. Still, it is a shame she has no fortune to speak of. It would take a man with his own money to see past the lack of dowry."

Darcy's gut clenched and he swallowed back the bile which rose in his throat. Richard desired to marry Elizabeth.

Chapter Seventeen

A SLEEPLESS NIGHT gave Darcy some much-needed perspective. Richard was the second son, and even the second son of an earl needed to marry well. *He could not possibly consider Elizabeth as a bride.*

All those calm soothing thoughts disappeared shortly after breakfast. Lady Catherine made an appearance in the study and, in strident tones, demanded to know what her nephews had planned for the day.

Richard leaned back in his chair—a behavior both men knew their aunt despised. She observed him through narrowed eyes. He said, "Oh, I thought I might walk over to the Parsonage and visit Mrs. Collins and her friend."

Lady Catherine sniffed. "Why would you care to visit them?"

Richard shrugged. "I am sure you need Darcy here for estate business, and I must have something to do."

Darcy glared at his cousin, all his jealousy of the previous afternoon back in full force. *How dare he dismiss me like that?*

However, Lady Catherine acknowledged that she did indeed have business for Darcy to attend to, and thus he was stuck. Darcy spent the whole of the afternoon going over the account books with her steward, and when Richard came back, he stayed only long enough for tea before he saddled his horse and left Darcy alone to attend his aunt and cousin in the pre-dinner hours.

Darcy swore to himself that evening that he would not be dismissed again, but on Thursday, Richard just as easily foisted Darcy off into the clutches of Lady Catherine. "Have you discussed your plans for Georgiana's Season with Darcy?" he asked their aunt after breakfast.

Richard's innocent smile did not fool Darcy. Yesterday, he had only suspected his cousin of courting Elizabeth; now he was certain. *What other company could draw him to the Parsonage?*

The realization that his cousin might steal Elizabeth's affections while he sat in the drawing room at Rosings Park robbed Darcy of his composure. Even his patience with Lady Catherine wore thin, and he barely stopped himself from snapping at her that afternoon when she made another of her thinly veiled allusions to his supposed marriage to Anne.

He met Richard at the stables when he returned from his ride. "We need to talk," he said when his cousin had dismounted and handed the reins to a groom.

"Of course. Just let me change..."

"No. Now." Richard raised an eyebrow at the demand, but nodded in agreement.

Darcy led the way toward one of the private paths around the circumference of the park, and once he was sure no one could hear him, he turned to Richard. "What do you mean by abandoning me to our aunt and cousin each afternoon?"

It was a fair question: the agreement between the cousins was that Richard would deflect Lady Catherine's attention and Darcy would keep the Earl and Countess from asking any uncomfortable questions about their son's trips to France.

He did not expect Richard's answer. "You have at your disposal a simple way to rid yourself of their attentions," he snapped. "Tell the truth for once and admit you will not marry our cousin."

Darcy stepped forward, his fists clenched. "As I said, I have never indicated I would. If they choose to believe…"

"Because you have never told them you will not!"

"Do you really think that will improve the situation?" Darcy retorted icily. "Aunt Catherine will only become abusive once she has no reason to curry my favor—that is, if she believes me at all."

"You will never know until you have tried."

Darcy snorted. "You know our aunt as well as I do. If she believed I was not determined to marry Anne, she would be impossibly rude to any woman I courted."

"She will be impossibly rude to your wife," countered Richard. "Consider the engagement period a trial to see if your future bride can handle the family pressure."

Darcy nearly hit Richard. "I will not put any woman through such a trial," he hissed.

Richard shrugged, and some of the tension left his shoulders. "Perhaps it would not be totally fair," he said.

"It would not." Darcy breathed in through his mouth and let the air out through his nose. "I told you on the journey here, once we are engaged, I will explain to Lady Catherine."

Richard grinned. "Have you selected a lady to be your bride then?"

"What? No." Darcy waved him off. "When I have proposed to the woman I love, I mean."

"I see."

Darcy sighed; this conversation was the closest he and Richard had come to arguing in years. "May I count on your help, Richard?"

"You may."

This agreement did not dispel Darcy's notion that Richard courted Elizabeth, and with that uneasy suspicion came a new realization—if he intended to marry the woman he loved, his bride must be none other than Elizabeth Bennet.

Chapter Eighteen

SINCE THE FOLLOWING day was Good Friday, there were no calls paid to the Parsonage by any member of the household. After the service, Richard kept his promise to Darcy and entertained the ladies long enough for Darcy to steal a few minutes to himself.

He walked in the direction of the stables, but stopped halfway there. His fingers tapped the side of his leg in a nervous rhythm, and he knew he had neither the patience nor the control to ride. *A walk then,* he decided, and turned toward one of his favorite parts of the park.

He strode through a copse of trees into a hidden thicket. A small stream cut its way through the Downs, and the hills here reminded Darcy of Pemberley. His steps slowed as he neared the large oak which stood near the center of the grove. He and Richard had placed a bench here many years ago, and he often came here to think when Lady Catherine's demands became too much.

Today, however, Darcy did not seek a solution to bring his temper into check; rather, he sought clarity regarding the lovely and elusive Elizabeth Bennet. *Can I possibly be so lost to reason that I would consider marrying into such a family?*

He sat on the bench and pressed his back against the

tree trunk. *What would such connections do for Georgiana's prospects? How would a sister like Lydia Bennet influence her?* Darcy shuddered at the thought, but despite the multitude of arguments against the lady, he could not help but love her.

The crack of a twig alerted Darcy to the presence of another, and he leapt from his seat, his hand going to his hair to hide the evidence of his distress. He turned toward the path and barely concealed his surprise when he came face-to-face with the object of his thoughts.

"Mr. Darcy!"

Her lips were a perfect O of surprise, and he had a sudden wild desire to catch them in a kiss. "Miss Elizabeth," he said when he thought he had regained control of himself. "Forgive me; I had not thought to see anyone here."

Elizabeth smiled, and Darcy's restraint nearly deserted him yet again. "This walk has quickly become my favorite part of Kent. I walk here most days."

The word sounded innocent enough, but their hidden meaning took his breath away. *If you wish to see me,* they said, *this is where you may find me.*

As he always did when his emotions threatened to overwhelm him, Darcy fell back on formality. "I will leave you then to enjoy your walk, Miss Elizabeth." He bowed and turned back up the path before he did something he might later regret.

The encounter with Elizabeth convinced Darcy of one thing, however. *If Richard means to court Elizabeth Bennet, he will face competition.*

Darcy only wished there was a way to invite Elizabeth to Rosings. He knew he did not always show to his best advantage when he was out in public, but at his aunt's house he would be on familiar territory. He could not think of an excuse that would not rouse the curiosity of his relations, but Richard obligingly solved the problem for him that night at dinner.

"Aunt, I have enjoyed the company of Mrs. Collins and Miss Bennet greatly when I have called on them, and I wonder if we could not include them in our party Sunday evening."

"We have no need for further company, now that you and Darcy have come," she argued. "There is no need to fill up a table for quadrille, or gain extra conversation."

"All the same, I think it would be well-done of us to invite them. After all, you are his patron. You would not want him to think you took your duties lightly, would you?"

Richard's deft manner in handling Lady Catherine amazed Darcy, as always. The lady sighed and said, "Very well. We will ask them to come to dinner when we see them at church."

Darcy carefully concealed his satisfaction with this arrangement. That Richard had only asked so he could see Elizabeth did not matter to Darcy. Elizabeth would see them both.

Saturday dragged by and Sunday's sermon was even less inspired than he had expected of Mr. Collins. After the service, Darcy stood impatiently by while his aunt complimented the parson on his use of the Psalms in an Easter sermon.

"I knew it would be the right passage when I suggested it," she added, and Darcy frowned.

"Your ladyship does me a great service by this manner of advice," Mr. Collins said and bowed.

"Yes, it is so. I have always found, Mr. Collins, that a clergyman is only as wise as his patron. You would do well to keep this in mind."

"Of course, your ladyship."

"Now, we are going back to Rosings for an

afternoon respite, but if you and your party wish to join us tonight for coffee, you would be welcome."

Mr. Collins bowed once more, and Darcy wondered if his back ever grew tired of the motion. "You are too kind, Lady Catherine. We would be honored to visit you this evening."

Lady Catherine nodded. "Very well. We will see you then."

Darcy followed her to the carriage where Anne and Richard waited. "Are we to have company this evening?" Richard asked when they were all situated.

"Yes," Darcy answered. "Mr. Collins graciously accepted our aunt's invitation."

Nothing but the promise of an evening with Elizabeth could have made that Sunday afternoon bearable to Darcy. Lady Catherine was more cantankerous than usual, and Darcy was made to bear the brunt of her ill humor. Indeed, that did not change when their guests arrived. Mr. and Mrs. Collins sat with Elizabeth and Miss Lucas on one side of the room, while Lady Catherine kept her nephews beside the chair from which she presided over the gathering.

Elizabeth glanced their way more than once, and Darcy felt keenly all his aunt's rudeness in ignoring their invited guests. However, each time he tried to ask them a question, Lady Catherine directed another comment toward him and his attentions were drawn back toward Anne.

Less encumbered by his aunt's grasp, Richard rose from his seat a few minutes later and sat down next to Elizabeth. Darcy was torn between gratitude for his action and fierce jealousy of his ability to speak with Elizabeth. She smiled freely at his cousin, and Darcy gritted his teeth at the sight.

Though he tried to attend to his aunt, the quiet conversation between Richard and Elizabeth held most of his attention. Finally, Lady Catherine noticed this as well. "What is that you are saying, Fitzwilliam? What is it you are talking of? What are you telling Miss Bennet? Let me hear what it is."

Darcy blushed faintly at the rude manner with which she inserted herself into a conversation she was not party to, but he was secretly glad she had done so. His impatience equaled his aunt's. *At least I do not tap my fingers on the table while I await an answer.*

"Fitzwilliam! You will answer me!"

Richard finally turned toward them. "We are speaking of music, madam."

"Of music!" Lady Catherine leaned forward in her seat. "Then pray speak aloud. It is of all subjects my delight. I must have my share in the conversation, if you are speaking of music. There are few people in England, I suppose, who have more true enjoyment of music than myself, or a better natural taste. If I had ever learnt, I should have been a great proficient. And so would Anne, if her health allowed her to apply. I am confident that she would have performed delightfully. How does Georgiana get on, Darcy?"

Darcy had watched Elizabeth throughout his aunt's raptures, and the amusement he saw in her eyes increased his own embarrassment over his aunt's behavior. He glanced at Elizabeth again before he answered the question, a little hopeful that he might improve her opinion of his family. "She does very well, Aunt. I trust that were you able to hear her play, you would approve."

"I am very glad to hear such a good account of her, and pray tell her from me, that she cannot expect to excel if she does not practice a great deal."

Darcy stamped out the flare of irritation. Lady Catherine always gave her own advice; it was not a true commentary on what she believed of Georgiana. "I assure you, madam, that she does not need such advice. She practices very constantly."

Lady Catherine nodded sagely. "So much the better. It cannot be done too much; and when next I write to her, I shall charge her not to neglect it on any account. I often tell young ladies, that no excellence in music is to be acquired without constant practice. I have told Miss Bennet several times that she will never play really well unless she practices more, and though Mrs. Collins has no instrument, she is very welcome, as I have often told her, to come to Rosings every day and play on the pianoforte in Mrs. Jenkinson's room. She would be in nobody's way, you know, in that part of the house."

Now he did blush; his aunt had always been proud, but her rudeness became more and more pronounced as the years went by. The invitation to allow Elizabeth to practice on one of the many pianofortes available at Rosings would have been well done, if she had not indicated that she did not really want to extend it. The implication that she did so only because it was possible to place Elizabeth in a part of the house where she would not be inconvenienced was truly beyond the pale.

As usual, his aunt positioned Anne by his side when it was time for coffee. He smiled a little at his cousin and wondered if she knew what plans her mother had in store for her, and if she would go along with them if she did. He doubted very much that she would put up any resistance. Anne's entire life had been shaped by forces stronger than herself: first her mother, then her illness. *She does not know how to find her own mind.*

The whole time he drank his coffee, Darcy sought a way to draw the attention back to Miss Bennet and away from himself. Therefore it was with great pleasure that he heard Richard say, "Miss Bennet, you have promised to play for us."

Darcy watched with interest as she seated herself at the instrument, and with some degree of consternation when his cousin seated himself near her. *What game is Richard playing?* he wondered. *He knows as well as I that he needs to marry an heiress. What does he mean by singling her out in such a manner, when he cannot follow through on any expectations he might raise?*

What was more, his cousin's defection to Elizabeth's side left him yet again to entertain their aunt. "Pray tell me, Darcy, how does Mrs. Reynolds get on? Does she still keep so many servants at Pemberley?"

Darcy smiled a thin-lipped smile. "You must allow me the freedom to run my house as I choose, Aunt. Mrs. Reynolds has had the management of the household for many years; my mother trusted her implicitly. Surely you do not think Lady Anne's judgment was lacking?"

The reminder of her sister discomposed Lady Catherine for a bare moment, but it was enough time to allow Darcy to escape her side. Elizabeth's playing was unusually strong tonight, and he wondered if it was the company that brought out her latent talent, or whether she had indeed been practicing.

One look at her face drove all thoughts of her playing from his mind, for though she performed quite well, her beauty bewitched him. She played with her eyes half-closed, and her features mirrored the emotions of the music: first thoughtful, almost pensive, then questioning, and finally turning playful.

After a few minutes, she opened her eyes and said, "You mean to frighten me, Mr. Darcy, by coming in all this state to hear me? But I will not be alarmed, though your sister *does* play so well." She lifted her hands from the instrument and smiled at him. "There is a stubbornness about me that can never bear to be frightened at the will of others. My courage always rises with every attempt to intimidate me."

Her smile made Darcy go weak at the knees, and he placed a hand on the pianoforte to steady himself. "I shall not say that you are mistaken, because you could not really believe me to entertain any design of alarming you; and I have had the pleasure of your acquaintance long enough to know that you find great enjoyment in occasionally expressing opinions which in fact are not your own."

The pleasure of her laughter was immediately deflated when she turned to Richard and addressed her next remark to him. "Your cousin will give you a very pretty notion of me, and teach you not to believe a word I say. I am particularly unlucky in meeting with a person so well able to expose my real character, in a part of the world where I had hoped to pass myself off with some degree of credit." She looked at Darcy and raised an eyebrow. "Indeed, Mr. Darcy, it is very ungenerous in you to mention all that you knew to my disadvantage in Hertfordshire—and, give me leave to say, very impolitic too—for it is provoking me to retaliate, and such things may come out as will shock your relations to hear."

Though he welcomed her beauty, it was this wit he had missed most. "I am not afraid of you."

Were it not for Richard's presence, his joy in her teasing would have been complete. However, his cousin shot him a sly glance, and Darcy knew he was scheming. "Pray let me hear what you have to accuse him of. I should like to know how he behaves among strangers."

Indignation rose up in Darcy. *This method of gaining Elizabeth's attention is beneath you, Richard.*

Elizabeth, however, did not feel the undercurrents in the room, and she turned fully from the instrument, though she remained seated on the bench. "You shall hear then—but prepare yourself for something very dreadful. The first time of my ever seeing him in Hertfordshire, you must know, was at a ball—and at this ball, what do you think he did? He danced only four dances, though gentlemen were scarce; and, to my certain knowledge, more than one young lady was sitting down in want of a partner. Mr. Darcy, you cannot deny the fact."

An uneasy suspicion formed in the back of Darcy's mind. He well remembered that first ball, and he also remembered Bingley attempting to get him to dance with Elizabeth herself. He could not recall the exact phrasing of his refusal, but he knew it had been ungenerous. *Could she have overheard me?* He sought for a way to explain his unjust words, and finally said, "I had not at that time the honor of knowing any lady in the assembly beyond my own party."

Elizabeth shook her head slightly. "True; and nobody can ever be introduced in a ballroom. Well, Colonel Fitzwilliam, what do I play next? My fingers await your orders." She turned back to the pianoforte and rested her hands on the keys.

Darcy's heart sank. Her posture spoke clearly of her disinclination to forgive his offenses against her. *I must make her understand.*

He placed a hand on Richard's shoulder and shook his head. His cousin nodded his acquiescence, and Darcy drew a breath before giving the only explanation he could. "Perhaps I should have judged better, had I sought an introduction, but I am ill qualified to recommend myself to strangers."

The words were difficult to speak, and he could not tell from the set of Elizabeth's shoulders if she accepted his unspoken apology. She glanced back at Richard and said, "Shall we ask your cousin the reason of this? Shall we ask him why a man of sense and education, and who has lived in the world, is ill qualified to recommend himself to strangers?"

"I can answer your question without applying to him. It is because he will not give himself the trouble," Richard said, and Darcy had never felt more out of charity with his cousin.

True though this statement might be, it did not paint Darcy in the light he cared for Elizabeth to see him in. He clasped his hands behind his back and said, "I certainly have not the talent which some people possess of conversing easily with those I have never seen before. I cannot catch their tone of conversation, or appear interested in their concerns, as I often see done."

Elizabeth flexed her fingers slightly where they rested on the keys. "My fingers do not move over this instrument in the masterly manner which I see so many women's do. They have not the same force or rapidity, and do not produce the same expression. But then I have always supposed it to be my own fault— because I would not take the trouble of practicing. It is not that I do not believe *my* fingers as capable as any other woman's of superior execution."

Elizabeth looked at him through her lashes, a smile playing around the ends of her lips. Darcy's knees went weak again, this time with relief. Here then was a second chance, an opportunity to promise he would do better. "You are perfectly right. You have employed your time much better. No one admitted to the privilege of hearing you can think anything wanting. We neither of us perform to strangers."

Elizabeth accepted his apology with a smile and began playing with no direction from Richard. Darcy recognized the piece she had selected, but at first he could not place it. He listened to a few more bars and his eyes widened—it was a sonatina which had played on the night they met.

Lady Catherine voice broke into his fond recollections. "Miss Bennet would not play at all amiss if she practiced more and could have the advantage of a London master. She has a very good notion of fingering, though her taste is not equal to Anne's. Anne would have been a delightful performer, had her health permitted her to learn."

Darcy bit back his retort. He did not see anything lacking at all in Miss Elizabeth Bennet, save one thing: she was not yet Mrs. Fitzwilliam Darcy.

Chapter Nineteen

DARCY WANDERED THE park for much of the next morning, hoping to meet Elizabeth on another of her walks. The quiet country lanes gave him space to think, and he realized that he had very little time to settle matters with Elizabeth before he and Richard planned to leave Kent. Lady Catherine's manner was not inviting, and her nephews rarely stayed longer than two weeks. *Though I am sure Richard will not object to a longer visit,* he thought bitterly. *He is determined to woo Elizabeth.*

When he did not find Elizabeth in the park, his path was obvious, loathe though he was to spend any time in the company of Mr. Collins. He rapped on the door of the Parsonage and was quickly given entrance by the maid. With nary a word, he was escorted to a quiet sitting room where he was surprised to find Elizabeth sitting alone.

The chair she sat in was near a writing desk, and from the slight flush in her cheeks, he could easily tell she had been writing a letter she did not wish anyone else to see. *About me, perhaps?* he wondered, and immediately turned bright red himself.

"Miss Elizabeth! I did not expect... That is, I had expected to find all the ladies at home this morning."

"Mrs. Collins had business to attend to in the

village, and Maria accompanied her. Please, do sit down."

Elizabeth's courteous manner eased Darcy's nerves but a little. He took the chair she offered, though he wished he could remain standing. *You did not think to court a lady without ever being alone with her, did you, Darcy?* The mental reminder did nothing to calm him, and what little skill he had in the art of small talk evaporated.

Thankfully, Elizabeth was not likewise stricken dumb. "I hope this morning finds everyone at Rosings doing well."

Darcy swallowed. "Yes, very well thank you."

"Your aunt seemed in fine spirits last night."

Darcy's lips twisted into a wry smile. "Lady Catherine enjoys company above all things."

There was a brief pause, and Darcy knew she sought a new topic. "How very suddenly you all quitted Netherfield Park last November, Mr. Darcy! It must have been a most agreeable surprise to Mr. Bingley to see you all come after him so soon; for, if I recollect right, he went but the day before. He and his sisters were well, I hope, when you left London."

"Perfectly so—I thank you."

Darcy shook his head slightly. *You will never win over an intelligent lady like Elizabeth if you answer in single sentences.*

Elizabeth adjusted the folds of her gown and then looked up at him. "I think I have understood that Mr. Bingley has not much idea of ever returning to Netherfield?"

Darcy shifted, but the alarming creak his chair gave forced him to hold himself completely still. "I have never heard him say so; but it is probable that he may spend very little of his time there in the future. He has many friends, and he is at a time of life when friends and engagements are constantly interesting."

She frowned and shook her head, and he wondered what she found to disapprove of. "If he means to be but little at Netherfield, it would be better for the neighborhood that he should give up the place entirely, for then we might possibly get a settled family there." Here she paused and smiled a little self-consciously. "But perhaps Mr. Bingley did not take the house so much for the convenience of the neighborhood as for his own, and we must expect him to keep or quit it on the same principle."

This assurance at least Darcy could offer, and he hoped to regain her favor by it. "I should not be surprised if he were to give it up, as soon as any eligible purchase offers."

He waited to see if she had anything else to add, and when she did not continue, he knew the onus of conversation rested on his shoulders. *How does one go about asking a lady if she would be interested in accepting one's suit?* His usual direct manner of speech seemed woefully inadequate here.

He pondered all the subjects he could reasonably broach and finally settled on one that might lead them in the direction he wished to go. "This seems a very comfortable house. Lady Catherine, I believe, did a great deal to it when Mr. Collins first came to Hunsford."

She tried to hide a smile, but he caught it and was intrigued. "I believe she did—and I am sure she could not have bestowed her kindness on a more grateful object."

Ah, so she has as little patience with the man's ingratiating manner as I do. Darcy returned her smile. Then, by way of further directing the exchange toward the topic he wished to discuss, he said, "Mr. Collins seems very fortunate in his choice of a wife."

"Yes, indeed; his friends may well rejoice in his having met with one of the few sensible women who would have accepted him, or have made him happy if they had." Elizabeth's lovely eyes lit with amusement. "My friend has an excellent understanding—though I am not certain that I consider her marrying Mr. Collins as the wisest thing she ever did. She seems perfectly happy, however, and in a prudential light, it is certainly a good match for her."

A very good match for her, he observed, *but not one Elizabeth would have chosen for herself. Just what would you consider a good match, Elizabeth?*

That was far too bold a question for Darcy to ask, so he settled for commenting on the marriage. "It must be very agreeable to her to be settled within such an easy distance of her own family and friends."

Her eyes narrowed and she shook her head quickly. "An easy distance, do you call it? It is nearly fifty miles."

He frowned a little. If she considered fifty miles long distance, what would the miles between Hertfordshire and Derbyshire seem? "And what is fifty miles of good road? Little more than half a day's journey. Yes, I call it a *very* easy distance."

"I should never have considered the distance as one of the *advantages* of the match. I should never have said Mrs. Collins was settled *near* her family."

Her answer upset him a little, until he realized that in it, he had found a way to divulge his attentions. "It is proof of your own attachment to Hertfordshire. Anything beyond the very neighborhood of Longbourn, I will suppose, would appear far." He smiled, in hopes she would see the question his words held: *Would you be willing to leave your friends and neighbors for Derbyshire?*

She pursed her lips, and he held his breath as he

waited for her to understand his intent. The frown cleared a moment later, and her cheeks pinkened with a soft blush. That alone sent Darcy's heart racing, and her next words took his breath away.

"I do not mean to say that a woman may not be settled too near her family. The far and the near must be relative, and depend on many varying circumstances. Where there is fortune to make the expense of traveling unimportant, distance becomes no evil. But that is not the case *here*. Mr. and Mrs. Collins have a comfortable income, but not such a one as will allow of frequent journeys—and I am persuaded that my friend would not call herself *near* her family under less than *half* the present distance."

He drew closer to her; nothing could keep him away now. "*You* cannot have a right to such a very strong local attachment. *You* cannot always have been at Longbourn."

Until he saw the expression of surprise on her face, he did not realize how close he had gotten to her. Embarrassment overrode his desire to be as near her as possible, and he withdrew to the distance propriety demanded. He sought frantically for a topic that would ease the tension he could now feel, and finally settled on, "Are you pleased with Kent?"

It was a logical segue from the conversation on traveling, and he congratulated himself for that.

"Oh! Yes. I had never before been to the Downs. Is it always this lovely in spring?"

This at least was a comfortable topic for Darcy, and they managed a few minutes of light conversation before Mrs. Collins and Maria arrived home from the village. "Mr. Darcy!" Mrs. Collins said. "I did not expect you to call today, sir. I do apologize for being away."

"Pray, do not trouble yourself, ma'am. I had not planned it myself, but found myself in the neighborhood. Now, however, I must return to my aunt." He rose from his chair and bowed, and took his leave.

Chapter Twenty

*"**I DO NOT** mean to say a woman may not be settled too near her family..."*

The memory of Elizabeth's words added a spring to Darcy's step that not even tea with his aunt could remove. When she maneuvered him into the place beside Anne, he smiled and remembered how lovely Elizabeth had looked that morning; when she inquired about his plans to return to Pemberley, he imagined what it would be like to take Elizabeth there for the first time.

At that thought, his smile dimmed a little. He could not ask her to Pemberley without a formal engagement between them; he could not leave Kent yet.

"What is it, Darcy? What are you thinking of?"

"Would it trouble you, Aunt, if we stayed at Rosings a while longer? I know we came with the intention of staying only two weeks, but would you be very much annoyed if we stayed through till Saturday, rather than leaving on Monday as we had intended?"

On the other side of Lady Catherine, Richard froze, his teacup halfway to his lips. Darcy knew he would have much to answer for. *But once I make an offer for Elizabeth, all will become clear.*

Darcy focused his attention on his aunt, whose smile of feline delight raised a faint alarm. It was never a good thing when Lady Catherine looked so pleased with herself. "Of course you may stay, Darcy," she said. "Anne would not hear of you leaving when you wish to stay, would you, Anne?"

Darcy did not hear his cousin's dutiful agreement, so complete was his frustration. Richard smirked at him; both men knew he was caught. Convinced as she now was that he intended to finally pay his addresses to Anne, it would not be easy to escape Lady Catherine's clutches. *But I will manage somehow*, he promised himself.

They had no company that evening, and Darcy doubted the Hunsford party would be invited to join him again. Intent on forcing a proposal from Darcy before he left, Lady Catherine would not wish to divert any of his attention from Anne.

Darcy rose early the next morning, and instead of joining Richard for breakfast, he dressed and walked outside. The sun had just barely begun to burn off the predawn mist when he reached the grove's edge, and he pulled his coat closer against the morning chill. He rounded the bend that led to the copse, and his heart stopped. Elizabeth stood by the water, bathed in pale golden sunlight. In the distance he heard the call of a lark, and he knew he would always picture her like this, his herald of the morn.

He took another step toward her, and she turned around. "Mr. Darcy! I did not know you were such an early riser, sir."

They met on the path, and Darcy turned back with her in the direction of the house. "You will discover that early morning is the only time one is truly free when at Rosings." She had trusted him with her impressions of her cousin and his marriage; he could offer this veiled insight into his aunt.

"I see. Lady Catherine does like to arrange players

to her own wishes, does she not?"

Darcy looked over at her, a wide smile on his face. "Indeed she does. When next you are in Kent, your stay will give you ample opportunity to become intimately acquainted with her ladyship's ability to manipulate the lives of those around her."

Her cheeks tinged with a faint pink that he felt sure was not merely a reflection of the sunrise. Darcy mentally reviewed his words and realized he had as good as said he expected her to stay at Rosings when next he was in Kent. His own color rose to match hers, but he held her gaze. *Let her see my intent,* he thought. *It will not be long before I openly declare myself.*

They reached the open part of the park all too soon, and Darcy watched Elizabeth continue on down to the Parsonage. His presence there and absence from Rosings would raise questions on both ends which he did not wish to answer.

Richard met him in the main hall before the breakfast room. "I see you have been out already," he said, indicating Darcy damp boots. "What draws you from bed so early?"

Darcy waited to answer until they were seated with their coffee. "I wished for some time to myself. It seems these hours are the only ones Lady Catherine has not filled with endless activities of taking tea or calling on the local gentry."

Richard pointed at him with his knife. "You have only yourself to blame for that. Whatever gave you the idea of extending our stay?"

Darcy took a sip of coffee and considered his answer. Confident though he was of Elizabeth's acceptance, he did not wish to give his rival any more information than necessary. "I am considering some changes to the home farm at Pemberley and I wish to discuss them with Edgeley," he said, naming a prominent gentleman farmer in the neighborhood.

"And this will take an additional five days?" Richard pressed.

Darcy shrugged. "As we will by that time have stayed one day longer, what does it matter if we stay out the week complete?"

Richard laughed. "Oh, it makes no difference to me, Cousin—after all, I am not the one being courted with all the subtlety of a battle-ax."

Darcy grimaced. "I admit, I did not take that into consideration before I spoke. However, once I made the suggestion, she would not allow me to shorten our stay."

"Oh no; in fact, I believe she will entice you to stay till Sunday to have the banns read."

"Hold your tongue, Richard!" Darcy glanced over his shoulder, almost afraid he would see Lady Catherine standing there, triumphant smile in place. "If our aunt heard such things, you know it would be almost impossible to extricate myself."

Richard for once looked truly penitent. "I am sorry, William. I spoke without thinking. How do you plan to spend your day?"

"I believe I shall oblige our aunt today, so she will not fuss when I call on Edgeley tomorrow. And you?"

"Oh, I plan to call on the Parsonage this afternoon," Richard said casually. "As you know, I have scarcely met with a lady as uniformly charming as Miss Elizabeth."

Darcy gritted his teeth. "She is pretty, yes."

"Pretty?" Richard snorted. "Lord, William, have you lost your sight? She is entirely lovely and quite clever as well. When she gave you that set down regarding your behavior at the dance—'because I would not take the trouble of practicing'—I could scarcely keep my countenance."

The remembered rebuke stung more at its repetition than it had when she had first uttered it, but Darcy maintained control over his temper. "So you say," he replied blandly. "Well, if you will excuse me, Richard, I will need to change before attending to our aunt."

He left the room before Richard could respond, still vexed with his cousin's clear recollection of Elizabeth's words. It was not long, however, before the more recent memory of their morning meeting overcame his mortification, and he wore a smile when he answered Lady Catherine's summons to join her in the salon.

True to form, Lady Catherine continued, by means of various impertinent questions, to keep him with her for the whole of the afternoon. Darcy resolved to call on Edgeley the next day, and it was not until he recalled that Richard had visited the Parsonage that he felt any true consternation with the arrangement.

However, it was not only that day his aunt monopolized his time. By Thursday, Darcy wondered if he would have any time to himself before they left Kent. He had sat with her two afternoons and visited the members of the parish on the third, and he still had not spoken with Edgeley.

"And how was your afternoon, William?" Richard inquired a few evenings later. "I noticed you and our aunt had not finished your morning calls when I returned from Hunsford."

Darcy poured their after-dinner port and handed Richard his glass. "Yes, I fear her attentions are more assiduous than I had anticipated. I have barely been allowed to leave her side—or rather Anne's—since I suggested we might stay in Kent a few extra days."

Richard chuckled. "I told Edgeley you mean to call."

"Thank you, Richard. You see now why I believed that would require more than a day. With the exception of that first morning, I have not had a single moment to myself."

"You are far too agreeable, William."

Darcy knit his brows together—agreeable was one thing he had never been accused of. "I beg your pardon?"

Richard chuckled again at his baffled tone of voice. "You allow Aunt Catherine to control your life in a way you would not tolerate from anyone else. Do you not think my presence is required at these tea parties and afternoon calls?" He shrugged. "I simply tell her I have business of my own."

"Richard, you devil." Darcy stared at the rich plum-colored wine of his glass, then sighed. "But I am afraid that will not do for me. You forget that I am about to disoblige her in the worst possible way. It would be better for all involved, not the least..." He barely caught himself before naming Elizabeth. "...my future bride, if she is not already—"

"Most seriously displeased," the cousins chorused, a grin on their faces as they repeated their aunt's oft-used phrase.

"So you have a bride in mind then?" Richard questioned.

Darcy nearly choked on his port. "Why do you ask that?"

Richard bent his head to light his cigar, but Darcy thought he saw the familiar gleam of wicked humor. "You said you were about to disoblige our aunt. I assumed from that you had a woman in mind."

Darcy remembered suddenly that it was Richard's job to notice details others might overlook. "I am not yet engaged, if that is what you are asking," he said, after pausing for an instant too long.

"It was not," Richard replied cheerfully, "but we can leave it at that for tonight. Come, I am sure Aunt Catherine is requiring our presence."

Darcy followed him out of the room, filled with the sudden certainty that Richard knew a great deal more than he let on. That belief was solidified the next afternoon, when they called together at Hunsford Parsonage.

The ladies greeted them in the parlor, and a few minutes later the hurried steps in the hall announced the arrival of Mr. Collins. Darcy cast a sidelong glance at Elizabeth, who seemed as amused by the man's pompous behavior as he was. It was some minutes before the parson finally drew breath, and when he did, Richard stepped in to fill the gap.

Darcy leaned back in his chair, all his confidence suddenly gone. He could hold his own against his cousin in many things, but conversation was not one of them. However, as the call went on, Darcy suspected that Richard purposely chose topics he knew Darcy could not speak on.

"You will have to forgive my cousin," he told Mrs. Collins at one point. "He is not usually so inarticulate." Darcy protested, but Richard just laughed. "Did you not promise Miss Elizabeth you would practice, Cousin?" he gibed.

Darcy wished very much to speak with Elizabeth; the difficulty was, he could not say any of the things he wished to when they were in company. He looked over at her and suddenly he knew exactly what he could say to direct the teasing away from himself.

He sighed and glanced between Elizabeth and Richard. "You considered it ill-fortune to have met someone here who could expose all your faults— imagine my bad luck then to always have my cousin with me."

She and Richard both laughed, and it was only a few minutes later when the clock struck three o'clock, and he realized they had been there for nearly an hour.

Both gentlemen rose from their seats and made their farewells.

"You surprised me, William," Richard said when they reached the road. "I did not think you capable of laughing at yourself so easily."

Darcy glanced sideways at him. "Perhaps that is because when I am with you, I have no need to laugh at myself. You do quite a good enough job of it for both of us."

It was not truly a joke, but Richard laughed anyway and slapped him on the shoulder. "Well, better to laugh at yourself than to sit there with that stupid look on your face."

When they arrived back at Rosings, they found their aunt in an ill humor. Anne was feeling poorly, and Darcy had not been available to show his care of her, as he ought. He inquired of the physician who tended her and learned his cousin suffered a feverish headache. *Likely brought on by exerting herself for me*, he thought, with no very charitable feelings toward his aunt.

Darcy doted on his cousin—when they were younger, they had been quite close. But Anne had fallen ill when she was only eight and had never fully recovered. He would have liked to care for her as he did for Georgiana, but his aunt's ridiculous assumption regarding their future made that impossible. It was partly this sense of responsibility and remembered fondness that kept him from denouncing her plans, as Richard believed he ought.

On Saturday, Darcy and Richard sat with their cousin and took turns reading to her or simply keeping her company. It was not much, and Darcy chafed at his inability to do more.

The next day, their party was one short at church. Mr. Collins fawned over his aunt and pretended concern for Anne in a way that sickened Darcy.

However, before he could cut him down with one of his famous scathing remarks, Elizabeth met his gaze and said, "I do hope Miss Anne does not suffer long."

Her simple sincerity brought the first smile to his lips in a full twenty-four hours. "I will pass along your good wishes, Miss Elizabeth."

Of course, with Anne ill, they did not entertain that evening, and the company grew rather tiresome. Lady Catherine was more petulant than usual, and Richard escaped early with the ruse of a letter to write. She turned to Darcy after he left and said, "I suppose you are going to say you must write to Georgiana—well, I shall not keep you."

Darcy bowed over her hand and barely kept himself from running out of the room. A few minutes later he heard a quiet tap on his door and Richard walked in. "Managed to escape did you? Good, I am glad. You looked like you were about to lose that famous Darcy temper."

Darcy took a deep breath and shoved his hands into his hair. "I cannot stay with her tomorrow," he confessed. "Will you make my excuses? Tell her I have to visit Edgeley—I still have not spoken with him, and tomorrow is as good a day as any."

Richard nodded. "I will. I know your habit of saying things you later regret when pushed too far, so I think it is best you have a day to cool off. And perhaps Anne will be feeling better on the morrow. I am sure Lady Catherine would not be half so ill-humored if she were downstairs."

"Let us hope," Darcy murmured, and a moment later Richard left.

Darcy still felt out of sorts when he rose the next morning. He had swallowed a dozen sharp remarks the night before, and the taste of them was bitter on his tongue.

He pulled his dressing gown on and crossed the room to the window. The world was still dark, though he thought the eastern sky was a shade lighter than the deep azure in the west. He opened the latch and took a deep breath of fresh air, and suddenly he knew what he needed to regain his peace of mind.

Darcy was outside ten minutes later. He tilted his head back to welcome the mist; today's weather was not as fine as it had been on that other morning. However, he had no doubt that Elizabeth would come.

Today he reached the grove first. It was not yet dawn, and he sat down on the bench to watch the sunrise over the edge of the trees. When the grass shimmered with a silvery light, he stood and walked in the direction of the parsonage. It would not be long now, he felt sure.

He heard Elizabeth before he saw her, humming a light, pleasing melody. She did not seem surprised to see him, a fact which gratified him greatly. "Good morning, Mr. Darcy. I see we meet again."

"Indeed, Miss Elizabeth—it seems we are both in the habit of a morning walk." Darcy could easily imagine mornings spent walking through Pemberley with her, and he said the first thing that came to him. "For my part, however, they need not always be solitary walks." He fell in step beside her as she approached the brook.

She did not speak for a long moment, and Darcy knew she was parsing his last statement. A quick glance at her confirmed the blush he anticipated, and he knew he could say no more on the subject without a formal declaration.

He opened his mouth, intending to speak the words he had prepared—"My dear Miss Elizabeth, would you do me the honor…"

Instead, a voice he hardly recognized as his own said, "How did you leave Mr. and Mrs. Collins this morning?"

Her brow wrinkled, and he cringed at his own feeble conversation device. "I think I understand from my aunt," he said hastily, "that Mr. Collins is also a lover of the dawn."

Elizabeth smiled. "Oh yes, he rises early so he may have his sermonizing done before Lady Catherine might have other need of him."

Darcy smiled, but then a strange thought struck him. "And your friend? She does not mind having her life dictated by one so wholly unconnected with herself?"

Elizabeth frowned pensively. "I think," she said at last, "that Mrs. Collins is grateful enough for her own household that she would put up with anything."

"Surely that is not a recipe for marital felicity."

She shook her head. "I would not think so— certainly it would not be for myself—but then, as I have been reminded, our situations are not the same."

Elizabeth glanced up at him, and he forgot to breathe. If he had nearly declared himself earlier, then now so had she.

He could not think of anything to say after that, and they walked together in silence for some moments until they reached the point where the path veered toward the road. "And here is where we must part, I fear, Mr. Darcy." Elizabeth smiled up at him and then skipped along the path without giving him a chance to reply.

Darcy's visit with Edgeley took the whole of the afternoon, and he barely had time to change for dinner before the meal was announced. Anne was present, though still a little more pale and wan than usual, and Darcy appeased his aunt by offering her every possible solicitude. He knew the time grew near when he would tell her he would not marry his cousin, and he wanted her in the best possible mood when he presented Elizabeth to her. *Though Elizabeth is more than capable of holding her own,* he thought with a smile.

To his surprise, Darcy slept late the next day. When he arrived in the breakfast room, the footman informed him that Richard had already eaten and left for his round of the property. His first feeling of guilt that Richard had been left to handle their joint duty alone was squashed by the sudden conviction that he would take advantage of Darcy's absence to call at the Parsonage.

Much to his surprise, when his aunt came downstairs she announced her intention of doing likewise. "I have not called on Mrs. Collins since you arrived at Rosings, Darcy. You will join me this afternoon at the Parsonage."

For once, her dictatorial style did not bother Darcy in the slightest. The ladies of Hunsford received them most cordially when they arrived, and if Elizabeth seemed more quiet than usual, Darcy attributed it to her understanding that no more could be said between them until he paid his formal addresses.

It was the most comfortable afternoon he had ever spent in his aunt's company. In Elizabeth's presence, he was able to drown out Lady Catherine's gross improprieties and simply enjoy the rest of the company. When the visit ended, he could truthfully say to Mrs. Collins, "I enjoyed my time with you this afternoon, ma'am."

All of Darcy's good will disappeared the next morning, when Richard was again absent at breakfast. He set his coffee cup down with rather more force than necessary, then took a deep breath. *Remember all Elizabeth has said,* he reminded himself. *She welcomes your suit; do not fret.*

Still, by the time Richard returned in mid-afternoon,

he was tense, and he knew it was time to speak to his cousin openly regarding his intentions toward Elizabeth. "Would you mind joining me for a ride, Richard?" he said without preamble.

Richard blinked. "Of course, William. Just let me change. Shall I meet you in the stables in fifteen minutes?"

"I will have a groom saddle two horses."

Twenty minutes later, they were cantering across the fields to the far reaches of the estate. Neither man said a word until they reached the hedgerow that marked the boundary there.

When they slowed their horses and turned back, Richard shifted in the saddle to look at Darcy. "Do you know Miss Elizabeth does not like riding? I can hardly imagine it, can you?"

Darcy nearly growled at the thought of Richard knowing any personal details regarding Elizabeth. "What are your intentions toward Miss Elizabeth?" he asked abruptly.

Richard smiled. "She is a lovely lady—beautiful, charming, and sweet. I like her a great deal."

Darcy twitched reflexively and then had to adjust his seat in the saddle when his confused horse sidestepped. "I see."

Richard glanced over at him. "Of course, I might like her even more if my cousin was not in love with her."

Only years of training kept Darcy from letting go of the reins entirely. His jaw dropped, and Richard laughed heartily. "Did you think I would not see?" he asked. "One minute you told me I would regret being friendly to Mr. Collins—a point I must allow—and the next you practically invited yourself to his home."

"You... knew? All along?"

"From the moment I saw Miss Elizabeth and observed how suddenly tongue-tied you were. Even you, William, are normally more conversant than you are when Miss Elizabeth is in the room. But I looked at you when we left the Parsonage that afternoon and knew I would never get you to tell me the truth."

"Then why…"

"I thought if I gave the appearance of courting Elizabeth, you might finally make a move." The Colonel grinned. "It seems I was correct."

Darcy groaned when he saw how neatly he had been played. "All that time, all those suggestions that I tell Lady Catherine I would not marry Anne…" His eyes narrowed as something occurred to him. "You have been most assiduous in your attentions, Richard." His voice was dangerously soft. "In fact, one might say you had been trifling with her affections."

Richard tilted his head. "I cannot say I have ever received real encouragement," he answered at last. "However, if it will assuage your concerns, I will find a way tomorrow of letting her know I am not seriously courting her."

Darcy nodded. "Yes, I would advise you did, Cousin," he said, and then rode off before Richard could reply.

Chapter Twenty-one

IN THE MORNING, Richard renewed his promise to make his own situation clear to Elizabeth. Darcy kept to the study until he returned, sometimes reading a book, sometimes pacing the floor while he rehearsed his proposal.

"My dearest Elizabeth, you must allow... No, that is too bold, Darcy—entreat, do not demand. Loveliest Elizabeth, pray make me the happiest of men..." He snorted. "Hackneyed!"

"Not to mention, if our aunt heard those words you would not live to utter them to their intended recipient."

Darcy spun on his heel and found Richard leaning against the closed door. "How long have you been there?"

"Long enough to pray Miss Elizabeth is as patient as she is lovely," Richard returned. "Good lord, William—she will never be able to answer if you do not finish the question."

Darcy crossed his arms. "I am trying to find the right words. But speaking of her answer, did you deliver your message?"

Darcy could not interpret the slow smile that spread across his cousin's face. "Oh, yes."

"And?"

"And..." Richard stretched the word out so long that Darcy wanted to strangle him. "And, I do not think you need to worry about her answer."

"Why —" Darcy coughed to remove the frog from his throat – "why do you say that?"

Richard examined his fingernails. "Simply something she said."

"Which was?"

He tapped his chin. "How did she phrase it? I believe her words were, 'I wonder he does not marry.'" The colonel dropped all pretense of disinterest and strode across the room to slap Darcy on the back. "Congratulations, Cousin. Had I a fortune of my own, I might give you some competition, but as it stands, I am sure you will both be very happy."

Richard was gone before Darcy recovered his speech. He stared at the closed door for several long moments, Richard's—no, Elizabeth's words— resonating in his mind. "So, she wonders that I have not married," he said at last. "Well, Elizabeth, after tonight you will wonder no more. Before this evening is out, you will know the whole of my heart."

Darcy still had not worked out exactly how he would manage that when teatime arrived. He knew, however, that he must, for he and Richard were to leave Kent on Saturday. If he did not declare himself tonight, there would hardly be time to make the engagement known to their friends in the neighborhood. He was particularly determined to inform his aunt, if only to stop his cousin's taunts.

He had a half-formed idea of offering to escort Elizabeth into the house when she and the Collinses arrived and then stealing her away to someplace private where he might propose. With this in mind, he met the Hunsford party on the lane and noticed immediately that Elizabeth was not among them.

"Good evening," he said. "But where is Miss Elizabeth?"

Mrs. Collins's brows rose, and he wondered if he had been too obvious in his attentions. "My friend did not choose to come," she replied. "She stayed at home with a headache."

"Will you not do us the honor of walking into the house with us, Mr. Darcy?" Mr. Collins asked.

"No, thank you," Darcy said, his mind racing. *Elizabeth is home alone.* "I am afraid I was just on my way into the village on some business. Please make my excuses to my aunt—I did not have time to inform her."

Mr. Collins bowed low, but before he could speak, Darcy strode down the lane. Elizabeth was alone. That situation he had not known how to bring about, she had wrought with ease.

He remembered the concern on Mrs. Collins's face and his steps slowed for a moment. Would she be too ill to receive him? He shook the thought off and continued to the Parsonage with all haste. Unless she was in her bed, he would find a way to speak. "I will not leave Kent without asking her to be my wife."

He reached his destination in good time, and a servant ushered him into the little sitting room where he had first asked on Easter Monday if she would consider his suit. She sat in the same seat tonight which she had occupied then, and the memory agitated his emotions further.

Elizabeth stared up at him, and Darcy realized he had yet to speak. "I beg your pardon," he said. "I heard you were ill and came to see for myself if you were feeling any better."

Darcy barely heard her reply in the affirmative. He sat down in the chair opposite Elizabeth's for only a few seconds before he stood back up and paced the confines of the small room, turning his hat over in his hands.

None of the speeches he had prepared would come, but he would not remain tongue-tied tonight as he had done on that previous morning. He gathered his courage and reminded himself of what she had told Richard only hours ago, and then he turned to face her.

"In vain have I struggled. It will not do. My feelings will not be repressed. You must allow me to tell you how ardently I admire and love you."

Elizabeth gasped and pressed a hand to her chest. Such a display banished what little doubt lingered in Darcy's mind, and his nervous pacing ceased.

"After many months of loving you, I find that nothing will do except to ask for your hand in marriage." He flushed slightly, aware that she might well wonder why, if he loved her so deeply, he had not declared himself before.

He looked down at his hat, then up at her. "I am aware, of course, that in so doing, I go against every wish of my family—even against my own better judgment. The lowness of your connections has long prevented me from truly seeking you as the mistress for Pemberley, but my own heart would not be dissuaded.

"Those who know me best will be surprised by the imprudence of my choice, but I am sure they will understand when they have met you."

He placed a hand on the mantelpiece and drew himself up straight. "And now, my dear Miss Elizabeth, will you not end my suffering and promise to be my wife?"

Here he stopped to finally take a breath. He looked over at her and found her gazing at him with some consideration in her expression. She blushed, and he felt the queer stirrings of unfettered joy deep in his heart.

"In cases such as this, it is, I believe, the established

mode to express a sense of obligation for the sentiments avowed, however unequally they may be returned. It is natural that obligation should be felt, and if I could *feel* gratitude, I would now thank you." She pursed her lips. "But I cannot—I have never desired your good opinion, and you have certainly bestowed it most unwillingly."

Darcy could not breathe for a moment, and he gripped the mantel to avoid toppling over. As if she had ascertained his distress, her voice softened. "I am sorry to have occasioned pain to anyone. It has been most unconsciously done, however, and I hope will be of short duration. The feelings which, you tell me, have long prevented the acknowledgement of your regard, can have little difficulty in overcoming it after this explanation."

Her meaning was clear, and yet he could not understand it—he had believed he had her favor far too long to accept this change in the situation graciously. The pain in his chest spread upward, and he had to swallow a lump in his throat before he could speak. "And this is all the reply which I am to have the honor of expecting! I might, perhaps, wish to be informed why, with so little *endeavor* at civility, I am thus rejected. But it is of small importance."

Elizabeth's eyes sparked with indignation, and despite himself, he could not help but admire their brilliancy. "I might as well inquire why, with so evident a design of offending and insulting me, you chose to tell me that you liked me against your will, against your reason, and even against your character? Was not this some excuse for incivility, if I *was* uncivil? But I have other provocations. You know I have. Had not my own feelings decided against you, had they been indifferent, or had they even been favorable, do you think that any consideration would tempt me to accept the man who has been the means of ruining, perhaps forever, the happiness of a much beloved sister?"

The blood which had drained from his face at her refusal rushed back. *So that is why she constantly mentioned Bingley.* The unexpected intelligence stole his power of speech, and she continued before he could form an answer.

"I have every reason in the world to think ill of you. No motive can excuse the unjust and ungenerous part you acted *there*." She rose from her chair and paced the room, before turning back to him. "You dare not, you cannot deny that you have been the principal, if not the only means of dividing them from each other, of exposing the one to the censure of the world for caprice and instability, the other to its derision for disappointed hopes, and involving them both in misery of the acutest kind."

Darcy barely withheld a snort. *Misery of the acutest kind? Is that not overstating things, Elizabeth? Bingley and your sister will learn to love others as soon as those around stop reminding them of their foolish infatuation.*

Apparently, she had expected an answer to her question, for after a moment's pause, she said, "Can you deny that you have done it?"

Her claims regarding Bingley and her sister restored Darcy to some of his equanimity. He rested one shoulder against the mantle and shrugged. "I have no wish of denying that I did everything in my power to separate my friend from your sister, or that I rejoice in my success. Towards *him* I have been kinder than towards myself." He could not withhold his bitterness. *Would that I had taken my own advice.*

Elizabeth took a deep breath, and Darcy braced himself for whatever might come next. "But it is not merely this affair on which my dislike is founded. Long before it had taken place, my opinion of you was decided. Your character was unfolded in the recital which I received many months ago from Mr. Wickham." Darcy dropped his hat in shock, and she looked at him with all the triumph of a vengeful Boadicea. "On this subject, what can you have to say? In what imaginary act of friendship can you here defend yourself? Or under what misrepresentation can you here impose upon others?"

Wickham! Darcy bent to pick up his hat and took the second to rein in his growing temper. "You take an eager interest in that gentleman's concerns," he bit out when he had straightened up.

Elizabeth, so bold, did not shy away from his anger. "Who that knows what his misfortunes have been can help feeling an interest in him?"

This was more than Darcy could bear. "His misfortunes!" he repeated sarcastically, wondering what story exactly Wickham had spun to Elizabeth. "Yes, his misfortunes have been great indeed."

"And of your infliction!" she cried out, and he finally saw in her expression the full weight of censure he had somehow missed before. "You have reduced him to poverty, comparative poverty. You have withheld the advantages which you must know to have been designed for him. You have deprived the best years of his life of that independence which was no less his due than his dessert. You have done all this! And yet you can treat the mention of his misfortunes with contempt and ridicule."

With his emotional lassitude broken, her words brought a wave of indignation and hurt; indignation that she could believe such things about him, and hurt that she did not first allow him to explain what had happened before accusing him. "And this is your opinion of me! This is the estimation in which you hold me! I thank you for explaining it so fully. My faults, according to this calculation, are heavy indeed!"

His temper carried him forward. "But perhaps these offenses might have been overlooked had not your pride been hurt by my honest confession of the scruples which had long prevented my forming any serious design. These bitter accusations might have been suppressed, had I with greater policy concealed my struggles and flattered you into the belief of my being impelled by unqualified, unalloyed inclination—by reason, by reflection, by everything."

He leveled a glare at her. "But disguise of every sort is my abhorrence. Nor am I ashamed of the feelings I related. They were natural and just. Could you expect me to rejoice in the inferiority of your connections? To congratulate myself on the hope of relations whose condition in life is so decidedly below my own?"

All traces of emotion vanished from her face. "You are mistaken, Mr. Darcy," she said in a voice so calm that Darcy felt a tremor of dread, "if you suppose that the mode of your declaration affected me in any other way, than as it spared me the concern which I might have felt in refusing you, had you behaved in a more gentlemanlike manner." Those words shocked him out of his anger, but she did not stop there. "You could not have made me the offer of your hand in any possible way that would have tempted me to accept it."

For an instant, Darcy feared his heart had stopped. He grabbed the mantle again to keep from falling, and listened with a dull pain in his chest as she continued to enumerate his flaws. "From the very beginning, from the first moment I may almost say, of my acquaintance with you, your manners impressing me with the fullest belief of your arrogance, your conceit, and your selfish disdain of the feelings of others, were such as to form the ground-work of disapprobation, on which succeeding events have built so immoveable a dislike;

and I had not known you a month before I felt that you were the last man in the world whom I could ever be prevailed on to marry."

Mortification mingled with the sharp pain of rejection. "You have said quite enough, madam. I perfectly comprehend your feelings, and have now only to be ashamed of what my own have been. Forgive me for having taken up so much of your time, and accept my best wishes for your health and happiness."

Chapter Twenty-two

ONCE DARCY WAS free of Hunsford Parsonage, his mortification, felt so keenly only moments earlier, simmered into resentment. *"I had not known you a month..."*

"And she criticized me for forming my opinions too early!" The anger welled up, red-hot, and he stopped on the road until it had passed. He kicked the grass when he started walking again, and a startled grouse flew from a bush nearby.

When Darcy reached the gate to Rosings Park and saw the windows ablaze with light, he realized how unequal he was to be in company. Lady Catherine would inquire impertinently about his absence, and he could not bear to face Richard's knowing smile.

Without missing a step, he turned toward the side of the house. Here, hidden behind the trailing ivy, was a door only a few knew about. From the entrance by the garden, it led to a staircase which opened out on the second floor in a linen closet. He and Richard had discovered it as boys and had delighted in the freedom it gave them from their aunt's strident voice and constant criticism.

Darcy had not used the secret entrance in many years, and it took him a few moments to find the exact location. Eventually he was successful, and he slipped into the house and up the rickety staircase. Now safe from detection, he closed the door and crept down the hall to his own room.

When the door shut behind him, he suddenly found himself at a loss. *What am I to do now?* The night was young—he doubted dinner was even over.

Slowly, almost mechanically, Darcy removed his jacket and cravat, but he still felt constricted. He slipped his fingers through the buttons of his waistcoat and allowed the garment to slide down his arms till he could catch it and place it over a chair. His fine linen shirt choked him, and he undid the tie at his throat. Finally comfortable, he crossed the room to the window.

His room overlooked the lane, and in the gathering twilight he could just make out the carriage leaving the estate, presumably returning the Collinses to their home. *What will Elizabeth tell her friend regarding tonight?* he wondered. He cringed at the thought of being an object of gossip, or worse, pity, at the Parsonage, and firmly resolved to leave on Saturday as planned, in order to avoid meeting any of them again.

The admission of one thought of Elizabeth triggered a flood, and soon the memory of her every word overwhelmed him. He had been so sure of her acceptance. Her entire demeanor over the last two weeks seemed to welcome him. Now aware of her true feelings toward him, however, he saw her actions toward him in a very different light.

Darcy groaned and poured a brandy, which he drank quickly. He poured a second and set the glass down on the small table by the window before he sank into the chair beside it.

"I have every reason in the world to think ill of you..."

Where did I go wrong? Darcy shoved his hands through his hair and pulled, as if the pain would ease the ache in his heart.

How long Darcy sat like that, he did not know. It was full dark when he finally looked up, and he realized he had not lit a candle when he entered the room. He felt over to the bureau and found a candle and matches by the silvery light of the moon. He struck the match and watched, mesmerized, as the flames burned through the wood toward his fingers. He blew it out just in time and struck another. This time he remembered his purpose, and a moment later, he carried the candle back to his seat.

Despite his best intentions, his mind continually strayed to Elizabeth's words and manner when she refused his suit. *"Had you behaved in a more gentlemanlike manner..."*

With a sudden shock, Darcy realized she had compared him unfavorably to George Wickham. *Wickham, a gentleman?* He snorted. *That, above all things, is ridiculous. When I think of what he would have done to Georgiana if I had not arrived in time...*

The possible implication of Elizabeth's approbation of Wickham struck Darcy, and he nearly dropped the candle. "Is that knave to insinuate himself with all the women I love?" The word hung in the air for a moment, paining him further, but he pushed the emotion aside.

"At least I can warn Elizabeth of his true nature," he finally decided. Darcy sat down at his desk and took out a piece of paper and his pen and ink. He considered for a moment, with the tip poised above the blank white paper, that she might wonder at first if he sought a different answer to his earlier question, and thus he began:

Be not alarmed, Madam, on receiving this letter, by the apprehension of its containing any repetition of those sentiments, or renewal of those offers, which were last night so disgusting to you. I write without any intention of paining you, or humbling myself, by dwelling on wishes, which for the happiness of both, cannot be too soon forgotten; and the effort which the formation and the perusal of this letter must occasion should have been spared, had not my character required it to be written and read. You must, therefore, pardon the freedom with which I demand your attention; your feelings, I know will bestow it unwillingly, but I demand it of your justice.

Two offences of a very different nature...

His rebuttal of her accusations regarding her sister and Bingley came easily. On one point only did Darcy stop to consider: he had thought that Miss Bennet felt only a passing interest for his friend; clearly, from what her sister had said this evening, that was not true. It was possible that he could be right and her sister wrong, but that seemed unlikely. If he had been wrong on this count, he would apologize, but he had seen no evidence to the contrary, and even Bingley had been convinced when Darcy had expressed his doubts to him; thus, he felt justified in what his beliefs had been, despite the fact that they were now proven inaccurate.

Darcy did not scruple to conceal his true objections to the marriage. He had seen Elizabeth's mortification in the face of her family's improprieties often enough that he trusted her understanding. In his mind's eye he saw her humiliation in reading these words, and affection for her crept back into his breast for the first time since her refusal.

Pardon me. – It pains me to offend you. But amidst your concern for the defects of your nearest relations, and your displeasure at this representation of them, let it give you consolation to consider that to have conducted yourselves so as to avoid any share of the like censure is praise no less

generally bestowed on you and your eldest sister, than it is
honorable to the sense and disposition of both...

With a few quick strokes of the pen, Darcy laid out
the whole of his part in the affair, much of which he
surmised from her words she had already ascertained.
That he had separated them he acknowledged with no
more sense of shame than he had borne this evening
when she had questioned him in the matter. That he
had contrived to keep her sister's presence in town a
secret from Bingley he now admitted, with the
confession that this perhaps was beneath him.

Darcy stopped here to blot the ink from his pen.
"Perhaps?" he muttered. "That is the worst kind of
hypocrisy—to claim in one moment that I abhor
disguise of any kind, and then to claim in the next that
falsehood has a place, if it is done with kind
intentions."

It was the first time in many years Darcy had seen
his own actions in this light. Though still unashamed
of his actions, this inkling of humility softened his
words as he turned his attentions to the matter of
George Wickham.

Darcy set his pen down and pinched the bridge of
his nose. A dull ache grew behind his eyes, and he
wished for nothing more than to lie down on his bed
and sleep away the twenty-four hours or more until
they were to leave Rosings, but he could not. He must
explain the truth of Wickham's nature to Elizabeth.

"But what can I say here that she will believe?"
Darcy sipped his brandy. "Wickham is above all things
a masterful storyteller; how many times did he escape
punishment when we were boys?" Clearly Elizabeth
had been drawn in by his tales and would scorn any
attempt on Darcy's part to cast aspersions on his
character.

Though every inch of family duty within him protested, Darcy knew the only way she might believe him was if he explained the depths of Wickham's depravity. He had heard a hint of partiality in her voice when she spoke of Wickham; indeed, he had called her on it and she had not denied it. If, by telling her of Wickham's dealings with Georgiana, he could prevent something similar from happening to her, he knew his sister would forgive him for breaking her confidence.

With respect to that other, more weighty accusation, of having injured Mr. Wickham, I can only refute it by laying before you the whole of his connection with my family.

Darcy took great care not to hide any of the details from her, knowing that if he seemed to prevaricate, it would only lend truth to Wickham's lies. He did not even conceal his own father's preference for his godson, though that pained him. It was a truth Wickham loved to brag on; he was sure Elizabeth had heard of it. He allowed the full truth of his father's care, up to and including the desire that a living should be provided for Wickham, should he indicate a wish to take orders.

Though he could not be sure, he suspected this was the first place where his rendering of the events differed from his rival's. From Elizabeth's words, he gathered that he had been accused of withholding that living from him, in fact of going against his own father's will for no reason beyond petty jealousy. He now explained the truth to her—a truth for which he had no one to corroborate, but which he could easily prove with access to his own bankbook from which the draft had been written.

When he reached the deepest point of Wickham's perfidy, the words came more slowly. Telling the story brought back all the emotions he had felt at the time, from anger and fear to guilt that he was unable to protect his sister against profligates such as Wickham. It was his responsibility as her elder brother to keep her safe, and he had failed—or near enough that he considered it a failure.

But last summer he was again most painfully obtruded on my notice. I must now mention a circumstance which I would wish to forget myself, and which no obligation less than the present should induce me to unfold to any human being. Having said thus much, I feel no doubt of your secrecy.

Darcy stared at the words and dipped his pen back in the ink to continue on. When he would have shied away from painful details, the thought of Wickham worming his way into Elizabeth's affections forced him to dig deeper, to reveal truths he had not considered himself.

He did owe the truth of the affair to Georgiana. She had shown more wisdom than he gave her credit for. And if her affectionate heart had led her to trust a man not worthy of her notice, was that not preferable to Miss Bingley's slyness? The pen drew the bitterness from his heart, and when he reached the end of the letter, he could even feel charity toward Elizabeth.

He closed by suggesting she verify the letter's contents with Richard, much as he deplored the thought that his words might not be believed.

...And that there may be some possibility of consulting him, I shall endeavor to find some opportunity of putting this letter in your hands in the course of the morning. I will only add, God bless you.

Fitzwilliam Darcy

Chapter Twenty-three

DARCY SET THE pen down on the table and examined the letter. He had kept his handwriting small, but still it took two sheets of paper. *Perhaps I should read over it to make sure of my phrasing.* He shook his head and folded the two sheets together and placed it inside an envelope. He probably should, but he would not. The sooner this letter was in Elizabeth's hand, the better.

A knock at his door startled him and he nearly fell over in his chair. "Who is it?"

The door opened to admit Richard. "I came to see how you fared..." His jaw dropped when he took in Darcy's ragged appearance. "Good Lord, William, what happened? When you did not come down for tea, I assumed you had gone to propose... and when you did not return for dinner, I believed you had found a more pleasant way to occupy your time."

Darcy flinched. "Your first assumption was correct."

Richard frowned. "You do not mean to say she refused you?"

Darcy glanced down at the envelope in his hand. "As it happens, Richard, not only did she refuse me, she did so in terms so strong that I felt I must be allowed to answer for myself."

Richard crossed his arms and leaned against the doorframe. "Should you not do the lady the honor of accepting her answer, however distasteful it is to you?"

"Not when that answer contains a defense of George Wickham."

Richard drew himself up, an immediate scowl on his face and a curse on his tongue. "What can she know of that blackguard?"

"A great deal, in fact. I did not tell you that he was a member of the local militia when we were lately in Hertfordshire." Darcy shrugged. "I must own that his presence in the country certainly contributed much to my own desire to quit it."

"Understandably."

"Indeed. With his usual inimitable charm, Wickham managed to ingratiate himself to Elizabeth, and last night she accused me of a great many things in regard to him." Here Darcy held up the letter. "I could not allow her to believe him a gentleman, so I wrote a letter explaining the whole truth of my connection with the man."

Richard narrowed his eyes. "The whole truth?"

Darcy rubbed his forehead where the headache lingered. "Yes. I have also named you as a witness whom she may question. Will you make yourself available for any quizzing she might give?"

"Of course. I cannot be content to let any lady think well of George Wickham."

"Quite so. I will return after I find her and we will repair to the Parsonage then."

Richard held up his hand. "I admire your eagerness, William, but may I suggest you call Vincent and allow him to dress you in fresh clothes before you walk out? I am not sure your current state of disarray would recommend you to the lady."

Darcy looked down at his rumpled shirt and grimaced. "Indeed. But may I count on you to put off Lady Catherine and then call on the Parsonage with me when I return?"

"Certainly."

Darcy rang for Vincent after Richard left, and it was a mark on the valet's discretion that he did not so much as raise an eyebrow when he was admitted to the room. He went to work with all his usual efficiency, and in less than half an hour, Darcy was presentable.

He exited the house the same way he had entered the night before. Force of habit sent him in the direction of the grove where he had often met Elizabeth, but he was not halfway there when a new painful thought overcame him. He had thought, when Elizabeth told him she loved to walk in the grove, that she was inviting him to join her there. However, her total disapprobation of him made that unlikely.

Mortification swept over Darcy. *Had I realized her words were a warning, rather than an invitation, I would not have plagued her with my presence.*

His headache returned, and Darcy pinched the bridge of his nose once more. He took a deep shuddering breath; the thought that Elizabeth disliked his company enough to warn him away hurt almost more than anything else. *"Had you behaved in a more gentlemanlike manner..."* The words rang in his ears and he winced. Yes, *almost* anything else.

With that thought in mind, he gave up on the grove. She would not go to a place where they had met so frequently. Instead, he walked on the edge of the park which fronted the road, in hopes he might catch sight of her.

He had almost given up hope that she should happen upon him when he spied her walking the lane that bordered the park. Her back was turned toward him, and it struck him that she had seen him first and was walking away to avoid conversation with him.

"Miss Elizabeth," he called out in a loud voice, for

once heedless of propriety. *I shall make it impossible for her to leave without being rude.*

She halted in her steps and paused for a moment, then turned back slowly. There was not even an attempt at a smile on her face; rather, her eyebrows were drawn together in an expression that spoke of both her reluctance to answer his summons and her annoyance at being caught.

Darcy swallowed his resentment and held out the letter, which Elizabeth took without question. That, at least, was gratifying. "I have been walking in the grove some time in the hope of meeting you. Will you do me the honor of reading that letter?" Without waiting for an answer he bowed and walked back toward the house.

Richard was in the breakfast room when he returned. "I began to wonder how long it took to deliver a letter."

Darcy rubbed the back of his neck. His headache had spread and he longed for food and rest, but their task was not complete. "The delivery took but a moment; chancing upon Elizabeth in the park took rather longer."

If Richard heard any possibility that she had been avoiding him, he very tactfully did not comment on it. "Shall we call on the Parsonage? If you wish me to be available to her questions, we should go."

Darcy poured a cup of coffee and stared into the rich brown liquid. "I do not believe I will stay long. After the events of the last day, I fear I have not patience to deal with Mr. Collins."

They were welcomed most cordially to the Parsonage, but Darcy was unaware of anything but Elizabeth's absence. *If she has not returned, then perhaps she is reading my letter.*

However, it did not take long for the clergyman's

obsequious manner to pierce his consciousness, and what little forbearance Darcy still had vanished. "I am sorry," he said abruptly, "but I have business with Lady Catherine this afternoon. Please excuse me."

Mr. Collins, of course, could not object to anything her ladyship might want, and Darcy bowed his farewell and exited the house.

Once back at Rosings, he paced the length of the library while he awaited his cousin's return. *Will she believe me, or has Wickham made too strong an impression on her sensibility to be overcome?* The thought wounded his pride, but there was a deeper concern that pride could not match—concern that Wickham had won her over, that despite all she now knew, she would be swayed by him in the same way Georgiana had been.

It was past noon when Richard finally returned, and Darcy's anxiety rode high. "Well?" he demanded as soon as his cousin entered the room.

"She still had not returned by the time I left."

Darcy considered this for a minute, and then said, "As much as I would like to believe she simply took me at my word, her speech last night makes that unlikely. Perhaps you should seek her out, Richard."

His cousin shook his head. "You do not give Miss Elizabeth the credit she deserves. She is a clever woman—surely she would see that you would not suggest she speak to me if you did not know I would corroborate your word." Darcy hesitated and Richard continued. "And there is more beside. Yesterday when we spoke, she said something about Georgiana which accidentally came very near the mark. If she recalled my reaction, that may give your words all the verisimilitude they require."

Darcy shook his head. "I hope you are right, Richard, for we leave on the morrow whether she has inquired of you or not. I cannot stand to remain here another day."

Chapter Twenty-four

"I CANNOT SEE why you must leave so early, Darcy," Lady Catherine complained the next morning.

Darcy paced on the other side of the room and scowled out the window. *What is taking Parker so long?* he wondered. *Surely the carriage should be ready to go by now.*

Undaunted by his lack of reply, his aunt continued her tirade. "Had you but stayed a little longer, we could have shared an early nuncheon with you of cold meats and cheese."

"Your cook packed us food, Aunt." Richard held the hamper up.

She looked at it and her nostrils thinned. "Very well, but why must you leave today? Anne had quite expected you to stay through till the end of April, did you not, Anne?" The young lady made a sound that might be taken for assent, and Lady Catherine continued. "I do not know why you need to be away so suddenly."

"I do not know why you expected us to stay a month when our original plan was two weeks." Darcy crossed his arms and glared at his aunt. "We have already extended our stay once; now we really must leave."

Lady Catherine opened her mouth, but the entrance

of a footman forestalled any further argument. "Everything is packed, Mr. Darcy," he said. "The carriage awaits you."

The two cousins bowed to Lady Catherine and Anne. "As always, our visit has been a pleasure," Darcy said, able to be civil now that he knew he was truly leaving.

"Goodbye, Aunt—Anne." Richard pressed a kiss to both hands and then the gentlemen left.

In the privacy of the carriage, Richard began to laugh. Darcy frowned and said, "What, pray tell, is so amusing?"

"The look on your face when our aunt suggested we stay longer. I thought you would run her through."

Darcy grunted. "I cannot abide her controlling behavior. I do not see how Anne manages. Do you remember what she was like as a child?"

"Ah, but that was before she fell ill—and before her father died," Richard pointed out, and Darcy shrugged his shoulders in concession.

A figure on the side of the road ended their conversation. "I see the estimable parson would like to bid us adieu," Richard said. Mr. Collins bowed so low his cravat dragged in the dirt. When he straightened, Darcy touched the brim of his hat in acknowledgment and then they passed.

An awkward silence filled the carriage. Both men were thinking of their visits to Hunsford, and neither could think of anything to say that would not bring up painful topics.

"I do not see," Darcy said at last, "how she could possibly compare me unfavorably to Wickham." Of all things, this offended him most. "I had thought her to be more insightful than that."

"You are unjust," Richard said. "Wickham is a great deceiver; you should know that better than most." A dull heat rose in Darcy's face at the implication, but Richard did not stop there. "You do not blame Georgiana for believing his lies. How can you blame Miss Bennet?"

"Georgiana is a girl of fifteen. Elizabeth is a young lady of twenty," Darcy protested.

Richard snorted. "That makes little difference in matters such as these. Miss Bennet is just as ignorant of the ways of rakes as Georgiana was." He studied Darcy through narrowed eyes. "I believe the true difference is that she hurt your insufferable pride. Well, perhaps instead of snorting like a wounded bear, you might consider how Miss Bennet feels, now that she realizes how wrong she has been in her estimations of you both."

The rest of the journey to London was silent. Richard did not know he had echoed Elizabeth's invectives against Darcy with the phrase "insufferable pride," but Darcy could think of nothing else.

He had been able to dismiss the charge when it came from Elizabeth alone. She did not know him so well, and she had clearly been blinded by her own partialities. However, with Richard's voice added to the accusation, it carried more weight. His cousin knew him well; the two men were as close as brothers—there could be no undue prejudice swaying his opinion. A seed of doubt settled in the back of his mind. *Am I overly proud?*

He had not yet found an answer when the carriage pulled up to Darcy House. "Come, Richard," he said, "Georgiana is most anxious to see you again. I do not think she has forgiven me for taking you away from London so soon after your return from France."

And indeed, she was waiting for them in the foyer, her lower lip caught between her teeth. She gave a cry of delight when she saw them, and Richard stepped forward and caught her and swung her around before setting her down.

"Come, let us go inside," she urged them both. "The calendar may say April, but it is still chilly in the evenings, and I have tea ready for us in the salon."

The two gentlemen allowed her to walk slightly ahead of them, and Richard turned to Darcy. "Be careful, William, or she will be a grown woman before we realize it."

"You need not warn me of this, Richard, I assure you." Darcy sighed, but he smiled after his sister.

Once she had poured tea for everyone, Georgiana turned to her brother with an eager expression on her face, and Richard chuckled. "Ah, you had best be on your guard, William. She is about to ask you for a very great favor—I know that look."

Georgiana turned pink, but her smile did not falter. "I do not know that it is a very great favor," she protested, and they all laughed. "I simply wondered, Brother, if we might leave soon for Pemberley."

Richard reached over and tugged on one of her curls. "She will not even let us rest for a night before she would send us across the countryside."

Georgiana looked down at the floor. "Of course, we may wait until you are refreshed after your trip to Kent. I only thought... It is April and you said..." She looked at Darcy uncertainly.

"You are quite correct, Georgiana—I did say we would return home in April. I shall speak with Mrs. Grigsby about closing... No, you and Mrs. Annesley should speak with her. I am sure Mrs. Annesley knows what steps need to be taken when closing a house for a few months." *It is time I started passing some of these domestic tasks on to Georgiana,* he thought.

She recognized the import of what he said and blanched, but she quickly rallied. "Yes, of course. We shall speak with her tomorrow."

Darcy turned to his cousin. "Well, Richard, will you return to Derbyshire with us?"

It was a loaded question. The Fitzwilliam family seat was quite near Pemberley, and Richard could not travel with them without visiting his parents. Darcy loved his aunt and uncle, but he knew Richard struggled with his overprotective parents and overbearing elder siblings. In fact, Darcy rather suspected he joined the Army in part to escape their control.

But the colonel nodded gamely. "I have not seen my family since last summer." He pitched his voice to a falsetto and added, "I imagine my mama doubts I am still alive."

All three cousins laughed at his apt imitation of the countess, and then Darcy said, "It is settled then. We shall leave town as soon as possible."

With this incentive, Georgiana lost little time in dealing with household matters, and they were packed into the carriage traveling north by the end of the week. The trip from London took just over two days by carriage, and by the time they reached Pemberley in the afternoon of the third day, they were all very glad to be finally at home. Georgiana craned her neck out the window to catch the first glimpse of Pemberley as they rounded the bend in the road, and in truth, Darcy was no less eager. Only Richard reclined back against his seat.

Late evening sunlight filtered through the trees. *How long has it been since I felt so much at ease?* The answer came readily, and with it the end of his peace: it had been ten days, since the eve of his disastrous proposal.

Chapter Twenty-five

NOTHING, HOWEVER, COULD drive Elizabeth from his mind. With every task he completed, he was conscious of how much easier or pleasanter it would have been with her by his side.

When he walked the estate with his steward, he remembered Georgiana commenting that he needed a wife who could walk with him, and he thought again of Elizabeth and the walks they had shared in Kent. How he had looked forward then to showing her the grounds of Pemberley and his favorite walks through the park! Those spots he had loved all his life lacked luster, now that he saw them without Elizabeth.

Not long after his return to Pemberley, one of his best tenants celebrated the birth of his first child. By rights, the mistress of the estate would visit the family —but Pemberley had no mistress.

When Darcy appeared on the Coombs' doorstep, the man could not hide his surprise. "Mr. Darcy!"

"Good day, Coombs. I hear your wife has provided you with a son."

Coombs snapped his gaping mouth shut and swallowed. "Yes, sir. That is… Well, yes, sir. May I ask, sir, why you are here?"

Darcy raised an eyebrow. "I should think that obvious, Coombs. I came to congratulate you."

Coombs nodded slowly. "Of course, Mr. Darcy. Would you like to come in and see James?"

Darcy took his hat off and followed Coombs into the cottage. Mrs. Coombs smiled up at him when he entered. "Mr. Darcy, this is such a surprise!"

He looked at her, then back at her husband. *Why are they both so shocked to see me pay this form of courtesy?*

Before he could think any more on the question, a babe was thrust into his arms. "This is our James—isn't he the sweetest lad you ever did see?"

Darcy held the child six inches out from his chest, and when James yawned and stretched, he panicked. *Please do not wake.* But young James had not yet learnt that the master of Pemberley was always to be obeyed, and the tiny eyes opened. On beholding an unfamiliar face, his mouth opened in a wail that would have scared years off the life of a grown man, had he not known where it originated.

Mrs. Coombs bustled over and took her child back into the comfort of her arms, "There, there, Jamesey— Mama's here. You aren't afraid of Mr. Darcy, are you?"

Darcy watched in wonder as the child immediately quieted and settled back to sleep. Never had he been more aware of his own awkwardness, or longed more for Elizabeth's ease of manner.

The incident did not quickly leave his thoughts. Late into the evening he pondered it, always coming back to one thing: his own tenants, who knew him to be a generous landlord, had been surprised when he also showed them courtesy.

"Your manners impressing me with the fullest belief of your arrogance…"

Was there truth in her words? Did he look down on those he saw as beneath him and not treat them with the same kindness he treated those of his own class?

Darcy paced the length of his study, an empty

brandy glass in his hand. *How do my fellow landowners see me? Would they be likewise surprised to receive a note from me on the birth or marriage of one of their offspring?* The answer came in an instant—they would not. Those common forms of politeness were *de rigueur* among the upper class.

Am I then so caught up with social standing that I cannot offer simple congratulations to a family without it being a noteworthy event? Was Elizabeth so right about me?

Darcy had long acknowledged he had not the ease or openness of manner that many did. Of course he had pride in his family and his land, but he had never taken the time to consider how that was presented to others. In truth, he had never cared enough for the opinion of others to care how they saw him, but now he wondered if it was more than how he appeared. *Am I truly prideful?*

Over the next few weeks, he examined his interactions with all he met: staff, tenant, and landowner alike. What was his first response in all of these situations? Was it one of habitual pride? Did he consider himself so far above even his friends? Were Elizabeth's accusations true?

Such self-examination is never a pleasant course of study, and therefore, Richard's return in late May was welcome for the diversion it offered. "Did you grow tired of your family so soon?" Darcy teased when they were seated in the study.

The late evening sun shone on Richard's face, and he raised a hand to shield his eyes. "You have no idea," he said, his face pulled into a grimace. "My dear mama had a list of eligible young ladies waiting when I arrived. Take heart, Cousin, that you have no parents trying to marry you off."

Darcy flinched and Richard groaned. "Oh Lord, William, I did not think. I did not mean —"

Darcy held up his hand. "I assure you," he said harshly, "I quite took your meaning. However, I cannot see how facing a list of women you do not wish to marry is any worse than being refused by the woman you do!"

"I put my foot in it this time." Richard rubbed a hand across his face, but Darcy quashed any feelings of sympathy.

Richard opened a cautious eye. "As long as I am in your black books already, may I say that I admire the lady for rejecting you? It would certainly have been an advantageous marriage, not only for her, but also for her sisters. For one to marry a wealthy man would have opened the door to others."

Darcy snorted. "Careful, you begin to sound like Mrs. Bennet. She expressed very similar sentiments when complimenting herself on snaring Bingley for her eldest."

Richard furrowed his brow. "I beg your pardon?"

"I told you of Bingley's close escape while we were on the road to Rosings—do you recall?" Richard nodded. "The lady he nearly married is Elizabeth's elder sister."

Darcy did not understand the comprehension that dawned on his cousin's face. "I am afraid," Richard said very slowly, "that you might owe part of your current misery to me."

Darcy rose from his seat and poured them both a brandy. "Whatever do you mean?" he asked when he handed Richard a glass.

His cousin took a sip of the liquor before he answered. "When I spoke with Miss Bennet the morning before you proposed, I spoke of the role you played in separating Bingley from an undesirable connection. I did not know the lady in question was her sister."

Darcy's free hand clenched into a fist, but he forced himself to relax. *Richard had no way of knowing,* he reminded himself. "It is no matter," he said when the flush of indignation had passed. "That was merely the last in her list of complaints against me."

Darcy stood by the window and observed the way the sunlight reflected through the brandy. The shifting amber hues at least gave him something besides Richard's guilty countenance to look at.

"You know Darcy," Richard said, and Darcy turned back to him, "it strikes me as odd that you would not consider the Bennet family to be suitable connections for Bingley, if you did not scruple to pursue Miss Bennet for yourself."

Darcy froze, his brandy glass raised halfway to his lips. *"Though the motives which governed me may to you very naturally seem insufficient, I have not yet learned to condemn them."*

The words from his letter taunted him. With Richard's comment, he could see them as they might have appeared to Elizabeth, and he sat back down and groaned. *My pride, my insufferable pride.*

"William?"

Darcy looked up, almost surprised to see Richard still sitting across from him. "I am fine, it is only..." He tilted his head. "You were not sure I had done rightly by Bingley when I told you of my involvement, were you?"

Richard shrugged. "It shows a certain lack of consideration —"

"For the feelings of others," Darcy completed, now completely numb.

Oh God, could Elizabeth have been right? Am I so conceited, so sure my own judgment is always correct that I disregard what others might feel?

Richard set his glass down on the small table

between them, and the loud clink startled Darcy. "You appear to have a great deal on your mind, William. I believe I will turn in for the night." He turned back when he reached the door. "Do not stay up the whole night, going over and over what she said. It is done—leave it at that."

But Darcy could not. *"Do you think any consideration would tempt me to accept the man who has been the means of ruining, perhaps forever, the happiness of a most beloved sister?"*

"And I treated her accusation with contempt." Darcy stood and paced the room, stopping now and again to look out at the park. "I might by now have shown Pemberley to Elizabeth, had I not been so full of vanity."

He sank into a chair near the window, where he could watch as the setting sun sent reflections of pinks and golds dancing across the stream. The picture tugged at his memory, and he followed the string until he saw Elizabeth standing before the brook at Rosings just after sunrise.

Lovely as the image was, he could not think of it without likewise remembering he had then believed her to return his affections to some extent, if not in equal measure. "Indeed, I went to Hunsford that night believing her to be expecting my addresses. Could there be a stronger sign of arrogance?"

All thoughts of Wickham were now gone. Darcy had for a time laid the greatest share of his sorrow at his enemy's feet—for surely, if Wickham had not deceived Elizabeth, she would have accepted him.

He snorted. "And yet again I disregarded her feelings, this time concerning Miss Bennet. Ah Elizabeth, how truly you named my faults, though I would not listen."

The knowledge that there would be no second

chance lingered in the back of his mind, but he pushed the thought aside. *I may never meet Elizabeth again, but I can honor her by taking her remonstrations to heart.*

Darcy was even more grateful than usual to be at Pemberley. Given his recent revelations, he knew he would be very bad company. Even Richard did not stay long, but returned to his London lodgings after only a week.

Now his only company was Georgiana, and for the first time, he selfishly wished she were elsewhere. He had not the energy to entertain her, and he could tell by her confusion each night that she wondered at his low spirits.

Business took Darcy to Matlock for two weeks in the middle of June, and not wanting Georgiana to be alone, he asked if she would wish to stay with their aunt and uncle. Her pensive frown should have told him she had something in mind, but he had forgotten her normally observant nature.

It was not until they were on their way back to Pemberley two weeks later that he realized his mistake. She waited until they were comfortably ensconced in the carriage and on the main road before she turned to him.

Darcy laughed. "Why do you look at me with such a serious expression, Georgiana? Have I done something to vex you?"

Georgiana frowned and shook her head impatiently. "Of course not, Fitzwilliam. You know you are the best brother—no one could be kinder to me. That is why I must ask what is troubling you."

Darcy crossed his arms over his chest. "Whatever makes you think something troubles me?"

She leaned forward and placed a hand on his shoulder. "Please, Fitzwilliam, won't you trust me? You were so good to me last summer when I... when I needed you." She blushed, but did not drop her eyes. "I only wish to be as much help to you."

Darcy swallowed. He could not refuse such a request, but everything in him revolted at the notion of exposing his misfortune to anyone, even to his beloved sister. He thought for a long moment and then said, "Do you recall me writing to you of Elizabeth Bennet last fall?"

Georgiana tapped her chin and then smiled. "Was she not one of the young ladies you wished I could meet?"

"She is." Darcy carefully considered his next words. "I have found myself thinking of her often, but… there are circumstances which are likely to prevent us from ever meeting again."

Georgiana clasped her hands together on her lap. "Fitzwilliam, are you in love with her?"

He shifted uneasily in his seat. It was this very question he had been trying to avoid, and in the end, he did not truly answer. "I will only say that I admire her more than any other female I have ever met, besides you and Mother."

"And these… circumstances, they are what has been troubling you?"

If by "circumstances" you mean my own foolish behavior. But this would tell Georgiana more than he wished her to know about the events of the spring, so he merely nodded and said, "They are."

She frowned. "If you admire her so very much, I do not see why you do not find a way around them."

Her innocence broke Darcy's heart. "You will find, dearest, that there are some things not even the stoutest heart can overcome."

"I suppose," she said, but she still looked doubtful. "But what if you were to meet her again?"

"That is unlikely ever to happen. The family is not

often in town, and Hertfordshire is quite a ways away from Pemberley."

"But if you were?" she pressed.

"Please, Georgiana, I cannot consider it."

The pain in his voice ended her questioning, and the carriage was silent for a good thirty minutes. "I am saddened I shall never meet Miss Elizabeth," Georgiana said finally. "I think, given your approbation, that I would like her very much."

Darcy smiled sadly. "I believe you would, Georgiana. I believe you would like her very much indeed."

Chapter Twenty-six

TO HIS SURPRISE, Darcy found that sharing even a part of his burden with Georgiana helped. Some of his melancholy lifted, and by the end of July, he was able to look forward to the coming visit with Bingley with a degree of pleasure.

He broached the subject with Georgiana in late July. "I invited Bingley and his sisters to join us here for a few weeks, in thanks for their hospitality last fall. Would you care to travel with me to London to bring them hither, or shall you stay here?"

"I will come with you, I believe."

"Good, I have a gift in mind for you, and it is one you had best choose for yourself."

She wrinkled her nose. "A gift?"

Darcy chuckled. "You will have to wait till we arrive in London to learn more—I must still have some power of surprising you."

Georgiana attempted to wheedle more information out of Darcy for the next week, but he deflected every attempt. Thus, when their first stop in London was not Darcy House, but a renowned music shop, he was rewarded with a girlish squeal.

"Oh, Fitzwilliam, are you sure? A new pianoforte? The one we have at Pemberley is perfectly suitable —"

"— for a novice," Darcy finished. "You, my dear

sister, are no longer a novice. If you are to truly excel, we must get you a new instrument."

The workshop owner was most solicitous, once he realized Darcy had every intention of making a purchase. Georgiana wandered the floor, stroking the veneer on this instrument, checking the action on another.

Darcy observed that though she looked at all the pianofortes available, she came back to one over and over. After the fourth time, when she actually sat down and played for a few minutes, Darcy turned to the man and said, "I believe we have made our choice. You will see that it is delivered to Pemberley?" He wrote a bank draft and left directions to the estate, then he and Georgiana left.

The coachman had hardly closed the door when she turned to Darcy, stars in her eyes. "Oh, Brother, you are too good to me! A Broadwood grand!"

Darcy leaned back in the seat and smiled indulgently. "Even one as unmusical as myself could tell it produced the best sound, Georgiana. Will you be happy to find it in your music room when we return to Pemberley?" The smile on her face was all the answer he needed.

Darcy stopped by Bingley's lodgings that night and found a warm welcome. "Darcy, I cannot tell you how glad I was to receive your letter last week, confirming your invitation to us. London has been quite dull this summer."

"Surely you did not stay in town? Did the Hursts not invite you to join them?" Mr. Hurst owned a small estate in Richmond, and though it was not as fine as Pemberley, it at least would have been cooler than London.

Bingley grimaced. "He did, but I only stayed a few weeks. It may surprise you, but even I grow weary of my sisters at times. I had thought to spend some energy looking for an estate of my own, but I will not be free of Netherfield until Michaelmas, and…"

Darcy could easily fill in the blank—"and my last attempt to settle down did *not* end as I had hoped." He examined his friend closely and saw sadness behind the cheerful smile. *He still regrets Miss Bennet.* Never had Darcy felt the justice of Elizabeth's reproach so strongly, and were he but certain of the constancy of the lady's regard, he would have confessed all to his friend on the spot.

Instead, he said, "Well, I hope you will not mind the presence of your sisters at Pemberley. I could not very well exclude them, when you all showed me such hospitality last autumn."

Bingley laughed. "Even if I did mind, I would not dare suggest you exclude Caroline from Pemberley's hallowed grounds. I left Richmond in part to avoid her constant comments on the subject."

Darcy groaned. "Perhaps we might stay in town and send the ladies on ahead?" he said, only half joking.

Bingley shook his head, and Darcy was glad to see mischief in his eyes. "I fear the estate would be nothing without its master."

"Very well, but you may warn her I have no intention of being monopolized. I will not be settling down anytime soon." He hid all traces of pain when he made that statement. "You will be ready to leave day after tomorrow?" Bingley nodded. "Good. Then I should go home to my supper."

The party left London early in the morning, and they had not been on the road for an hour when Darcy realized how right Bingley's veiled warning had been. Miss Bingley would not allow anyone else to speak, and she would speak to none but him. In the closed environment of the carriage, Darcy could not ignore her without giving her the cut direct.

By the time they reached the posting station where they took a light nuncheon, Darcy feared he could no longer withhold his scathing remarks. Therefore, he was glad to find a letter from his steward waiting for him.

"What news is it, Mr. Darcy?" Miss Bingley purred. "Nothing that will postpone our visit, I hope."

"What?" Darcy questioned sharply, and then regained control of his temper. "No, nothing as serious as that. However, my steward has some business he would like to discuss with me, and as I would prefer to be at leisure during your stay, I am sure you understand if I ride ahead and leave you to follow with the carriage."

From her expression, he could see she did not know if she should be gratified he wished to have no entanglements during her visit, or put out that he would leave. Bingley's ready agreement robbed her of either option, and the matter was settled.

After their repast, Bingley followed Darcy out to the stable where he mounted his horse. "Tell me truly, Darcy—will our visit inconvenience you in any way?"

Darcy shook his head. "Not in the slightest. The matter with my steward is very minor and could in truth probably wait another day. However..." Darcy glanced back at the inn.

"Ah, I see. You seek an escape from Caroline. Well, I cannot blame you there. We shall see you on the day after tomorrow."

"Watch out for Georgiana for me—I am trusting you with her care."

"Of course."

On horseback, Darcy was able to cover half the remaining distance before nightfall. He spent the night at a small roadside inn where he was well known, and set out again at first light. The rolling hills of the Midlands soon gave way to the more rugged countryside of Derbyshire, and Darcy spurred his horse on, eager to be at home.

Darcy turned off the main road about half a mile from the Pemberley drive and followed a shortcut that led directly to the stables. He waved to the tenant farmers he passed along the way, but he did not stop. This close to home, he would not allow any delays.

This approach gave the view of Pemberley from the side, with the stream seeming to flow out from the house itself. The first glimpse of Pemberley always filled Darcy with a combined sensation of pride and contentment, and latterly, a sense of longing. *If I could see Elizabeth here...*

In the stable, Darcy passed the reins off to a stable hand and gave explicit instructions on where to return the animal. He was pulling his riding gloves off as he headed toward the house when he heard a sound that did not belong.

Shock flooded him when he looked up, and he stood there ridiculously, one glove half off. He blinked, but still she stood before him.

"Miss Bennet!"

Chapter Twenty-seven

DARCY TOOK IN every detail of Elizabeth's appearance, from her slightly rumpled traveling gown to the light blush coloring her cheeks. She turned, and he spied one curl which the wind had teased free from her pins. It caressed her cheek, and Darcy's hands shook with the effort it took to restrain himself from starting forward to brush it back behind her ear.

An instant later, her actions registered. *She is leaving!* He covered the remaining yards between them in a few quick steps and bowed low before her. "Miss Bennet," he repeated, his voice calmer.

Elizabeth turned back, looked at him, and flushed cherry red. "Mr. Darcy."

She seems almost embarrassed, but why? Unless... Could she have believed better of me after reading the letter?

The thought gave him courage. "It is a pleasure to see you again. May I ask how your family is doing?"

She inclined her head. "They are all very well, thank you very much."

The quiet control in her voice did not satisfy him, and he pressed further. "Indeed, your mother and father, and your sisters?"

She smiled at last. "Yes, indeed, they are all quite well, thank you."

Darcy glanced at the couple who stood a few feet

away, and then back to Elizabeth. "Have you been in the country long?"

"Only a few days, sir."

Sir—how he hated such formality from her.

Elizabeth again made a motion as if to leave, and Darcy sought frantically for a topic, any topic, that would keep her with him. "And what do you think of Derbyshire so far?" he asked, finally recollecting that she must be traveling.

Real animation sparkled in her eyes. "It is beautiful." A breeze caught the errant curl, and she tucked it back with an economical, practiced gesture. "I have never seen anything like the Peaks before."

A genuine smile crossed her face, and Darcy caught his breath. *My memory did not do her justice.*

Ironically, it was that which impressed upon him the immensity of the moment. Elizabeth was here, in Derbyshire—at his home, even! The wave of panic he had been holding in swept over him. He had not the slightest idea what to say next, and he had an inkling that he had repeated himself several times in their short conversation. After standing in awkward silence for a few minutes, he bowed once more and excused himself.

Darcy had not gone many steps before reason woke him and he realized he had thrown away his one chance to redeem himself in her eyes. "She may never think well enough of me to return my love, but if I can show her that I have taken her criticism to heart, then perhaps she will at least think better of me," he murmured, and his steps toward the house quickened to a near run.

Mrs. Reynolds started when he walked through the front door, but he did not have time for the explanation of his early arrival. "Yes, I am home early. I see we have visitors; will they take the tour of the Park?"

"Indeed, sir, for the young lady professed an avid interest in walking the grounds."

Darcy smiled. He had fond memories of the pleasure Elizabeth took in a walk. "If you would be so kind as to tell Mr. Jones I will require his attention later this evening, I believe I will walk out and join them."

Darcy bounded out of the house with an eagerness he had not felt since that dreadful day in Kent. Then his hopes had been dashed; he prayed his much more modest hope of making her think better of him would not likewise be crushed.

A question to the gardener told him which path Elizabeth and her companions had followed, and he set out after them. The entire time he tried to see his home through her eyes, wondering what she might think of it.

The river wended its way through the valley in a series of bends, and it was around one of those turns that Darcy first caught sight of Elizabeth, farther down the path. He sped up, eager to be with her again, and the next twist brought them face-to-face.

Elizabeth seemed to have regained some of her composure, and she smiled at him when they met. "I was just admiring your grounds, Mr. Darcy. I had no idea Pemberley was so delightful—this walk in particular is all that is charming."

She blushed then, and with a greater understanding of her than he had previously owned, he knew she had heard the possible meaning he could take from her words. *Ah, Elizabeth, do you think I would mind if you were intimating a desire to be mistress of my home?*

Feeling it was safer not to follow that train of thought, he turned slightly toward her companions and said, "May I ask to be introduced to your friends, Miss Bennet?"

Some of the archness Darcy loved so much returned

to Elizabeth's expression. "Certainly." She held out a hand to the lady and said, "May I introduce my aunt and uncle, Mr. and Mrs. Edward Gardiner."

Darcy caught Elizabeth's glance and could not mistake her meaning. This was the very couple he had once disdained to be related to, and yet everything about them proved them to be very worthy people, at least on outward appearance. Rather than the vulgarity he had expected, they exhibited dignity and refinement in both fashion and demeanor.

My pride once again! He bowed to them and said, "Welcome to Pemberley, Mr. and Mrs. Gardiner."

The couple returned his salutation with a level of composure which told him they did not know the whole of his acquaintance with their niece. Darcy honored her discretion; he knew many young ladies would not keep quiet when they had received an unwanted proposal. His hopes that he might yet gain her affections rose higher, and with an idea of bettering himself in her eyes, he turned back to walk with her uncle.

"I understand you have a profitable business in town, Mr. Gardiner."

The older gentleman smiled, and Darcy caught a glimpse of the liveliness he admired in Elizabeth. "Indeed I do, sir. I own, however, that I would like it to be less profitable at times. We had intended to visit the Lakes this summer, but there is so much requiring my presence that I could not take that much time away from my warehouses."

"I hope you are not disappointed with Derbyshire, sir."

Mr. Gardiner shook his head quickly. "Oh no, not at all. I believe Mrs. Gardiner was actually quite pleased with the change in plans—she grew up in Lambton."

"But you were perhaps looking forward to the sport

in the Lake District?"

Mr. Gardiner nodded and smiled ruefully. "I did anticipate a spot of fishing, I confess."

"If that is all, sir, you must avail yourself of my stream while you are here."

"I could not impose upon your hospitality, Mr. Darcy."

Darcy smiled. "Nonsense! I had planned to do some fishing myself while at home, and your company would be most welcome. I will, of course, supply any tackle you might require; simply ask Mrs. Reynolds about it when you come."

The invitation was sincere; though he had originally struck up the conversation in an effort to prove to Elizabeth that he had changed, he had discovered Mr. Gardiner to be a very amiable gentleman—yes, a gentleman, despite how close he lived to his warehouses.

The party stopped for a while on the riverbank when Mr. Gardiner noticed a water-plant he had never before seen. The two gentlemen descended from the path to the water's edge and took a closer look. Darcy, who was more familiar with the native flora, finally pronounced them to be May-blobs, harder to identify in August without their distinctive yellow flowers, and they walked back up to the path, their curiosity satisfied.

Before they could resume their walk, Mrs. Gardiner spoke. "I fear the exercise has fatigued me more than the rest of the party. If you would not mind walking with Elizabeth, Mr. Darcy, I should very much like the support of my husband's arm."

Darcy took great care that nothing in his countenance should display how little he minded such an arrangement. Elizabeth did not need his arm, so he simply walked in step with her, as close as propriety would allow.

However, once they had begun walking again he realized he did not know what to say to her. *I cannot ask again after her family; that would be too ridiculous.* All other topics—their last meeting, his letter—were obviously out of the question.

After a short silence, Elizabeth obliged him by speaking first. "Your arrival was very unexpected, Mr. Darcy, for your housekeeper informed us that you would certainly not be here till tomorrow; and indeed, before we left Bakewell, we understood that you were not immediately expected in the country."

Her message was clear—if she had known he would be home, she would not have come. Never had Darcy been so grateful to his steward. "Mrs. Reynolds did not misinform you," he answered. "I, and the rest of the party I was traveling with, intended to arrive tomorrow, but I received a note from my steward indicating he had business to discuss with me, so I rode on ahead of the rest. They will join me early tomorrow, and among them are some who will claim an acquaintance with you—Mr. Bingley and his sisters."

The instant the words were out of his mouth, he wished them back. He could not help but recall the last time those names had been mentioned between them, and the emotion of that moment temporarily robbed him of speech.

He regained his equanimity with effort and said, "There is also one other person in the party who more particularly wishes to be known to you. Will you allow me, or do I ask too much, to introduce my sister to your acquaintance during your stay at Lambton?"

Darcy held his breath, suddenly aware of all the implications of his request: first, that he had mentioned her to Georgiana with enough warmth that his sister would want to meet her, and secondly, that he himself wanted them to be acquainted. He feared the request was in fact rather impertinent, but rather than deny him, she smiled slightly and nodded her head.

"I would be glad to wait upon Miss Darcy during our stay at Lambton."

Relief was not the only emotion he felt at her acquiescence. In the months since Kent, he had spent much time going over her words, turning them over in his mind. It had seemed at the time that her opinion of him was so decided that her mind could never be changed. He had hoped that his letter would at least show her that George Wickham was not a man to be trusted; he had not dared believe that it would improve her opinion of him.

That it had done so seemed obvious. There was none of that teasing in her manner which he now realized had been her way of baiting him into behaving badly. Instead she seemed shy, unsure of herself in a way that was most unlike her. It charmed him and sparked the tiny ember of hope that had never truly died.

They walked steadily on, and Pemberley House appeared before them long before he would have liked. Anxious not to let this time with her end, he said, "Would you care to come inside while we wait for your aunt and uncle? Perhaps you would like to rest from the walk."

She shook her head decisively. "I assure you, Mr. Darcy, I am not the least bit tired, though I do thank you for the consideration."

He led her instead to a small bench positioned at the base of the pond in front of the house, beneath the shade of an ancient oak. "Your aunt and uncle were some ways behind us. There is no reason we should not sit in comfort, if we are to wait."

For a fraction of an instance, he feared she would refuse, but she smiled graciously and said, "Indeed, you are correct," before sitting beside him.

Her proximity very nearly did Darcy in. It certainly robbed him of his ability to speak, and instead he occupied himself with surreptitiously observing the way a stray shaft of sunlight danced around her face, bathing her features in golden light and turning her brunette hair the color of rich, dark honey.

Elizabeth seemed about to say something, but changed her mind. He watched her with great curiosity, for she did not often seem at a loss for words. Finally she began talking of the things she had seen in their travels so far, and, as he was well familiar with the sites of Matlock and Dove Dale, he could easily join her in conversation.

When the Gardiners at last arrived, Darcy did not know if he should be glad or sorry their tête-à-tête was at an end. The weight of unsaid words grew heavier with every moment, and he knew that at some point, if things progressed as he hoped, they would have to be discussed. However, time spent with Elizabeth was always desirable, and time alone in her company was infinitely more precious.

"Would you care to come into the house for some refreshment before returning to Lambton?" he inquired of the group.

Mr. Gardiner shook his head. "Thank you, sir, but I think my wife would prefer to return to the inn for a brief rest before our dinner engagement tonight."

"Very well. I trust we will be able to entertain you at Pemberley some other time during your stay."

Mr. Gardiner called his carriage up and climbed in first, leaving Darcy with the task of handing the ladies up. He took Mrs. Gardiner's hand first and passed her on to her husband, and then he turned to Elizabeth.

Though they had often been in company, there had been little opportunity to touch her, and the effect of her hand in his was startling and profound.

Once they were all seated, Mr. Gardiner gave the order for the coachman to take them back to the inn, and Darcy watched them drive away. He forced himself to turn away before they reached the end of the drive, not wanting the Gardiners to be aware of the depth of his regard for their niece.

He walked slowly back to the house, turning over in his mind every expression, every word of Elizabeth's. That she was more pleasantly disposed toward him was obvious. How far that approbation extended he dared not guess. Experience had taught him that he knew little of the lady's heart, and he would not allow himself to believe he had a place there until he heard it from her own lips.

Chapter Twenty-eight

THE DARCY CHAISE rattled up the lane shortly after ten o'clock the next morning. Darcy, who had been waiting for that sound since breakfast, soon stood in the open doorway to welcome his guests.

"Good morning, Darcy!" Bingley said.

"Good morning, Bingley. You must have left quite early; have you had breakfast yet?"

Miss Bingley sighed and covered her mouth in a delicate yawn. "Oh my, no, Mr. Darcy. We could not eat at the inn, for your sister insisted we must be at Pemberley in time to break our fast."

Darcy raised an eyebrow at Georgiana, but she flushed and shook her head. *I believe I know who it was...*

But Bingley spoke before he could finish the thought. "That is untrue, Caroline! It was you who refused to wait another minute, even though the hostler had prepared a meal for us!" He turned to Darcy. "I do hope it will not inconvenience your staff to serve us?"

"No, of course not. Georgiana, will you inform Mrs. Reynolds?"

Once they were seated around the table, he turned to Bingley. "Bingley, the strangest thing happened yesterday—you will never believe. Do you know who I saw when I arrived home?"

"I daresay I do not," Bingley replied and then took a sip of coffee.

Darcy waited until Bingley swallowed before he said, "Miss Elizabeth Bennet."

Bingley's jaw dropped. "I say! What was she doing in this part of the country?"

Darcy feigned some ignorance. "I believe she is touring with her aunt and uncle."

"Would these be the same noble pair who live on Gracechurch Street?" Miss Bingley interjected while spreading jam over a slice of warm bread.

"They would," Darcy said coldly, tired of her constant insinuations against that family.

Georgiana saved the moment. "Brother, is this the Miss Elizabeth Bennet you told me about in your letters?"

"The very one." The Darcy siblings shared a long look which spoke of their conversation in the carriage.

Georgiana's eyes sparkled. "Oh, I do hope she is still in the area, as I would so like to meet her."

"I should imagine they have moved on." Miss Bingley waved a hand, as if to shoo away a fly. "You know how holidays are, Georgiana dear."

Darcy's dislike of Caroline Bingley grew with every moment. "In fact, they have not, Miss Bingley. There are staying in Lambton for a while. Miss Bennet has expressed a willingness to meet you, Georgiana. Would you like to drive into town with me this afternoon?"

"Oh no!" Georgiana's immediate negative surprised him, but she quickly followed it with, "Let us go now. Perhaps they have plans for the afternoon; I would not want to miss her."

It was a possibility that had not occurred to Darcy, but now that it had been presented he could not deny its likelihood. As eager as his sister to see Elizabeth, he quickly ordered his curricle made ready.

After the order had been given, he turned to see Bingley rocking back and forth on his feet. "I say, Darcy, do you suppose you have room for one more?"

Bingley's interest in seeing Elizabeth could only come from a desire to hear something of her sister, and guilt smote Darcy. "There is not room in the curricle, Bingley, but you may ride along beside us. I am sure Miss Bennet would be glad to see you again."

The animals set off at a brisk pace, and soon the small party left the park and was on the main road. "Fitzwilliam," Georgiana said at this point, "do you think Miss Bennet will like me?"

Darcy glanced over at her, startled. "Whatever makes you wonder such a thing, dearest?"

Georgiana twisted her hands together in her lap. "I know what people say about me. They say I am proud, but I simply—I do not always know what to say."

The uncertainty in her voice tugged at his heart, and holding the reins in one hand, he pressed his other on her arm. "Do not fret yourself overmuch, Georgiana. Miss Bennet is the most amiable lady of my acquaintance. I am sure she will give you the credit you deserve, if you allow her the time."

Earnestness shone in his sister's eyes. "Oh yes, I will!"

Very soon, they were driving down the narrow streets of Lambton that led to the inn. Darcy glanced up at the window and he caught a glimpse of Elizabeth looking down at them. The hope that her eagerness might match his own did much to brighten his mood, and he hopped out of the curricle with more than his usual energy. Georgiana took his hand, and they entered the inn.

"Are Mr. and Mrs. Gardiner and Miss Bennet available?" he queried.

"Aye, sir, they are in the sitting room above stairs."

He smiled his thanks to the maid and they walked upstairs. Mr. Gardiner opened the door with such alacrity that he knew they were expected, and they walked into a pleasant parlor.

"Good morning, Mr. Gardiner, Mrs. Gardiner... Miss Bennet."

Darcy watched with fascination as color rose in Elizabeth's cheeks. He almost missed Mrs. Gardiner's reply, but subtle pressure on his arm from Georgiana reminded him of his surroundings. "Good morning, Mr. Darcy. I say, we did not expect to see you so early."

"My sister was very eager to meet Miss Bennet. May I introduce you? Georgiana, this is Mr. Edward Gardiner, Mrs. Gardiner, and this is Miss Elizabeth Bennet."

"I am very pleased to meet all of you," Georgiana said, her voice soft.

"It is a pleasure to meet you as well," Elizabeth said warmly. "We heard such wonderful things about you yesterday." Elizabeth held out her hand, which Georgiana gladly took, but still she hardly looked up.

Darcy, eager that his sister and his beloved should get along, had to stop himself from interjecting. *At some point Georgiana must learn to do for herself.* He stood aside and watched with pleasure as Elizabeth patiently asked question after question, with a few additional asides from her aunt. There was nothing in her expression that indicated she felt the same disgust of Georgiana that she had shown toward Darcy in Kent, nothing that said she was found to be overly proud. He relaxed enough to recall that Bingley was still waiting downstairs.

"Miss Bennet, there is someone else who came with us. Mr. Bingley is downstairs, and most eager to meet you again. May I call him up?"

Her quick smile was the only answer he needed, and he felt a brief pang that his own presence did not inspire such ready warmth. Bingley soon joined them, and as always, his affability threw Darcy's reserve in sharp relief. "Miss Elizabeth Bennet! It is so good to see you once more."

"And you, Mr. Bingley."

"You are in good health, I trust."

"Indeed, we are. Travel can be so invigorating, and we have not been gone long enough to grow weary of each other." Elizabeth and her aunt shared a quick smile at the joke.

Bingley, however, did not seem inclined to ask after their journey or the sites they had seen. "And… your family?" There was the barest hesitation. "Are they all well?"

She smiled ever so slightly, but her response was measured. "I believe so, or they were a week ago when we left Hertfordshire."

"You have not been traveling long then."

Elizabeth shook her head. "Not at all. My aunt grew up in Lambton, and this was the first place she wished to see."

"It is a very fine part of the country, I have always thought."

"Oh yes. There something in the wildness of the rocks and peaks that is far grander than anything I had anticipated."

Darcy felt a ridiculous pride in his county. He had not put those rocks there himself, and they had no more connection to him than being the landscape he was most used to. However, it was suddenly of the utmost importance that they should please Elizabeth.

He turned his own attention to Mr. Gardiner, though he followed the other conversation with half an ear. "Mr. Gardner, I hope you have not forgotten your promise to come fish with us."

Mr. Gardiner raised his eyebrows. Darcy had so often received such a look from Elizabeth that he read it in an instant. "Do not tell me you doubted my offer."

His companion gave a quick negative. "Indeed I have not, sir, though I confess I was not sure you would find time, once your guests arrived."

"I assure you, sir," Darcy said dryly, "we have nothing but time. There is little to occupy us beside the idle occupations that make the summer so enjoyable. Will you join us then tomorrow morning?"

"At what time?"

"Shall we say noon? I am afraid some of my guests are still accustomed to town hours."

Mr. Gardiner chuckled. "No need to make excuses, Mr. Darcy. I shall be delighted to join you, whatever the time. So, noon it is then."

Bingley and Elizabeth continued to talk, and rather than join them, Darcy simply observed, enjoying the chance to see her smile and hear her laughter. After believing her lost to him forever, it was enough to be in the same room with her, to see her once more without the dreadful look of contempt she had worn when she told him she could never be prevailed upon to marry him.

The recollection pained him, and he closed his eyes briefly. When he opened them, he heard Bingley say, "It was a very long time since I have had the pleasure of seeing you, Miss Bennet. Why, it is above eight months. We have not met since the twenty-sixth of November, when we were all dancing together at Netherfield."

Darcy saw Elizabeth's smile and knew she had interpreted this comment the same way he had. With every moment, he was surer that Bingley's attachment to Miss Bennet was more permanent than he had believed. He tried to imagine how he would feel if some well-meaning friend tried to divide himself from Elizabeth, were he ever lucky enough to be the recipient of her affection. *Can Bingley ever forgive my interference?*

But Darcy's attention could not wander long from Elizabeth. "I understand you live primarily in town," she said to Georgiana.

"Yes, but I prefer to remain at Pemberley."

Elizabeth laughed, and the rich sound shot straight to Darcy's heart. "Indeed, I could easily understand why. Pemberley is so lovely; I cannot imagine ever wishing to leave. To borrow a phrase, what are shops compared to rocks and nature?"

Loath as Darcy was to interrupt this intercourse, they had now been with the family above half an hour. "Georgiana, will you not invite Miss Bennet and the Gardiners to dine with us?"

She blinked, but obediently said, "Oh yes, of course. I do hope you will join us for dinner at Pemberley while you are in the area."

Anxiety to be accepted made her sound diffident and proud. Darcy saw the look of understanding on all three faces and blessed them for their patience. In time, Georgiana would become accustomed to giving invitations, and he hoped her performance would improve with practice. He remembered Elizabeth's dictates to him and smiled briefly before formalizing the invitation.

"Indeed, we should be very glad to see you at Pemberley for dinner. Perhaps the day after tomorrow?"

Mrs. Gardiner glanced at Elizabeth, but rather than answer, she turned her head away. He caught a glimpse of her expression, though, and knew her to be merely confused and perhaps embarrassed by the attention. For a brief moment he wondered if he was being too particular in his attentions. *Surely she must know I still love her.*

In the end, it was Mrs. Gardiner who accepted the invitation, leaving Darcy with little insight into Elizabeth's mind or affections.

Chapter Twenty-nine

THE LADIES WERE still in bed when Darcy and Bingley rose at ten o'clock for breakfast. Bingley was unusually quiet, and Darcy could only guess from the pensive look on his face that his mind was filled with questions he could ask Mr. Gardiner—questions that might lead to discussion of his fair niece, perhaps?

A footman showed Mr. Gardiner into the breakfast room promptly at noon. "Good morning, sir," Darcy said solicitously. "I trust the day finds you well?"

"Indeed, who would not be well on a morning like this?" Mr. Gardiner asked. "It is a fine day to be out of doors."

"Indeed you are right, sir," Darcy agreed. "I believe we will find the servants waiting with tackle and a hamper packed with provisions for the late afternoon, if you will follow me."

Darcy led the way out of the house and gestured for the servants waiting on the lawn to join them. More familiar than anyone with his own land, he took them down a small, little-known path to his own favorite fishing hole.

"Why, Darcy, I do not think I have ever seen this part of Pemberley," Bingley remarked.

"Mr. Bingley, I would venture to guess there is more you have *not* seen of Pemberley than that you *have*,"

Mr. Gardiner said.

"You are likely right, sir," Bingley agreed. "However, I did expect to have seen the best places for sport."

"Surely a gentleman may be allowed some secrets at his own home," Darcy protested. "Now, choose a pole and let us enjoy this fine morning."

Darcy sought in vain for a topic they could discuss without revealing Miss Bennet's London visit, and in the end, it was Mr. Gardiner who broke the silence. "It was very good of you to invite me to fish with you this morning, Mr. Darcy. I am not insensitive to the fact that you must wish to be with your private party while you are at home, and I am hardly more than a stranger to you."

"Indeed, sir, you must not think so. Both Bingley and I became well enough acquainted with your nieces last fall that I daresay we feel we know you as well."

Mr. Gardiner finally looked away from the water, and Darcy flushed at the comprehension in his eyes. However, he did not flinch from his steady gaze. *If I am to be deemed worthy of Elizabeth, I must first reveal my intentions.*

After a long moment, Mr. Gardiner smiled. "My niece did not tell us she was so well acquainted with you, Mr. Darcy."

Darcy did not know how to answer the question, but for once, Bingley's innocence proved useful. He laughed and said, "My friend is so very reserved, it takes twice as long to get to know him as it takes him to get to know you. I declare, during the first year of our acquaintance, I lived in fear of that keen, penetrating eye."

Darcy huffed and rolled his eyes. "Bingley, you will make me sound like some dreaded arbiter."

"As well you might seem to one who does not know you," Bingley retorted frankly. He turned back to Mr.

Gardiner. "But lest I give you a false impression, Mr. Darcy is the best and most loyal of friends. Once he does decide to trust you, his friendship is absolutely unwavering. I have never seen him turn from anyone in his own circle."

Mr. Gardiner's eyes widened, and Darcy felt his cheeks heat once more. Still, this sort of constancy was the very image he wanted Elizabeth's uncle to have of him. "I take my time making a decision, sir, but once I do, my... opinions remain unchanged."

A silent exchange passed between the two gentlemen: Mr. Gardiner questioning, Darcy promising. Finally, Mr. Gardiner looked up at the sun as it rose higher in the sky. "I imagine Mrs. Gardiner and my niece have arrived at Pemberley by now."

Darcy jerked on his pole and the line flew out of the water. He cast again, then said, "I was not aware they intended to visit today."

Mr. Gardiner tended to his own line and did not look away from the stream. "Yes, they were much impressed by Miss Darcy's courtesy yesterday morn and wished to return the favor as early as they could."

Darcy smiled; this was very like Elizabeth, and one of the things he loved about her. Her understanding of what was appropriate was unerring, her courtesy flawless. His own interest in the sport faded now that he knew she was nearby, and after a few minutes he said, "If there are guests at the house, perhaps I should go welcome them. Bingley, Mr. Gardiner, feel free to stay as long as you wish. When you are ready to leave, my servants will direct you and Bingley back to the house."

Mr. Gardiner bowed, and Darcy saw a hint of a smile on his face, but it did not bother him to be seen through so easily. He strode quickly through the trees and saw that the Gardiner's carriage was indeed parked in the drive. Thus assured that Elizabeth was inside, his pace quickened even more. Once inside the house, an inquiry of Mrs. Reynolds gave him the location of the ladies.

When he joined them in the large salon his sister favored, tea had just been set out. He quickly took in the seating arrangements and sighed; Elizabeth and his sister were seated on opposite sides of the room. Miss Bingley and Mrs. Annesley sat on either side of Georgiana, and Mrs. Hurst and Mrs. Gardiner beside Elizabeth.

How am I to encourage their conversation? He took a plate for himself and sat down near his sister. He soon saw that with his presence, her own reserve eased and she was able to present herself to better advantage. He equally saw that Elizabeth and her aunt were very much impressed with her.

Miss Bingley had sat up quite straight when he walked in and her glance over at Elizabeth did not need any interpretation. He immediately realized that his actions made his intentions clear to more than just Mr. Gardiner, and he wondered if he should have been more discreet. A quick look over at Elizabeth showed no discomposure on her part, however, a fact which eased his mind as much as it quickened his pulse. If she did not object to his intentions, then perhaps her feelings toward him were not as wholly set as they had been in months past. Perhaps...

Conversation started once more and did not allow him to ponder these thoughts any longer. Darcy sought a topic that would lead to conversation between Georgiana and Elizabeth, and eventually he turned to his sister and said, "Have you told Miss Bennet of your new pianoforte?"

She smiled and said, "No, we had not gotten to music yet. Do you play, Miss Bennet?"

"Not as well as I should like—I ought to take the time to practice." The smile she offered Darcy held no reprimand, and he took it as an olive branch.

"I am sure you do not give yourself enough credit. I confess, music is one of my greatest joys. My brother was good enough to have a new instrument sent to me this last week. Perhaps when you are with us for dinner tomorrow night you might play for us."

"If you would like."

"Oh yes, very much so."

Darcy leaned back in his chair, a smile on his face. Even if his dreams did not come true and Elizabeth never accepted his hand, he could not think of a better friend for Georgiana. Elizabeth was as open and vibrant as his sister was quiet and reserved, and she had a quick understanding of people and their motives that would do his innocent sister well.

Before he could congratulate himself too greatly on securing their friendship, Caroline Bingley's voice ruined the moment. "Pray, Miss Eliza, are not the –shire militia removed from Meryton? They must be a great loss to *your* family."

Georgiana paled, and Darcy cursed the impulse that had led him to disclose Wickham's membership in that corps. However, before he could deliver a stunning retort to Caroline, Elizabeth took the matter calmly in her own hands. "Of course we were as sorry as any family to find the diversity of the company materially diminished, but I daresay we have been able to cope well enough. After all, we managed without the militia for many years, and we shall continue to do so."

Her answer quickly put paid to any notion on Miss Bingley's side that she missed Wickham, and that lady colored when her insult was so easily rebuffed. Darcy could easily guess what her intent had been—to cast Elizabeth as a lady with poor discernment, who was not above befriending a common soldier. *A year ago, that might have made a difference in my opinion of her, but today, nothing Caroline Bingley says could sway my affections. Were Elizabeth to tell me her own sister had actually married a soldier, I would not love her any less.*

It was but a few minutes later when Mrs. Gardiner indicated to Elizabeth that they would soon need to return to Lambton in order to meet their afternoon appointments. Darcy rose when they did and offered to escort them to their carriage.

After he had handed them up into the carriage, Mrs. Gardiner smiled down at him. "Thank you very much for your hospitality, sir. If you would be so kind as to tell Mr. Gardiner we have returned to the village, I would appreciate it."

"Of course, Mrs. Gardiner."

"Then we shall see you tomorrow night for dinner."

Darcy smiled, and his eyes drifted to Elizabeth. "I greatly look forward to it."

Elizabeth blushed, and Mrs. Gardiner nodded to their driver. Darcy stepped away from the carriage, and this time, he did not turn until it had disappeared down the lane.

When he returned to the salon, he found Caroline abusing Elizabeth in the strongest language she dared use. "How very ill Eliza Bennet looks this morning, Mr. Darcy! I never in my life saw anyone so much altered as she is since the winter. She is grown so brown and coarse Louisa and I were agreeing that we should not have known her again."

She clearly expected some kind of response from him, some token agreement perhaps. It was foolish on her part, he reasoned, for she obviously was driven to speak thus because she had seen his regard for Elizabeth had not faltered. *Why then does she expect me to join in her censure?*

He could not leave the sentence hanging, however, and he said, "I perceived no other alteration than her being rather tanned, and that is no miraculous consequence of traveling in the summer."

Miss Bingley flushed beneath her own tan, but she was not quieted. "For my own part, I must confess that I never could see any beauty in her. Her face is too thin; her complexion has no brilliancy; and her features are not at all handsome."

Mrs. Hurst tried to catch her sister's eye, but either Miss Bingley did not notice or did not care to be stopped, for she tilted her head slightly and continued with her litany of Elizabeth's perceived flaws. "Her nose wants character; there is nothing marked in its lines. Her teeth are tolerable, but not out of the common way; and as for her eyes, which have sometimes been called so fine, I never could perceive anything extraordinary in them. They have a sharp, shrewish look, which I do not like at all; and in her air altogether, there is a self-sufficiency without fashion which is intolerable."

Darcy had maintained his composure as well as he could, but these sly remarks on Elizabeth's *fine eyes* raised his ire past what he could conceal. He had long regretted making that comment within Miss Bingley's earshot; he was beyond tired of hearing her bandy it about.

She was not done, however. "I remember, when we first knew her in Hertfordshire, how amazed we all were to find that she was a reputed beauty; and I particularly recollect your saying one night, after they had been dining at Netherfield, '*She* a beauty! I should as soon call her mother a wit!' But afterwards she seemed to improve on you, and I believe you thought her rather pretty at one time."

This was the outside of enough. He could bear Miss

Bingley's mockery of his good opinion of Elizabeth with fortitude. But to hear his mistaken first impressions displayed before his sister, who was now looking at him with mild reproach, infuriated him.

"Yes, but *that* was only when I first knew her, for it is many months since I have considered her as one of the handsomest women of my acquaintance."

Miss Bingley snapped her mouth shut, and Darcy stood and bowed with severe formality. The gentlemen were still fishing at the river, and he felt quite sure that they would be better company than Caroline Bingley.

Agitated as he was on quitting the room, he could not help but realize he had just made his feelings abundantly clear, and it struck him that perhaps it was time he made his intentions likewise clear to Elizabeth.

Nothing stopped him from declaring himself but an uncertainty of her own heart. That she had softened toward him was obvious. He recalled, with gratitude and pride, her manner in quelling Miss Bingley's inappropriate reference to Wickham. Clearly she no longer held Wickham in any esteem. But had she transferred that regard to him? He could not say, and after his disastrous proposal in Kent, he was unwilling to venture a guess.

He resolved, therefore, to return their visit with one of his own on the morrow. The company of Mr. and Mrs. Gardiner he had found enjoyable, and any time spent with Elizabeth was greatly to be desired. During this interview he would attempt to gain, by some measure, a sense of her opinion of him. If it had indeed improved, he would, in the manner befitting her station, ask her uncle for permission to court her.

He blushed when he thought of the impropriety of his addresses toward her in Kent. Not only had his words been insulting, the very manner of address had been indecorous. He had not sought permission from anyone, for he had not believed his attention would be anything less than desirable to the interested parties. He would not make that mistake again.

And if he found Elizabeth alone? He remembered their private conversation in the Hunsford parsonage and shifted uneasily. He had thought then that he had gained a suitable understanding of her wishes, and he had been wrong. However, in this setting he thought it unlikely, and he had some certainty of her approbation to at least assure him she would not be adverse with sharing a few words with him in private. From there… well, fate had brought her as far as Derbyshire. Surely fate could do a little more for him.

Chapter Thirty

DARCY WAS ALREADY awake when the sunlight crept through the closed curtains into his bedchamber. The similarity of this day to the one in April did not escape him, and the lingering fear that Elizabeth might once more repudiate him checked his impulse to ride to Lambton at first light.

That caution could not curtail his wildly tumbling thoughts, however. Darcy looked out at the grounds, lit as they now were by the early morning light. "I might yet bring Elizabeth here as my wife," he murmured. He let the curtain fall and rang for Vincent.

His valet turned him out in short order, and Darcy went downstairs. He was glad to find the breakfast room empty; he wanted no company on this visit to Lambton, nor the questions that might attend such a request for solitude.

He tapped his fingers against the side of his coffee cup, his eyes never leaving the clock. When at last it read eleven o'clock, he could wait no longer. He went to the stables and saddled his own horse, over the protests of the stable hand.

The ride to Lambton proved little enough time to calm Darcy's mind. What kind of fool was he to once again declare himself to the woman who had once refused him—and in terms so violent they still left a mark in his heart? He checked the reins and the horse pulled back, confused. Darcy glanced over his shoulder at Pemberley. "What purpose can there be for such an interview?"

He turned around, but then he remembered Elizabeth's smiles in the last few days—sweet, genuine smiles that were so much more inviting than any he had ever seen from her before. His pulse raced and he knew, foolish though it might be, that he could not let her leave Derbyshire without making one more attempt to win her heart.

The serving maid at the inn met him with a slight smile, and he knew it was not only the members of his own party who had gathered his feelings toward Miss Bennet. Not even this lack of privacy could squelch his excitement, and he returned her smile with one of his own before he took the stairs.

At the top of the stairs, a door swung open and Elizabeth burst out of their private rooms. Her cheeks were pale, and he thought he spied unshed tears in her eyes. In her hand she clutched a letter, but before he could ask her what was the cause of her distress, she exclaimed, "I beg your pardon, but I must leave you. I must find Mr. Gardiner this morning, on business that cannot be delayed; I have not a moment to lose."

"Good God! What is the matter?" Darcy took a breath and collected the emotions roiling inside him at the sight of her obvious agitation and said, "I will not detain you a minute, but let me, or let the servant, go after Mr. and Mrs. Gardiner. You are not well enough; you cannot go yourself."

Elizabeth took another step forward and he detected a tremor in her step. She put a hand on the doorframe, and just when he would have insisted she sit down, she pressed the letter to her heart and drew a shaky breath. "John!" A manservant appeared at the foot of the stairs. "Please fetch my aunt and uncle for me – they are walking in the village. Go, and do not tarry a single moment!" she commanded, and the catch in her voice made Darcy's heart ache. The man nodded and dashed off.

Elizabeth moved back into the parlor and sat down, and though propriety would have ordered Darcy to leave her alone, her pale features and watery eyes made it impossible for him to do so. He sat down in the chair beside her, and nothing but a doubt of her feelings kept him from taking her hand in his.

"Let me call your maid," he offered, desperate to be of some use. "Is there nothing you could take, to give you present relief? A glass of wine; shall I get you one? You are very ill."

She swallowed hard, and he could see the effort with which she held back tears. "No, I thank you," she replied. "There is nothing the matter with me. I am quite well; I am only distressed by some dreadful news which I just received from Longbourn."

The tears flowed freely then, and Darcy waited with impatient concern for her to collect herself. She wiped her eyes, but to no avail; tears still streamed from them and it was many moments before she was able to speak at all.

Finally, she said, "I have just had a letter from Jane, with such dreadful news. It cannot be concealed from anyone. My youngest sister has left all her friends—has eloped; has thrown herself into the power of—of Mr. Wickham. They are gone off together from Brighton. You know him too well to doubt the rest. She has no money, no connections, nothing that can tempt him to —she is lost forever."

Darcy sat in stunned silence while she dabbed at her eyes once more. *Has Wickham not caused enough mischief in my life? Would that Richard had dispatched him earlier!*

Her next words fixed his recriminations back on his own person. "When I consider that *I* might have prevented it! *I* who knew what he was. Had I but explained some part of it only—some part of what I learnt—to my own family! Had his character been known, this could not have happened. But it is all, all too late now."

But was it your place to share that story? Darcy wondered, his concern for Elizabeth shifting to self-reproach. *Should not that task fall to the one who had long been witness to his depravities? Why did I remain silent, rather than let the whole world know what he is?*

His guilt drove him to speak more forcefully than he usually would have. "I am grieved indeed; grieved—shocked. But is it certain, absolutely certain?"

"Oh yes! They left Brighton together on Sunday night, and were traced almost to London, but not beyond; they are certainly not gone to Scotland."

Darcy's mind whirled. There still remained a chance of recovering Lydia. If she could be found and brought home before news of this indiscretion was known to the general public, there would not be a very great scandal. Elizabeth and Jane especially would be free of the reproach which now threatened their own characters.

To this end, he asked, "And what has been done, what has been attempted, to recover her?"

Elizabeth clenched her handkerchief in her hand. "My father is gone to London, and Jane has written to beg my uncle's immediate assistance, and we shall be off, I hope, in half an hour. But nothing can be done; I know very well that nothing can be done. How is such a man to be worked on? How are they even to be discovered? I have not the smallest hope. It is every way horrible!"

With every word from Elizabeth's mouth, Darcy's

own path became clearer. He knew how to discover Wickham, and he had the means of working on him. Any guilt which was not Wickham's belonged to him. It was his fault that none knew the truth of Wickham's character. Elizabeth had only kept it secret on his behalf.

Elizabeth, however, was not done, and her next words drove his sense of responsibility higher. "When my eyes were opened to his real character... Oh, had I known what I ought, what I dared, to do! But I knew not–I was afraid of doing too much. Wretched, wretched mistake!"

Darcy's heart beat with tender, ardent affection. Though she regretted her silence now that her own sister's honor was at stake, he admired her integrity— her willingness to keep Georgiana's name unsullied. He respected her no less for wishing that the same could be said of Lydia.

Darcy knew if he stayed by Elizabeth any longer, he would not be able to keep himself from reaching out to comfort her. He tapped his hand against his leg as he paced the room.

Where would Wickham go in London? To one of his friends from University? Darcy's lips curled in a sneer. *No, he owes them too much money. Mrs. Younge then—yes, he will be looking for a place to stay.* He thought back to his own business with Mrs. Younge and soon realized he had her address, or the very least, the one she had given him as a forwarding address.

Darcy turned back to Elizabeth, and he saw to his chagrin that she had her face buried in her handkerchief and was crying once more. The impropriety of his being there finally struck him and he said, "I am afraid you have been long desiring my absence, nor have I anything to plead my excuse of my stay, but real, though unavailing, concern. Would to

Heaven that anything could be either said or done on my part that might offer consolation to such distress!" He held her gaze, hoping she might see the sincerity in his eyes, the depth of that honest concern. "But I will not torment you with vain wishes, which may seem purposely to ask for your thanks. This unfortunate affair will, I fear, prevent my sister's having the pleasure of seeing you at Pemberley today."

Elizabeth swallowed and attempted a smile, but it faded after only a second. "Oh, yes. Be so kind as to apologize for us to Miss Darcy. Say that urgent business calls us home immediately. Conceal the unhappy truth as long as it is possible. I know it cannot be long."

More than ever, Darcy wished they had a formal agreement, that he might offer some more personal comfort. Words seemed paltry in the face of such acute misery, but they were all he had.

"I assure you, Miss Elizabeth, you may depend upon my discretion." She smiled a little, but it did not reach her eyes. "I am very sorry your visit to Derbyshire should end on such a note; indeed, sorry that such an event has come to pass at all. I hope for the sake of all your family that this entire affair may be resolved reasonably well."

He bowed, and she inclined her head. "Please pass along my compliments to your aunt and uncle. I have greatly enjoyed getting to know them."

Darcy was not, by nature, a neck-or-nothing rider—in fact, he despised men capable of that kind of disregard for an animal's well-being. But when he arrived at Pemberley stables that afternoon, his horse was covered in a thick lather of sweat. "Walk him around the grounds until he cools off, and then rub him down well. Oh, and give him an extra helping of oats this evening," he ordered the surprised stable hand.

His anxieties spent, his mind was clear to focus on the recurring problem of George Wickham. He knew where he would find him, knew how to sway the man to do his bidding, but the one thing he had not yet arranged to his liking was his own departure from Pemberley.

He gazed at the house from the end of the drive and abruptly turned off to one of the footpaths. "What excuse can I concoct which my guests will accept?" He walked up the steep incline to a bluff overlooking the Derwent. It was one of his favorite places, one he had wanted to show Elizabeth someday.

He realized a moment later that Elizabeth herself had provided the solution to this problem. *"Tell her that urgent business calls us home…"*

"Very well. It is an excuse I can tell for myself. What is more, I can easily disguise the nature of Elizabeth's departure if I cover it with my own haste."

Darcy walked back to the house and found the whole company waiting for him in the drawing room. "Mr. Darcy!" exclaimed Caroline Bingley. "We had quite despaired of your ever joining us. Surely a round of country calls does not take the whole day."

"I beg your pardon, Miss Bingley. I was not aware I had pledged myself to any engagement at home." The words were too pointed for the meaning to be missed —Miss Bingley flushed bright red and her eyes sparked with anger.

Darcy ignored her reaction and continued. "As it happens, I have been called to town on a matter of some urgency, and rode to Lambton to inform Miss Bennet and the Gardiners that I would not be at home to receive them for dinner tonight."

He despised the quick flash of triumph he saw in her eyes. "You are, of course, all welcome to stay. I hope my business will be finished within a week, and then I will be able to rejoin you."

Before the rest of the party could react or ask any further questions, Darcy turned to his sister then. "Georgiana? May I speak with you in my study?"

His sister obediently followed him down the hall, and he shut the door behind them. Once they were private, he led her over to the small couch by the window. To everyone else, he would not breathe a word of Lydia's disgrace, but he would not lie to Georgiana—not when the subject was George Wickham.

"Fitzwilliam?"

"I am afraid I have some rather unsettling news, my dear—news which we must keep to ourselves."

Her blue eyes filled with concern. "What is it? What is wrong?"

"One of Elizabeth's sisters—a girl just your age—has eloped with Mr. Wickham."

Her cheeks paled and she sank onto the settee. "Oh no, not him!"

"Indeed. They left together from Brighton on Sunday. She just had news of it this morning, and they are traveling back to Longbourn so Mr. Gardiner can assist Mr. Bennet in tracking them down."

Georgiana placed her head in her hands. "Oh, that poor girl!"

Darcy bit his tongue—it would be no good to share his own opinion of Lydia Bennet. Though not usually wise in the ways of women, he was smart enough to realize that if he laid censure on that girl's head, Georgiana would take it to heart.

"That is why I am leaving. I have hope that I may be able to find where Wickham went when they might not."

She sat up, a look of determination in her eyes, and

Darcy had never been prouder of her. "What would you like me to do, Brother?"

"Stay here. Entertain our guests; keep the true nature of my absence from them. I depend upon you for this, Georgiana."

Darcy was surprised when she bit her lip and looked down—the action did not fit with the courage she had just displayed. He knelt in front of her and tilted her chin up so he could look her in the eye. "What is it, dearest?" he asked.

"Fitzwilliam… If I, that is, if you had not…" She sighed, then straightened her shoulders. "Would you have come after me in this manner?"

Darcy pulled her close and pressed a kiss to her forehead. "In an instant," he promised, his voice thick. He felt the tension ease out of her body, and he pulled back to look her in the eye. "Is this what has troubled you, Georgiana? Did you think I would leave my sister in the clutches of such a man, knowing what misery he would bring upon you?"

Her smile was sheepish, but happy. "It was my own folly which led me to him."

"Never," Darcy denied. "His avarice and desire for revenge led him to you. Now, I trust we finally understand one another?" Georgiana nodded. "Good. Then I will see you after I return from London."

Chapter Thirty-one

DARCY HAD NEVER been so glad he kept horses at the posting inns along the London Road. Fresh horses gave him extra speed to reach London before nightfall the next day—at least two days ahead of when Mr. Gardiner could be expected in town.

"Good evening, Remington," he said to his surprised butler as he rushed through the door of his London townhouse. "I apologize for showing up unannounced —there was no time to send word. I will be here but a week, and I am quite alone. You need not open up all the rooms. The breakfast room only, I think, and my study of course."

"Yes, Mr. Darcy."

Darcy heard the bustle of servants below as he climbed the stairs toward the master suite, and he felt a pang of remorse for the maids who would lose sleep so the house would be ready when he rose the next morning. "Remington," he called over his shoulder, "they need not do the work tonight. I can take breakfast on a tray in the morning. It is late—let us rest for the night."

"Very well, Mr. Darcy."

The ever-efficient Vincent had already unpacked Darcy's valise and laid out his nightshirt and dressing gown. "Will you be needing anything else, sir?"

"Just a word, Vincent," Darcy said. "You are no doubt wondering why I brought you with me on such a short trip. After all, ordinarily I would simply let one of the senior footmen handle my toilet, if I planned to be back in Pemberley in less than a week."

"I did wonder, but you never do anything without a reason, Mr. Darcy."

Darcy laughed. "How well you know me, Vincent. I have come to London in search of George Wickham. I needed somebody with me who could readily identify him, but whom he might not know as easily." He gazed steadily at his valet. "Will you help me?"

Vincent nodded. "Of course, Mr. Darcy."

"Thank you. I shall need to start quite early in the morning, so if you will see that a breakfast tray is ready for me at six o'clock, and then come and dress me at seven, that would be sufficient."

"As you please, sir. Good night, Mr. Darcy."

"Good night, Vincent."

After two days of travel, six o'clock came quickly, even for an early riser like Darcy. By the time Vincent came in at seven, however, he was fully awake and ready to start the business of the day.

After they were seated in the coach, Vincent looked over at him. "Have you any idea where we might find Mr. Wickham, sir?"

Darcy nodded. "I have a clue, however slight it might be. We are going now to the address Mrs. Younge gave when she left us. I doubt she is still there, but they will have a forwarding address."

As they approached the City, traffic thickened with London's financiers on their way to work. Their own progress slowed to a crawl until they crossed Blackfriars Bridge. Once over the Thames, they were able to pick up the pace, and it only took them another ten minutes to reach their destination.

When he saw the house, Darcy almost doubted they had the correct address. He had pictured Mrs. Younge in a dilapidated house, but there was no sagging roof or peeling paint here. *You forget,* he told himself, *that she once appeared quite respectable to your eyes.*

"Shall I come with you, sir?" Vincent asked.

Darcy glanced at the house and shook his head. "I would rather you stay out of sight. You are unknown to Mrs. Younge, and I prefer it remain that way."

Vincent nodded, and Darcy exited the carriage and took the steps to the door. A footman answered his knock, and Darcy gave his card. "Would you please tell the proprietress of this establishment that Mr. Fitzwilliam Darcy of Pemberley in Derbyshire has come to call on her?"

The man allowed Darcy into the foyer and went in search of his mistress. Less than five minutes later, Darcy stood in front of a tired looking middle-aged woman. "I am Mrs. Davies. How may I be of service, Mr. Darcy?"

"I apologize for bothering you, Mrs. Davies. I am looking for a woman who was formerly in my employ —Mrs. Younge. I just learned we have more matters of business to conclude."

"Mrs. Younge..." She frowned and was silent so long Darcy feared she could not recall Mrs. Younge at all. At last, she said, "Oh yes, she stayed with me about a year ago, is that right?"

"That is near the time I last spoke with her, yes."

"She is not here any longer, I am afraid. She only stayed about a month, then she started a boarding house of her own."

Darcy smiled politely. "Would you happen to have a forwarding address?"

"I believe I do somewhere, though it has been months since I have needed it. Wait here, I will see if I can find it."

She hurried out of the room, and Darcy tapped his foot nervously. *If she has lost Mrs. Younge's address…*

She had not. A minute later, she returned, with a triumphant smile. "Ah, I knew I still had it. She is located on Edward Street."

Darcy stood and bowed. "Thank you, madam. You have been most helpful."

"Harry will see you to the door, Mr. Darcy. I am glad I had the information you required."

Once Darcy was in the carriage, he let out a soft huff of air. "Mr. Darcy?" Vincent asked. "Did you find her?"

"I did. Take us to Edward Street, Broderick," he called out to the coachman, and they set off.

Darcy shook his head. Edward Street, in the heart of the City. *Could Miss Lydia be that close to her uncle's house, hidden in plain sight?* He had expected a seedier neighborhood, here in Southwark perhaps, or even in Lambeth. *But we may not find our fugitives with Mrs. Younge,* he reminded himself.

Mrs. Younge's boarding house was as respectable looking as any other building on Edward Street, but this no longer amazed Darcy. *After all, this whole affair hinges on the ability of the unscrupulous to appear creditable, does it not?*

"Mr. Darcy?"

Darcy looked at the neat brick townhouse and then back at Vincent. "First let me see if I can learn anything from Mrs. Younge. If not, I will explain your task, Vincent."

"Yes, sir."

Darcy walked up the front stairs and rapped on the door three times. A servant opened the door slightly and said, "Who be there?"

Darcy blinked. *It seems the manners of the mistress have been passed on to the servants.*

"You will tell the lady of the house that Fitzwilliam Darcy desires to speak with her."

The man looked him up and down and said, "Wait here."

Darcy had never suffered the indignation of being left to wait on a front step before, and he liked it little more than he had imagined he would. Luckily, the servant came back with an alacrity that was more admirable than the rest of his manners. "Mrs. Younge is not at home."

Darcy raised an eyebrow at the obvious lie. "Very well. I shall have to return another time."

"She don't intend to see you ever."

"I am sure she does not." Darcy nodded his head slightly and went back to his carriage.

"Drive down the street and then pull over," Darcy ordered Broderick.

Vincent looked at him expectantly. "Yes, Vincent, now we come to the part you are to play. Mrs. Younge would not even receive me, which tells me she has seen Wickham since his arrival in town. I wish you to make inquiries of anyone leaving the house and see if he remains here, or if he has moved on."

"Very well, Mr. Darcy."

Darcy handed him a pocket full of money. "Here is enough coin to hire a hack home at the end of the day, and to buy yourself a meal while you wait. As soon as you have a definitive answer, come back to Grosvenor Square."

"Yes, sir." Vincent stepped out of the carriage and soon disappeared into the melee.

"Take me home, Broderick," Darcy called out, and the carriage started back down the street.

The staff of Darcy House had never seen the master so agitated. He entered the house at a slight run and retreated immediately to his study, pausing only to order that Vincent be brought to him as soon as he returned. His coat and hat were tossed on a chair in the foyer and the study door shut before any of them had time to so much as acknowledge his command.

Darcy did not even attempt to do any business, though there were papers sitting on his desk that he needed to read. He knew the limits of his attention, knew he could not focus until he heard news of Wickham.

Do you not think Mr. Bennet is in the same agony of suspense? his conscience whispered. *Is it your right to deny a father any news of his daughter? Would you be happy if the positions were reversed and it was Georgiana who was lost?*

But thoughts of Georgiana only strengthened his resolve. If he had made Wickham's true character known to the general assembly at Meryton, this could not have happened. *"I, who knew what he was..."* Elizabeth's guilt-stricken words kept him firmly on course. He would discover the fugitives; he would right this wrong—for her sake.

Darcy knew not how much time had passed before someone knocked on the door. "Enter!" Vincent walked inside with a smile on his face. "Yes?"

"Mr. Wickham was there earlier this week, Mr. Darcy. He sought a room, but the house is full."

Darcy bounded up from his chair in anticipation. "You heard this from someone who saw him?"

"I did. The man even knew Wickham's name."

Darcy smiled at last. "I had not dared hope for such luck. I will return to Mrs. Younge tomorrow and confront her with this bit of truth. Thank you, Vincent."

The same servant answered the door the next morning when Darcy arrived, but this time he anticipated the man's rudeness. When the door opened, he did not wait to be acknowledged but pushed his way past the servant into the foyer.

"Here now! You can't go pushing your way into other people's homes!"

"I am afraid it is not polite to leave visitors waiting on the front step, even if they are to be denied. You may tell Mrs. Younge I am here."

The footman's beady eyes glared at Darcy beneath his bushy eyebrows. "I told you she wouldn't be seeing you."

"I do recall that, yes. However, you find I am here anyway."

Darcy removed his hat and gazed about the room, which seemed to annoy his adversary further. The man harrumphed out of the room and returned a few minutes later, a gleam of triumph in those same black eyes. "Like I said, she don't want to see you."

Darcy sighed. "Very well, I shall just have to remain here until she changes her mind." He took a seat on the divan in the foyer.

"You can't stay here!" the man blustered.

"Unless you plan to remove me yourself—which I do not recommend—I believe I can."

Darcy pulled out the morning paper he had brought with him and settled in to read. The servant glared at him for some time before he finally left the room.

Though he projected an image of calm indifference, Darcy's heart raced. He took a large risk by demanding to see Mrs. Younge in this way. If she chose to ignore him, he had no other cards to play. He was now convinced that the couple was not within the house. If they were present, Mrs. Younge would have received him, if only to keep him from accidentally discovering them. He had no leads, therefore, beyond whatever intelligence this woman could offer.

Several servants wandered through the room, and he knew they had been sent to see if he remained. He smiled coolly at all of them and then went back to reading his paper.

It was more than an hour later when the first footman returned. "Follow me."

Darcy folded his paper neatly and tucked it back under his arm. The footman led the way into a small sitting room located at the front of the house. Mrs. Younge stood by the windows, her thin lips set into a deep scowl.

"Mrs. Younge."

"Mr. Darcy, I must protest this invasion of my home."

Darcy allowed confusion to show on his features. "I was not aware I had mounted an invasion. I simply wish to speak with you."

She tossed her head and sniffed. "Now that you have, you may leave."

"I am afraid, madam, that I cannot. You see, I have business to conduct with you."

"Aye? And what might that be?"

"Has Mr. Wickham come to visit you lately?"

"And what if he has? He's a good man, a far sight better than yourself."

Darcy tilted his head and examined her flushed cheeks. *She knows something.* "I wish to know where he is."

She snorted. "If I knew, why would I tell you? I told ye before and I'll tell ye again—George Wickham is worth five Mr. Darcys. If not for you, he would have all the ready he deserved."

Darcy found it surprisingly easy to keep his temper in the face of her unfounded accusations. One thought of Elizabeth's tear-stained face was all it took to keep his resolve coolly in place.

"Ah yes, money. That always has been at the crux of the story. It is too bad that you do not know where

Wickham is. I was prepared to pay handsomely for such information."

Darcy laid his hand on the door, but Mrs. Younge called him back. "Exactly how much money would you be willing to give, assuming someone knew where he was?"

Darcy shrugged. "That does not really signify, since you do not know. Good day, madam." He left before she could say another word.

Chapter Thirty-two

THE NOTE ARRIVED the next morning before Darcy even finished his breakfast. He read the short message quickly and could not withhold a victorious smile.

> *Mr. Darcy, I may have the information you seek.*
> *Mrs. Younge*

Though his first instinct was to rush to the City, Darcy waited until past noon to set out. *The longer I wait, the more anxious she will become.*

Indeed, when he arrived at the now familiar boardinghouse just after two o'clock, the footman opened the door before he could even knock. "Mrs. Younge will see you in the drawing room, sir."

"Thank you." Darcy handed his hat to the footman and entered the drawing room.

Mrs. Younge was seated on the chintz divan when he entered the room. "Good afternoon, Mr. Darcy. Please, have a seat."

Darcy shook his head. "I prefer to stand, thank you."

Her nostrils pinched together and her fingers flexed around the edge of her seat, but a moment later she smiled. "Of course, if that is what you wish. Did you receive my notice this morning?"

"That is why I am here. I confess, it confused me. I

thought you said you did not know where Wickham was—in fact, you said you would not tell me even if you did."

"Well, as to that... perhaps..." She traced the brocade pattern of the upholstery with one finger. "You see, I cannot guarantee he went where I suggested; that is what I meant when I said I did not know his location."

"I see." Darcy kept his voice carefully neutral.

Mrs. Younge tilted her chin up. "If you are willing to pay, I may be willing to give you the address of the house I recommended."

"With no guarantee I would find Mr. Wickham within? I think not." *For as soon as you have my money in hand, you will certainly send Wickham a message, warning him to move.*

He tilted his head slightly and remained silent for long moment. When Mrs. Younge finally fidgeted, he shook his head. "No, I do not think that will do at all."

She crossed her arms and glared at him. "What do you want then?"

"Tell me where he is. If I find him within, I will come back and pay you the agreed upon amount. If I do not, then you have not actually given him up, and you will not have helped me at all."

"No pay if you don't find him?" Darcy held her gaze for a long moment and finally she nodded her head. "Very well. You've always been a sly one; I should have known you'd make it like that."

She stood and walked toward a writing desk, but stopped in the middle of the room. "Here now, we haven't discussed the subject of payment."

"Indeed we have not." Darcy observed her narrowly for a moment and then said, "If I find Wickham at the address you give, I will pay you one hundred pounds."

She laughed, as Darcy had known she would. "One

hundred pounds to betray a confidence? My loyalties are not so cheap. One thousand pounds."

"That is at least two years income—not even Wickham is worth that much. Two hundred."

"Five hundred and not a farthing less."

"Agreed. The address, madam."

Some minutes later she handed him a piece of paper. "They will be there, him and that girl of his. Nowhere else for them to go, is there?"

Darcy kept his face blank at the mention of Lydia, and Mrs. Younge sighed in disappointment. "Trust me, madam. If this is information is correct, you will shortly be a much richer woman."

The drive took him across the river to one of the poorer neighborhoods in Southwark. Darcy heard children crowding around the coach, awed by the sight of such finery. They pulled to a stop in front of a rickety, rundown building, and when he got out, the children fell back apace, daunted by his formidable demeanor. He took in their dirty faces and pinched expressions, and compassion overwhelmed him. He pulled a footman aside and said in a low voice, "See to it that each of these children is given a guinea." Then, without a backward glance, he rapped swiftly on the door.

The maid who answered the door was almost as dirty and unkempt as the children, and Darcy nearly took a step backward. "Yeah?"

Darcy was past being surprised by the rudeness of servants, and stated his business directly.. "I wish to call on Mr. Wickham, if he is available."

She snorted. "They're here. They never leave, do they? Hiding from someone, I wager." Her eyes narrowed. "They been hiding from you?"

"No, they have not." It was the truth—neither the gentleman nor the lady was aware that he was involved in the hunt.

She looked him over but finally decided he could be trusted. The door opened wider and Darcy stepped inside. The maid pointed down a dimly lit hallway. "They're the second door on the left."

Darcy stared after her retreating figure for a moment, then shook his head and went in the direction she indicated. He knocked at the door he presumed to be theirs. After a few seconds with no answer, he knocked again, more loudly.

This time, he was gratified to hear noise from inside and a voice mutter, "All right, just a minute." The door swung open and Darcy took advantage of Wickham's momentary amazement to slip inside the room. "Darcy! What in blazes…"

"Good afternoon, Wickham. I presume you can have no doubt what I am doing here."

The other man's face twisted into a snarl. "You do like to ruin my little elopement parties."

Darcy refused to allow the reference to Georgiana to rile his temper. "Be honest for once. Do you have any intention of marrying Lydia Bennet?"

Wickham pushed his greasy hair out of his face and laughed. "Good God, no. And if you can convince her of that, I would be in your debt. In truth, she wears on my nerves already."

"Why did you elope if you did not intend to marry her?"

He shrugged, and Darcy could see lines of exhaustion around his eyes. "Elopement was her idea, not mine. I… ah, I found it expedient to leave Brighton in rather a hurry, and as she wished to join me…"

He let the sentence dangle, and Darcy could easily fill in the blanks. Wickham had never been one to deny himself female companionship, even if it was under false pretenses.

That thought led him too close to Georgiana, and he knew he needed to get to his purpose, or he would not be able to hold his temper. "Would it be possible to speak with Miss Bennet?"

Wickham rose from his seat and went to the bedroom door. "Lydia, my love, we have company."

From his seat, he could easily see past Wickham into the room. Lydia Bennet lounged on the bed, twirling the ribbons of her bonnet between her fingers. Her vaguely dissatisfied expression gave way quickly to eagerness, and he wondered who she supposed he might be that would excite such warm feelings.

Darcy rose when she entered the room. "Lord! Mr. Darcy, what are you doing here?"

Wickham coughed. "Well, clearly you have some things to discuss. Lydia, love, I shan't be gone long."

The door shut behind him, and Darcy could not help but be slightly amused by his eager desire to have Miss Bennet talked out of this elopement. He bowed to her. "Good afternoon, Miss Bennet. I am here on behalf of your family—they are quite distraught to know your whereabouts."

She laughed. "What a joke it will be when they find out what I have been up to!"

He could not help but stare at her in disbelief. "Miss Bennet, it is not a joke to run away from the family in whose care you are in, nor to throw your entire household into frantic worry."

She brushed aside his concerns. "I am sure by now that Kitty has told them all about my love for dear Wickham and they are not the least bit concerned."

It did not surprise him in the least to learn that her sister was complicit in her scheme, at least in part. "On the contrary, they were all so upset that Jane felt she needed to pull Elizabeth away from her holiday in Derbyshire." He remembered again how distraught she had been and his features tightened into something like disapproval.

If Lydia saw it, she did not care. "La, how silly they all are! They all know how wonderful my dear Wickham is; they have nothing to worry about if I am with him."

"I am afraid they do. As your family, it is their place to worry about your reputation."

She wrinkled her nose. "My reputation! But we are to be married."

He shook his head slightly at her naiveté. "But you are not yet, and you have been living with him for over a week now."

"That does not signify. We will be married, and then this will all be a good joke."

Her selfish belief that she had managed to pull a prank on her family irritated Darcy to the extreme. He could not forget Elizabeth's tears or his own feelings when his own sister had narrowly avoided such a fate. *But if she is not to be reasoned with, there is only one thing left to be done: I must see that they marry.*

Wickham walked back in and looked at Darcy in query. Darcy shook his head slightly, and an ugly look flashed across Wickham's face, so that Darcy almost feared to leave Lydia alone with him.

A glance at his watch told him it would be past dinnertime when he arrived at Darcy House, so he stood and bowed. "Wickham, Miss Bennet, I am afraid I cannot stay any longer tonight. May I please visit with you again tomorrow?" he asked, hoping the promise of his return would keep the young lady safe from Wickham's anger.

Wickham rubbed at the crease in his forehead, and Lydia sighed. "Oh Lord, come if you want. It will be better than sitting around in these rooms with nothing to do all day, I daresay."

It was nearing dusk when Darcy stepped into his carriage and absently gave the order to return to Grosvenor Square. He paid no heed to the houses and buildings passing by the window; instead he focused all his thoughts on how he could finesse Wickham into marrying Lydia Bennet without being taken for all he was worth.

Chapter Thirty-three

THE NEXT MORNING Darcy dispatched a servant to Mrs. Younge's with a bank draft for the agreed upon amount and set off himself for Wickham's lodging. When he arrived, the couple was clearly just getting up from breakfast. Lydia was dressed, though barely, and Wickham had not yet taken the trouble to put a jacket on. A maid followed Darcy into the room to take the tea things, and he was mildly surprised the establishment offered that much service.

"Good morning," he said cordially.

"Darcy." Wickham looked at him and then at Lydia. "Darling, why don't you go down the hall and visit with the ladies you met the other day? I believe Darcy and I have some things to discuss."

Lydia pouted. "Why must a lady always leave the room? I have just as much right to hear what he has to say as you do—more, since he came from my family!"

Darcy shrugged. "It does not matter to me if you stay, Miss Bennet. However, I am afraid the conversation would be very tedious for you—matters of business which go back very far in our history." The two words "business" and "history" used together sealed it—Lydia was out of the room before he finished the sentence.

When she was gone, the two men sat down. "Well,

Darcy, have at it. Why have you truly come?"

Darcy studied his childhood friend for a moment before he answered. The last three years had not been kind to Wickham. His dissipated lifestyle had hardened his fine features, and he now appeared older than Darcy, rather than two years his junior.

Wickham squirmed beneath his keen gaze, and Darcy finally answered. "To see that Lydia has not been harmed."

"And you have seen that. Why did you return today?"

Darcy raised an eyebrow. "How can I tell her family that she is unharmed if she remains in your house, unmarried?"

Wickham laughed. "Your rigid morality does not apply to me, Darcy. Why should it matter to you if Lydia Bennet is ruined or not?"

Darcy leaned back in the chair, the picture of nonchalance. "Do you have anything to drink, Wickham?"

The other man grunted and rose from his seat. He came back a moment later with two glasses of brandy —very poor quality, Darcy supposed—and handed him one. "Now talk."

"Lydia Bennet is nothing to me, I assure you." That statement had the benefit of being wholly true. If she was not related to his Elizabeth, he would not give a tuppence for the foolish, headstrong girl. "However, something—my rigid morality, I suppose—balks at the idea of you ruining any girl, even one as ridiculous as her."

Wickham laughed. "You are a fool, Darcy."

"I may be, but I cannot help but be disturbed by the way you seduce young girls." Darcy twisted the glass around in his hands. He had not drunk much of it—his guess had been correct, the brandy was very poor. "It is a pity that Mr. Bennet does not have much he can offer a prospective suitor."

Wickham held up his hands and shook his head quickly. "Oh no, do not go there. I will not marry her, I told you that yesterday."

"Why not? She is a likeable enough girl."

"Oh yes, I daresay we would rub along together tolerably well. But you know my goal, Darcy—you saw through me well enough last year. I must marry a wealthy woman."

He rose from the table to refill his brandy glass after this pronouncement, which gave Darcy the chance to master the anger that crossed his face before Wickham turned back around. He nodded his head slightly, though he really wanted to slam his fist down the other man's throat for bringing up Georgiana so casually. "I am sure you do. That is why I lamented the Bennet estate."

"Only five thousand to be split between Mrs. Bennet and the girls. Not enough to tempt me, I can assure you."

Darcy winced at the unconscious echo of his own words regarding Elizabeth, but he did not lose sight of his goal. "But surely you do not expect to find someone as wealthy as my sister to marry. There are not many young ladies with thirty thousand pounds to their name; fewer still that you might have an introduction to."

Wickham took a long drink of his own brandy and rose to fill the glass. "That is true, I suppose. I do not need that much, my living is not so extravagant." Darcy nearly choked on his brandy. "I wager that... ten thousand would be enough to satisfy me."

"And how would you live? You cannot go back to the regiment now that you have tarnished the reputation of a young lady in the protection of your colonel, especially if you do not return married to her."

"I had rather thought I might go into the Regulars. Army life suits me, I've found."

Darcy could easily imagine that. Though most Army men were decent, upstanding fellows, the profession also drew a fair number of profligates. "How do you intend to purchase your colors?"

Wickham frowned. "Damn, I hadn't thought that far."

Knowing he had baited the hook well, Darcy rose. "Well, I see I cannot convince you to do the right thing, and I must be off. May I return one more time, just to check in on Miss Bennet? I did make a promise to her family after all..."

"Yes, of course." Wickham did not rise to see him out, and Darcy almost laughed at the morose expression on his face.

The next day when he arrived, Lydia was nowhere to be seen, as he had expected. "Good morning, Wickham."

"Morning, Darcy!" Wickham answered in tones far more jovial than had been used between them in many years.

He put on a false expression of surprise. "Why so glad to see me, Wickham? Is Miss Bennet about?"

Wickham faltered. "Ah... no. She stepped out again, but I daresay she'll be back shortly. You know, Darcy, as I think about it, she's not that bad a girl. Talks too much, of course, but what else can you expect from a woman?"

"Indeed."

"You know, if it wasn't for the financial concerns..." Wickham shuffled in place and then looked up at Darcy. "I mean, I'd do the thing right, of course I would."

This was not at all Darcy's impression of Wickham,

but he knew exactly what had brought about the change. "Would you?"

"Damn it, you know I would! She's... well, I've got to marry sometime; I might as well marry her."

Darcy coughed to hide his laughter. *He is playing right into my hands... Oh George, it is truly sad that you can be so easily led.* "That is very romantic of you."

Wickham cut off the comment with a wave of his hand. "Oh, you know what I mean."

"I daresay I do. But if you need to marry for money, then none of these sentiments toward Miss Bennet matter in the slightest. Her father can only provide the smallest token of a dowry; we discussed that yesterday."

Wickham tapped his fingers nervously on the table. "I do believe I have a solution to that as well, Darcy."

"And what might that be, pray tell? Do not tell me you intend to take up a profession, for I shall not believe it."

Wickham shook his head. "No, something much simpler. Here, let us sit down." He waited until they were both seated before he continued. "It occurs to me that you have taken a keen interest in our marriage. It seems the logical answer is for you to pay for it."

Darcy shook his head. "If I would not pay you to marry my sister, why do you think I would pay you to marry... Miss Bennet?"

He swore to himself. He had nearly slipped and said, "Marry Elizabeth's sister" instead—he had barely caught himself.

Wickham glowered at him. "It's your bloody morals that will answer if you do not."

Darcy snorted. "I daresay my conscience will not suffer if I allow the chit to have the reward she asks for."

Wickham gripped the edge of the table and leaned

forward. "Come, Darcy. You must know I need the money."

"That I can readily believe. I do not see why you expect me to provide it."

Wickham crossed his arms and pouted exactly like the petulant child he was. "Well, will you or won't you?"

Darcy leaned back. "I suppose that depends on how much it will cost me."

"I want a commission."

"Naturally." Though it went against Darcy's nature to provide a living for such a man, he would not leave Elizabeth's sister without an income.

"And the ten thousand I mentioned last night."

"Of course."

"And I want all my debts paid off."

Darcy blinked; this was not expected, though perhaps it should have been. "Do you have a list of those?" he asked after only a moment's hesitation.

"I can make one for you if you like."

Darcy nodded, and Wickham pulled out a piece of paper. After considerable thought, he handed Darcy the list, which was longer than even Darcy had thought it would be.

"Do we have an agreement then?"

"Ten thousand, plus a commission, plus the retirement of all your debt."

"Agreed."

Darcy rose and looked down at Wickham. "I did not believe you would ever do the right thing, George. I am glad to have been wrong for once."

Wickham stood up and shook his head. "You know as well as I that nothing but your money could convince me to marry that girl."

"I will share the news with her family," Darcy said after a long pause. "I believe they will want her to come stay with them for the duration of your engagement, but I will leave that up to them."

Wickham smiled sardonically. "Your rigid moral code again. What does it matter? She has been in my bed this last week."

Darcy frowned. "If you care for your financial security, you will not utter those words to anyone else."

The smug expression on Wickham's face made Darcy want to hit something, but he controlled his anger. "Very well, if you would have it be that way."

"And I need not tell you that if her uncle arrives this evening to find Lydia missing, you will never see another penny of Darcy money."

Wickham smiled at Darcy, some of his self-assuredness returning now that financial gain was at hand. "So we are clear then."

"I believe we are." Darcy eyed the man for a long moment and then held out his hand. "Though it goes against everything in me to do business with you, I am glad nonetheless that you could be persuaded to do the right thing—even if it was only for your own sake."

Wickham took his hand and shook it. "And I am glad you could be persuaded to support me, as has always been your duty. A pleasure doing business, Darcy."

Darcy rose from his seat, but before he reached the door, he turned back and gave Wickham a hard look. "There is one thing we have not discussed, Wickham."

"What is that, Darcy?"

"You will not receive a penny of this money, nor the benefit of your commission, until I see you married to Lydia Bennet. That will happen within the next two weeks by a special license I will provide. If you choose to decamp before the wedding, you will never gain another farthing from me. Do I make myself clear?"

A pettish, mulish expression crossed Wickham's

face, and Darcy knew he had been right to demand this condition. "I should have known you would have the last word," he muttered.

"Yes, you should have. Well, Wickham, what will it be—marriage to Lydia Bennet and comparative easy living, or poverty by yourself? And I warn you, if you choose the latter, I will ruin your good name so thoroughly that you will not be able to deceive any other young lady into taking you."

Wickham stared at him for a long moment and then nodded curtly. "Very well then. Buy the license, and we will meet with a clergyman."

"A wise choice. Felicitations on your upcoming marriage, George."

The gesture Wickham gave in reply left no doubt as to his true sentiments, but nonetheless Darcy was satisfied when he left the lodgings. Wickham valued his own livelihood too much to back out now.

Chapter Thirty-four

WITH THIS HAPPY news to report, Darcy finally felt comfortable informing Mr. Gardiner of his niece's location. "Gracechurch Street," he ordered Broderick, and then chuckled to himself. *It is lucky I heard Miss Bingley mention the Gardiner's address so often.*

Wickham's lodgings in Southwark were not four miles from the City, but they were leagues separated in fashion. The Gardiners' house was large and handsome, and Darcy felt another aspect of his pride fall by the wayside. He climbed the stairs and knocked on the door, which was opened by a liveried servant.

"Yes, sir?"

"Is Mr. Gardiner available?"

"No, sir—he and Mr. Bennet are out for the day."

Darcy wondered that he had not considered Lydia's father would still be in London. "I do not wish to disturb him while he has company. Tell me, will Mr. Bennet be long in town?"

"I believe he is to return home on the morrow."

"Very well. I shall call again then. Inform Mr. Gardiner that a gentleman came by on business and will inquire around tomorrow afternoon."

The next morning he went back to Gracechurch Street directly after breakfast. His card guaranteed him entrance into the house, and he was shown straightaway into Mr. Gardiner's study.

"Mr. Darcy, to what do I owe this honor? I take it you were the gentleman who called yesterday?"

"I am." Darcy took the seat indicated. "I am not unaware of the task that kept you from home yesterday, sir. Did your niece tell you I happened upon her shortly after she received Miss Bennet's letters?"

Mr. Gardiner's expression darkened. "Indeed she did. I understand you have had some unpleasant dealings of your own with Mr. Wickham. Though I do not know their nature, having spent the last week searching for the scoundrel, you have my full sympathies, Mr. Darcy. We had no idea of his true character."

"That is the point of my visit," Darcy cut in, glad of the segue. "Even while I was still with Miss Elizabeth, it rapidly became clear to me that this whole affair was partly my own fault, however indirectly." Mr. Gardiner opened his mouth to object, and Darcy held his hand up. "Had I made you aware of what Wickham really is, or had I given your niece leave to do so, this could never have happened."

Mr. Gardiner leaned back in his chair, a frown on his face. "You cannot have known he would behave so infamously."

Darcy shifted in his seat and his gaze dropped to the floor for an instant. He knew exactly how Wickham behaved when left alone with a vulnerable fifteen-year-old girl; he knew, and he had not taken steps to ensure that no other young lady would be treated as his sister had been.

"I assure you, I knew enough. But as I was saying, while I was still talking with Miss Elizabeth, I realized that I had a distinct advantage over yourself and Mr. Bennet. Neither of you knew where they might go on entering London. I still had the last forwarding address of a friend of his. I resolved to come to London and seek them out, and I have done so."

Mr. Gardiner leapt to his feet. "Am I to understand, sir, that you know where my niece and this blackguard have been concealing themselves?"

"I do."

"Then let us go at once." When Darcy did not move, Mr. Gardiner sat back down. "I do not understand. Is there any reason we cannot retrieve Lydia this instant?"

"May I be frank with you, sir?" Mr. Gardiner nodded. "Your niece has already been alone in his company for almost a week. Another few minutes will do no further harm, and the extra time will give me a chance to explain the arrangements I have made with Wickham."

"The arrangements you have made?"

Darcy nodded. "I will explain more fully in a minute, but first allow me to tell you how I found them." Mr. Gardiner nodded and settled back in his chair, and Darcy took a deep breath.

"It took me several days to discover them, and when I did, I easily learned he had never had any intention of marrying her. He found it expedient to leave Brighton, which I am sure you can understand, and when he told Lydia of his intentions, she insisted on going with him. She assumed his plan was then to go to Scotland, but he never promised anything of the kind."

Darcy pinched the bridge of his nose. "My first thought, I admit, was to find your niece and bring her home, hoping the matter could be hushed up well enough if she returned in good time. However, she would have none of it. She was content with his vague promises that they would eventually marry. When I pointed out the certain evils to her reputation, she brushed them off."

Mr. Gardiner sighed heavily. "Yes, that sounds like

Lydia. I am afraid my sister has spoiled her, as we are all liable to do with children who remind us too much of ourselves."

Darcy kept his own counsel on that point and moved on. "That discovered, I then determined that the only thing was for them to marry."

"Agreed."

"I know Wickham, however; the grudge between us is longstanding and bitter. If he suspected I had any true interest in the matter, there would be no way to accomplish the feat."

Mr. Gardiner smiled knowingly, but like the gentleman he was, he did not ask what Darcy's true interest was. "It took me two days to work around to it, but I finally was able to settle on exactly how much money it would take to convince him to marry Miss Lydia."

"Tell me the sum and I will have my solicitor draw up papers this afternoon."

"You do not take my meaning, sir. It is all arranged between us; I shall provide Miss Lydia's dowry. In addition, I shall buy his commission and take care of his debts, as well as provide one thousand pounds to settle on your niece."

"This is too much!" Mr. Gardiner cried. "Am I to accept such charity from a gentleman I hardly know?"

Darcy stood and used his imposing height to full advantage. "I assure you, sir, there is no arguing with me. As I said, this could not have happened if I had been more open regarding my dealings with Mr. Wickham. I am determined to take care of the matter myself."

"We will return to this point shortly, I assure you. Is there anything else you have arranged with the gentleman?"

"In addition to the funds already mentioned, they

will receive an amount to live on until his first paycheck arrives from the army. I will pay for the wedding, and I will be there myself to make sure he follows through. I do not need to tell you that he is not the most dependable of men."

"No, you most certainly do not. Ah, Lydia." Her uncle sighed and shook his head in resignation. "Could you not have chosen a better man to elope with?"

Darcy had to hide a smile at the sentiment. "As to their location, I will gladly give you the direction now. I am sure you and Mrs. Gardiner will want to bring Lydia into your house for the fortnight preceding the wedding. That will at least give the affair a veneer of respectability, however thin it might be."

"Indeed." Mr. Gardiner rose and shook Darcy's hand. "May I attempt once more to change your mind? If you will not allow me to pay for my niece's wedding, at least allow me to settle Wickham's debts in Brighton."

A frown furrowed Darcy's brow for a moment as he considered the request. *Perhaps I am once again being inconsiderate to the feelings of others,* he realized. *I cannot assume Mr. Gardiner is any more willing to sit idly by while others handle his affairs than I would be.*

"Very well," he agreed. "I will give you the complete list of his debts, both in Brighton and in Meryton, and allow you to divide the responsibility with Mr. Bennet as you see fit."

"Thank you, Mr. Darcy. When my brother hears how generous—"

"No!" Darcy exclaimed, then drew in his breath. "I apologize, Mr. Gardiner. However, I must insist you do not tell the Bennets of my involvement on any account."

Mr. Gardiner gaped at him. "Then what am I to say? They will never believe Wickham to be so easily tempted into matrimony."

"I leave that to you, sir, but I must remain anonymous." The thought of Elizabeth receiving him simply out of gratitude made Darcy ill. *I will have her love, or not at all.* "I go back to Pemberley on Monday. Perhaps we may visit my solicitor together that morning before I leave to finalize the arrangements."

"Yes, I believe that would be satisfactory. May Mrs. Gardiner and I have the pleasure of your company tomorrow afternoon for dinner?"

Darcy hesitated, and understanding his concern, Mr. Gardiner added, "You may be assured, Wickham will not be present. As to Lydia, I cannot promise…"

"Have Mrs. Gardiner send an invitation in the morning. If I have discharged all my responsibilities, I will gladly accept."

"I hope you may. Again, I thank you, Mr. Darcy, on behalf of our family. This is a debt we can never repay."

Darcy shook his head. "The debt was mine. Were it not for my… want of consideration, Wickham would never have been received by the neighborhood as he was. Though I cannot undo the wrong my reserve has caused, I can at least seek to temper it by whatever means in my power. I am only glad I was able to discover them."

"As am I. Until tomorrow I hope, Mr. Darcy," Mr. Gardiner said, and Darcy bowed and left.

Chapter Thirty-five

A LETTER ARRIVED for Darcy the next day, addressed in a fine, feminine hand.

Mr. Darcy,
Mr. Gardiner tells me we owe the restoration of our niece to your efforts. Please allow us to show our gratitude by way of dinner this evening.
M. Gardiner

Beneath it was a postscript, clearly added by Mr. Gardiner:

We retrieved Lydia last night. She is presently confined to her room until she learns to express some remorse over the upset she caused the family; this may last until the wedding.

The note from Mr. Gardiner ended Darcy's only concern with accepting the invitation, as was no doubt the intent. Though he enjoyed the company of Mr. and Mrs. Gardiner, he had no wish to spend any more time with Lydia Bennet. He quickly penned an acceptance and sent it back with the waiting porter, and then called for both Remington and Vincent.

The butler and the valet were before him in only a few short minutes. "Remington," he said, addressing the senior servant first, "I will be returning to Pemberley on the morrow. However, I will be back in town on Tuesday fortnight following."

"Very good; how long will your stay be, Mr. Darcy?"

"Quite brief: only a matter of days."

"Very well, sir."

Darcy nodded, and Remington bowed and left.

Darcy took a breath and turned to his valet. His business with this man was far less ordinary. "Vincent, you more than proved your worth on this trip. I wondered if there was any way I might compensate you for your help." Vincent's eyes widened, and Darcy smiled. "I do like to acknowledge extraordinary service, Vincent."

"Yes, Mr. Darcy."

The valet didn't say anything else, and finally Darcy prodded a bit. "Have you no aspirations, Vincent? Is there anything you have ever wished for?"

Vincent opened and shut his mouth a few times. "Ah, out with it, Vincent."

"If it would not inconvenience you in any way, sir, might I stay in London these two weeks?"

"A holiday of sorts? But your mother lives in Dorset, does she not? That is where the letters I frank for you are sent."

"Yes, sir, and I visit her every spring in the week you give me. But I have never been able to…" He shrugged.

"A holiday," Darcy repeated. "Very well. Your last task shall be dressing me tomorrow morn, and then I shall expect you to be waiting when I return to town in a fortnight."

"Thank you, Mr. Darcy."

"You are quite welcome, Vincent. As I said, the service you rendered was invaluable. Now, I expect you will want to begin packing for my return home."

Vincent bowed and left the room, and Darcy mused

over what he had said. The thought of rewarding Vincent for his help had only occurred to him when he had read Mr. Gardiner's postscript. It bothered him greatly that for her bad behavior, Miss Lydia was to be rewarded with the fulfillment of her dearest wish. Had it not been for Elizabeth...

And he had suddenly realized exactly how important it had been to his own future that Lydia and Wickham marry. A scandal involving the Bennet family would have been a very difficult obstacle to overcome. He would have married Elizabeth regardless, but the censure from his family would have been great, and the possible ramifications, even on their children, hard to accept.

Therefore, when Mr. Gardiner greeted him that evening with, "You must allow me to thank you once again, Mr. Darcy, for all you are doing for my niece," Darcy's answer was instantaneous and heartfelt.

"You must concern yourself over it no more, sir. I assure you, I could do no less."

Mr. Gardiner exchanged a look with his wife, and Darcy knew they both understood what he did not say. To her he said, "Mrs. Gardiner, I trust Mr. Gardiner has told you my one condition?"

"Indeed, Mr. Darcy, though I cannot imagine why you wish for such secrecy."

"I assure you, I have my reasons," he said. "May I trust that you will not divulge to your nieces the part I played in bringing this event to pass?"

She inclined her head in an elegant nod. "You may."

Dinner was a pleasant affair. As promised, Lydia was not seen at all. The Gardiners once again proved themselves to be more truly genteel than some of the members of the Ton, and when Darcy left their house, he satisfied himself that if he were to marry Elizabeth, not all of his new relations would be a burden.

The trip back to Pemberley was uneventful, and Thursday evening Darcy was able to share his after-dinner port with Bingley and Mr. Hurst. Hurst soon nodded off in the corner, and Darcy was able to turn the conversation toward more personal matters.

"I hope your sisters were not upset by my sudden departure?"

"Not at all!" Bingley assured him. "They understand that a gentleman occasionally has estate issues he must attend to." His face clouded. "In truth, your departure left them another opening to tease me about purchasing a home myself."

Darcy took a slow sip of port while he considered his next statement. "Bingley, would you like to return to Netherfield Park for the hunting season?"

Bingley nearly choked on his own wine. "Darcy, I thought you would be glad never to see Hertfordshire again."

Darcy winced. "I have lately learned that my own judgments of people are often hastily formed. Perhaps it is time I revisit the neighborhood."

Bingley raised an eyebrow. "You have lately learned?" he repeated. "I have tried to tell you that many times. May I ask whose advice you were more willing to listen to?"

Darcy waved him off. "That is no matter. Do you wish to return to Netherfield?" *For I will only know Miss Bennet's feelings for sure once I have observed her—without my own prejudices blinding me.*

Bingley hesitated. "If I return, there may be... That is..."

Darcy could easily read what he did not say—Bingley was yet uncertain of his own ability to act uninterested around Miss Bennet. The memory of Darcy's own recent encounter with Elizabeth flashed through his mind. He knew his feelings had been transparent enough for those who wished to see them.

"Your sisters are to go to Scarborough to visit your aunts, are they not?" Bingley nodded. "As a small hunting party, with no hostess, we would not be expected to entertain."

Bingley brightened. "Why, I had not thought of that! Darcy, you are a genius. Yes, let us go to Netherfield."

Darcy hid a smile. Bingley had forgotten one little fact, just as Darcy had hoped. As they were already acquainted with the neighborhood families, they could not escape the necessity of social calls. *You will have to see Jane Bennet at least once,* Darcy mused, *and if I know her mother, she will not let that call be our only visit.*

Bingley's announcement the following morning brought Darcy's party to an official end. Despite the fact that she had planned a holiday of her own, Miss Bingley complained that she should not be allowed to join them. "For you know you need a hostess, Charles."

But he was firm with her for once. "No, Caroline, I do not. It is to be a hunting party, with gentlemen only. There is no need for you to be there, as we will not be required to invite guests over."

Miss Bingley looked to Darcy for support, but he remained silent. She left the breakfast room in a huff, but some time later found him alone in the park. "Mr. Darcy, I confess I am rather confused as to your acquiescence regarding this hunting party. Did you not agree it was best Charles remains removed from… such society?"

"Your brother is his own man, Miss Bingley. He is able to make his own decisions. If he wishes to return to a property he has legally let, I cannot stop him. As to your other concern, I hope my presence will keep him from making further mistakes."

This half-truth pacified the lady, who smiled coyly at him. "You do look after Charles, rather as though you thought him to be your own brother." She placed a hand on his arm.

Her meaning could not have been clearer, and Darcy took a step away from her. "Friends are as important as family," he said. "As Bingley will never be my brother, the best I can do is treat him with the kindness of a friend." This subtle emphasis on *never* was not missed by the lady, and Darcy bowed and retreated before she could comment further.

The next day saw the departure of the Hursts' carriage for the North, and Darcy had never been so glad to get rid of any guest. "I suspect your sister will be unhappy with me for a time," he told Bingley that evening.

"I cannot imagine that."

"Yes, well, I found it necessary to disabuse her notion that I would one day propose."

Bingley stared at Darcy for a full minute, and then started laughing. "So that is what she meant!"

"I beg your pardon?"

"When she returned to the house yesterday afternoon, she muttered to herself about greener pastures and cutting her losses."

Darcy rolled his eyes. "I pity the northern men."

Bingley shrugged. "Oh, I would not say that. Perhaps their lack of patience for the subtle cat and mouse of relationships will free Caroline to find her honest streak. She may deal famously with them!"

"Enough of your sister, if you please," Darcy said, and Bingley laughed at his discomfort. "When do you return to London?" He had now been at Pemberley for a week, and the date of Wickham's wedding fast approached.

"I thought I might leave tomorrow, after a late breakfast."

"Excellent. I will only be a day behind you then."

"Does Georgiana not join you?" Bingley asked.

"No, she expressed a desire to stay at Pemberley."

In truth, Darcy had flatly refused to bring his sister into such proximity with Wickham, and when he had informed her of his reasons for keeping her at Pemberley, she had been most agreeable.

"Make him do the right thing, Fitzwilliam. Make sure Elizabeth's sister is the last young lady he ensnares with false promises."

Those words, fiercely spoken, still echoed in Darcy's head four days later when he stood up beside Wickham at his wedding. Though he knew these vows would not keep Wickham from dallying with other females, at least he would not be able to promise marriage to innocents.

After the ceremony, Mr. and Mrs. Wickham set off immediately for Hertfordshire, where her family expected them for a wedding visit. As Darcy watched them drive off in the carriage he had purchased for them, he could not help but feel that each had gotten exactly what they deserved: Lydia, an officer who would treat their vows just as flippantly as she treated every other decorous mode of behavior, and Wickham, a wife so thoroughly ridiculous that she could not be ignored.

Mr. Gardiner turned to Darcy when they were out of sight. "Well, that is over at any rate. I daresay they will be as happy as they deserve."

"I quite agree, sir."

"Were it not for Jane and Elizabeth, I would not have cared as much for Lydia, for she brought this all on her own head."

Darcy nodded. "Yes, but we could not let the more worthy Miss Bennets suffer the consequences of such a scandal, could we, sir?"

Mr. Gardiner shook his head. "Indeed we could not.

Mr. Darcy, you have been kind throughout this entire fiasco. Would you allow Mrs. Gardiner and myself the chance to thank you once more over dinner this afternoon?"

"I would be delighted, Mr. Gardiner." The gentlemen shook hands and retreated to their own carriages.

Chapter Thirty-six

THE HUNTING PARTY had now been in Hertfordshire for three full days, and no one had indicated an inclination to visit the local residents. Darcy had known Bingley would be reluctant, but now he found he was none too eager himself.

Surely I imagined the softening in Elizabeth's attitude toward me. How could she possibly forgive all the things I said about her and about her family?

Those words, *"had you behaved in a more gentlemanlike manner,"* cropped up once again, and he felt the full justice of their reproof.

But I may at least provide reparations for one of my faults, he reminded himself. *Is that not why I came in the first place?*

This reminder strengthened his resolve, and on the third morning at Netherfield he broached the subject with Bingley. "We have not yet paid any calls to our acquaintances in the neighborhood."

Bingley shifted in his seat. "Is that truly necessary? We are just here for the hunting; can we not remain secluded?"

Darcy shook his head. "Bingley, many in Meryton showed us kindness while we were here a year ago. We would be remiss if we did not repay their courtesy."

"Surely most of the gentlemen will come by for a

visit."

Darcy set his coffee cup down and leveled a stern glare at Bingley. "I almost think you are avoiding someone. That is most low spirited of you, Bingley." Bingley flushed, but did not speak. "Come. Let us visit the Bennets this afternoon."

"Shall I be teased into giving another ball, do you think?"

Darcy sobered. "As to that, have you heard the neighborhood gossip, Bingley?"

Bingley leaned back in his seat. "That Miss Lydia ran off from Brighton with Wickham and is now married? Yes, I did."

"It is partly for this reason I wish to call on the family. We must show the general neighborhood that the Bennets are not beyond respectable society."

This was the truth. Bingley had not heard, or had not comprehended, the malicious nature of the gossip. Everyone knew Lydia and Wickham had lived together prior to their marriage. It would only take one perceived snub to set the whole neighborhood against her family. No matter what transpired with Elizabeth, Darcy did not wish that for her or her sisters.

Bingley straightened and said, "My word, Darcy, are things as bad is that? Yes, of course we must visit."

Once the idea was in his mind, Bingley would not be stopped. He insisted they leave immediately after breakfast, though that was far from the fashionable hour for calls. They rode over, as the weather was fine, and were admitted without delay to Longbourn.

When Darcy entered the sitting room, he could not keep his eyes from seeking out Elizabeth. She sat by the window, and he watched for a minute as the sunlight cast shadows and highlights on her rich, dark hair.

Mrs. Bennet's voice soon drew his attention,

however. "Oh, Mr. Bingley, it is so good of you to visit us, and so soon after your return to Netherfield! I did hear that you had intended never to come back to Hertfordshire; I am glad to see that it was entirely false."

"Yes ma'am, I…"

"And Mr. Darcy. I am glad to see you as well."

"Mrs. Bennet." He bowed.

"My daughters, you see, are all here, except Lydia who is recently married. Jane, do stand up and greet our guests."

Miss Bennet had been sitting in the corner of the room, diligently plying her needle. At her mother's behest, she rose and offered a curtsy. "Good afternoon, gentlemen. It is good to see you after so long."

Her cheeks were rosy pink, and for the first time Darcy considered how her own reserve might be a means of shielding her emotions from her mother's perceptions. *For surely if Mrs. Bennet suspected her daughter of truly having affection for a gentleman, her effusions would be intolerable.*

His gaze traveled from the eldest sister to Elizabeth, and his heart sank when he saw her intent on her work, apparently unaffected by the proceedings. *Even Jane, known for her evenness of temper, shows more reaction.*

He dropped his eyes to the floor to hide his disappointment. *When we were at Pemberley together, she smiled and spoke to me with what I thought was at least a lack of ill will. Does she fear her openness might have led me to believe her feelings are greater than they truly are? Why does she not look at me?*

At last, he could bear her silence no longer, and he walked closer to where she sat. "Good day, Miss Elizabeth."

She looked up from her handwork at last. "Good day, Mr. Darcy."

"Have you heard lately from Mr. and Mrs. Gardiner?" he asked, and cursed himself the next instant. He had seen her aunt and uncle far more recently than she, and if she had heard from them, it would have been regarding Lydia. *That is one topic I should know well enough to steer clear of!*

Indeed, her expressive eyes questioned him, and after she answered in the affirmative, he remained silent.

A few minutes later, she spoke. "How is Miss Darcy?"

Darcy smiled. "She is very well. She bade me tell you that if you are ever in Derbyshire again, you must call on her."

He wondered when Elizabeth colored and looked down. "Thank Miss Darcy for me," she said quietly. "She is too kind."

Darcy would have pursued the subject further, but Mrs. Bennet's voice intruded just then. "It is a long time, Mr. Bingley, since you went away," she said after the tea had been brought in.

"Yes, indeed, it has been many months."

"I began to be afraid you would never come back again. People did say you meant to quit the place entirely at Michaelmas; but, however, I hope it is not true. A great many changes have happened in the neighborhood, since you went way. Miss Lucas is married and settled; and one of my own daughters."

She simpered and smirked at Bingley, and Darcy felt vaguely sick to his stomach at the performance. "I suppose you have heard of it; indeed, you must have seen it in the papers. It was in the *Times* and the *Courier*, I know; though it was not put in as it ought to be." She pursed her lips. "It was only said, 'Lately, George Wickham, Esq. to Miss Lydia Bennet,' without there being a syllable said of her father, or the place where she lived, or anything. It was my brother Gardiner's drawing up too, and I wonder how he came to make such an awkward business of it. Did you see it?"

Darcy could scarcely keep his tongue in the face of such a ridiculous ramble. Several snide remarks regarding the necessity of hushing up the marriage sprung to his mind, but a quick glance at Elizabeth showed him her mortification was great. He bit the corner of his lip to keep from responding and instead let Bingley, to whom the speech had been addressed, answer.

"I did, ma'am, congratulations," he said, all genuine joy. "Weddings are a fine thing indeed."

Though Bingley did not look at Jane Bennet when he said the last, Darcy knew where his mind went, and he kept his gaze focused on that lady. She blushed slightly, but no more than might be expected when faced with such a mother.

Mrs. Bennet was not satisfied to let the subject rest. "It is a delightful thing, to be sure, to have a daughter well married, but at the same time, Mr. Bingley, it is very hard to have her taken away from me."

Darcy barely controlled a snort. He had purposely chosen the regiment with the desire to keep Lydia and Wickham as far from himself as possible—if all his wishes came true and Elizabeth consented to marry him, he did not want to see Wickham every time they were obliged to visit Longbourn.

"They are gone down to Newcastle, a place quite northward, it seems, and there they are to stay I do not know how long. His regiment is there; for I suppose you have heard of his leaving the –shire, and of his being gone into the Regulars. Thank Heaven! He has *some* friends, though perhaps not as many as he deserves."

After the other indignities he had been subjected to in the short time they had been sitting there, this comment rolled off Darcy's back. That she referred to him was obvious, that she knew nothing of the true situation was equally so. *So the Gardiners have been true to their word—excellent.*

Thankfully, though, Elizabeth chose this moment to interject. "Do you know how long you plan to be in the country, Mr. Bingley?" she asked, and Darcy felt a pang of jealousy that she had not addressed him. *Fool!* he rebuked himself. *She wishes him to marry her sister; you have nothing to be jealous of.*

Bingley glanced over at Darcy, but he remained impassive. *He may get himself out of this one.*

"We will stay a few weeks at least," Bingley answered after a moment's hesitation.

"When you have killed all your own birds, Mr. Bingley, I beg you will come here, and shoot as many as you please on Mr. Bennet's manor." That absurd comment could come from no one but Mrs. Bennet. "I am sure he will be vastly happy to oblige you, and will save all the best of the covies for you."

Despite his own intentions, Darcy wondered why any man would choose to connect himself with such a family. Even if the sisters were all perfectly amiable—which was doubtful indeed—or the father truly intelligent and genial, what man would desire such a woman for a mother-in-law?

Mrs. Bennet spent the whole of the afternoon fawning over Bingley in a manner that would satisfy even the Prince Regent. There was not a consideration she did not extend, not a compliment she did not offer. Indeed, he was convinced that if Bingley had indicated a liking for the chair in which he sat, she would have insisted he take it with him back to Netherfield.

Again, it was Elizabeth who calmed his thoughts.

She kept her head bent over her work, but he could easily see the red flush in her cheeks. It reminded him of how he had felt when Lady Catherine interrogated her at Rosings, and he realized once again that she was not the only one in the world with relations to be ashamed of.

He bent himself back to his original object. Jane Bennet's feelings were not easy to discern, but he would not make the same mistake he had made the previous year and assume that if he could not see them at a glance, they must not exist. Bingley, he could easily see, felt the same regard he had in November. If anything, time had strengthened that bond.

Miss Bennet was quiet, but that could easily be because she was embarrassed. If she had loved Bingley before, seeing him again would be painful. Her mother's behavior would not make that any easier. Her smiles were just as sweet and unaffected, though, and he finally decided it would take more than one visit for him to know the truth.

The afternoon shadows lengthened, and Bingley rose. "I am afraid we must go. Thank you so much for your hospitality this afternoon."

"Oh, it was nothing! Nothing at all. Indeed, I was so glad to see you I... well. Now if only we could have you come and dine some evening soon. You are quite a visit in my debt, Mr. Bingley, for when you went to town last winter, you promised to take a family dinner with us, as soon as you returned. I have not forgot, you see; and I assure you, I was very much disappointed that you did not come back and keep your engagement."

"I... I apologize if my sudden departure overthrew any of your plans," Bingley stammered.

A light gleamed in Mrs. Bennet's eye, and Darcy knew exactly which plans Bingley's absence had upset.

"Bingley," he said, with rather more force than necessary, "do we not have plans for hunting before we lose the light?"

"Indeed we do!" Bingley answered, relief coloring his tone.

"Well then, we will let you return to Netherfield," Mrs. Bennet said, a trifle ungraciously. "However, you will soon receive an invitation from me, Mr. Bingley, depend upon it."

"I shall await it with pleasure, madam," he said, and the gentlemen were finally allowed to leave.

Chapter Thirty-seven

THE PROMISED INVITATION arrived the following morning, asking Darcy and Bingley to join the Bennet family for a small dinner party the next evening. "If others are to be there, it cannot be wholly for our benefit," Bingley said, and Darcy chose not to debate the point.

He, however, was quite sure the party was given only as a means for throwing Bingley and Miss Bennet together again. *Perhaps this will give me the necessary opportunity to observe her and see if she truly cares for Bingley,* Darcy thought as they handed their coats and hats to the Bennets' servant the next night.

Darcy paused momentarily when they entered the sitting room; though he had been prepared to see others, he had not expected Mrs. Bennet to have invited four families in addition to themselves. He glanced quickly about the room and saw none of the other ladies held a candle to either of the eldest Bennet girls, and he comprehended her motives. *By offering a contrast to her daughter's beauty, she thinks to draw Bingley in once more. Does she think Miss Bennet has nothing more to offer a gentleman than a pretty face?*

"Good evening, Mr. Bingley, Mr. Darcy," Mrs. Bennet said to them when they were both in the room. "Mr. Bingley, you may sit by me if you like."

Darcy was at first surprised that she did not once again thrust Jane at Bingley, but when his friend sat next to Miss Bennet after only a second's hesitation, Darcy applauded her cunning. *How better to convince Bingley to sit by her daughter than by offering herself as the only alternative?*

At that moment, Darcy became conscious of Elizabeth's attention on him. He looked at her and saw the smile on her face, and he readily discerned her thoughts. *Did I not prove myself better than that, Elizabeth?* he wondered with a mix of ire and shame. *Do you still believe me to be so set against your family?* He turned his attention to Bingley, who was likewise giving him a half-teasing look which he easily read to be part defiance and part fear.

Dear God, am I really so overbearing that they both believe me to control his actions? Perhaps there is more to what Elizabeth said on this count than I wished to believe.

He was now just as determined to discover Jane Bennet loved his friend, as he had earlier been to believe she did not. With such a positive frame of mind, it was not long before he was convinced of it. Bingley's demeanor during dinner showed him to be just as much in love with Jane as he ever had been, and in Jane's ready smiles he now saw the only form of encouragement the demure lady would ever give. That she smiled more readily and more sweetly at Bingley was plain to see, and he soon settled into the knowledge that if his friend married her, he would indeed have a loving wife.

Unfortunately, with that off his mind, he was free to think of other things. He had barely noticed when he sat down that he was seated next to their hostess, but now her inane chatter pierced through his mind. He looked around and realized that Elizabeth was seated on the far side of the table from him. *Did she ask not to be near me?*

Though he soon dismissed this as ridiculous, he could not keep his mind from his own concerns now that Bingley's were sorted, and he could acknowledge now that this had been part of his intent in coming to Hertfordshire. *If only I could make her love me....*

But first he must suffer through this meal with her mother. *Ah, Darcy, be careful. If you have your way, she will someday be your mother-in-law.* That thought in mind, he attempted to be pleasant, but it was not easy.

Her dislike of him was his one consolation. Though she was not quiet for more than thirty seconds at a time, to him she spoke but little, and when she did, it was always with the coldest civility—a welcome change from her usual volubility.

Far from minding her rude reception, Darcy relished the long moments of relative solitude in which to observe Elizabeth. He watched her, and she watched Bingley and her sister. Her dark eyes went from one to the other, and Darcy knew the minute she decided they might yet be happy. He detected the slight ease of tension in her shoulders that only one intimately familiar with her would have noticed, and a happy smile crossed her face.

Freed from that concern, Elizabeth now looked down the table toward Darcy. He barely managed to shift his own gaze in time, and he flushed at the realization that he had nearly been caught watching her. He kept his eyes firmly on his plate for the rest of the meal, though he greatly missed seeing her.

When the ladies withdrew, Darcy did not expect to have much to say to the other gentlemen, but he found the concerns of those in Hertfordshire were not so different from those in Derbyshire. Conversation turned to the harvest and land management, and though no one in the room owned an estate even half so large as Pemberley, the thoughts they shared he could easily relate to.

At last though, it was time to rejoin the ladies in the drawing room. When he entered, Darcy looked about anxiously for Elizabeth, though he tried to appear nonchalant. He easily found her standing next to the coffee table, and thought to join her. However, she was surrounded by a bevy of ladies, and he wondered again if she had not planned it so on purpose that she would not be left alone in conversation with him. Unwilling to intrude where he was not wanted, he passed by as if he had not wished to talk with her at all and joined some of the other gentlemen standing against the wall.

He could not stay away for long, however, and as soon as his coffee cup was empty he walked back to the table and asked her to refill it. She poured the coffee and said, "Is your sister at Pemberley still?"

Is there to be no conversation between us that does not revolve around my sister? "Yes, she will remain there till Christmas."

"And quite alone? Have her friends all left her?"

"Mrs. Annesley is with her. The others have gone on to Scarborough, these three weeks."

She smiled, but there was none of the invitation in her eyes that he had thought he'd seen at Pemberley. He paused for a long moment, but when she said nothing else, Darcy's hopes vanished. If her smile did not answer his question, her silence had. If she could not even hold five minutes' conversation with him, what chance was there that her feelings toward him had changed? He waited until one of the young ladies returned, and then he retreated.

What a fool I am, to think her opinion of me would have changed that much, he berated himself as he walked away. *A woman who has once been offended as I offended her... Can I expect her to now welcome my attentions? Did she not make her feelings plain to me on that occasion? Why should I believe them to be different now, merely because I wish it so?*

Darcy was quite eager to leave his downcast thoughts behind, so when Mrs. Bennet called for whist players, he readily agreed. He felt a momentary pang when Elizabeth was seated at a different table, but he was not sure he could bear the pain of being with her, seeing her, talking to her, if she did not care for him at all.

I will ignore her for the rest of the evening. This resolve Darcy could have easily followed if he had not been able to hear, over the sound of others, her voice. He would turn to see what she had said, or what she laughed at, and he would miss his turn of play and lay down the wrong card. The frustration in losing was outmatched by the pull of Elizabeth, and he was quite unable to keep himself from watching her.

By the time Darcy and Bingley left shortly before supper, he knew that even if she did not love him now, he must find a way to change that. This was yet another motive to bring Miss Bennet and Bingley together, for surely their marriage would put him frequently in Elizabeth's company.

The whole way home Bingley could not stop talking about Miss Bennet, and that reminded Darcy of one task remaining. That evening when they retired to the library with their brandy, he cleared his throat. "I have something I must confess, Bingley."

Bingley laughed. "This sounds serious." When Darcy did not laugh, he sobered. "Indeed, Darcy, what could you possibly need to confess to me?"

Darcy set his glass down and clasped his hands behind his back. "I am afraid I have abused your trust in a most unkind way."

"Come now, what is it?"

"Do you recall last winter when we left Netherfield?"

Bingley's smile dimmed. "Indeed I do, though I admit I would rather not."

"Yes, and it is that which I must confess. I knew when you left that you were quite in love with Miss Bennet, and I did not approve."

Bingley sat up straight. "Yes, you and my sister made that clear enough, but Darcy—"

"I am not through, Bingley. What you do not know —what we have never told you—is that she came to town last winter as well."

Darcy watched his friend assimilate that bit of information. Bingley blinked and said, "Jane Bennet was in London last winter?"

"Yes. She came to stay with her aunt and uncle. I believe Caroline called on her there."

"She was in town, and you did not tell me?" Some of the warmth left Bingley's blue eyes.

"I did not." Darcy drew a breath and offered the only explanation he could, paltry though it was. "I did not believe her to share your feelings, and I told myself I did not want you to suffer the pain of a broken heart."

Bingley stared at him without speaking for so long that Darcy shifted uncomfortably. "I cannot comprehend what might have given you the belief that you had the right to interfere in my life in that manner," he said finally.

Darcy winced at the uncharacteristic steel in Bingley's voice. "It was wrong of me, Bingley. It was done with your best wishes at heart, but I realize now that I undertook too much in the guise of protecting a friend from harm."

"Indeed you did! If I am to be hurt, it must be from my own cause and not because someone else has done it to me. By God, am I not a man, capable of making my own decisions?" Bingley slammed his glass down on the table between them and stood up.

Darcy bowed his head. "You are, and I apologize once more. I do have a penance to offer, if you will accept it."

"I cannot believe you have anything to say that will make this right. When I think how much Jane must have suffered, believing me to have toyed with her affections..." He paused and his eyes narrowed further. "And if my sisters visited her, she must have believed I knew she was in town and chose not to visit her myself! Indeed, she must think I no longer care for her at all."

"As I said, I kept you from her because I did not believe her feelings to be the equal of yours. Trust me, Bingley, you would not want to be in an unequal marriage." Darcy cleared his throat, and when the lump did not disappear, he took a sip of brandy. "However, I have observed her these last few days and I now believe I was mistaken."

Bingley, who had turned away, turned back fast. "What was that?"

"It is now my belief that Jane Bennet cares for you very much indeed, and if you were to declare yourself to her, you would be received quite warmly."

"Are you sure of this?"

The irony that he was being asked to vouchsafe for another's feelings when he had so misjudged Elizabeth's struck Darcy hard, but he nodded. "As sure as one can ever be of another's feelings," he qualified, unwilling to be held accountable should he be mistaken yet again.

"And what guarantee do I have that you will not continue to interfere in our affairs?"

"Only my sincere promise."

"Then if I were to propose to Jane Bennet while you are away next week…"

"I would think that a very wise course of action." Darcy looked away. "My pride led me astray, Bingley. Though I do believe you should think about what kind of family you marry into, that should not override the value of affection. What is marriage without love and affection, after all?"

Bingley rocked back on his heels, and Darcy saw with relief that some of the anger had left his eyes. "Well… I am not quite sure what to say. I am still upset with you, but if Jane accepts me, I believe I will find it in my heart to forgive you."

Darcy rose. "I hope she does, and not just for my own selfish gain. Now, I believe I should go to bed, as I have to be up early tomorrow morning to leave for London."

"Good night, Darcy. Despite my feelings tonight, I am glad you finally chose to tell me the truth."

From the door of the library, Darcy glanced over his shoulder and saw his friend staring into his still-full glass of brandy, a pensive frown on his face. *I wish you greater luck with your lady than I had with mine,* he thought and exited the room.

Chapter Thirty-eight

DARCY LEFT NETHERFIELD early the next morning with the intention of spending a week in town. His steward had forwarded a business proposal by a neighboring landowner to him. The gentleman wished to put a mill on the stream that formed the boundary between his property and Pemberley, and he asked if Darcy would make it a joint venture.

The business should have been conducted in short order. Everything was extremely straightforward; the gentleman in question was a trusted friend of Darcy's, and as the mill would not actually stop the flow of water downstream, there was no true downside to the scheme.

Darcy, however, could not focus. Every day out of Hertfordshire increased his restlessness—he had heard nothing from Bingley, and he would not feel sure of his welcome back at Netherfield until he knew his friend's engagement was accomplished.

The solicitor's patience with Darcy's lack of attention wore thin, until one day he actually ventured to suggest that Mr. Darcy might conclude his business with greater alacrity if he concentrated on the matter at hand, rather than on whatever else was occupying his thoughts. The rebuke was mild, but Darcy took it to heart and applied himself to reviewing the various papers and contracts attached to the mill.

Once the business was finalized, he had no reason to stay in London, and his agitation increased with every day that passed with no news from Hertfordshire. He had been in town for an additional three days when a knock at his study door pulled him from his book. "Come in."

A footman entered and cleared his throat before announcing, "Lady Catherine de Bourgh to see you, Mr. Darcy."

Darcy stifled a sigh. Lady Catherine was the last person he wished to see right now, but he could not ignore her. "She waits in the salon?" The footman nodded. "Very well. Inform her I shall wait upon her momentarily."

Darcy looked around at his solitude with no little regret, but he joined his aunt a moment later. "Lady Catherine, this is a surprise. What brings you to London?"

Lady Catherine's already thin lips were pressed together so tightly that they almost disappeared. She paced in front of the fireplace for a moment and then said, "Have you heard that your friend Bingley has proposed to Miss Jane Bennet?"

Relief shot through Darcy. "I had not heard confirmation, but I knew he intended to do so. She accepted him then; I am happy for them both."

She glared at him. "You do not mean to tell me that you approved this match?"

Darcy frowned. "It is not my place to approve or disapprove of the various connections Bingley wishes to form. He is his own man, Lady Catherine, and capable of making his own decisions."

She snorted. "I am afraid I do not see that your trust in his judgment has been rewarded. To marry into such a family, one that can do nothing but lower his standing in Society! True, he is only a few generations removed from trade and thus does not have the position you do, but even what little he has will be lost."

These were familiar words, and Darcy was heartily ashamed to hear his own former beliefs parroted back at him. *Is this what I sounded like to Elizabeth, so vain and unpleasant? How can she ever truly forgive me?*

He swallowed his own misery and spoke carefully. "Lady Catherine, you do not know Jane Bennet. She is a lady above reproach who can only increase the happiness in Bingley's life. She returns his regard and that is all that should matter to any of us."

Lady Catherine pounded her cane against the floor, a sneer curling her lips. "What does love have to do with marriage? Do you think I loved Sir Lewis, or that your mother loved your father? No! We married for position, for what the marriage might bring to our families and our own social standing."

Darcy's hand clenched at the mention of his mother, but he forced himself to relax. Lady Catherine had never understood or believed that Lady Anne actually had great affection for her husband. "That does not negate the fact that Bingley has made his own choice, whatever we might think of it. Now please, tell me what your reason was for coming all this way, for I cannot believe it was simply to inform me of my friend's engagement."

She tossed her head back, her eyes flashing. *She looks like an angry horse,* Darcy thought, and fought back an absurd desire to laugh. He sipped his tea and waited for his aunt to tell him the purpose of her visit.

"Indeed not! I am here to discuss a much nearer concern, though on the same subject—your own engagement."

All amusement was at an end; Darcy nearly choked

on his tea when she uttered those words. *My engagement? Surely she does not refer to Anne!*

Lady Catherine's next sentence did not illuminate the matter. "She would not give me the answers I wished for, so I came to you that I might hear them with my own ears."

A frown creased Darcy's brow. "Lady Catherine, I am afraid that I did not follow you. Perhaps it would be best if you started at the beginning. Of whom are you speaking?"

"Miss Elizabeth Bennet," Lady Catherine said, her upper lip curled into a sneer. "I have come to you directly from speaking with her, and I must say I left most displeased with the lady."

Elizabeth? Lady Catherine visited Elizabeth? "What took you to Hertfordshire?" Darcy asked, trying to calm his racing heart. "Did you bring a message to Miss Elizabeth from Mrs. Collins?"

Lady Catherine shook her head. "No, I came on business of my own."

Darcy raised a hand to his temple to massage away the headache he felt building behind his eyes. "What business could you possibly have with the Bennet family?"

Lady Catherine paced in front of the fireplace. "Surely you can understand my concern! I heard, on what I took as good authority, that you were to follow your friend to the altar—that not long after he married the elder Miss Bennet, you would wed her sister. In short, Mr. Collins told me that you, Fitzwilliam Darcy, had made an offer of marriage to Elizabeth Bennet."

Darcy started. *How did Mr. Collins know...* Then he realized the connection must have been assumed, since he was Bingley's closest friend and Elizabeth Jane's sister. *The rapidity with which truth is twisted into gossip shall never cease to amaze me.*

"Why did you drive to Longbourn?"

"To hear it contradicted!"

Darcy's stomach knotted, for Lady Catherine held the answer to the question he could not bring himself to ask. "And what did Miss Elizabeth tell you?"

"She thwarted me time and again. I asked her if you were engaged, and she refused to answer. I told her how our close relationship entitled me to know your concerns, and she said that did not entitle me to hers."

Darcy coughed to hide the laughter he could not contain. This sounded so very much like Elizabeth— and in truth, she echoed his sentiments. *Why does my aunt always assume she may impose on my life whenever she wishes?*

"Well, I finally managed to get an answer out of her, though I suspect that is merely because when faced with a direct question, even she would not lie."

Darcy slumped. "Your quest was satisfied then, I take it." *I was right—Elizabeth will not have me. She cannot forgive my past injuries.*

He almost missed Lady Catherine's reply, but the lady's voice was strident enough to pierce his mournful thoughts. "Indeed it was not! I then asked her to promise that she would never enter into such an engagement, and she refused! Can it be borne? You have been intended for Anne all your life but that matters little to her. Nothing matters to her but what she may gain from an alliance with you."

She spat those words out with such force that Darcy nearly took a step backward. His mind raced. "Lady Catherine, I am not sure I understand you. Do you mean to tell me that Miss Bennet refused to promise *not* to become engaged to me?"

"Is that not what I just said? She cares nothing for your good reputation and consequence in Society; the degradation that would come if you were to ally yourself with such a family did not sway her a bit."

"Perhaps your question merely surprised her and she was not sure how to answer," Darcy suggested, still unable to believe his aunt's conclusion.

"I think not. I laid out all the consequences she might expect if she were to pursue you—the censure she would receive from your family, from all your connections, and do you know what she said in reply? 'The wife of Mr. Darcy must have such extraordinary sources of happiness necessarily attached to her situation, that she could, upon the whole, have no cause to repine.'"

It was just as well she did not look at her nephew when she uttered those words, for she could not have mistaken the flush that swept over his features. Darcy turned toward the fireplace and rested a hand on the mantle.

"She speaks of your wealth, of your position, of course. Insolent girl, to aspire to such a match! She is determined, you see, to have you!"

His back to his aunt, Darcy felt free to grin foolishly. Of one thing he was certain—Elizabeth Bennet would never consent to marry him for his fortune. That she had made perfectly clear.

"Darcy, do you attend me?" Lady Catherine rapped her cane against the floor. "Do you hear what I am telling you? This girl believes she can usurp what belongs to my Anne!"

"Yes, it is quite shocking." Darcy's mind raced. He needed to be in Hertfordshire; he couldn't stay away from Elizabeth any longer. *But first, my guest must leave.*

Darcy rang for a servant and then looked at Lady Catherine, a disinterested mask firmly in place. "Aunt, I appreciate the concern for my wellbeing that brought you here with this message."

A footman entered the room. "Yes, Mr. Darcy?"

"Please call for Lady Catherine's carriage."

"Darcy! What do you mean by doing this?"

"I am simply tending to your comfort, Aunt," Darcy reassured her. "You cannot have taken time to truly relax at your house before you came here."

"I arrived in town late last night, and determined…"

"To come directly to warn me. Yes, I quite understand, and indeed, your words have had an impact you can scarcely believe." This was the moment when he should inform her that he would not marry Anne, but he hesitated. *If I tell her that now, she will not leave my house until she has convinced me otherwise. What is more, she might easily make the connection to Elizabeth.*

Though he hated the deception inherent in the omission, he chose not to mention Anne at all. Instead, he said, "Now I must beg of your ladyship to return to your own house where you may have all the comforts you have denied yourself in coming to me so early."

She huffed. "You will take into account what I have told you? This Bennet creature is determined to have you, Darcy—take heed."

Excitement rose in Darcy's breast at the thought. "I shall indeed heed your words, Lady Catherine. You have been a tremendous help."

Chapter Thirty-nine

"SHE COULD HAVE, on the whole, no cause to repine."

Once again, Elizabeth's words echoed in Darcy's head, but this time their effect was far more pleasant. He could not believe her feelings had undergone so material a change as they seemed to indicate, but Elizabeth was not one to dissemble. *Had she truly been decided against me, she would have told Lady Catherine so directly.*

He had made preparations to return to Hertfordshire as soon as Lady Catherine left, and then he had slept but a little, trying to guess what Elizabeth might have meant. Now he was only an hour from Netherfield, and some of his earlier certainty vanished. *For I once approached Elizabeth with a presumptuous belief she would accept me, and instead I was rejected. It would be far better to expect rejection and find welcome!*

It was not long before his carriage turned down the graceful sweep toward Netherfield Park. The view was not the same as the tree-lined drive he loved from Pemberley, but were Elizabeth to accept his hand here in Hertfordshire, the local landscape would be second in his heart only to Derbyshire.

The carriage rolled to a stop in front of the house, and Darcy jumped out. "Good afternoon, Mr. Darcy," the butler said after opening the door. "Shall I have your things taken to your room?"

"Yes, thank you. Is Bingley in his study?" Darcy asked, already walking in that direction.

"No, sir—he is visiting the Longbourn family."

Darcy swallowed a sigh of disappointment. He had hoped to arrive in time to join Bingley for his regular call. "Very well. I will await his return in the library."

Though the book he had been reading before his trip to London still sat where he had left it on the end table, Darcy did not pick it up. He did not even take a seat. The library provided a first-floor view down onto the lane; from here he would know the moment of Bingley's return.

He paced in front of the tall windows, pausing in every pass to look out at the clear, fall day. Lady Catherine's words had offered hope enough that he chafed at every minute's delay. He must know once and for all what Elizabeth's feelings toward him truly were. If they were still what they had been in April, he would remove himself from her presence forever, but if...

All the glorious possibilities of that "if" ran through his mind, and his fingers flexed. *Oh Elizabeth, how I would love you, if you would let me!*

"The wife of Mr. Darcy must have such extraordinary sources of happiness..."

All Darcy's hopes rested in those words. He was quite certain she had never before considered happiness as the resulting outcome of marriage to him!

Hoofbeats stopped Darcy in mid-stride and he turned back toward the window. "At last," he muttered when he saw Bingley hand the reins of his horse to the waiting stable hand.

He realized suddenly how odd it would appear if Bingley knew how anxiously he awaited his arrival, and he finally picked his book up and sat down. The words made no sense to him, however, and he turned the pages without being aware of his actions.

Bingley entered the room a few minutes later. "Darcy!" He held his hand out and Darcy rose to take it. "This is a welcome surprise. Why did you not write to say you were coming?"

Darcy sat back down and marveled at the cheerful, open expression on his friend's face. *I would not be so forgiving were our positions reversed.*

"I apologize, Bingley, but I heard congratulations were in order and decided to forgo the note in favor of a visit. I hope I am welcome?"

Bingley laughed and moved to the sideboard. "How could I do otherwise, when Jane has so sweetly forgiven me? Come, let us drink to my good fortune." He poured two glasses of claret and handed one to Darcy. "I hope you may soon find so worthy a woman for your bride."

The drink hit the back of Darcy's throat just as Bingley uttered the wish, and he choked, sputtering a little. "Darcy? Are you all right?" his friend asked in concern.

"I am fine, Bingley—I just inhaled a little wine, I believe." He coughed again and cleared his throat. "Now, tell me what plans you have made. When are you to marry?"

"November twenty-six—exactly a year after the ball when I realized I must propose."

Twin emotions of humor and jealousy shot through Darcy. He tamped down the latter and only said, "You have become a romantic worthy of the poets, Bingley."

His friend shrugged, a happy smile on his face. "Jane loves me; she has consented to be my wife. I defy even you to remain stoic in the face of such joy."

"And you will live here at Netherfield?" Darcy asked, turning the focus away from his future happiness.

Bingley nodded. "At some point, of course, we wish to purchase a home of our own, but Netherfield will do quite nicely for the present."

"Indeed." Darcy's mind turned to a vacant estate he knew of in Derbyshire. *If Elizabeth accepts me, how much happier she would be to have her favorite sister not fifty miles away. After all, fifty miles of good road…*

"Darcy?"

Darcy glanced up and saw Bingley looking at him curiously. "I apologize once again, Bingley. I am afraid my conversation skills are not up to snuff at the moment; the journey was more fatiguing than usual. Will you excuse me until supper?"

"Of course."

When Darcy joined Bingley that evening, he had regained control over his wayward thoughts and devised a plan that would give him the earliest access to Elizabeth, without rousing any suspicion. "I was not wholly honest with you earlier, Bingley."

"Good lord, Darcy, another confession? Well, out with it then."

"This omission of truth was not nearly as grievous as the first, I assure you. You asked what brought me back to Hertfordshire, and I dissembled a bit. My aunt visited me yesterday afternoon, you see."

Bingley's face darkened. "Did she? Jane says she caused quite a disturbance two days ago at Longbourn."

"Yes, I was afraid she had. Did Miss Bennet know the nature of the call?"

"No, she spoke only to Miss Elizabeth, and Elizabeth has not told Jane a word—which concerns my lady greatly, as they are not in the habit of keeping secrets."

"I see. It is my hope… I would like to apologize to Miss Elizabeth, in my family's name. May I join you tomorrow at Longbourn?"

Bingley smiled. "And that was your great secret? Of course you may, Darcy." He grinned. "Your presence may be the very thing to distract Miss Elizabeth from her role as chaperone."

Chapter Forty

DARCY'S PRESENCE THE following afternoon was surely a surprise to the whole family, but only Mrs. Bennet was rude enough to comment on it. "Mr. Darcy! We did not know you were back from town, sir."

"Yes, I arrived late yesterday afternoon."

He spoke to Mrs. Bennet, but his eyes were on Elizabeth. Her complexion seemed a little paler than he recalled. *Does she wish I had not come?*

"After sitting so long in a carriage, I am sure Darcy would welcome a walk. May I invite all the ladies to join us?" Bingley asked.

Mrs. Bennet and Miss Mary quickly answered in the negative, but Darcy kept his gaze on Elizabeth. If she refused to join them, he would have his answer. Instead, she smiled slightly and nodded her assent, and his relief was so great, he almost missed Miss Kitty announcing her intent to walk with them as far as Lucas Lodge.

The autumn sun warmed their backs when they set out. Bingley and Miss Bennet quickly fell behind, and Darcy smiled. *Bingley wastes no time.*

The silence between the remaining three was uncomfortable. There was much Darcy wished to say to Elizabeth that he could not say in the presence of her sister, and he wished Miss Kitty would hurry so they might reach the lane to Lucas Lodge a little faster.

At last, however, they were there, and Miss Kitty turned to look at her sister. "Lizzy, would you care to join me? I am sure Maria would be glad of a visit from you."

"No, Kitty, you may go along without me." The younger girl nodded and ambled down the drive.

Darcy took courage from the fact that Elizabeth did not seem unwilling to be alone with him. They resumed their walk without a word, but despite the awkwardness of the silence, Darcy would not speak until he knew how to broach the subject.

He had just settled on the right words when she suddenly turned to him and said, "Mr. Darcy, I am a very selfish creature; and, for the sake of giving relief to my own feelings, care not how much I may be wounding yours."

Darcy remembered well the last time she had given relief to her own feelings, and his gut clenched.

"I can no longer help thanking you for your unexampled kindness to my poor sister. Ever since I have known it, I have been most anxious to acknowledge to you how gratefully I feel it. Were it known to the rest of my family, I should not have merely my own gratitude to express."

Darcy cringed at the word gratitude. That was the one thing above everything else that he did not want from Elizabeth; it was the very reason he had kept his involvement in the affair secret. "I am sorry, exceedingly sorry, that you have ever been informed of what may, in a mistaken light, have given you uneasiness. I did not think Mrs. Gardiner was so little to be trusted."

He was rather vexed with the lady until Elizabeth said, "You must not blame my aunt. Lydia's thoughtlessness first betrayed to me that you had been concerned in the matter; and of course, I could not rest till I knew the particulars."

Darcy sighed; he could easily imagine that Lydia had been unable to keep the secret. She seemed to delight in sharing anything that was inappropriate.

Then he looked at Elizabeth, and the earnest expression on her face drove Lydia from his mind. "Let me thank you again and again, in the name of all my family—" she paused slightly and looked away for a moment— "for that generous compassion which induced you to take so much trouble and bear so many mortifications, for the sake of discovering them."

Her gratitude, though unwelcome, did offer him an opening to express his feelings for her. "If you *will* thank me, let it be for yourself alone. That the wish of giving happiness to you might add force to the other inducements which led me on, I shall not attempt to deny. But your *family* owe me nothing," he emphasized, and her eyes widened. "Much as I respect them, I believe I thought only of *you.*"

He paused, giving her the opportunity to speak, to tell him he must not go on. *She must know what I am to say next. If she stops me now, I will know her feelings are unchanged.* However, her only response was a sudden blush, and he took courage in her silence.

"You are too generous to trifle with me. If your feelings are still what they were last April, tell me so at once. *My* affections and wishes are unchanged, but one word from you will silence me on this subject forever."

For a moment he heard nothing but the sound of his own heart pounding in his ears. Elizabeth looked at him and moistened her lips with the tip of her tongue. "I… my feelings last April were so wrong… I did not know then what I spoke of. I view you quite differently now…. In truth—that is, I wondered—oh, I almost feared you might not care for me still."

She turned away then, but he had seen enough of the happiness in her countenance and heard the joy in her voice that allowed him to piece together her jumbled sentences into an acceptance. *My Elizabeth— you are my Elizabeth now,* he thought to himself in exultation.

After a moment he became aware that it was his turn to speak. "Miss Elizabeth, allow me to assure you that I will never stop caring for you. I would be glad to spend the rest of my life proving that to you, if you will allow me."

She looked at him then and smiled, and the expression in her wonderful brown eyes made his heart race. "I will."

Darcy gently, hesitantly, took her hand in his. "I would have there be no further misunderstandings between us. Elizabeth, will you agree to be my wife?"

Elizabeth looked down at their joined hands and then up at him. Her voice was firm when she answered. "Yes, Mr. Darcy."

Darcy knew he should never forget this moment as long as he lived. How beautiful she looked with the sun warming her upturned face. The soft breeze played with her one of her curls, and he lifted a hand to brush it from her face.

Then, with trembling hands, he raised her fingers to his lips. "Elizabeth," he breathed, unable to say more. Her eyelids fluttered and she swayed into his embrace. Darcy brushed a kiss across her forehead, and her soft sigh nearly did him in. "I believe we should return to our walk, my dear," he said with great reluctance.

Elizabeth straightened and attempted to retrieve her hands, but he kept her right in his left. "No, I think I will keep this for now," he murmured, and she flushed scarlet.

They walked a ways before either of them regained

the power of speech, but finally Elizabeth looked over at him with teasing eyes. "I fear Lady Catherine will not be pleased with our current understanding."

He laughed slightly. "I am afraid not. She has always believed I would marry Anne, though I never gave her any reason to believe it."

"She came here the other day..." Elizabeth's sentence trailed off, and Darcy wondered at her uncertain expression.

"Yes, she told me."

"So she did visit you then! I half-feared that she might."

"Why did you fear it?"

Elizabeth did not answer, and he knew with a sudden surety what she had thought. "Elizabeth, surely my behavior in the last few months has shown you I no longer share her beliefs."

She tilted her head in consideration. "Yes... I suppose it was simply insecurity; a fear that as your aunt, her words might carry more weight with you than they had with me."

"Indeed, her visit did sway me—though not in the way she wished. It taught me to hope, as I had scarcely ever allowed myself to hope before. I knew enough of your disposition to be certain that, had you been absolutely, irrevocably decided against me, you would have acknowledged it to Lady Catherine frankly and openly."

She laughed. "Yes, you know enough of my *frankness* to believe me capable of *that*. After abusing you so abominably to your face, I could have no scruple in abusing you to all your relations."

Darcy's jaw dropped a little. *Her memory of that scene is far different from mine.* "What did you say of me, that I did not deserve? For, though your accusations were ill-founded, formed on mistaken premises, my behavior to you at the time had merited the severest reproof. It was unpardonable. I cannot think of it without abhorrence."

Elizabeth's fingers tightened around his, and Darcy could hardly believe the chagrin in her voice when she spoke. "We will not quarrel for the greater share of the blame annexed to that evening. The conduct of neither, if strictly examined, will be irreproachable; but since then, we have both, I hope, improved in civility."

"I cannot be so easily reconciled to myself," Darcy said. "The recollection of what I then said, of my conduct, my manners, my expression during the whole of it, is now, and has been many months, inexpressibly painful to me."

He stared straight ahead, but instead of the idyllic country lane, he saw the parsonage at Hunsford. "Your reproof, so well applied, I shall never forget: 'Had you behaved in a more gentleman-like manner.' Those were your words. You know not, you can scarcely conceive, how they have tortured me—though it was some time, I confess, before I was reasonable enough to allow their justice."

Her expression was full of surprise. "I was certainly very far from expecting them to make so strong an impression. I had not the smallest idea of their being ever felt in such a way."

Those words, spoken to reassure, only deepened Darcy's self-disgust. "I can easily believe it. You thought me then devoid of every proper feeling; I am sure you did. The turn of your countenance I shall never forget, as you said that I could not have addressed you in any possible way that would induce you to accept me."

The remembered pain almost overshadowed the current joy until Elizabeth said, "Oh! Do not repeat what I then said. These recollections will not do at all. I assure you that I have long been most heartily ashamed of it."

There was one more question he had regarding the past, and he posed it then. "What first brought you to change your mind? Was it my letter? Did it, did it *soon* make you think better of me? Did you, on reading it, give any credit to its contents?"

She considered for a moment. "I confess I did not wish to give credit to your words at first," she admitted. "You remember enough of my feelings toward you at the time to understand that I would not want to believe anything you said." He nodded, and she continued. "However, when I read what you had to say of Wickham, it was so close to what he himself had said that I began to wonder. Then I considered that you surely would not have said something like that about your sister if it was not true, and I had to accept your word."

He sighed and shook his head. "I knew that what I wrote must give you pain, but it was necessary. I hope you have destroyed the letter. There was one part especially, the opening of it, which I should dread your having the power of reading again. I can remember some expressions which might justly make you hate me."

Despite their current good understanding, Darcy looked at Elizabeth with some anxiety. He could not help but feel he did not deserve her, and he trembled lest she might come to the same conclusion.

Instead, she laced her fingers more tightly through his and said, "The letter shall certainly be burnt, if you believe it essential to the preservation of my regard; but, though we have both reason to think my opinions not entirely unalterable, they are not, I hope, quite so easily changed as that implies."

Her cheeky good humor brought a smile to his lips,

but he could not quite let the subject rest. "When I wrote that letter, I believed myself perfectly calm and cool, but I am since convinced that it was written in a dreadful bitterness of spirit."

He glanced over at her and saw the way she tilted her head slightly as she considered. "The letter, perhaps, began in bitterness, but it did not end so. The adieu is charity itself." Then she smiled up at him. "But think no more of the letter. The feelings of the person who wrote and the person who received it are now so widely different from what they were then, that every unpleasant circumstance attending it ought to be forgotten. You must learn some of my philosophy. Think only of the past as its remembrance gives you pleasure."

He heard the lightheartedness in her voice, but the subject had depressed him slightly and he could not think thus. "I cannot give you credit for any philosophy of the kind," he argued. "*Your* retrospections must be so totally void of reproach, that the contentment arising from them is not of philosophy, but, what is much better, of innocence. But with *me* it is not so. Painful recollections will intrude, which cannot, which ought not, to be repelled."

He closed his eyes briefly. "I have been a selfish being all my life, in practice, though not in principle."

That confession triggered an avalanche of words he could not hold in, and what a relief it was to finally have someone with whom he could share his thoughts! "As a child I was taught what was *right*, but I was not taught to correct my temper. I was given good principles, but left to follow them in pride and conceit. Unfortunately, an only son (for many years an only *child*), I was spoilt by my parents, who, though good themselves (my father, particularly, all that was benevolent and amiable), allowed, encouraged, almost taught me to be selfish and overbearing—to care for none beyond my own family circle, to think meanly of all the rest of the world, to *wish* at least to think meanly of their sense and worth compared with my own. Such I was, from eight to eight-and-twenty; and such I might still have been but for you, dearest, loveliest Elizabeth!"

He stopped walking and faced Elizabeth, catching her other hand once again and holding both to his chest. "What do I not owe you? You taught me a lesson, hard indeed at first, but most advantageous. By you, I was properly humbled. I came to you without a doubt of my reception. You showed me how insufficient were all my pretensions to please a woman worthy of being pleased."

Elizabeth's forehead creased and curiosity flickered across her expression. "Had you then persuaded yourself that I should?"

Darcy laughed, a low, self-deprecating sound. "Indeed I had. What will you think of my vanity? I believed you to be wishing, expecting my addresses."

To his surprise and amazement, Elizabeth blushed. "My manners must have been in fault, but not intentionally, I assure you." Her smile was earnest, beseeching him to believe her. "I never meant to deceive you, but my spirits might often lead me wrong. How you must have hated me after *that* evening!"

Darcy started, and Elizabeth pulled at her hands, trying to get away. He held her closer and exclaimed, "Hate you! I was angry, perhaps, at first, but my anger soon began to take a proper direction."

She sighed, and he imagined she was looking for a new topic. "I am almost afraid of asking what you thought of me when we met at Pemberley. You blamed me for coming?"

His jaw dropped and he shook his head quickly, but she saw neither gesture, for her eyes had drifted to the ground. Darcy placed a hand under her chin and tilted her head up. "No, indeed; I felt nothing but surprise."

"Your surprise could not be greater than *mine* in being noticed by you," she said ruefully. "My conscience told me that I deserved no extraordinary politeness, and I confess that I did not expect to receive *more* than my due."

"My object *then* was to show you, by every civility in my power, that I was not so mean as to resent the past; and I hoped to obtain your forgiveness, to lessen your ill opinion by letting you see that your reproofs had been attended to. How soon any other wishes introduced themselves I can hardly tell, but I believe in about half an hour after I had seen you."

He and Elizabeth shared a smile at that, and then he said, "Georgiana was particularly delighted by your stay in Derbyshire. She had wished to make your acquaintance for some time, and for the opportunity to land so neatly in her lap was more than she had wished for."

"She is a sweet, unaffected young lady—exactly what I have always wished for in a younger sister." The allusion both to her own younger sisters and to the fact that Georgiana very soon would be her own sister made her blush again.

Eager to see that delicious shade of pink spread further across her face, Darcy said, "Georgie, too, has always wished for a sister—she will be very happy when I tell her those wishes are to come true." Her entire face was pink now, and he took pity on her. "She was most disappointed when you left so suddenly."

"Yes, as were we all. Lydia has not yet learned to time her escapades for the convenience of the rest of the family."

Her wry humor drew a chuckle from Darcy, but he sobered quickly. "I am sorry this incident happened at all, and only glad I was able to help as far as I was."

"When did you decide to follow them?"

"Almost from the moment I learned of the event. I confess I spent most of the time we were together thinking about how I would find them and what I would say to him."

She stared at him. "Is that why you were so quiet?"

"I was not aware that I was, but if I was so, then yes, that was the reason. Why, what did you think to be the cause?"

"I supposed... that is, I knew how repugnant Wickham was to you, and I thought..."

"Surely you did not believe that would be enough to put an end to my affection for you?" Elizabeth's silence told all, and in a moment of daring, Darcy placed his hands on her neck and caressed her jaw line with his thumbs. The pink of her cheeks deepened once more, but he would not let her look away. "I would never blame anyone else for the actions of George Wickham."

She smiled, and he ran his hands slowly down her arms and reclaimed her hand. "Your sister perhaps made her own bed, but I could not leave things like that, not when you were so unhappy. Your tears, Elizabeth, will always command me."

Silent understanding flowed between them, and Darcy knew they need not speak any more of Wickham. He examined his watch and said, "It is nearly dinner time. We should go back to the house, or your mother will wonder where we have been."

"We are not the only ones," Elizabeth retorted pertly. "What could become of Mr. Bingley and Jane!"

"Ah, but your family knows they are engaged. No one will wonder if they do not come home until dinner time."

"I must ask whether you were surprised?"

Darcy shrugged. "Not at all. When I went away, I

felt that it would soon happen."

"That is to say, you had given your permission. I guessed as much."

"Come now, Elizabeth, permission? Bingley is a grown man; he can make his own decisions."

Elizabeth raised an eyebrow. "You did not discuss it with him?"

"On the evening before my going to London, I made a confession to him, which I believe I ought to have made long ago. I told him of all that had occurred to make my former interference in his affairs absurd and impertinent. His surprise was great. He had never had the slightest suspicion. I told him, moreover, that I believed myself mistaken in supposing as I had done, that your sister was indifferent to him; and as I could easily perceive that his attachment to her was unabated, I felt no doubt of their happiness together."

Elizabeth smiled slightly, and he knew he had not successfully defended himself. "Did you speak from your own observation when you told him that my sister loved him, or merely from my information last spring?"

Darcy cleared his throat. Surely the answer she wished to hear was the latter, but he had never been the kind of man who could be guided simply by the impressions and beliefs of another. He hoped she would understand that. "From the former. I had narrowly observed her during the two visits which I had lately made here, and I was convinced of her affection."

"And your assurance of it, I suppose, carried immediate conviction to him."

"It did. Bingley is most unaffectedly modest. His diffidence had prevented his depending on his own judgment in so anxious a case, but his reliance on mine made everything easy. I was obliged to confess one thing which for a time, and not unjustly, offended him. I could not allow myself to conceal that your sister had been in town three months last winter—that I had known it, and purposely kept it from him. He was angry. But his anger, I am persuaded, lasted no longer than he remained in any doubt of your sister's sentiments. He has heartily forgiven me now."

"They are very happy together."

"Not nearly so happy as we are, my Elizabeth." She smiled tenderly at him and placed her hand on his arm, where it remained until the house came into view.

Darcy then allowed Elizabeth to be swept away from him by her elder sister, knowing there were already far more questions to be answered than he cared for. During dinner he found himself looking so often at Elizabeth that he felt sure someone must notice and comment, but no one did. She did not look at him but once, and were it not for the joy only he could read in that look, he might have feared she regretted her decision.

Chapter Forty-one

THAT EVENING WHEN they sat down in front of the fire with their port, Bingley opened the conversation Darcy had feared at Longbourn. "Wherever did you disappear to with Miss Elizabeth this morning, Darcy?"

Darcy shifted in his seat. "Did she not already answer that question? We walked, and talked as we walked, and as we paid more attention to our conversation than to where we were going, we were soon far from Longbourn."

Bingley tapped his fingers on the side of his glass. "I do seem to recall a time when the lady would not have tolerated your presence for that long."

Darcy could not suppress a smile. "Thankfully, that time is past."

Bingley lowered his glass. "Darcy? Is there something you wish to share?"

Darcy considered for a moment. He had not intended to tell anyone until the information became public, but there was no doubt in his mind that Elizabeth was telling Jane even as they spoke. "I have asked Miss Elizabeth to marry me, and she has accepted."

For the first time, Darcy had the pleasure of seeing his friend absolutely speechless. Bingley opened and closed his mouth several times before he finally took a large swig of his port and immediately rose to refill the glass, downing that quickly as well.

"Darcy, I think there is something amiss with my hearing. Did you just tell me that you have proposed to Miss Elizabeth?"

"I did."

Bingley leaned against his desk and crossed his arms. "Sister to Jane Bennet?"

"The very same."

"Whose relations you thought beneath me?"

Darcy squirmed. "I admit that, yes."

"Tell me, what could possibly induce you to make a match you deemed unsuitable for me?"

"It was hypocritical of me, I confess."

"I am glad you see that."

The sarcasm was unmistakable. "In my defense, Bingley, when I kept you from Jane last winter I was equally eager to get away from Elizabeth. It was only when I met her in Kent last spring that I realized my... affections could not be swept away as neatly as I had hoped."

"Last spring?" Bingley frowned. "Was that why you were in such poor spirits when you returned to town?"

Darcy sighed—he had not intended to mention Rosings. *At this point, I might as well make a clean breast of it.* "Yes. I proposed to Elizabeth once before in Kent, and she pointed out the same flaws in my reasoning that you just highlighted. She refused me."

"She never did!" Bingley rocked back on his heels, a smile spreading across his face. "Well, Jane does say she is quite independent."

Darcy smiled wryly. "Very much so."

Bingley straightened and stared at Darcy. "But if you proposed in April, then when she came to Derbyshire —"

"I had not seen her since the morning after she

refused me." Darcy swallowed—despite their recent understanding, he still could not think of that day without pain. "I assure you, it was awkward for both of us. However, if we had not met her there, neither of us would have been reunited with our ladies. It was that encounter which convinced me we must return to Hertfordshire."

"I did not know I owed all my good fortune to chance."

"Not chance, Bingley—Providence. For if I had not left you at the posting inn on the way to Pemberley— do you recall?" Bingley nodded. "If I had been but a half hour later coming to Pemberley, I should not have known she was in the country. That is too great a coincidence to be the work of chance, do you not agree?"

"Quite so."

The gentlemen soon returned to their private thoughts, but the next morning saw a rejuvenation of Bingley's fine spirits. "I do believe I am in your debt, Darcy," he said over breakfast.

"How so?"

"News of your engagement will surely take attention from my own. Why, your ten thousand a year will quite put my mere five thousand in the shade!" He laughed when Darcy groaned. "There is no avoiding the inevitable, my friend. You will certainly be Mrs. Bennet's favorite son-in-law."

"I am willing to be the second favorite. Perhaps I might do something as shocking as immigrate to the Americas." Bingley's jaw dropped, and it was Darcy's turn to laugh. "Ah! I see you had not thought of every possibility before teasing me, Bingley. Let that be a lesson to you."

"Darcy, you would not..." Bingley recovered himself. "But of course you would not leave Pemberley or Georgiana."

"No, I am afraid leaving the country is not an option, even if I wished it, or Elizabeth would agree."

The acknowledged engagement between Bingley and Miss Bennet gave them leave to call directly following breakfast. When they were admitted to the Longbourn sitting room, Darcy saw a hint of a scowl on Mrs. Bennet's forehead and wondered at it. "Mr. Bingley," she simpered, "why, have you come again, sir? But of course you could not stay away from Jane." To Darcy she offered the barest smile. "And good afternoon to you, sir."

Familiar as he was with Elizabeth's expressions, Darcy saw the amusement in her eyes. He wished he might approach her, but would that give away their attachment? Suddenly, every action carried more weight than it had before.

In the end, it was Bingley who greeted her first. "Miss Elizabeth, you are looking quite fine today. The fresh air yesterday must have been good for you."

Elizabeth took his hand but looked at Darcy, and he nodded in acknowledgement at the question in her eyes. She smiled then at Bingley and said, "Indeed, Mr. Bingley, I have scarcely enjoyed a walk more."

Darcy's face warmed and he resisted the urge to loosen his cravat. The laughter in Bingley's eyes when he glanced at him told Darcy his friend knew exactly how he felt, and took great pleasure in his discomfort.

However, Darcy's glare lost its heat when Bingley turned to Mr. Bennet and said, "Mr. Bennet, have you no more lanes hereabouts in which Lizzy may lose her way again today?"

Mrs. Bennet answered before her husband could. "I advise Mr. Darcy, and Lizzy, and Kitty, to walk to Oakham Mount this morning. It is a nice long walk, and Mr. Darcy has never seen the view."

Darcy bit back a sigh. The plan was not quite to his liking. Thankfully, Bingley was on hand to smooth everything over. "It may do very well for the others, but I am sure it will be too much for Kitty. Won't it, Kitty?"

The girl agreed, but it was her father Darcy watched. The shrewd man raised an eyebrow at Bingley's none-too-subtle handling of the players, and Darcy knew it would not be long before he pieced together Bingley's remarks with his own disappearance with Elizabeth the previous afternoon. *I shall have to apply for his consent this evening, then.*

Once they were well away from the house, Darcy broached the subject with Elizabeth. "If it is acceptable with you, my dear, I should like to speak with your father after dinner."

Elizabeth looked at him with some amazement, and Darcy could easily understand why. He had always been such a picture of restraint that he himself was surprised by his impatience. But now, even without Bingley's lack of discretion, he should not wish to hold his joy privately. "Given Bingley's comments this morning, I imagine he already understands more than we are aware," he said, "and I should prefer to tell him myself, up front. Do you not agree, Elizabeth?"

"Yes, of course." He heard a note of anxiety in her voice, which she explained the next moment. "Do let me speak to my mother, however."

Darcy smiled. "That is a pleasure I shall gladly relinquish to you."

She smiled saucily. "Oh, do not think you shall escape unscathed, sir. I cannot promise she will ever approve of you, but your houses and lands she will hold in the highest esteem."

"So I have been warned by Bingley," Darcy agreed, taking Elizabeth's hand to help her over a log that had fallen in the path. He was absurdly pleased when she did not attempt to reclaim it afterwards.

"Yes, how did the revelation to Mr. Bingley occur?"

"In much the same manner as yours to your sister, I imagine," Darcy retorted.

Elizabeth laughed and pulled away to run the last few yards up the hill. "Look at the view!" she exclaimed, her eyes roving over the landscape below. "Have you ever seen such beauty?"

"Never," Darcy vowed.

Elizabeth glanced over at him and smiled self-consciously when she realized he looked not at the hills of Hertfordshire, but at her own countenance, now flushed with exercise and what he hoped was happiness.

"In truth, I can think of one place better," Elizabeth told him. "Pemberley must be the most perfect place on earth." She smiled, and Darcy wondered what would next come out of her charmingly pert mouth. "Jane asked me last night when I first knew I loved you, and I told her it was the moment I saw Pemberley."

Her smile faltered when he did not answer. "Mr. Darcy? I assure you, I was not in earnest, sir."

To hear her say so freely and naturally that she loved him affected Darcy more than he had anticipated, and his hands shook from a desire to touch Elizabeth. When he could finally trust his voice, he said, "I believe we should turn back, Elizabeth."

"Turn back? But we only just arrived."

"Yes, but if we stay any longer, I will not be able to keep from kissing you."

Elizabeth's eyes widened at this bold declaration, but she did not look away, and his resolve was sorely tested. "Come, Miss Elizabeth—back to the house," he said firmly. "The walk is long enough that we shall likely find dinner waiting for us."

She set off down the hill and he followed a few steps after. "Do walk beside me, Mr. Darcy," she requested. "There is one matter further which we have not discussed."

"And what is that?" Darcy asked when he reached his rightful place by her side.

"The small matter of a wedding date, sir."

"What did you and Miss Bennet decide upon last night?" Darcy asked, and then chuckled at the look she gave him. "Come, Elizabeth, she is your sister. Of course you discussed it together."

"We did," she confessed.

"And?"

"Jane and I always imagined standing up for each other at our weddings."

"And I cannot think of a gentleman besides Bingley whom I should want at mine," Darcy answered. "So we are to have a double ceremony with Bingley and your sister."

"So long as that suits you, my dear."

Darcy drew in a deep, satisfied sigh. "Elizabeth, so long as the day concludes with you as my wife, I care little for the details." Elizabeth's only answer was to take his arm once more.

When they reached Longbourn, the sun was already setting. Darcy's prediction was proven correct; dinner had been laid out and their arrival was all that was wanting. Bingley glanced over at him and Darcy smiled in reply, but further discourse must wait until they were alone.

Dinner seemed an interminable affair. Darcy could not eat from nerves and was reduced to subtly rearranging the food on his plate to give the appearance of an appetite. As soon as he saw Mr. Bennet leave the table after dinner, Darcy followed him into the library.

Mr. Bennet turned with some surprise when he realized he was not alone. "Mr. Darcy, is there something I can do for you?"

"Yes, sir." Darcy surreptitiously wiped his palms on his breeches and said, "I should like to have your consent to marry your daughter."

Mr. Bennet stared. "Which one? You shall have to specify."

Darcy raised an eyebrow at this odd remark, but he obliged Mr. Bennet. "Miss Elizabeth, sir. I have asked for her hand, and she accepted."

Mr. Bennet sat down, hard. "Elizabeth accepted you?"

Darcy refused to flinch, though the incredulity in the man's voice rubbed salt in an old wound. "Indeed she did, sir, yesterday afternoon."

Mr. Bennet looked at Darcy over steepled hands. "That is where you were when you were getting lost."

"Yes, sir."

"Mr. Darcy, I realize I need not ask if you have the means to provide for a wife." Mr. Bennet fixed him with a stern glare. "However, pecuniary gain has never been Elizabeth's goal, nor is it mine for her. I will not have my favorite child sacrifice her happiness at the altar of wealth and position."

"And she will not, sir. I promise you, I will do everything in my power to make Elizabeth happy for the rest of her life."

Mr. Bennet crossed his arms and leaned back in his chair. "She has accepted you, you say?" he asked a second time.

"She has."

"Very well then, I cannot do any less. I give you my consent, Mr. Darcy."

"Thank you, sir."

Mr. Bennet held up his hand. "Do not thank me yet.

I wish to see Elizabeth now, if you please."

Darcy shook his hand and wondered at the odd turn of phrase. It was only when he reached the drawing room that he realized Mr. Bennet's meaning. *He hopes to change her mind!*

One glance at Elizabeth calmed his spirits, for he could clearly see a love in her eyes that would not be easily overturned. When he was near enough to speak without being overheard, he said, "Go to your father; he wants you in the library." She flushed and rose from her seat.

Darcy looked around the room and saw Bingley sitting on the other side beside Jane. Both returned his gaze with varying degrees of sympathy, Jane all smiles and Bingley with a wide smirk across his face. He made his way over to them and waited for Elizabeth's return. It was so long in coming that he began to worry that her father had convinced her he did not deserve her. Finally, however, she appeared, and the smile on her face reassured him that no such disaster had befallen him.

Darcy's reception the following morning told him that all the members of the household were now aware of their engagement. Mrs. Bennet watched him in silent awe, but the rest of the family was effusive in their outpourings of good wishes. *If only I could guarantee it would remain this way,* Darcy thought, eyeing his future mother-in-law.

It did not. As dinner progressed that evening, her natural garrulous behavior overcame her reverence for his income, and she began to pay those little compliments he so despised. "Oh my. Mr. Darcy, it is such a pleasure... I never knew... Would you care for the potatoes, sir? Kitty, for heaven's sake, pass the potatoes! Do you not know he has ten thousand a year?"

Darcy caught Elizabeth's eye across the table and they both took a quick swig from their water goblets to hide their laughter.

Kitty was not so wise. "I do not see why his fortune should mean he receives the potatoes any sooner than the rest of us," she complained, and Darcy bowed his head.

"Kitty! Hold your tongue! Mr. Darcy, I do apologize for my daughter. She does not know…"

"Mrs. Bennet, there is no apology necessary. Miss Catherine is quite correct; I do not require any special treatment. After all, you are soon to be my family."

The lady of the house dropped her fork and looked at him, all astonishment. "Why… Mr. Darcy… that is… Why, I have always said Lizzy could not be so clever without reason."

Mr. Bennet rose from his seat. "When my wife has expressed all her gratitude, sir, you may join me in the library for a glass of port."

Between the two gentlemen there now subsisted a most genial understanding. Mr. Bennet had approached Darcy on his arrival at Longbourn that afternoon. "Mr. Darcy, I understand I owe the marriage of not just one, but two, of my daughters to you."

Darcy knew immediately what he meant. "I beg you not to think of it, sir."

"No! This will never do!" Mr. Bennet cried. "Not think of the greatest kindness which has ever been done my family? You must allow me to repay you."

"Never!" Darcy declared. "What I did, I did for Elizabeth, and that, sir, requires no payment."

"Well-spoken, Mr. Darcy. I think we will deal together quite nicely, though you are a great deal too sensible for my taste."

Thankfully, the next day was free of the attentions from Elizabeth's family. Jane and Bingley were sequestered in one corner of the sitting room and he and Elizabeth were in the opposite corner. Ostensibly, both couples were acting as chaperones to the other, though in practice no one paid attention to anyone but their own lover.

Darcy held Elizabeth's hand in his own, and the way she absently traced patterns on the back of his hand drove him to distraction. "I have a question for you, my dear," she said.

He recognized the playful tone in her voice and hid his smile. "Yes, Elizabeth?"

"I wish you to tell me how you ever fell in love with me." He heard her amusement and waited for her to continue. "How could you begin? I can comprehend your going on charmingly, when you had once made a beginning; but what could set you off in the first place?"

There was much he did not know about Elizabeth, but he began to think she voiced these outrageous opinions in order to hide how deeply she truly felt on the subject. Despite her laughter, he suspected she honestly wished an answer, and so he considered for a moment. "I cannot fix on the hour, or the spot, or the look, or the words, which laid the foundation. It is too long ago. I was in the middle before I knew I *had* begun."

Her next words gave him more insight into her mind, and he cursed his own wayward tongue. "My beauty you had early withstood, and as for my manners—my behavior to *you* was at least always bordering on the uncivil, and I never spoke to you without rather wishing to give you pain than not. Now be sincere; did you admire me for my impertinence?"

Though he wished to counter her beliefs regarding her beauty and her manners, he answered the question instead. "For the liveliness of your mind, I did."

She shook her head. "You may as well call it impertinence at once. It was very little less. The fact is, that you were sick of civility, of deference, of officious attention. You were disgusted with the women who were always speaking, and looking, and thinking for *your* approbation alone."

Darcy started. *Did I not tell Bingley exactly that only a year ago?*

"I roused and interested you, because I was so unlike *them*. Had you not been really amiable, you would have hated me for it; but in spite of the pains you took to disguise yourself, your feelings were always noble and just; and in your heart, you thoroughly despised the persons who so assiduously courted you."

Her smile was so saucy, and her picture so precise, that Darcy had to laugh—but Elizabeth was not done. "There—I have saved you the trouble of accounting for it; and really, all things considered, I begin to think it perfectly reasonable. To be sure, you knew no actual good of me—but nobody thinks of *that* when they fall in love."

Now to this Darcy must protest. "Was there no good in your affectionate behavior to Jane while she was ill at Netherfield?" The lady in question, hearing her name, looked up. Darcy smiled and shook his head, and she turned her attention back to Bingley.

"Dearest Jane! Who could have done less for her? But make a virtue of it by all means." She waved her free hand in a gesture of largess. "My good qualities are under your protection, and you are to exaggerate them as much as possible; and, in return, it belongs to me to find occasions for teasing and quarreling with you as often as may be; and I shall begin directly by asking you what made you so unwilling to come to the point at last? What made you so shy of me when you first called, and afterwards dined here? Why, especially, when you called, did you look as if you did not care about me?"

Darcy examined her expression; beneath her teasing smile he saw that same curiosity he had noted earlier. "Because you were grave and silent, and gave me no encouragement."

He could not keep a defensive note from creeping into his voice, but she smiled, and for the first time he noticed a dimple that winked in and out of existence. The sight so transfixed him that he almost missed her next words.

"But I was embarrassed," she protested.

With an effort, Darcy tended to the conversation. "And so was I."

"You might have talked to me more when you came to dinner."

Darcy stroked the soft skin on her inner wrist with his thumb. "A man who had felt less, might."

Elizabeth blushed and laughed. "How unlucky that you should have a reasonable answer to give and that I should be so reasonable as to admit it." Darcy smiled; it amazed him that he could discompose Elizabeth simply by telling her he loved her.

"But I wonder how long you *would* have gone on, if you had been left to yourself. I wonder when you *would* have spoken, if I had not asked you! My resolution of thanking you for your kindness to Lydia certainly had great effect. *Too much*, I am afraid; for what becomes of the moral, if our comfort springs from a breach of promise? For I ought not to have mentioned the subject. This will never do."

Darcy barely contained his laughter at the rapidity with which her mind worked. "You need not distress yourself," he assured her. "The moral will be perfectly fair. Lady Catherine's unjustifiable endeavors to separate us were the means of removing all my doubts. I am not indebted for my present happiness to your eager desire of expressing your gratitude. I was not in a humor to wait for any opening of yours. My aunt's intelligence had given me hope, and I was determined at once to know everything."

Elizabeth smiled slyly. "Lady Catherine has been of infinite use, which ought to make her happy, for she loves to be of use. But tell me, what did you come down to Netherfield for? Was it merely to ride to Longbourn and be embarrassed, or had you intended any more serious consequence?"

Darcy settled back in his seat, his lips turned up in a faint smile as he remembered. "My real purpose was to see *you*, and to judge, if I could, whether I might ever hope to make you love me. My avowed one, or what I avowed to myself, was to see whether your sister was still partial to Bingley, and if she were, to make the confession to him which I have since made."

"Shall you ever have courage to announce to Lady Catherine what is to befall her?"

He pulled his hand from hers and rose to his feet. "I am more likely to want more time than courage, Elizabeth. But it ought to be done, and if you will give me a sheet of paper, it shall be done directly."

"And if I had not a letter to write myself, I might sit by you and admire the evenness of your writing, as another young lady once did. But I have an aunt, too, who must not be longer neglected."

And thus their quiet discussion shifted to the writing tables, where they each pulled out a sheet of paper and pen and wrote letters to their aunts. Darcy could well imagine the joy Elizabeth shared in hers and knew he would need to soon write a letter to Georgiana, who would welcome the news. However, his first duty was to inform Aunt Catherine, and so he began—

> *Dear Lady Catherine,*
>
> *I hope this letter finds you in health. I have news to impart which I fear you will not like. I am engaged, and my future wife is none other than Miss Elizabeth Bennet. I am sorry if this angers you, and I am especially sorry if it hurts Anne. I never had any intention to marry her; she was never more than a dear cousin to me. I deeply regret any actions of mine that might have been misconstrued as deeper intentions.*
>
> *Miss Bennet and I would be honored if you chose to join us at our wedding. I hope you will wish us joy.*
> *Yrs&etc,*
> *Fitzwilliam Darcy*

He then drew out another piece of paper and dipped the pen back in the ink. The letter to Georgiana was far longer, filled with all the effusions of joy he could not express to anyone else but Elizabeth. When he was done, he folded them both and put them in his jacket pocket to seal later with his own wax and signet.

Chapter Forty-two

DARCY SOON DISCOVERED that the general knowledge of their engagement was not the perfect solution he had anticipated. When no one had known of their relationship, he and Elizabeth had been allowed—nay, encouraged—to spend time alone together. Now they were constantly under the chaperonage of some one or other of her sisters, or occasionally Mrs. Bennet.

More than once, Darcy caught Mr. Bennet laughing at his obvious discomfort. His conversations with that gentleman were longer and more detailed than they had ever been before, and he soon came to appreciate Mr. Bennet's wit as being the source of Elizabeth's. That very lack of decorum which he had previously despised had created the atmosphere which had allowed her spirit to flourish.

Each morning, Darcy waited in the study for the post with some anticipation. Neither his aunt nor his sister would be long in replying to this news, he felt certain. On the morning four days after he sent word of his engagement, a letter from each fulfilled his trust.

The letter addressed in Georgiana's hand was thick and he set it aside to share with Elizabeth later. Lady Catherine's letter he studied with some apprehension, but eventually he decided to open it himself, as her manner of expressing herself was not likely to be something he wished Elizabeth to read.

Mr. Darcy,

You can have no doubt as to my reasons for writing you, Sir. I have lately received such news that I could not believe, had it not been in your own hand.

I speak of course of the letter you sent to inform me of your impending marriage to that nobody, Elizabeth Bennet. What can you be thinking, Sir, to marry such a girl? Did I not warn you of her arts and allurements? But this is always the way of things when people do not heed my words — they make foolish decisions which cannot be undone.

I most certainly will not attend your wedding. It would give your bride a consequence she does not deserve. For the sake of your dear mother's memory, you shall always be welcome at Rosings Park, but I shall never wait on Miss Elizabeth Bennet.

I remain,

    Your affectionate aunt,

    Lady Catherine de Bourgh

Darcy reached the fireplace in two strides and tossed the letter on the flames. He jabbed at it with the poker until it caught fire, and then he watched with grim satisfaction as it burned to ash. *Elizabeth will never read those vile words.*

He set the poker down and paced the room, his fingers tapping against his leg. "Lady Catherine must be answered," he decided finally, and sat down at the writing table.

Her ladyship's language having been so harsh, Darcy felt no need for civility in his reply.

Lady Catherine,

Your manner in referring to my intended is insupportable. I find myself in a position I had never anticipated. Henceforth, your ladyship, you are unwelcome at all Darcy properties. I will not tolerate the society of one who cannot see the value of Miss Bennet, or who would abuse her in such a fashion.

Fitzwilliam Darcy

Darcy sealed the letter and left the house. He was halfway to Longbourn when he met Elizabeth on the path. "This is an unexpected pleasure, Elizabeth. I had thought to find you at home."

She grimaced. "I left my mother and Aunt Phillips deep in wedding discussions."

Despite his agitation, Darcy smiled at her comical expression. "Then perhaps I might walk a ways with you," he suggested. "Or do you suppose our chaperones would be too shocked to learn we managed to find a few moments to be alone?"

Elizabeth's eyes sparkled up at him. "I think we can be held blameless, since we stumbled upon one another quite by accident. If we do not hurry back to Longbourn, who is to know?"

Darcy chuckled and offered her his arm, and they walked some ways in companionable silence. Elizabeth's presence soothed him, and he almost forgot his earlier aggravation until she asked, "What sent you from Netherfield this morning?"

He stiffened in remembered anger, and Elizabeth turned to face him. "What troubles you, Mr. Darcy?"

"Elizabeth, we are to marry in less than a month. Do you think you could call me by my name?"

She raised an eyebrow. "I do not think that is what rests so heavily on your mind."

He sighed. "No, I apologize. I received a letter from Lady Catherine. She is displeased by our match."

Elizabeth smiled. "Did you really expect her to be otherwise?"

"It was the manner in which she expressed her displeasure that angered me. The language she used when referring to you, Elizabeth..." He ran a hand through his hair.

"I can well imagine. After all, my arts and allurements have drawn you in."

His jaw dropped. "Did she address herself to you with those same words?"

"It does not matter," she said. Darcy grunted—it mattered a great deal. "Fitzwilliam, look at me." His name on her lips calmed him as nothing else could, and he met her eyes at last.

Elizabeth stepped closer to him. "It does not matter," she repeated softly, and placed a hand over Darcy's heart.

He opened his mouth to argue, but she flexed her fingers and the words escaped him. "I told your aunt," she said quietly, "that even if your whole family stood against me, I could not lose the happiness I would find in being your wife."

"You could have, on the whole, no cause to repine," Darcy said. Confusion marred her lovely features, and he explained. "My aunt shared your words with me."

"Then why did you..." She dropped her hand and took a step back. "Why did her opinion matter so much to you?"

Darcy took Elizabeth's hand and pressed it back to his heart. "Not her opinion of me, Elizabeth—her opinion of you!" His impassioned tone caught her by surprise, and she tried to step away. Darcy caught her around the waist with his other hand and held her close. "But I must admit," he said, his voice much quieter now, "that I feared perhaps your... affection for me might be swayed by her words."

There was a long pause, in which Darcy dared not meet Elizabeth's gaze. "I do not need your aunt's words, or anyone else's," she said finally, "to tell me you are at times a proud, disagreeable man."

Darcy flinched, and this time it was Elizabeth who held him in place. Her free hand somehow found its way to the back of his neck, forcing him to look her in the eye.

"However, you are also the best man I have ever known."

Inexpressible warmth stole over Darcy. Elizabeth had seen him at his very worst, and she still loved him.

Elizabeth smiled up at him, and Darcy could no longer resist her. He covered her hand with his own and closed the remaining distance between them. He was close enough now to feel her sudden intake of breath when she realized what was about to come. "Elizabeth," he whispered, and she raised her face toward his.

In the heartbeat before he kissed her, he recalled the proud pretensions that had kept them apart for the last year. Then his lips met hers, and they all melted away.

There was none for Darcy but Elizabeth.

About the Author

Nancy Kelley is a Janeite, an Austenesque author, and a blogger. During the writing of *His Good Opinion*, a version of Mr. Darcy took up residence in her brain; she fondly refers to him as the Darcy in My Head, or DIMH.

If Nancy could possess any fictional device, it would be a Time-Turner. Then perhaps she could juggle a full-time library job, writing, and blogging; and still find time for sleep and a life. Until then, she lives on high doses of tea, of which DIMH approves.

You can find Nancy on Twitter @Nancy_Kelley, at nancykelleywrites.com and on Indiejane.org.

Acknowledgements

First, to Jane Austen for writing a book so beloved and enduring that readers 200 years later still want to know more about her characters.

There are far more people to thank than I can possibly list here, but I can at least start. First, to my entire extended family for instilling a love of reading in me; second, to Mr. Roher, the junior high English teacher who told me I should write a book; third, to National Novel Writing Month for giving me the impetus to take writing seriously, fourth, to the online Jane Austen community who has been so supportive and enthusiastic as I've worked on *His Good Opinion*; and finally to the band of critique partners, beta readers, and editors who took my first draft and turned it into what you see today: Jessica Melendez, Kate Dana, Rebecca Fleming, Haley Whitehall, Jaymi Elford, and Carissa Reid. Special thanks goes to Jennifer Becton who very kindly shared her indie publishing expertise.